A
Forever
Love

OTHER BOOKS BY MICHELE ASHMAN BELL

An Unexpected Love

An Enduring Love

A Forever Love

A Novel

Michele Ashman Bell

Covenant Communications, Inc.

This is a work of fiction. The characters, names, incidents, places, and dialogue are products of the author's imagination, and are not to be construed as real.

Cover image "Picture This . . . by Sara Staker"

Published by Covenant Communications, Inc.
American Fork, Utah

Printed in the United States of America
First Printing: August 1999

06 05 04 03 02 01 00 99   10 9 8 7 6 5 4 3 2 1

ISBN 1-57734-506-1

Library of Congress Cataloging-in-Publication Data

Bell, Michele Ashman, 1959-
    A forever love : a novel / Michele Ashman Bell.
        p.   cm.
    ISBN 1-57734-506-1
    I. Title
    PS3552.E5217F67 1999
    813'.54--dc21   99-38400
                                              CIP

This book is dedicated
to my sisters and best friends
Alicia, Nicole, and Erika,
and my niece, Lindsay.
Thanks for sharing everything with me—
joys, sorrows, failures, successes, and advice.
I love you.

Acknowledgments

I'd like to acknowledge the following individuals
for their help in the research of this book:

My brother-in-law, Matthew Miller, for his legal expertise,
Christine Miller, Genetic Counselor at the
University of Utah,
my sister-in-law, Teresa Bell, for
location research and photographs,
Kendall Brady and Don C. Atkinson
for their contagious passion for sailing, and
Julie Christensen for her medical knowledge.

Also, thanks to Tina Foster, Amy Bell, Lynelle Spencer
Caren Tucker, and Joyce and Arden Larson,
for their input and valuable suggestions,

and Joel Bikman and Robby Nichols
at Covenant for their creativity and hard work
and the wonderful people who work in the bookstores
who support and promote my books.

As always, sincere thanks to
Valerie Holladay, valued friend and editor.

Prologue

When Alex regained consciousness she was surrounded by thick darkness. The air was hot and heavy, making it difficult to breath. Her hands were tied in front of her and her feet were bound tightly together. Then she realized she was in the trunk of a moving car.

Panic and fear collided in her chest. What was going on? Who would do this to her and why? With all the willpower she possessed, she forced herself to stay calm, to breath slowly, and to think clearly. But her heart pounded and her nerves sparked with terror. A thousand thoughts tore through her mind at once. She searched for one that made sense out of what was happening, but found nothing.

In less than one week, she and Rich would be going to the temple to be married after almost an entire year of waiting. She'd met Rich and they'd fallen in love while she was visiting her sister, Jamie, and her husband in Island Park, Idaho. Jamie had been expecting a third time after two devastating miscarriages, and Alex had come, hoping to offer some support. Rich was her brother-in-law's business partner, and everything she'd ever hoped for in a man but thought she'd never find. He'd nearly lost her because of his fear of commitment, but had realized his mistake before it was too late. Alex was a new member of the Church, which meant they would have to wait almost a year to be married in the temple, but she knew there was no other place to be married.

But now Alex wondered if her abductor would let her live to see the day.

Please, Heavenly Father, this can't be happening! she thought as her body shook with fear, and tears of helplessness slipped down her cheeks. But there was no denying it. She'd been kidnapped.

Chapter 1

It was the last thing anyone expected on a relaxed Friday evening as Alex McCarty stretched out on the living room floor, discussing her wedding plans with her sister, Jamie. Jamie's husband, Steve, and Alex's fiancé, Rich, were only minimally interested in the "girl talk," preferring to discuss last night's big game.

"I can't believe it's only six more weeks until the wedding," Jamie said. "And you'll be in San Diego for two weeks, for that fitness convention. Are you going to be able to get everything done?" Seven and a half months pregnant, she winced and shifted uncomfortably. After three previous miscarriages, she was understandably nervous about this pregnancy. Even this far she was still afraid to hope, and no one dared suggest anything could go wrong. Nevertheless, it was at the forefront of everyone's thoughts and fears as they nervously and anxiously awaited the blessed event.

In fact, it was because of Jamie's difficult pregnancies that Alex had taken time off from her work as a national fitness instructor and lecturer to visit Jamie in Island Park, Idaho, and offer moral support. During her visit, Alex had gained a testimony of the Church and was baptized. She had also met and fallen in love with Rich Greenwood, Steve's best friend and business partner.

After a fire had devastated the outdoor equipment rental business that Rich and Steve ran together, Steve decided to go back to school for a law degree. He'd always wanted to be an attorney, but had let other interests get in the way of actually going after this goal. He and Jamie, with their adopted daughter, Andrea Nicole, moved to Salt Lake City, where Steve was applying to the University of Utah Law School.

His mission president had gone to the "U" law school and was a partner at one of Salt Lake's most prestigious law firms. Steve hoped President Simon's letter of recommendation would help.

Steve and Jamie enjoyed living in Salt Lake. They had found a cute duplex in the Sugarhouse area of Salt Lake City, close to the University campus, nestled in the northeast benches of the Wasatch Mountains.

When Steve and Jamie decided to leave Island Park, Alex and Rich agreed that there was nothing to keep them there either. They had discussed their future, fasting and praying to know where to make their new home after the wedding. Rich had already left the recreation business even before the fire to pursue painting full-time. With his growing reputation as an artist and Alex's travel demands for her work, moving to Salt Lake to be near the airport was the perfect solution.

Alex's mother was a frequent visitor, spending more time in Salt Lake than she did in New York. Alex still traveled occasionally back to California, but she was beginning to feel that Salt Lake was home. She and her mother shared an apartment in a complex just south of Jamie and Steve. Rich had an apartment in the same complex. With everyone living in close proximity, it was easy to spend time together.

When he wasn't painting, Rich devoted every possible moment to the new house they were building. Alex joined him whenever she wasn't traveling for her work. She loved the location they'd chosen— high enough on the east bench of Bountiful, north of Salt Lake City, to have a spectacular view, but secluded enough to give them privacy.

Their floor plan allowed plenty of space for Rich's art studio, a workout room in the basement, a nursery close to the master bedroom, and an extra bedroom upstairs to be used for company. Alex and Rich had encountered a few problems with the house—but Alex refused to think about those tonight.

As Jamie continued to shift positions, trying to get comfortable, Alex empathized with her sister's aching back, swollen ankles, and constant heartburn. Nevertheless, she knew this was what Jamie wanted. Jamie had waited so long to have a baby and nearly lost hope of ever having children. Then she and Steve had adopted little Andrea Nicole.

Has it been almost a year since they brought Nikki home? Alex mused. *And fourteen months since I met Rich?* It was difficult to remember life before Rich; she couldn't imagine it without him. And now, finally, after nearly an entire year of waiting, she was getting married in six short weeks—and in the temple, no less.

"Alex," Jamie repeated. "I asked you a question, but you look like you're off in never-never land."

Before Alex could respond, an unexpected knock came at the door. Four surprised faces looked at the door, and then at each other.

"You didn't arrange something with the home teachers, did you, honey?" Jamie asked her husband suspiciously.

"No, I swear, I didn't, " Steve said, holding his right hand up to promise on his honor. "I learned my lesson last time."

"I wonder who it could be," Jamie said, struggling a little to stand and answer the door.

"I'll get it, honey." Steve hopped to his feet and raced to the door. He opened it to find a stranger who was definitely in the wrong neighborhood. The man wore black jeans and a black t-shirt under a black leather vest. A chain hung from a belt loop and was tucked into his pocket. He had tattoos on both forearms and had two earrings in one ear. Alex suspected he had a Harley in the parking lot.

"Hello," the stranger said gruffly. "My name is Clint Nichols. I'd like to talk to you about my daughter."

"I'm sorry," Steve said, obviously confused, "but are you sure you have the right address?"

"Are you the Dixons?"

Exchanging a puzzled look with Jamie, Steve nodded his head slowly. Jamie joined him at the door, curious to find out what this was all about.

The man looked satisfied. "Then you're the right ones. I was told you adopted my baby daughter."

"Steve," Jamie's voice grew weak, along with her knees. Steve placed a supportive arm around her.

"What is this?" he demanded, glaring at the stranger. "Who are you?"

"I told you," he repeated. "My name is Clint Nichols. I'm the baby's father and I want to talk to you about her."

Steve and Jamie didn't speak for a moment, then Steve motioned for the man to come inside. Inviting the man to take a chair, Steve sat beside Jamie, her face ashen, her eyes wide and full of fear.

"Now, Mr. Nichols," Steve said, "do you want to tell me what this is all about?"

The man took a deep breath. His words sounded rehearsed, as if he had practiced his lines to make sure he said them right. "Several days ago I went to a funeral for a woman I knew. Her name was Coralyn. I learned she had a baby and gave it up for adoption."

"Sh–she died?" Jamie gasped.

The man nodded. "In a car accident. I heard about it from the people at the diner where she worked. I stopped in there on my way to deliver a load to Missoula."

"Why are you here? Why are you telling us this?" Jamie asked. The fear in her face tore at Alex's heart. After all she had been through, was Jamie about to lose her daughter now?

Jamie and Steve had been warned that adoption carried some risks. But when Jamie's obstetrician, Dr. David Rawlins had placed the baby in her arms and told her that the child's mother didn't want to keep her, both Jamie and Steve had felt an instant bond with the tiny girl; they felt surely that it was meant to be. They had already made their decision even before the lawyer who had drawn up the papers assured them there was practically no risk of the unknown father stepping forward. Alex and Rich had been at the hospital with them, and Alex had helped Jamie with little Nikki for those first difficult weeks while the infant struggled with the drugs in her system. She had been diagnosed with fetal alcohol syndrome, a legacy of a mother with a substance abuse problem.

Alex forced herself to listen as Clint Nichols continued to speak. "Me and Coralyn, well," he paused, "we had somethin' goin' for a while. And when I heard she died, I wanted to pay my respects to her, so I made arrangements with another trucker to finish my run and I went to the funeral. Coralyn's sister Bonnie told me that Coralyn talked about me and even said she thought I was the baby's father."

Steve and Jamie sat with both hands clasped together between them. Alex was grateful that little Nikki was asleep in her room. This guy didn't seem like a convicted kidnapper or thug, but they all felt a serious threat from his mere presence. Alex hated to think what he might have said or done if he had seen Nikki.

"'Course I didn't want to bother you people 'til I knew for sure. Bonnie said Coralyn told her the names of the people who adopted the baby on the legal papers, and all's I needed was to get the name of the county the baby was born in and the date of the adoption."

Alex frowned at this information. She had always thought adoption papers were sealed documents.

As if he could read her mind, Clint looked uncomfortably around at the four suspicious faces staring at him. "I know it don't seem like I'm a nice, upstandin' fella and all," he said, somewhat defensively, "but if this is my child—one I had no idea was mine, mind you—I thought I should take some responsibility for it. I really did love Coralyn, but she was a stubborn woman and wouldn't let no man control her life again." When no one spoke right away, he mumbled, "I just want to do what's right."

Jamie spoke at last, the pain evident in her voice. "But she's ours— we've adopted her legally. She's been *sealed* to us." Her eyes pleaded for the stranger to understand and go away.

Clint shrugged. "You gotta see it from where I stand," he argued. "You see, I didn't even have no say in what happened to this kid when she was born. If Coralyn had told me she was pregnant, I'd-a stayed with her and helped her out. She didn't give me no choice, though. So now I feel an obligation to try and make it right to her. 'Specially now that she's dead and left four other young'uns with her sister."

Steve spoke up now. "You said *if* this child is yours. Are you sure without a doubt that she is?"

Clint stuck out his chin. "Accordin' to Bonnie I am," he said, "but she did say Coralyn had a lot of men friends and wasn't exactly positive about it. Now I found out that accordin' to Idaho state law there's something called a 'Putative Father Statute' that allows the natural birth father to reclaim the child at any time if he hasn't signed a form releasing all parental rights. I asked a lawyer friend of mine about this," he stated proudly.

Alex didn't like where this conversation was headed. She watched nervously as Steve leaned forward on the edge of his seat and said tersely, "Listen, Mr. Nichols, I don't know what you plan to do—"

"I plan to take care of my child, the way any father would," Clint interrupted.

Steve's eyes hardened. "As I was saying, Mr. Nichols, I don't know what you plan to do, but unless you have a positive paternity test proving that you are, in fact, the baby's father, I really don't see any need to continue this conversation. I think it's time for you to leave."

Clint Nichols looked confused. "Wait! What do you mean, paternity test?"

But Steve was clearly out of patience. He marched to the door and yanked it open. "Mr. Nichols, if this is as important to you as you say it is, I'm sure you'll figure it out," he said curtly. "Until then, we'd better not see you anywhere near our home again or I'll call the police and have you arrested for harassment."

"But—" the man stumbled to his feet. "I-I just—"

Steve's voice was glacial. "I mean it, Mr. Nichols. You'd better leave."

Almost as if it was his cue, Rich stood to add force to Steve's words. His tall, well-built frame was imposing, although Alex knew he would never consciously hurt a soul. Clint Nichols looked at both men, then turned on his boot heel and left. Steve slammed the door behind him and locked it.

For a moment no one spoke, then Jamie burst into tears. Her worst nightmare had just come true.

Chapter 2

The next few days Steve stomped around the apartment and Jamie jumped whenever the phone or the doorbell rang. As time passed and Clint Nichols didn't reappear, she started to breath a little more easily. Nevertheless, she asked Steve to give her a blessing, which had offered her some comfort as well as the assurance that nothing would divide their family.

Soon after, Alex received a blessing of her own, one that left her humbled with the incredible power she felt as the stake patriarch placed his hands on her head and began to speak. As the words rolled over her, tears formed and began to slip down her cheeks. When the flow of words came to a close, the patriarch lifted his hands and Alex felt the corridor from heaven slowly close as the powerful feeling of the Spirit softened to a whisper, the words of her blessing echoing in her mind.

Receiving her patriarchal blessing had been a goal for her for a long time. She yearned to know what was expected of her in this life, what the Lord had planned for her to accomplish. She had been told that she had the gift of discernment and would be able to know in whom she should place her trust, and that she would be blessed to marry a worthy man in the temple and have a posterity. That assurance gave her great peace and she knew that part of the prophecy would be fulfilled in just over five weeks, on July 16, just two days after the anniversary of her baptism one year ago.

Her blessing had also cautioned her to never lose faith in times of trial. She had been told that she would be tested and tried to the limits of her endurance, but if she would remain faithful, she would be able to withstand these trials.

As she basked in the warm glow that snugly enfolded her, Alex sensed that the others in the room were waiting for her. She opened her eyes and looked around, overwhelmed with the love she saw on the faces most dear to her in the world—her mother, Jamie and Steve, and of course, her fiancé and best friend, Rich Green.

"That was wonderful, Alex." Jamie stepped forward and hugged her gently.

Steve was next, then her mother, who was in town visiting. Judith McCarty was a writer for a popular woman's magazine, *New Woman*, whose office was located in New York. She had been pleasantly surprised with the West when she came to Island Park, Idaho, to visit her two daughters.

"Oh, honey," Judith said, teary-eyed. "That was just beautiful."

"It was, wasn't it?" Alex held her mother close. There were times when she wondered if her mother would ever join the Church, but with each occasion that their family experienced a strong outpouring of the Spirit, she felt more encouraged. Judith had recognized those times when the Spirit was present, and Alex had faith that someday her mother would get baptized, and their family could be sealed with her father, who had died years before. Ironically, it had been his death, shortly after his baptism, that turned Alex and her mother away from the Church, but had led Jamie to it. In fact, it had been Jamie's baptism into the same church that seemed to have robbed Alex of her father and Judith of her husband, which had led to a painful rift in the family. One that had been healed this last year, Alex remembered gratefully.

Now, overcome with emotion, she turned to Rich. Neither of them said a word as she looked into his eyes, but their hearts spoke volumes. She'd never known how deep love could grow between a man and a woman; she wouldn't have believed that she could love Rich more now than she had the day he'd finally managed to overcome his fears and propose to her. Only the bond of marriage would bring them closer together, she thought. Then they could truly be of one heart.

He pulled her into a warm embrace and held her close. There weren't many hours in the day that her mind didn't picture, if only briefly, what it would be like to kneel across the altar in the temple from this man she loved with all her heart, and be sealed to him for eternity. The knowledge that, no matter what happened in this life, she and Rich would always be together, was a blessing and a comfort she could hardly wait for.

"I love you, Alex," he said softly in her ear. Unable to speak, her heart full, Alex could only hold him tightly as tears of happiness spilled down her cheeks.

* * *

Rich's hand was warm around hers as he led her through the sheet-rocked structure that was to be their home. "Don't peek just yet," he warned.

"How can I peek? You've got a blindfold on me. What in the world are you doing anyway?" Alex asked. "I thought we were going out to dinner." She and Rich had planned on having dinner together so they could discuss house plans and wedding preparations. There were still so many decisions that needed to be made right away so the house would be finished on time and reservations made for the reception center, flowers, and tuxedos. At the thought of everything that needed to be coordinated, Alex felt her head begin to ache.

"Rich—" she began.

"I know, I know," he said placatingly. "We're almost there. You just need to climb these stairs."

She stumbled. "Rich, I'm going to fall. I can't see, remember?"

Rich's voice was mellow and soothing. "Alex, I won't let anything happen to you. I promise. Here's the first step." With his help, she made it up the stairs. *One good thing about not being able to see,* she thought. *I can't concentrate on maneuvering the steps and worry about wedding plans at the same time.* Carefully, she inched her feet up the steps, not wanting to take a major tumble backwards.

At the top of the stairs, Rich patted her shoulder. "Now wait here. I have to do something."

Alex held her tongue and wondered what in the world he was up to.

"Okay, I think it's all set. I'm going to take off the blindfold." His tone was exuberant, but Alex scarcely noticed over the rumbling of her stomach.

"Rich, I really am hungry. Can we just—"

The blindfold slid away. She couldn't believe her eyes. They were in the master bedroom, and it was lit up like Times Square. Rich had strewn white Christmas lights across all the walls, while dozens of candles surrounded a blanket laid out on the floor, which held a large bucket of fried chicken and several cartons of side dishes.

"Oh, Rich. This is incredible. I can't believe you went to all this work." Alex threw her arms around Rich and gave him an ecstatic hug.

"I just wanted us to have dinner alone, without interruptions," Rich explained, smiling warmly at her. "The only place I could think of was our own house."

Alex sighed as she looked around. "It's so beautiful like this. We should always use candles. They're so much more romantic."

Rich looked gratified at her appreciation. "Oh, wait, I forgot something." He slipped out of her arms, and a moment later soft music filled the room.

"There now, would you like to dance?" he murmured invitingly.

Alex melted back into his arms. "I'd love to."

As they moved in time to the slow rhythm, Alex felt as though she was floating in Rich's arms. The music, the candles, the starlit sky showing through the skylight, all made the moment magical and dreamlike.

"Is this what married life is going to be like?" she asked softly.

"Like what?" Rich asked.

"You—full of surprises, candles and moonlight. Dancing. Picnics in the bedroom?"

"Probably not," Rich said, practically. Alex pulled back and looked at him with disappointment.

"It will be much better than this," he chuckled.

Alex smiled and rested her head against his shoulder again as he glided her around the room.

"Thank you," Alex sighed.

"For what?" Rich asked, as he steered her expertly, but gently, around the floor.

"Oh . . ." Alex sought for the right words. "For being wonderful. For being everything I could ever want in a husband. For being my best friend."

Rich chuckled again. "Don't build that pedestal too high. I'm bound to fall off."

Alex shook her head. "I doubt it, because I love everything about you. Even your flaws," she whispered in his ear and ran her fingers through the back of his hair.

"Flaws? *Moi?*" Rich said, pretending to take offense. "Whatever can you mean?"

At that, they both giggled and he whirled her around one last time as the song ended. "We'd better eat," he said lightly. "I don't know if I can handle too much romance."

Despite his tone, Alex was aware of how long and difficult this wait had been for both of them. But she knew nothing could stand in the way of their goal for a temple marriage. It didn't mean they hadn't had their temptations, but their commitment to each other and to their goal had kept them strong.

And with only six weeks to go, she wasn't about to let anything stop them from achieving their goal now.

* * *

The days passed like a whirlwind, filled with the fast-paced excitement of getting ready for the wedding and keeping the house moving. For most issues, they were able to agree, or at least compromise, on decisions about the house, but they did disagree on a few things, which frustrated Alex no end. She'd lived alone several years, worked hard at her career, planned her life, made her own decisions; the idea of not being in complete control and having to compromise was difficult for her. Like when the builder had suggested they put a fireplace in their master bedroom. Alex had loved the idea, Rich didn't. Or when Alex had suggested a bay window in the kitchen so they could have a bigger view of the mountains behind them. Rich had axed that idea as well. But her biggest frustration was the front porch. The house plans didn't call for an overhang, or any kind of cover, for the front entrance, but Alex felt something was needed there to protect people from the rain and snow when they came to the door.

Rich had argued that it would put them way over budget. And while Alex appreciated that Rich was very cost conscientious and conservative in their spending, she nevertheless felt that down the road, the extra cost would be balanced by the pure enjoyment of having the additions.

Alex had been more frustrated during this stage of her relationship with Rich than she had at any other—and that was saying something. She hated to remember the times she doubted he'd ever be ready for a commitment, the time she had gone to Europe on a fitness tour and left Rich behind to make up his mind about their relationship. He had nearly ruined her trip, except that she was determined to enjoy it, regardless of his decision. Those days seemed long ago, and now Alex felt like they were having their first real arguments over building the house. She found herself wanting to strangle Rich when he was being so logical and practical and stubborn, even though she loved him.

She knew they would find some way to compromise, but she wished he would just try to see things from her perspective. She was sure he would like her suggestions if he'd just give them a chance.

Chapter 3

Frantic with all the wedding preparations, Alex still had to find time to schedule a visit with her gynecologist, Dr. Chandler, who was also Jamie's doctor. For several months Alex had tried to ignore the growing pain in her abdomen and problems with her monthly cycle. She hadn't expressed her fears to anyone, even Rich, but now that her marriage was rapidly approaching, the possibility of having children— or not having them—was foremost in her mind. For several years during her struggle with anorexia, her monthly periods had ceased. She'd been told by doctors at the time that the strain her eating disorder placed upon her body not only jeopardized her own health, but could also affect her ability to bear children later on. At the time, she'd ignored them.

Those words haunted her now. There was no reason to believe she couldn't have children, but what if . . . ? *What if . . .?*

As she sat in the waiting room, Rich beside her, she tried not to worry. When her name was called, she squeezed Rich's hand, then disappeared through the door where the nurse stood waiting. After her exam, they were going to pick out the flowers and the menu for the reception.

Rich watched as women of various ages, some obviously pregnant, others not, took turns checking in, waited for their names to be called, then disappeared into examining rooms. Rifling through the collection of magazines on the table in front of him, he glanced over the prenatal, women's, and baby magazines, hoping to find something he could read that wouldn't make him blush. He preferred not to look at pictures of nursing mothers or pregnant women modeling underwear.

To his relief, he found a token *Sports Illustrated,* not caring that it was six months old.

By the time he finished the magazine, he noticed that several women had come and gone, and Alex was still in the examining room. As he wondered why her exam was taking longer than the others, he felt a vague discomfort creeping over him and he sent a brief prayer heavenward that Alex would be healthy and well.

At the sound of a door opening, he glanced up quickly. One look told him that she was very upset. His heart pounded as he noticed her red-rimmed eyes. The magazine fell to the floor as he jumped up and rushed to her.

"Honey, what's wrong?" he asked tenderly, trying to keep his own fear out of his voice.

She looked at him with tear-filled eyes.

"Alex?" he asked again, more urgently.

"Let's talk when we get outside," she whispered. He took her arm gently and they quickly left the office.

Outside in the warm sun, Alex leaned against the brick building and drew in several deep breaths. Birds chirped merrily in the trees, a jet overhead stretched a long trail of white smoke across the sky, and the fragrance from a late-blooming lilac bush scented the air with its sweet perfume. But all Rich could think about was whether or not Alex was okay.

"Tell me what's wrong," he begged. "What did the doctor say?"

Alex's mind raced a million directions. She thought of Jamie's fears and her troubles carrying a baby to term, of her own expectations that she would one day marry and have children of her own. Of course, she would. She'd never expected anything different. *First comes love, then comes marriage, then comes baby in the baby carriage . . .*

She shook her head to clear away her thoughts.

"This is killing me, Al," he said, his throat tightening. "What did the doctor say?"

"Oh, Rich," was all she could say. She wiped her eyes with the already damp Kleenex and drew in another deep breath. "I'm so stupid, Rich. Why didn't I take better care of myself?"

His face showed his concern. "What do you mean? What did you do?"

Alex wished she had a baseball bat she could pound against the wall behind her, to vent her rage, her frustration, her fear. "All those years I starved myself, risking my health to be thin," she whispered. "It was so stupid." Rich looked at her blankly, not understanding. "What do you mean? What's wrong? You're doing a lot better now. I remember the first time we met, when I could barely get you to eat a peanut butter sandwich—" He stopped at the pain that ravaged her face.

Alex closed her eyes tightly, not wanting to see Rich's face when she said the words. She swallowed. "The doctor says I have cysts—all over. She thinks I might have . . . endometriosis. I have to go in for laparascopic surgery. That's the only way we can know for sure. She's pretty sure that's why I'm having so much pain in my abdomen and why my periods are so bad."

"Endometriosis," Rich said slowly. "I don't know what that means."

"She said it's web-like tissue that implants itself in the pelvic area. It attaches itself to the female organs and then outside of the intestine. She says no one knows for sure what causes it, and without treatment it can become worse. "

"Did she say that your anorexia caused this?" Rich asked, struggling to make the connection.

"No, not really, but she said my eating disorder could have aggravated the problem," Alex explained. "I can't help but wonder if . . . I'm seeing . . . the consequences of my stupidity." She had to force herself to say the words clearly. It was hard to talk, she was so distraught.

"Is there anything they can do about it?" Rich asked, hopefully.

Alex shrugged. "She said they could do surgery to remove the tissue, but it generally grows back."

Rich didn't know what to say. He searched for words of comfort to give her, but nothing came. So he pulled her into his arms and held her close. Knowing the pain she must be feeling, he was surprised when he heard what sounded like a weak laugh. Her tears one minute and her laughter the next made him wonder if she was going to fall apart in his arms.

"What is it, honey?" he asked, pulling back to see what she had found to laugh about.

"It's ironic, really," she said. "One way to cure endometriosis is getting pregnant."

Rich was overcome with relief. "That's great. We both want children. In fact," he said with a grin, "as soon as we're married, we can get working on that right away."

Alex looked away. "You don't understand," she said. "Endometriosis *prevents* women from getting pregnant—from ever being able to conceive."

Rich shook his head with confusion. How could the cure for the problem be something that wasn't physically possible? Then how could they cure the problem? It seemed a vicious cycle.

After a few moments of silence, Alex said softly, "We may never be able to have children, Rich. Could you live with that?"

Rich didn't answer. Instead he pulled her close again and rocked her gently. "C'mere," he said. "You're forgetting that your patriarchal blessing tells you that you *will have* a posterity."

"I know, I've thought about that," she said softly, leaning her cheek against his chest.

In his arms she felt safe. His convictions buoyed her up, giving her courage and hope. Rich was her rock, her pillar, her strength. Whenever her emotions threatened to overwhelm her, Rich helped her stay strong and gave her the ability to face her challenges, even though she didn't want to. This wasn't a problem she'd ever wanted to experience, but that wasn't how trials worked, on a pick-and-choose basis.

She prayed with all her might that her body would be able to function properly and bear children, but she knew Rich loved her no matter what. With him by her side, she would be able to face this challenge, just as she had her eating disorder.

"We'll just do everything in our power to correct the problem, then have faith that the Lord will take care of the rest. And He will, Alex. I know He will," Rich assured her.

"You're right," she said hoping his words would convince her and make her doubts disappear. "The doctor wants me to come in for some blood studies and to schedule the surgery. She wants to go in with a scope to see exactly what's going on inside."

Rich paled as the reality of her surgery hit him. He gulped, then said bravely, "And we'll fast and pray and do everything else in our power to overcome this problem. Right?"

She hugged him tightly. "Okay." During the days when she'd starved herself to death to stay thin, she hadn't bothered to think of her future. How she wished she would have. What she would give to go back and undo all the damage she'd caused her body by her anorexia. Rich stroked her hair and held her close.

"I don't know what I'd ever do without you, Rich." Looking up at him, she could read the love and concern in his eyes. His heart seemed to beat in perfect rhythm with hers, a complete synchronization of their souls, united together.

She still feared the outcome, but felt encouraged after talking with Rich. His assurance and love seemed to overshadow her fears and give her hope. As the years passed and she remained childless, would it continue to give her strength?

* * *

That night Rich and Alex joined Steve and Jamie at their duplex. Judith was still in town and wanted to fix dinner for everyone. As the women prepared dinner in the kitchen, Alex told her sister and mother about her doctor's appointment. Even though they had no answers for her, she felt their love, concern and support. And while talking to her family didn't change her condition, she felt better knowing that they were going to pray for her and they'd be there to help her any way they could.

Alex watched her mother move efficiently around the kitchen and wondered if Judith would make her presence in Salt Lake permanent now that both of her daughters were there. She had started dating Jamie's former obstetrician, Dave Rawlins, when she had first come to visit Island Park, and although her two daughters now lived in Salt Lake, she was still able to see a lot of the good doctor. He had scaled down his practice in Idaho Falls to only a few patients that he saw on Mondays and Tuesdays, which left him plenty of free time to travel to Salt Lake and be with Judith when she was in town. An associate of his at the hospital had offered Dave the use of his condo near the mouth of Emigration Canyon, on the east side of the valley.

With all the time Judith spent in Salt Lake, it was difficult for her to not feel the influence of the Church. Judith had actually gone through the missionary lessons, seen several church films and other productions, had been through a temple open house, and even attended a session of general conference. She agreed with the gospel teachings, even to the point of giving up her coffee, but still she wouldn't commit. Alex wasn't exactly sure why, and the subject seemed a little too sensitive to approach head-on, so it was left untouched.

After a delicious dinner of shrimp scampi over pasta, everyone relaxed in the living room to watch Rich's video footage. He'd become a regular "videoholic" since buying a new video camera. He'd been recording the construction of the house and planned to record their wedding and honeymoon as well. But he'd gone crazy with the darn thing, Alex thought ruefully.

Last month she and Rich had gone to Boise for his parents' remarriage. They'd gotten divorced soon after Rich returned from his mission, but in the years since had managed to rebuild bridges and rekindle their love. It had been a wonderful and extremely moving ceremony, and it seemed to Alex that he hadn't turned off the videocam for even a minute.

"This is my family," he narrated as his parents appeared on the screen. His older brother and his wife and two children were next. They'd moved back to Idaho after living in Chicago for several years. Rich's younger sister, Jenny, smiled briefly as the camera focused on her.

"The only one missing is my younger brother Ben," he told his audience.

"Doesn't he get home from his mission soon?" Steve asked. Jamie had her feet in her husband's lap and he was massaging them gently. She'd been retaining water and her feet ached constantly.

"He gets home from Scotland two days before our wedding." Rich fast forwarded to the next event on tape, an art show in Sun Valley. Rich and Alex had traveled there from Boise after the wedding. Rich's friend Colt Bywater, whom they'd all met, had handled the show. An extremely talented artist himself, he had supported Rich from the beginning and worked to promote Rich's art and set up shows for him.

"There's Colt talking with a woman from Vail, Colorado," Rich continued to narrate. "She's a collector and is interested in setting up a show in Vail sometime this fall."

Alex was proud that Rich's art was doing so well although Rich worried at times he wouldn't be able to provide for a family on an artist's income. But he was determined to build a lucrative career and take care of her. Alex didn't doubt him for a second. She knew that with her income alone, they would be fine financially, but Rich was determined to be the patriarch and provider of the home. She respected and supported those feelings. Besides, once they had a family—if they had a family—her income would drop substantially.

"There's Alex looking at the displays," he said, "and there's Alex, feeding the ducks." A moment later, he said, "There's Alex at Red Fish Lake, trying to skip rocks." Everyone laughed as Alex attempted over and over to skip rocks across the surface of the water, with no luck.

"Okay, you can fast forward through all of this, please," Alex said, embarrassed that she was the focus of so much camera time.

As the others patiently listened to Rich's narration of the Sun Valley trip, Alex excused herself to make a phone call. She needed to check in with her business manager, Sandy Dalebout, about her upcoming fitness conference in San Diego. Although the timing was horrible, Alex was excited because Julianne, her friend from England, would be going with her. The two of them were working together to create a personalized exercise video they were sure would revolutionize the fitness industry.

Sandy picked up on the first ring. "Hey," she said, "I was just thinking about you."

"Good things, of course," Alex kidded.

"Of course," Sandy agreed. "Now, I've got some good news and some great news. Which do you want first?"

Alex smiled at her enthusiasm. "Either one. I'm glad things are going so well."

Ever since she joined the Church, Sandy had become an inextinguishable fireball. She was in the church choir, she went on splits with the missionaries, she was the Relief Society compassionate service leader, and she was addicted to genealogy. Alex realized her enthusiasm was due to a desire to share what she had with everyone around her, and she wasn't the type to bulldoze people into her way of thinking. Still, Alex didn't plan on leaving Sandy alone with her mother quite yet.

"How are your mom and sister doing?" Sandy asked.

"Jamie's only got six weeks left until her baby's due, and my mom is doing great."

"Is your mom still taking missionary lessons?"

"No, she finished those a while ago."

"Is she going to get baptized?" Sandy asked in her classic "to-the-point" way.

"Uh, I don't know. I think eventually," was the best she could come up with.

"Alex," Sandy spoke slowly and clearly, "until your mother is baptized and is worthy to go to the temple, your family can't be sealed. She needs to get baptized. Your father is waiting for this work to be done."

Alex didn't answer. When it was put that way, she felt neglectful.

"You realize this is the ultimate act of love you, your sister, and your mom can do for your father, don't you?"

"Yes," Alex said softly, "of course, I do."

"Then you'd better talk to your mother. Maybe she just needs some gentle persuasion. Maybe I should talk to her."

"No," Alex said quickly. Sandy's approach was anything but gentle. "You're right. I should talk to her."

"Good girl. This work is much too important to wait."

Alex knew her friend was right. In a little over a month Alex would be an endowed temple recommend holder and would be worthy to be sealed to her parents. Judith was the one missing piece. Right then Alex made the mental resolve to have a long, heart-to-heart talk with her mother. She would just have to approach it very carefully.

"So, are you ready for my great news?" Sandy's excitement grew to new heights.

"Yes, what is it?" Alex never knew what to expect from Sandy.

"I'm moving."

"Sandy, that's great. Did you finally find a home?" Sandy had been looking for her own place somewhere in the hills of Los Altos, but hadn't had any luck so far.

"No. I'm moving to Paris."

Chapter 4

"What?" Alex shrieked. "Why in the world are you moving to Paris?"

"It's exciting, it's challenging, it's something new and different," Sandy explained reasonably.

Alex digested this new information carefully. "But won't that make it a little difficult to manage your clients?" she asked.

"Well," Sandy said carefully, "I guess there is a drawback to my moving. You're going to have to find a new manager."

"Oh, Sandy." Alex drew in a deep breath, trying to gather her thoughts so she could convince Sandy of the absurdity of her idea. "I know you get this wild hair every once in a while, but you can't just leave a thriving business just like that."

"I know it seems sudden but I've actually been thinking about this for over a year," Sandy said. "You're the last client I've told."

"A year? Without saying anything? And then—*Paris?* You don't even speak French." Alex got a sinking feeling in her stomach. Sandy's mind was apparently made up.

"Au contraire," Sandy replied with an exaggerated French accent. "I've been taking classes. My teacher thinks I have quite a knack for the language."

"But what about a job? Where will you work?" Alex asked desperately.

Sandy's voice was patient. "A dear friend of our family is a designer in France. He's offered me a job. You've heard me talk about Jean Pierre Ramone."

Alex scanned her memory quickly. She didn't recall Sandy saying anything about knowing the famous French designer. "I guess I wasn't really paying attention when you mentioned him," she admitted.

"Well, I've known Jean Pierre for years. You remember that my father was in the military? I grew up a total 'army brat.'"

"Yes, that I remember," Alex agreed. Despite her own challenges growing up, dealing with the death of her father and her subsequent anorexia, she had never envied Sandy's life, although Sandy had thrived on it. It had suited her personality completely.

"We lived all over the world when I was growing up, and we met Jean Pierre in Switzerland, before he became famous, when he was just beginning to market his designs," Sandy said nostalgically. "He was the nicest man, even then. And success hasn't changed him a bit."

"So, this Jean Pierre wants you to come work for him?" Alex could hardly continue the conversation. All she could think about was, what was she going to do without Sandy? She knew it was selfish to put her own needs before Sandy's, but Sandy had been a wonderful manager and a treasured friend. She was downright irreplaceable!

"Oh, Jean Pierre has heard me complain often enough about how confined I start to feel after being in one place too long, so he offered me a job."

Alex had heard Sandy talk about getting itchy feet every four or five years. Sandy called it "wanderlust," the desire to see new places, experience new things. Alex didn't know what to call it. But right now she didn't like it one bit.

"But Sandy," she persisted, "what will you do? You can't design clothing or even sew, can you?"

Sandy laughed. "Hardly. But I can arrange fashion shows, manage publicity affairs, and even arrange for private parties and showings. Just think about all the places I'm going to see and the people I'm going to meet. Alex, I've never felt more right about anything in my entire life. And if it helps," Sandy paused for just a moment, "I've fasted and prayed about it, and I feel like the Lord wants me to go. The Church needs strong members to go out into the world and have an influence, make a difference, spread the gospel. Look at what you were able to do when you went on the EuroTour last year. You were giving out Book of Mormons left and right."

Alex couldn't argue with that. And if anyone was capable of making a difference it was Sandy.

"Hey, Alex," Sandy said soberly, "don't think this is completely easy for me. I'm going to miss you tons." She cleared the emotion from her throat. "You know you're more than just a client to me. That's why I told you last, it was just too hard. But with you getting married and moving to Salt Lake anyway, it seems like the best time to make the change."

Alex had to agree she had a valid point.

"Besides, I'll pop in now and then. I'll make it to New York, L.A., and even Salt Lake City once in a while. And you and Rich can come and see me in Paris anytime you want. And I expect you to come by when you're on your honeymoon," she said sternly.

Now that Alex was getting used to the idea, she thought she wouldn't mind having a reason to go to Europe occasionally. "When do you plan on leaving?"

"I've already started making arrangements here, so I'll go over as soon as we finish the convention in San Diego. But I'll be back for your wedding," she promised.

"You'd better be back for my wedding," Alex scolded. "I didn't spend a fortune on that bride's maid dress for you to ditch my reception."

"I'll be there. Hey, maybe I'll bring you back a Jean Pierre original."

"Just get your body here, that's all I care about."

"I hope someday you'll be able to stand in my wedding line," Sandy said. "Who knows, maybe I'll meet my future husband in Europe. Heaven knows I've looked all over America for him."

"I hope you do, Sandy. I just want you to be happy," Alex said, trying to be supportive although she was fighting back an overwhelming sense of loss. Sandy wasn't only her business manager, she had been one of her best friends ever since Alex had moved to California.

"Oh, just one other thing," Sandy added. "Not to end this call on a sour note, but I thought you'd be interested to know. I saw your old boyfriend Jordan Davis on the news. Apparently he was arrested for selling drugs, but there wasn't enough evidence to convict him. So he was acquitted and released. He still looks like a Mr. Universe-in-the-making, and just the glimpse I got of his face tells me he still has a major attitude."

Alex closed her eyes at the mention of Jordan's name. Jordan had stepped into her life at a time when Alex had been hurt and vulnerable, and he had come in with flattery and compliments, playing like a master upon her wounded ego. From the beginning, he'd had a way about him that seemed to convince women that they should be grateful he was paying them the slightest bit of attention. Alex deeply regretted not being able to see through his manipulative facade earlier.

"Is he still in the Bay area?" she asked. She had no intention of going anywhere near there. She'd given up her apartment and had no ties to the area except Sandy, and now Sandy would be leaving.

"Who knows?" Sandy answered. "He could be anywhere. I'd hate to think where you'd be if you hadn't dumped him when you did."

* * *

At the University of Utah, in the lobby of the Student Services Center, Jamie pushed Nikki's stroller back and forth while she waited for Steve to talk to a financial aid counselor. Nikki stared at all the people, her small purple dinosaur tucked securely under one arm and a box of animal crackers in her other hand. Jamie and Steve had some savings left from their business back in Island Park, but until their home sold, they would need help with school expenses. Steve had planned on getting work at some point, but recently he had devoted all his time to preparing for the law school entrance exam.

"Oh, look at the cute baby," a young red-haired girl said to her friend as they passed Jamie and Nikki.

They stopped and fussed over Nikki, who, true to form, relished the attention and waved one gooey, cookie-covered hand, smiling and jabbering for them.

"She is so cute," the other girl said. "I want a baby. They look like so much fun."

Then they looked closer at Jamie. "Wow," the redhead said, "and you're expecting another one already?"

"I am," Jamie admitted, smiling and blushing a little.

"Gee, that's going to keep you busy," the girl remarked.

"But think how close they'll be," her friend said. "Especially if it's another girl. Do you know what you're having?" she asked.

"No, we've decided not to find out. We want it to be a surprise," Jamie answered.

"Our English professor is having a baby," the redhead girl told

Jamie. "She isn't due for two months, but she's having some problems and has gone into labor early."

"That's too bad," Jamie said, able to empathize with their teacher's predicament. "I hope everything works out for her."

"Yeah," the other girl laughed. "The whole department is in a panic. Mrs. Duncan's replacement isn't available to cover for her yet, and they don't know who they're going to get to finish out the term."

Without warning, the question popped out of Jamie's mouth, "What does she teach?"

"Journalism," the girls said together.

Had there been a light bulb above Jamie's head, it would have turned on and blinded them. *Wouldn't it be perfect if...*

"Are they looking for someone temporary to take her place?" Jamie asked suddenly.

"Yeah—like someone who can start today," the redhead said. "Why, do you know someone?"

"I think so. She works for *New Woman* magazine in New York, but she's here in Salt Lake for a while."

"I love that magazine," the girl said enthusiastically.

"Me too," her friend added. "Do you think she'd do it?"

"I bet she'd love to. And I should know, she's my mother."

"Your mother?!" Both of the girls shared an excited look. "You should go over to the English Department right now and tell them before they get some boring old retired professor to fill in."

Jamie laughed. "I promise, my mother would be anything but boring. And I think it might work out." Judith had always talked of taking a leave of absence from her job to teach. This was perfect!

"I need to get to a phone and call her," Jamie said, searching the area for a pay phone.

"Here," one of the girls thrust out a cellular phone. "You can use this."

"Thanks." Jamie dialed the number to the apartment her mother was sharing with Alex. It took several rings but her mother finally answered.

Quickly Jamie explained what was going on and what the two students had told her.

"Are you sure the department hasn't already found someone?" Judith asked.

"No, but the sooner you contact them, the better your chances are. That is, if you want to do it," Jamie added quickly. She didn't doubt what her mother's response would be.

"Want to? I'd love it. This is something I've always wanted to do. Jamie, this is perfect!"

Jamie smiled and nodded at the two girls who were listening to her side of the conversation. "I thought so too, Mom. Do you want me to go over to the department and talk to them for you?"

"No, no. I'll call them from here." Judith's voice sounded distracted, as if she was already thumbing through the Yellow Pages.

"Steve's almost done, then we're going straight home. I'll call you as soon as we get there."

"Okay, hon. And thanks. Tell those two girls they get an A-plus if I get the job."

Jamie laughed. "I will. Good luck, Mom."

Turning off the power, Jamie handed the phone back to the girl and said, "She's interested. She's calling right now. And she wants me to get your names so she can make sure to give you A-pluses if she gets the job."

"Hey, that's great!" the redhead said. "I'm Brittany Rogers and this is Morgan Foster."

About this time Nikki started protesting the lack of attention and discomfort of the straps that kept her confined to her stroller.

"I better go find her dad so we can get going." Jamie picked up Nikki's toy dinosaur that she'd thrown down and handed it back to her. "Thanks again, you two."

"Hey, good luck with your baby. I hope it's a girl and she's as cute as this one."

Jamie smiled. "Thanks."

Heaving their overloaded backpacks over their shoulders, the two students waved and took off out the front doors.

Cute girls, Jamie thought as they walked away. Watching them reminded her of her own college days at BYU. The thought brought a smile to her face.

"Hey there, beautiful," a familiar male voice said in her ear. "What's your major?"

Jamie turned and grinned at her husband. "Early childhood development." She patted her stomach. "Very early childhood development."

They both laughed and he kissed her cheek. Kneeling down by the stroller, he tickled Nikki under the chin. She giggled and squealed with delight.

"So, what have my two girls been doing?" He stood up and tucked a handful of papers inside the front flap of his day-planner.

"Oh, not much," Jamie said nonchalantly. "Just waiting around for you. Oh, and it looks like we found a job for Mom teaching journalism in the English Department."

"That's good," Steve said, half listening. Then it sunk in. "You what?"

Jamie quickly explained what had happened in the previous several minutes.

"Wow," Steve said admiringly. "You sure work fast."

"Hey, you don't get opportunities dropped in your lap like this every day." Jamie stepped aside as Steve took over Nikki's stroller, and she linked her arm through his.

"I don't get opportunities dropped in my lap like that *ever*," he laughed. "Your mother would love teaching. And I think the students would really like her, too."

"Let's get home so we can find out what's going on," Jamie said eagerly. "I'm *dying* to know what she found out."

* * *

But instead of going home, they went straight to the apartment complex where Alex, Judith, and Rich all lived. After knocking and waiting for several minutes, they turned away, disappointed. At the sound of the door swinging open, Jamie's heart jumped. Judith waved a hand, beckoning them inside. She was on the phone.

"Lunch would be great, Max. Sure I know the place. I'll meet you at one. We can talk more then."

She gave Steve and Jamie a thumbs-up and laughed at something Max said. "It *is* a small world. I can't wait to see you either. Bye."

Judith hung up the phone, clapped her hands, and said proudly, "How about that!"

"What happened? Who was that? Did you get the job?" Jamie asked excitedly.

"I called just in time. They were about to hire one of the teachers who retired last year. I caught Max just before he made the call."

"Max who?" Jamie asked.

"Maxwell Thorpe, dean of the English Department. He and I knew each other years and years ago. He was actually one of my professors back at NYU when I was going to school. Can you believe it?"

"No," Jamie said, amazed at the coincidence.

"Anyway, I'm meeting him for lunch to talk about the position. He already knew of my job with *New Woman* and previous work in newspaper and thinks I would be ideal for the department. As a formality he wants to discuss some of the details with me at lunch. Honey," Judith said, giving her daughter a quick squeeze, "I don't know how to thank you. This is so perfect! It doesn't really surprise me, though. The minute the phone rang this morning, with you calling me about this position, I knew. The Lord wants me here in Salt Lake. I know this is the right thing to do."

Jamie smiled. She agreed completely.

Chapter 5

The next night the family gathered around Steve and Jamie's dinner table for pizza. Nikki was in her high chair getting more pizza in her hair than in her mouth. Judith had gone back to New York to make arrangements to take a leave of absence from *New Woman,* and they were discussing her new job offer and trying to solve Alex's challenge of losing her business manager.

"You know," Steve said, taking a moment to swallow a bite of pizza, "there is a very simple solution. Rich could be your manager."

Alex wiped her mouth with her napkin and then looked at Rich for his reaction. He inclined his head, as if considering it. "It's weird you would even mention that," she said, turning to Steve. "I was just thinking the same thing this morning."

"It's perfect," Steve said. "With Rich's accounting background, he'd be great in negotiating contracts and deals for you. And he could handle the scheduling and arrangements for your lectures and appearances."

Alex turned to Rich. "What do you think?"

"I think it sounds great," he said. "But I want you to feel good about it."

"I do," Alex answered. "It's a great arrangement." She knew he would have her best interest in his every decision.

"It's ideal," Jamie agreed, as she leaned over Nikki, picking globs of cheese out of the little girl's hair, while Nikki bounced her purple dinosaur in a pool of juice from a tipped-over cup. "Nikki, you're such a mess. You need a bath."

"Bubbos!" Nikki shouted. "Bubbos!" She clapped her chubby hands together.

"Yes, you can have bubbles," Jamie told the toddler.

"What are you going to do with two kids under fourteen months?" Alex asked with wonder. Nikki wore her out after an hour, but Jamie seemed to have enough endurance to climb Mount Everest.

"I'll probably pull out my hair," Jamie responded, then she smiled. "But I'll have fun doing it."

"When do you go in for your next doctor's appointment?" Alex asked, hoping she didn't sound too anxious. With Jamie's past record, Alex thought the doctor should see her on a weekly basis instead of monthly.

"I see Dr. Chandler at the end of the week," Jamie replied. "As much as I miss Dr. Rawlins, I'm really enjoying having a woman obstetrician."

"I'm glad everything's working out," Alex reached over and rubbed her sister's stomach. She loved feeling the baby inside move and kick and roll around. She swallowed the lump that formed in her throat and pushed her fears to the back of her mind. Changing the subject, she said, "With Mom teaching at the 'U,' she'll be around to help out when the baby comes."

"And after the LSAT is done, I'll be able to spend more time at home," Steve added, gathering up the plates and stacking them in front of him.

"But you can't stay at home, honey. If you don't work, we don't eat. Besides, you're going to be busy marketing your new idea," Jamie said proudly.

"What new idea?" Alex asked. Steve had come up with some pretty crazy inventions since she'd known him. Had one of his nutty ideas actually worked?

"Well," he said a little hesitantly, "I haven't really wanted to say much since I'm still waiting for the buyer of Delaney's Department Store to call me back with their decision, but it's possible that they'll want to carry my gourmet fortune cookies in their gift shop."

"You mean your idea of fortune cookies that fit any occasion?" Rich couldn't hide his surprise.

"Yeah, can you believe it?" Steve seemed dumbfounded himself. "I finally decided it was time to quit thinking so much and start acting on my ideas. So I had a prototype made—a sample of fortune cookies—and took them around. The buyer at Delaney's happens to be

Chinese, if you can believe it, and she thought it was a great idea. She especially loved the cookies about turning forty, since she'd just had her fortieth birthday. She actually laughed out loud when she read some of the sayings. I also made up some cookies for retirement, graduation, weddings, 'sweet sixteen,' and birthdays."

"Steve, that's wonderful." Alex was so excited for him. With the setback he and Jamie had had when his outdoor rental business was completely devastated, Alex was happy to see him get a lucky break.

"We'll see. If they decide to go ahead with it, we'll need to have a serious brain-storming session and come up with a lot more sayings. Believe me, Confucius isn't a whole lot of help right now."

"That would be fun," Alex said. She liked the idea of helping Steve fill his cookies with clever sayings. "You know, the more I think about it, the better I think it is. I've always thought fortune cookies never seemed to apply to a situation exactly, but you could have them at any occasion, even baby showers and missionary farewells."

"And we're even thinking of coloring the cookies to make them more fitting—you know, green and red for Christmas, pink and red for Valentine's Day," Steve added.

Jamie stood and lifted her daughter from the high chair. "Time to get you in the tub, young lady," she said.

Just then the phone rang. Steve leaned back in his chair and answered it. Alex could tell by the tone in Steve's voice, he wasn't happy about who was on the other end.

"I'm sorry, Mr. Nichols, but until you have any proof, you cannot see *our* daughter."

Jamie froze.

"Here—" Alex jumped to her feet. "Let me take her."

Woodenly Jamie handed Nikki over and sank down on her chair, listening numbly as Steve spoke. Alex carried Nikki to the bathtub. After a quick scrubbing she bundled the baby in a towel and dried her off.

"You smell clean and pretty," she said, rubbing the toddler with the towel. Her wet hair sprang into black, corkscrew curls all over her head.

"Pwity," Nikki said.

"Yes," Alex repeated, nodding. "You're very pretty."

Rich poked his head inside the bathroom. "Hey, girls, need any help?"

Alex looked over her shoulder at Rich. "Is everything okay in there?"

"Steve's off the phone now, but Jamie's very upset. I thought I'd give them some time alone," he explained, slipping into the bathroom and closing the door behind him.

"Here." Alex handed him the baby. "Take her to her room while I straighten up in here. And if you feel really brave, you can try to get a diaper on her."

"You got it," Rich said, snuggling his nose into the child's neck and making her giggle. "Come on, princess. Let's get that bottom of yours covered before you have an accident."

Alex wiped the water off the floor around the tub where Nikki had splashed up a storm. As she stacked all the toys in a basket to drain, she wondered what would happen if Mr. Nichols continued to pursue this ridiculous notion that he was actually Nikki's father. Certainly positive proof of his parenthood didn't qualify him to take the child. Wasn't the bigger issue who would provide a better home and upbringing for Andrea Nicole?

Alex paused at the door before going into Nikki's room, watching Rich try to get the baby to hold still long enough so he could fasten the sticky tabs on her diaper. As she stood there, she felt her throat tighten at the thought that Rich might never be a father. More than anything she wanted to have children. His children. Rich would make such a wonderful father—loving, giving, fun, but firm. For the first time she realized why Jamie, for so many years, had become almost obsessed with having children.

Nikki squirmed and twisted on the changing table, thrashing like a lion in a net to get free. Rich struggled and fumbled with the diaper, all the while trying to coax the child to lay still. "I'll give you a million dollars if you'll hold still," he bribed through clenched teeth, but she continued to wiggle.

Alex tried not to laugh but couldn't help it when Rich finally said, "There—got it," and held up Nikki. One tab was stuck to her stomach, the other hung hopelessly off the other side, unattached to anything.

He looked up at Alex. "How long have you been standing there?" he demanded.

"Long enough," she said.

"Why didn't you offer to help?" He glared at her.

Alex arched her eyebrows in amusement. "What? And miss the biggest laugh I've had all week?"

"She's pretty strong for a one-year-old. How do you get her to hold still?" Rich looked completely baffled.

"The principle of distraction, Rich. You have to get her mind off the diaper. Watch." Alex grabbed a brightly colored stuffed clown whose nose honked when she squeezed it. "Lookee, here, Nikki. Look who I have."

She held the toy out to Nikki, who grabbed it and squealed with delight as she honked the clown's nose over and over. Quickly laying the child on the changing table, she whipped off the mutilated diaper, smoothly slipped on a new one, and fastened it.

"There," she said. "All done."

"Very good," Rich said. "I'm impressed." He stepped closer. Alex held the toddler in her arms as she received a kiss from Rich.

"Kisses," Nikki shouted. "I-na kisses."

"You want a kiss, too?" Rich leaned down and received a wet, slobbery smooch from the baby. He pulled a face and wiped at his mouth. "Your turn," he said to Alex.

Bravely Alex puckered up and received the same slippery kiss. "Ooo, thank you, Nikki. Time for 'jamas."

"Bawnee jamas. Bawnee jamas."

"Okay, okay," Alex said, digging through Nikki's top drawer. "You can wear the Barney pajamas."

They got the little girl dressed, then took her into the living room with them where Steve and Jamie sat together on the couch. An awkward silence hung in the room.

"Clint Nichols is going ahead with the DNA test," Steve explained. "He said if it takes every last cent he owns, he's going to find out if Nikki is his—one way or the other."

Chapter 6

Back in New York, Judith hailed a taxi in front of her Manhattan apartment. The rain had been pouring all morning and didn't show any sign of letting up.

"Doubleday's coffee shop," she told the taxi driver.

She was meeting with Wally Sharp from *New Woman* to talk about her unexpected opportunity to teach at the University of Utah. She hoped he would be open to giving her a leave of absence, and at the same time, keep her in mind for some freelance projects.

Sitting at a booth, waiting for Wally, Judith watched the people on Times Square scurrying, under umbrellas, to get to their destinations. Wally was late, as usual.

Judith's thoughts were jumbled as she pondered the changes that were occurring not only in her life, but in both of her daughters' lives as well. Here she was, ready to make a monumental career change. Not only would it allow her to be closer to her daughters, she would also be closer to Dave Rawlins. That proximity would certainly have an impact on their relationship, and she wasn't sure she was ready for that.

She looked up to see a pair of young women enter the shop, shaking the rain from their umbrellas.

"Morning ladies," the man behind the counter called. "Can I get you an espresso?"

"Good morning," one of the young women answered. "No, thank you, but we would like two hot chocolates and a couple of blueberry bagels with cream cheese."

Judith watched the girls find a booth by the window and wait for their order. When they removed their coats, Judith realized who they were. They wore name tags indicating they were sister missionaries. Mormon missionaries. She watched them pause just a moment before beginning their meal and bow their heads quickly, obviously blessing their food. No one else would have noticed, but Judith had been watching and would have been disappointed had the girls done otherwise.

With Wally still not in sight, Judith decided to go over and visit with the girls.

"Excuse me," she said. "I noticed that you were wearing name tags. Are you Mormon missionaries?"

"Why yes," one of the girls said. "We are."

"Are you LDS?" the other sister asked.

"Well, no," Judith answered, somewhat hesitantly. "But both of my daughters are and I've taken the missionary lessons."

"That's wonderful," the first sister said. She had long dark hair, and beautiful, exotic features. Judith guessed she was Polynesian. Her name tag said Sister Corlett.

"How's your missionary work going here in Manhattan?" Judith asked.

"Great," the girls exclaimed together. They laughed, then the other sister, who was fair-skinned, her light brown hair pulled up into a clip on the back of her head, explained, "We've received a lot of help from the members lately, and it makes a big difference. The members here are really great." Her name, Judith noticed, was Sister Bond.

"Do you get invited for dinner much?" Judith asked.

"Occasionally," Sister Corlett said. "But the members here are very busy and usually work until late in the evening, so we don't get together with them much except on Sundays."

"Would you like to come to my house for dinner sometime?" she invited.

"Sure," Sister Bond spoke up. "We'd love to."

Judith jotted her address down on the back of one of her business cards. "Would Wednesday work for you? Say around 7:00?"

"If we could make it at 7:30, it would be better. We're meeting with our ward mission leader at 6:00," Sister Corlett explained.

Judith added her phone number to the card and handed it to the sisters. Through the window next to the sisters, she saw Wally step out of a cab that had stopped in front of the coffee shop.

"I'll look forward to Wednesday," she said as the sister missionaries thanked her again. Leaving them to their meal, she greeted Wally with an affectionate hug. She'd enjoyed working with him on the magazine, and she loved New York. But as much as she loved her job, she was excited for the new challenge of teaching at the University. Even more, she looked forward to living near her daughters and grandchildren and seeing more of them. And, she wouldn't deny it, she looked forward to seeing more of Dave, as well.

* * *

That night Rich brought Chinese food over to Steve and Jamie's apartment for everyone to enjoy. Nikki played with her chopsticks and covered herself from head to toe with fried rice.

"What time does Julianne get in on Friday?" Rich asked Alex, scooping the rest of the sweet and sour sauce onto his plate. Alex had worked with Julianne, an international exercise and fitness consultant from England, during the two-month Supertour in Europe the summer before, and the two girls had become good friends. Alex was proud of Julianne, who, the previous year, had successfully made it through her treatment for anorexia and bulimia. She'd been hospitalized twice and had starved herself to the point that she'd actually gone into shock and nearly died of heart failure. But she'd fought long and hard and had made it through the battle—though not without a lot of scars. She'd nearly ruined her health and her career, and instead of bringing her family closer together, the experience had pulled them further apart.

Alex had received a fax of Julianne's itinerary earlier that day. "Around ten in the morning," she replied. "I thought I'd let her get a little sleep first then maybe we could do something fun that evening, like take her out to dinner. She's so excited about coming to Salt Lake."

"I can't wait to meet her," Jamie said. "You've talked so much about her, I feel like I know her already. Is she still trying to decide whether or not to join the Church?"

Alex nodded. "It's been so hard for her to have her parents take such a negative stand against her getting baptized. She's got an aunt and uncle who are members, and they've been a great support for her. She's actually living with them right now. I'm sure if and when Julianne does decide to join the Church it will be because of them. And of course, because of Andre." Andre was Julianne's boyfriend. They'd met when Alex and Julianne had attended church in France while on the Supertour.

"You and Julianne leave for San Diego on Monday, right?" Rich asked, reaching over to steal a piece of egg roll from Alex's plate. She slid her plate toward him so he could have the rest. "Right. We'll meet Sandy in San Diego Monday, then the conference starts Wednesday." Rich and Andre planned to fly to San Diego, on Saturday, after the conference. Andre was still in New York making arrangements for Alex's latest project. When they returned from San Diego, Alex and Julianne would begin work immediately on a revolutionary type of home video workout; Andre would be instrumental in organizing, arranging, and directing the production.

Alex continued. "We'll go to Sea World, and the zoo, of course. And we'd like to do some shopping."

"Sounds like fun," Jamie responded enthusiastically while attempting to get the chopsticks away from Nikki, who screamed in protest. Jamie knew her little girl was spoiled, but it had been hard not to dote over her daughter after all they'd been through to adopt the child.

"We're also going to hang out at the beach and do some snorkeling," Rich was quick to add. "And we've talked about chartering a boat and sailing to Catalina Island or something."

"Now *that* sounds fun," Steve said.

"Oh, Nikki, you have made such a mess," Jamie exclaimed, looking at her daughter in despair. It would take a high-pressure hose and rubber suits to pick up after Nikki's mess.

"Here," Alex offered. "Let me help you clean her up."

Jamie wiped the baby while Alex picked up clumps of rice. Rich and Steve went into the living room to watch a baseball game.

"How are you doing?" Jamie asked her sister.

"I'm fine," Alex answered, wondering what Jamie was getting at. "Why?"

"I just wondered if you'd made your appointment for the surgery yet." Jamie tossed the dishcloth into the sink and looked at her sister sympathetically. "I can imagine how you must be feeling."

Alex was kneeling on the floor as she cleaned. She sat back on her heels and shrugged. "It's hard. I try not to think about it too much, but when I do I can't seem to imagine anything but the worst possibilities. You know what I mean?"

"I do that, too," Jamie said. "I think it's our way of preparing ourselves for the worst, even though we're hoping and praying for the best."

Alex nodded in complete agreement.

"You know," Jamie gave Nikki a bottle to quiet her down and keep her still so they could talk. "When I first found out I was pregnant, I cried for days I was so happy. Then about a week later, I started crying again."

"Because you couldn't believe you were really pregnant?" Alex could imagine feeling that way herself.

"No, because I was already terrified I was going to lose this baby, too. I think in a way I began mourning the loss of this child, somehow trying to prepare myself just in case I did lose the baby." Jamie rocked Nikki on her lap as the child sucked apple juice contentedly from the bottle. "I was so scared I would miscarry again."

"Are you past that now?"

"Kind of," Jamie said. "I mean, I'm farther along with this baby than I have been with any of the others, but I just don't dare hope for the best, completely."

The sisters looked at each other, realizing that they shared the same deep, emotionally searing feelings. Although Alex didn't know the pain of losing a child, she was beginning to understand the agony of not knowing if she'd ever conceive and actually give birth to a child of her own.

"I'm so glad I have you to talk to." Alex looked into her sister's understanding eyes.

"And I'm glad to have you," Jamie said with an encouraging smile. "We'll be okay, Al. We just have to believe and have faith. I mean, look at me. What if I would've given up when I was so down and discouraged. I wouldn't have Andrea Nicole, and I never would have gotten pregnant. I mean, why would I even consider putting myself through all that pain again, unless I believed it could be different this time?"

Alex had wondered that herself.

"Well, I have faith that it's going to turn out okay. I just know it is, for me and for you." She reached over and gave Alex's hand a squeeze.

Alex clung to her sister's hand, and to her faith, hoping that hers would be as strong.

* * *

That evening before going back to their apartments, Rich and Alex drove out to their property to check on the progress of their home. Hand in hand they walked through the house, examining the workmanship, imagining the final product, sharing dreams of their future. They made some decisions about cabinets and lighting and agreed on a wood floor in the kitchen instead of tile. Alex hadn't fully understood until now how enormous the task of building a house was. It seemed as though there were major decisions that needed to be made on a daily basis.

"Rich," she began. "About that bay window—"

Rich frowned. "We've been through this before," he said. Alex felt herself start to tense up.

"But you know—"

Rich interrupted her. "Not tonight, Alex. Please. Let's just enjoy the evening."

Alex took a deep breath. She'd heard that couples building their own homes often ended up calling off the wedding. She was beginning to see why. She knew what she wanted, and he apparently knew what he wanted. The problem was, it wasn't the same thing. But because of what she felt for Rich, she took a deep breath and tried to put her frustration aside.

They stopped in the master bedroom, pausing underneath the open skylight. Looking up at the stars emerging in a darkening sky, they stood together, still hand in hand. Alex couldn't help the mental picture that came to her mind of a handsome oak fireplace with a cozy fire. It would be the perfect addition to this room. But she knew enough not to even mention it.

"It's been a long year, hasn't it?" Rich said softly, wrapping his arms around her.

Saving the fireplace discussion for later, Alex nodded and leaned her head against his shoulder. "It seems like an eternity."

"You know," Rich said, pausing a moment to brush a kiss on Alex's brow, "we're going to be awfully close to Las Vegas when we go to California. I hear the Graceland chapel is an unforgettable experience. Elvis himself performs the ceremony, and for an extra twenty bucks he'll sing 'Love Me Tender.'"

"Gee," Alex said, grinning. "It's tempting. I mean you are my 'hunka, hunka, burnin' love,' and everything. But I think I'll pass. I want this marriage done right. I haven't waited this long just to blow it at the last minute."

"This has been a long year, but you are definitely worth the wait, Mrs. Alexis McCarty soon-to-be Greenwood," Rich whispered, his lips meeting hers.

When she could speak, Alex chuckled. "My feelings exactly, Mr. Richard can-you-believe-we've-almost-made-it Greenwood."

Deciding that they'd lingered long enough, they made their way back to the truck in the dusk. Rich held her arm to help her negotiate the path. "I meant to ask you earlier," he said. "Did you ever get a copy of your patriarchal blessing?"

Alex kept a copy of it with her in her planner, so they sat in the truck reading it together. When it came to the part about the gift of discernment, she read it very slowly so she could absorb the full meaning.

You have been blessed with the gift of discernment. You will know in whom you should place your trust. You have been blessed with a close relationship with the Spirit. As long as you remain faithful to the gospel and obedient to the Lord's teachings, praying morning, noon, and night for protection from the adversary, listening carefully for the whisperings of the Spirit, you will be led by the hand and be a source of wisdom and counsel to others.

"You do have a good gut instinct," Rich said. "Like with Elena. You could tell there was something wrong, and I just couldn't see it." Elena had acted as Rich's agent when he first decided to market his artwork. She was someone Alex would prefer to forget entirely. Still Alex was surprised that this gift of discernment referred to in her blessing was evident to other people. Until she'd received the blessing, she'd never thought of herself as someone with particularly good instincts.

"I've learned my lesson," Rich continued. "I trust your judgement, and you're the first person I want to talk to about anything. You always listen and try to understand. I'm glad you don't mind sharing your blessing with me."

Alex was surprised. "Did you think I wouldn't?" she asked. "Blessings are so personal I didn't want to overstep my bounds," Rich said earnestly.

Alex turned to face him squarely. "Rich," she said, "I want us to share everything, always. I want you to feel like you can talk to me about anything, good or bad, happy or sad. You do feel that way, don't you?"

Rich signaled his agreement with a kiss, then directed her to keep reading. She continued:

> *You will be tried and tested to the limits of your endurance. There will be many challenges for you to face, but if you remain faithful, staying close to the Lord, you will be blessed and protected. Your faith will carry you through many hardships.*

As she read further she slowed again to carefully take in the meaning of another phrase:

> *You will be blessed to find a worthy priesthood holder who will take you to the temple and there you will be sealed for time and all eternity. You will be blessed to have a posterity. The priesthood power will be a great blessing in your life and will protect you and your family from the evils of the world and the power of the destroyer. Pay strict attention to the counsel your priesthood leaders give you. You will be blessed for your obedience.*

You will be blessed to have a posterity, she repeated to herself silently. Even though she didn't completely understand how that was to come about and what part her health problems played in the whole scheme of things, the Lord had promised her a family. For now that would have to be enough.

Chapter 7

Waiting anxiously at the terminal, Alex scanned the passengers as they exited the plane. She hadn't seen Julianne for nine months, and that had been before her friend had recovered from her eating disorder. Julianne had seemed lifeless and distant back then, with pale, gray skin and dark, sunken eyes. Her hair had thinned to the point that Alex could see patches of scalp. Julianne's condition had scared Alex and helped her renew her determination to never let her own tendencies for anorexia take control of her life again.

A tall, blonde woman stopped in front of her. "Alex!"

Alex looked at her in astonishment. "Julianne?!" The two friends shared a warm embrace, then Alex stepped back and looked at Julianne from head to toe. She was still thin, but her cheeks glowed with vibrant color and her eyes were bright and lively.

Alex was nearly speechless but finally managed to say, "Julianne, you look wonderful. It's so good to see you."

They stepped away from the crowd of people and walked toward the baggage claim.

"You look wonderful yourself," Julianne said. "Knowing I was coming to see you and we'd be at the conference together was all the incentive I needed to work even harder to get better and get my weight up. I feel so good. I don't think I realized just how sick I was."

"I'm so proud of you for sticking with it," Alex said, remembering her own struggles and what Julianne had gone through. "I'll bet you're exhausted though. Traveling can do it to you."

"A bit. I didn't get much sleep, but I'm sure I'll be fine. I'm just so excited to be here." She looked around the bustling airport. "I can't wait to meet the rest of your family and go to Temple Square."

"They're anxious to meet you, too." Alex put her arm around Julianne and gave her another squeeze. "We are going to have so much fun together."

At Alex's apartment, Julianne realized she was more tired than she thought, so after a quick bite to eat, she rested for a while on Alex's bed. When the phone rang, Alex snatched it up at the first ring so it wouldn't disturb Julianne. It was Alex's mother.

"Hi, honey. Did your friend get there okay?"

"She did and she looks great," Alex said proudly. "She made her goal weight and has maintained it now for four months." As she spoke, she put a lid on the salad bowl and wrapped the fresh bagels in plastic. "She's lying down right now."

"I'm so glad she's doing better. Did she say much more about the treatment?"

Alex sighed. "Only that it was the hardest thing she's ever been through in her life and that she discovered emotions and learned things about herself she's never understood before. You remember what my doctor always said—you 'heal from the inside out.' I guess there were a lot of issues that caused her to have an eating disorder. Once she faced those issues and discovered the power they had over her, she was able to understand her actions and learn to take control of her life."

Alex had talked to her mother about Julianne and her struggles with her eating disorder. Growing up, the slender British girl had had great potential as a professional ballet dancer until a car accident had shattered the bones in one foot. After that, she was never able to dance *en pointe* again. Her parents had always had very high expectations of her, especially her father, and they had treated her as if it were her fault. She was always seeking their approval and couldn't bear their disappointment. So she tried to be perfect every other way she could.

"I've always felt they wouldn't love me if I weren't a dancer," Julianne had confided to Alex. "They admitted to me that they were terribly disappointed in my accident. Their dreams had been shattered along with the bones in my foot."

"*Their* dreams? What about *your* dreams?" Alex had asked in disbelief. Julianne had merely shrugged.

Alex wrapped the spiraled phone cord around her index finger and continued, "It's still hard for her, especially since she became interested in the Church. Of course, her parents are completely opposed to the idea of her joining. She's been living with her aunt and uncle, and they've really been a strength to her. They're already members. Plus she's got Andre. He's been by her side through a lot of this, too."

Judith knew how hard Alex had worked to overcome her own eating disorder, and had tried to be supportive. "I'm sorry to hear about her family," she said. "At least she has good friends, like you."

Alex asked Judith about her meeting with Wally and her plans for coming to Salt Lake. Judith recounted the high points, then she said something unexpected. "I meant to tell you, I ran into the missionaries the other day. I invited them over for dinner."

Alex knew her mother loved feeding people. "That was nice of you," she said, "especially as much as those elders eat."

"Oh, but they weren't boys. These were sister missionaries," Judith corrected her. "They're darling girls. We had a wonderful visit and I'm having them back again on Sunday. I'm already looking forward to seeing them again."

Alex smiled to herself. Her mother couldn't help pulling these two girls under her wing. It was instinctive for Judith to reach out to someone in need.

"We had a nice talk. I told them all about you and Jamie and said I'd even met with the missionaries myself. You know, honey," Judith's voice grew softer, "these girls were so easy to talk to."

Alex felt a tingle run through her. She knew it wasn't by chance that her mother had run into the missionaries. The Lord was guiding her mother—slowly but surely.

"I felt like I could ask them anything so I talked to them about temple marriage."

"You did?" Alex couldn't hide her surprise.

"I think that out of all the things I'm struggling with about the Church, temple marriage is the biggest."

Alex was surprised. "Temple marriage? Why? I don't understand."

Her mother's voice grew quiet. "I'm going to admit something to you, that I've never said before. I . . . I know the Church is true, Alex."

Alex gasped. It just came out. "What?" Had she heard her mother correctly? "Really? You mean it?"

Judith didn't answer right away. Alex heard a sniffle. *Was her mother crying?*

"Mom? I don't understand. What is it?"

Judith's voice was shaky. "Because, Alex, I love Dave. We've talked about getting married, but I don't know what to do—I still love your father." She could barely get the words out.

Although Alex loved her father deeply, she felt her mother deserved another chance at happiness. Judith had been alone for nearly twenty years, and Alex couldn't think of a more wonderful man for her mother than Dr. Rawlins. He was kind, humorous, intelligent, and compassionate. He'd helped Jamie through three miscarriages and had also helped Alex face her own eating disorder. The two sisters had watched his growing relationship with their mother with a mixture of satisfaction and excitement.

Alex didn't know what to do or say. "Mom," she tried to soothe her, "The Lord understands your feelings. Things will work out. Don't worry." But that didn't satisfy Judith.

"But, Alex dear, I love both of them," she argued. "If I get baptized, I can only be sealed to one of them—and I want it to be Samuel. I don't know if David will understand that."

Alex could hear the pain in her mother's voice. She tried to reason with her mother and at the same time offer words of comfort. "Mom, I know there are other women who've lost the husband they were sealed to and have been remarried. The Lord doesn't expect you to go through your life alone. I just know it will be okay. You have to have faith that it will."

"I guess," Judith answered, her voice still trembling. She didn't sound convinced.

"Have you prayed for help?" Alex asked.

"Constantly, darling. I've about worn out the Lord and my knees over this one." Judith paused. "But I'll tell you—I've realized I don't want to lose Dave."

"Have you talked to him about this?" Dr. Rawlins was so easy to talk to, Alex knew he would understand her mother's concerns. Alex had just talked to Dr. Rawlins herself about her examination, and they'd had a long discussion about cysts and endometriosis. He'd given her every reason to believe that she would be able to have children and that the problems she had were manageable.

"I don't know what I'd say," Judith faltered, ". . . or how I'd even bring it up."

Alex said another quick prayer for guidance to say the right thing. "This involves both of you, Mom," she said, "and I think Dave would be able to help you sort through it. Don't forget, he's been married in the temple once before. He probably has some idea how you're feeling."

Judith was quiet for a moment. Alex could tell she was thinking. "Maybe you're right," Judith finally said. "I just don't know how I'd even bring it up. I don't want to hurt him, but I don't see any way around it."

As Alex hung up the phone, she closed her eyes a few moments to express her thanks in a brief prayer. After a long year of waiting and praying, her mother was ready to embrace the gospel and be baptized at last. She was even considering the next step in her relationship with Dr. Rawlins. *Help Mom to have the strength and courage to take those steps,* Alex prayed. *And bless those two sister missionaries who made a spiritual connection with her. Help them to help her.*

* * *

Julianne didn't sleep long. Rich was out at the construction site, so Alex and Julianne decided to go out and say "hi" and look around at the house. When the freeway took them past downtown Salt Lake, Julianne noticed the temple in the distance.

"I can't wait to go to Temple Square tomorrow," she said. "And I want to take Andre when we get back from San Diego."

"Things are pretty serious between you and Andre, aren't they?" Alex looked over at her friend quickly then back to the road.

Julianne gave a heavy sigh. "We've talked about marriage, but there are so many obstacles still to overcome."

"Like what?" Alex asked curiously.

Julianne ran her fingers through her blonde, chin-length hair. "The fact that I'm not a member of the Church yet is the biggest. He's determined to wait until we can get married in the temple. I don't know if I can wait that long. Plus, I haven't even decided about getting baptized yet."

Alex could tell this was weighing on her friend's mind. Remembering her conversation with her mother, Alex knew that

Julianne, like her mother, would be able to find out for herself if she had the desire. "Julianne, you just need to listen to your heart. Things will work out, you'll see," she promised.

The conversation turned to Andre, who had told Julianne he wanted to move to the U.S., a decision that his stay in New York had helped him to make. He felt there was more opportunity for him to become a film producer in America than there was in Europe.

"He's pretty excited about our exercise video," Julianne said. "And he's thrilled to have a chance to finally do what he loves."

Alex was equally thrilled to have Andre on her team. "He's not the only one excited about this project," she said. "Sandy is looking forward to spending all of her time in San Diego promoting us."

"It is going to be successful, isn't it, Alex?" The doubt in Julianne's voice caught Alex off guard. She turned to look at her friend, and the car nearly swerved into the next lane. Fortunately, there were few cars on the road, and none in the lane beside her.

"Of course it is," Alex said adamantly. "We've done the market research and talked to all the experts. Everyone agrees we've found an untapped market."

Julianne gave Alex a worried look. "I hope they're right. I'd hate to let all our investors down."

Alex reached out to squeeze Julianne's hand, careful to keep her eyes on the road to avoid a second lapse. "I've had my doubts and concerns about this whole thing, too," she confided. "But Juli, I really feel good about it. Personalized workout videos that are geared to individuals make so much sense. Women these days are so busy with work or family, or trying to juggle both, that there isn't much time left in the day to run to the gym and work out."

Alex and Julie had created a questionnaire for women and men to fill out, asking them exactly what they wanted from their workout, what their trouble spots were, what their limitations were, and what their goals were. From that, Alex and Julianne would design specific workouts to fit their needs. Alex hadn't had one negative response from anyone she'd asked about it. Even the men were responding positively to the concept.

Alex continued. "I know there's a need for this type of product. We can even put an extra personal touch in the video by using their name and helping them with exactly the areas they feel they need to focus on. That will make the video even more effective at motivating them and giving them encouragement through the workout."

"I guess I just worry. You know me," Julianne confessed. "I don't handle failure very well."

Alex gave her friend a reassuring smile, "Well, I can guarantee this is not going to fail. We're going to have so many orders for these crazy videos we won't be able to keep up. We'll have to hire dozens of staff members to help shoot the videos. Andre's going to be so busy he won't have time to produce any of those commercials and corporate videos like he wants."

Julianne was silent for a moment, then she said, "You know what?" She looked at Alex and grinned. "I think you're right. And I'll tell you something else—I'm glad we thought of it first."

Alex knew they were taking a risk, but she was convinced it was the right thing for them to do. She often felt that the Spirit was guiding her life in every aspect, even in her business decisions. She realized that Julianne didn't have the reassurance of the Holy Ghost to help her, which made Alex doubly grateful to have this constant companion in her life.

Help Julianne feel the Spirit, she prayed. *Give her an opportunity to see what a difference it makes to have the Spirit.*

Chapter 8

Saturday morning Alex and Julianne went shopping in downtown Salt Lake City. Alex needed to have a final fitting for her bridal gown, order the flowers, and double check on the reception center and refreshments. Afterwards they were going to visit Temple Square.

Rich hadn't seen Alex's dress yet. She wanted to surprise him. But even though he hadn't seen it, she knew he would love it. Every time Alex put on the dress she felt like a princess. It was a Victorian style gown with intricate beading across the shoulders and down the front of the bodice. The long, sheer sleeves were also beaded. The waistline came just below her natural waist and dipped into a point in front. Her skirt was billowy and full, with layers of organza, satin, and netting.

Julianne gasped when Alex walked out of the dressing room.

"Alex. You look breathtaking." She walked a circle around Alex "oohing" and "aahing" over each tiny detail.

"How does it fit?" the sales clerk asked.

Alex sighed happily. "Like a glove. The tailor did a wonderful job."

"I'll make sure and let them know. The gown is beautiful on you. You made a good choice," she complimented Alex.

Alex smiled and looked in the mirror again. Even with less than six weeks to go, her wedding still seemed so far away. But she knew the next few weeks would fly by with the San Diego trip and the wedding preparations yet to make.

When she and Julianne finally made it to Temple Square, they wandered the grounds slowly, filling their lungs with the heady fragrance of millions of flowers, feeling the sweet breeze whisper through the trees.

"It's amazing," Julianne exclaimed as she looked up at the majestic spires, reaching heavenward.

"What is?" Alex asked, noticing how quiet Julianne had become as they'd strolled the grounds.

"Outside on the street, life is busy and chaotic. People are blasting their horns, annoyed at the other drivers. Others are rushing to get to their jobs, or get errands done, and who knows what. But you step inside the temple grounds, and there's a whole different feeling. The atmosphere is so peaceful and serene. It's almost as if I don't want to go back out there," Julianne said, pointing beyond the gate. "I like how this feels in here. Even though I know the world is still out there, somehow I feel protected, safe."

Alex nodded in understanding. "You've said you aren't sure about getting baptized. But when you receive the gift of the Holy Ghost, that's how it feels because you can have the Holy Ghost with you always. Even though the world is full of problems and dangers, you have the constant reassurance, that 'peace' you referred to, that comes from having the Holy Ghost with you."

Julianne looked at the temple. Alex could tell she was thinking about what she said. Pieces of the puzzle were starting to fit into place; the picture was beginning to take shape. Alex could see that Julianne was searching and yearning. *That's what it takes,* Alex said silently.

"Come on," she said, walking toward the visitors' center. "There's something I want to show you."

Alex would never forget how she felt when she herself had first seen the statue of Christ inside the visitors' center. She wanted Julianne to have the same moving experience. As they made their way to the statue, Alex prayed that Julianne's heart would be receptive to the Spirit.

Around the circular ramp they walked toward the statue, a reverent silence surrounding them.

At last they emerged into the room containing the statue that stood gloriously in front of a background of the swirling blue heavens.

Julianne stood, speechless.

Alex glanced at her face, completely understanding her awestruck expression and the feelings that were no doubt overwhelming her. Julianne blinked several times, a veil of moisture covering her eyes, and reached for Alex's hand. She held it tightly in hers without speaking. No words were necessary.

They remained that way, feeling they were in a dimension removed from the "real" world, feeling the presence of that sweet, unmistakable spirit, until a group of noisy tourists wound their way up the ramp toward them. The two girls left, but Alex was sure Julianne wouldn't forget what she had felt.

* * *

That evening Rich barbecued hamburgers for the two girls. Julianne had wondered what an American barbecue was all about, so Rich and Alex decided to treat her to one. Rich was the only man Alex knew who could barbecue and record videos at the same time. He wanted to get Julianne's first barbecue on video for her.

Along with the hamburgers, they had baked beans, potato salad, chips and salsa—which Julianne went wild over—and corn on the cob. They feasted until their stomachs were stuffed and their eyes bulged. Julianne enjoyed her hamburger, wasn't sure about the baked beans and potato salad, but loved the salsa and the corn on the cob. Her favorite thing to do was to roll the cob on the cube of butter.

As they relaxed on Rich's balcony that overlooked the Wasatch Mountains to the east, Alex and Julianne told Rich about their day. Alex blushed under Rich's gaze as Julianne described how exquisite Alex looked in her wedding gown. Even though Alex knew Julianne was embellishing the truth, she let her go on. She wanted Rich to anticipate seeing her in her gown as much as she anticipated wearing it.

"The house looks great," Julianne said to Rich. "How much longer until it's finished?"

Alex got up from the table and grabbed the pitcher of lemonade. She began refilling their drinks, curious to hear Rich's reply to Julianne's question.

Before answering, Rich cleared his throat then took a drink from his glass. "It depends," he said slowly. "We still have a few final decisions to make."

Alex knew he was referring to the porch, the bay window, and the fireplace, and she just couldn't understand why he was so adamantly opposed to the ideas. They still hadn't reached a compromise and they were getting down to the wire.

Alex set down the pitcher and playfully circled her arms around his neck and nuzzled his ear, "Rich honey," she said sweetly, "I know we would be glad in the long run if we spent just a little more and really got what we wanted in the house."

"A little more?" He turned and looked at her in disbelief, as if he couldn't believe she was serious. "Alex, changes like this would cost at least ten thousand dollars or more. We've already gone over our budget with the other upgrades we've made. Maybe down the road we can add those things you want, but right now we just can't do it."

With a frustrated sigh, Alex released her hug and started clearing dishes. She didn't want Julianne to know she was upset, but Rich could be so obstinate sometimes and it hurt that his mind was so closed. He wouldn't even *consider* the improvements her ideas would make to the house.

Trying to keep the conversation light, she turned to her friend and asked, "What do you think, Julianne? Don't you agree the home would look better with a front porch. Plus, it would provide shelter in bad weather. People wouldn't have to stand there and get rained on while they're waiting for us to open the door."

Julianne wiped her mouth with her napkin, then put it on her plate and said, "Actually, I think I'm going to stay out of this debate." She speared one last strawberry from her plate with her fork and popped it into her mouth.

Alex didn't like how she was starting to feel inside. Rich was making her so mad. Why couldn't he just try to see her point of view about the improvements?

But he couldn't. He wouldn't. Alex looked at him, his jaw clamped stubbornly shut, the way he avoided her gaze, unwilling to discuss the issue any further, and wondered if this was how married life was going to be. Disagreeing and having to compromise, or having to give in completely.

For the first time since their engagement, Alex tasted a side of marriage that left a bitter aftertaste. She'd only focused on the fun and togetherness of marriage. But she couldn't help seeing the "real" side of it now.

Why couldn't he give in? Why did she have to be the one?

Chapter 9

"I just don't feel good about going," Alex protested over the phone to her sister. "I don't want to leave you here with all of this going on!" Alex knew there was a very real threat that at any time Jamie's pregnancy might end in a miscarriage, as her previous pregnancies had. At the same time, Jamie and Steve faced the heart-wrenching prospect that Clint Nichols would find a way to prove paternity and take Andrea Nicole from them.

"Besides," Alex continued, "if I stayed home I could have my surgery sooner and get it over with." Alex had scheduled her surgery for the Tuesday after they returned from San Diego, even though she and Julianne had already planned to start shooting their workout video on Wednesday. The doctor had explained that it was a simple outpatient surgical procedure; the two tiny incisions would be a little tender, but otherwise she'd feel fine the next day.

"Alex, I appreciate you offering to stay home, but having you stay here won't change anything," Jamie opposed her adamantly. "Besides, Steve found out what is involved in taking a paternity test. He has a friend who works in the Genetic Testing Lab at the University Medical Center."

To establish paternity, a blood sample was needed from the baby and both parents. Since the mother was dead, it would be difficult to get any kind of tissue sample for DNA testing from her. If cause of death were questionable, an autopsy would have been performed and slides of tissue samples prepared, but that was unlikely in this case.

Jamie explained all this to Alex, concluding, "If alcohol was suspected in the accident, a drug/alcohol test would have been done on the mother and a blood sample taken, but we don't know if that was done."

Alex couldn't help but think it would cost a lot of money to have the mother's body exhumed to take a tissue sample, and she said so. "Exactly," Jamie said. "I don't think Mr. Nichols knew exactly what he was up against when he came up with this crazy scheme of his. I still haven't figured out what's in it for him."

"And besides," Alex added, "what's the chance that he's even the father? Mr. Nichols said himself that Coralyn had a lot of 'men friends.' It sounds to me like Coralyn herself didn't even know for sure."

"Well," Jamie said confidently, "Steve and I have spent a lot of time in prayer about this and we both feel really calm about it. I know Nikki is supposed to be with us, and Heavenly Father is going to make sure it stays that way."

When Alex asked how long it would take to get the results of the test, if Clint Nichols went ahead with it, Jamie answered, "Steve's friend said around a month or so. They check the samples in five different DNA spots for matches. It's pretty involved and is quite expensive. He said to plan on a month's time."

Alex realized that staying home from her convention really didn't make any sense. Even if the man did have the test, the results wouldn't show up until a few weeks after she returned from San Diego.

"Well, okay," she said. "If you're sure you're all right. I just hate to leave you if you need me."

"Alex, I would tell you if I did, but I don't," Jamie promised. "I'm actually surprising myself at how calm I am about this. I'm going to the temple tomorrow, and we're going to carry on as if everything is normal, because I know nothing is going to change. This is just one of those crazy obstacles the adversary throws in your way to test you. But I've got it from a better source that everything's going to be okay."

Alex believed her sister's words. "I just don't want you to get upset and go into premature labor or something, especially while I'm gone," she teased.

"At the rate I'm going, I'll probably go past my due date. So don't worry about us. You have fun and be careful, and we'll see you in a couple of weeks."

Alex still felt a strange hesitancy, unable to shake off a feeling in the pit of her stomach that something wasn't right. But what Jamie said made sense, and Alex couldn't see that staying home would change anything anyway. "And you're sure you don't mind addressing the rest of those wedding invitations for me?"

"Not at all. It will give me something to do while I sit here and retain water and get fat," Jamie laughed. "Listen, if you go to Sea World, Nikki would love a little stuffed Shamu."

Alex promised to bring one back. As she said good-bye, she noticed the lateness of the hour and realized that she still wasn't through packing. Turning her attention to last-minute preparations, she set her worries aside but prayed that everything would be okay.

* * *

The convention center was an enormous group of buildings set right on the waterfront of the San Diego Bay. From their room in the Marriott Hotel, Julianne and Alex had a beautiful view of the harbor and the bridge stretching to Coronado Island.

After traveling from the dry climate of Utah to the balmy, breezy climate of San Diego, the girls changed their clothes before meeting Sandy in the lobby for dinner.

While Julianne was in the bathroom, Alex took a moment to pray, grateful to have arrived safely, but mostly to ask the Lord to watch over her loved ones—Jamie, Steve, and Nikki, Judith and Dave, and of course, Rich. She missed him already.

Downstairs in the lobby, fitness participants from all over the country were still arriving and getting settled into their hotel rooms. The lobby buzzed with the energy of so many aerobic instructors, personal trainers, and health and fitness enthusiasts.

Before Alex and Julianne even had a chance to sit down, Alex saw Sandy coming out of the elevator. Sandy looked radiant, her naturally curly hair hanging in glossy red waves about her shoulders. Her skin was bronzed and glowing, her startling blue eyes, bright and lively. She looked wonderful.

"Alex," Sandy cried when she finally spotted her. She rushed over and they greeted each other with a hug. Then Sandy turned and cried, "Juli, darling," and hugged her too.

"Sandy," Alex couldn't help stating the obvious, "you look wonderful. Did you just win the lottery?"

Sandy laughed. "Me? Are you kidding?"

"Whatever's going on in your life must be working, I've never seen you so radiant."

"It's nothing, really," Sandy said. "I'm just happy to see both of you. We're going to have so much fun." Then she added, "I guess it might also be that I just secured a lovely apartment in Paris, thanks to Jean Pierre. We were having some trouble finding me a place, but with the Internet and a few phone calls, I'm all set. That was the final detail to be made before I moved, and I'm so relieved. I was getting a little worried."

"Are you sure there's nothing going on between you and Jean Pierre?" Alex asked, still not sure how keen she was on Sandy's decision to move to Paris.

"Good grief, Alex," Sandy exclaimed. "He's like a father to me. Especially now that my own father has passed away, Jean Pierre has been a great help and support to me. The last five years have been so busy, I feel like I've neglected him, but that's all going to change." Sandy paused to wave to some friends, then added, "My mother is even going to join me in Paris for the rest of the summer. She adores Paris and her French is flawless. She can be my interpreter. Plus, she and Jean Pierre are very close friends. But enough of this chit-chat. I've got reservations for dinner. We can talk while we eat. I'm anxious to hear all about you two. Julianne, you look fabulous, by the way." Sandy turned and headed toward the hotel restaurant. "C'mon," she called over her shoulder.

Alex and Julianne exchanged humorous glances before following Sandy. Sandy's level of intensity always amazed Alex. The woman was a whirlwind of energy; it seemed like her motor ran on high constantly. Alex wondered if the Eiffel Tower would still be standing after a tornado like Sandy arrived in France.

* * *

After dinner the three women walked in the evening shadows along the waterfront toward the convention center. Sandy wanted to show them the display she had set up to advertise the personalized workout videos they were calling *Just for You*. The aroma from the fragrant flowers around them mingled with the salty breeze from the ocean. The air was warm and relaxing.

Along the way, Sandy advised them about the details of the conference. "Julianne," she said, "Your kick boxing workout videos arrived this morning. I was getting a little worried, but they made it. And, Alex, we have your cookbook and your videos also on display. You might want to take a moment tonight and autograph some of the copies of the cookbook, before they go on sale in the morning. I know you'll both be busy with your own lectures and presentations, but the more time you can spend at the booth, the more we can pitch the new product. The public loves you both, and they'll be more inclined to listen to you than Kristi or Pam, the temporary help I've hired for the convention. They'll be running the booth."

"Okay," both Alex and Julianne agreed.

"Every participant is receiving information about the *Just for You* videos in their registration packet, and there's an ad and an order blank in each convention brochure. We've made a point to make sure everyone knows that part of the proceeds from the sale of the video are going to the National Eating Disorder Foundation."

They entered the Expo Hall, where all the booths and displays were set up. The enormous room was swarming with activity. Alex looked around for the ProStar booth. She knew she was also supposed to spend some time there, promoting her new signature bodywear and aerobic shoe. Nickolas Diamante, the president of ProStar and her dear friend, had been hoping to attend the convention, but he was unable to get away this year. Alex had enjoyed her experience as the ProStar spokesperson, which had proven to be highly productive and financially rewarding. During the last nine months, both she and Robbie Tyler from the Chicago Bulls had made numerous personal appearances, and some commercials as well, promoting the ProStar line in the United States. Several of the ProStar brand shoes had become top sellers, surpassing many of the already established market trendsetters.

Nickolas, or Nicko as Alex called him, had known all along that his product was good. He'd done everything possible to ensure a quality product, and he felt that he and his staff had chosen the perfect fitness icons to represent his line.

On the way to their booth, Julianne ran into some acquaintances from England and spent a few moments visiting with them. Sandy busily made last-minute changes and arrangements with Pam and

Kristi about the booth, so Alex took time to sign her cookbooks. She'd been pleased not only with its success, but at the milestone it signified in her life. Truly it represented the victory over a long hard battle with her anorexia, and she was grateful for the treatment she'd received that had helped her overcome it. Without treatment she knew she would have never been cured. Julianne echoed her feelings exactly, and had even admitted that she doubted she'd still be alive today without treatment. Getting help had been the hardest thing either of them had ever done, but it had helped both of them gain control over their lives again. Alex hoped and prayed that her book would be able to touch lives and help others gain the strength they needed to face their own challenges, whatever they were. She wanted to give encouragement and hope to people.

As she set down the copy of the cookbook she'd just signed, she had a strange feeling, as if someone had been watching her. Quickly she turned and looked over her shoulder, but found no one there. *That's odd.* She could have sworn someone was there. A chill ran up her spine. Trying to shake the feeling, she left the cookbooks and joined Sandy's lively conversation with the two booth workers. But she couldn't help taking one more look around, just to see if anyone was watching.

"Here she is," a voice said. Alex turned to see Sharla Mitchell with several people coming toward her. Sharla had been a presenter herself at one time, but was now a convention administrator. She was in charge of lining up the fitness professionals to present at the conferences and making sure they had everything they needed for their lectures or workshops.

"Nice to see you Alex," Sharla said, giving her a quick hug. "I wanted to welcome you to the convention and see if there's anything you need. Are your accommodations okay? Does the schedule work for you?"

"Everything's great," Alex said. "I can't think of anything else you could do for me."

"Well, just in case, we are assigning each of our presenters a personal assistant this year. They will act as your right-hand man—or woman—whatever the case may be." Sharla motioned to the individuals behind her, three girls and a man. All were dressed in similar black warm-up pants and light blue polo shirts to show their association with the convention.

"Great idea," Alex said. She remembered in the past she'd had problems with overhead projectors and sound systems and would have been glad to have someone take care of the unexpected problems while she continued with her presentations.

"Your assistant will be Dylan Mansfield," Sharla said, as the young man stepped forward.

He was probably in his mid-twenties, about Alex's height, lean but muscular, and had thick blonde hair. He extended his hand and gripped Alex's fingers.

His voice was very deep. "Hi, Alex. It's nice to meet you at last."

"Dylan is very excited to help you any way he can," Sharla explained. "I'll let you two get acquainted while we find the rest of our presenters."

"Thanks, Sharla," Alex said. She watched the woman and other assistants leave, then turned to Dylan. "So, you got stuck with me, huh?"

"Not at all, Ms. McCarty," he said, fairly quivering with excitement. "I was the first one to sign up, and I requested you specifically. I'm your biggest fan."

Alex laughed. "You are?"

"Oh, yes," he nodded earnestly. "I've followed your career and attended almost every workshop and presentation you've given. I've got all your videos and recorded every one of your ESPN workouts."

Alex was impressed at his devotion. "Wow, Dylan. Sounds like you really are my biggest fan."

"It's such a thrill to finally meet you in person. Although," he said, with one eyebrow raised, "we have met before. Twice. Do you remember?"

She thought back at the many appearances she'd made and tried to recall when she might have met this young man. Nothing came to mind and she shook her head. "Sorry."

Dylan looked surprised. "The first time we met was in Orlando, three summers ago," he reminded her. "You called a few members of the audience up to the front to do a demonstration. I was one of those people you called up front."

"Oh," she nodded, as if she, in fact, remembered. But his face seemed completely unfamiliar. She met so many new people during her workshops there was no way she could remember every name and face. "When was the other time?" she asked.

"I auditioned to be on your ESPN workout series. I made it to the final cuts, then lost out to Chip Sterling."

Alex remembered vaguely how the final decision for the series had been made, but didn't remember any details about Dylan. "I'm sorry that didn't work out for you," she said.

Dylan shrugged. "Well, I didn't take it personally. I'm sure you didn't have anything to do with the decision."

Alex didn't answer. She had, in fact, been the deciding factor in who ultimately was chosen. She didn't remember Dylan at all, only that Chip had been clearly superior to all the others who had tried out. Tactfully she said, "I'm sure you would have done a great job."

The young man nodded confidently. "I know I would have. I've been teaching at several of L.A.'s top health clubs. I have celebrities come to my classes all the time."

Alex looked around. She didn't plan on standing there talking to Dylan all day, but he didn't seem in a hurry to go anywhere. "Well, keep up the good work," she encouraged. "Maybe someday you'll have a show of your own. And I appreciate your willingness to help out."

"Oh, no," he protested. "It's such an honor just to be your assistant. I'm planning to attend every session you present, and I'm available anytime to help you. Anytime," he said with emphasis, "morning, noon, or night. Whatever you need. Don't hesitate to call."

"Well . . . thank you," Alex said, feeling awkward. His puppy-like eagerness was a bit embarrassing. "I appreciate that. You never know . . ."

He shoved something at her. "Here's a card with my room number, telephone number, and beeper number. If I'm not with you and you need me, this is how to reach me."

"Thanks, Dylan. I'll be sure to do that." She was ready to leave, but he showed no sign of going.

"Anytime," he said again.

She nodded. "Got it."

He stood there, as if he was waiting for an assignment.

"I guess that's all for now," she said. His face fell. "Oh, there is one thing," she said, trying to erase the disappointment from his face.

He perked up. "Yes?"

"I do need to get a list of times of appearances from the ProStar booth. I'm not sure when they have me scheduled there." Alex wouldn't have minded stopping by the booth herself, but Dylan was clearly thrilled to be able to be of service.

"I'll get right on it," he announced.

"Just leave it with the front desk at the hotel. They'll get it to me." She turned to leave.

"Are you sure there's nothing else I can do? Any errands to run, letters to mail, something to drink?" he asked persistently.

Alex had an impression of a pesky fly buzzing around a horse. "I can't think of anything right now, but I'm sure I will later."

"I'll see you soon then, Ms. McCarty," he said formally.

That was all she needed. "You can call me Alexis, Dylan," Alex said dryly.

His face lit up. "Oh, thank you—Alexis."

He hurried off, eager to take care of his task. Alex shook her head in dismay. Boy did he need to get a life!

Chapter 10

The next day the convention swung into full motion on a grand scale. Every meeting room and convention hall was filled with fitness classes, lectures, workshops, and actual workouts with music, action, and energy.

Alex spent time at the booth between lectures and presentations, answering questions about her signature workout shoe and talking to people about her personalized workout video. She was amazed at the response as she began to realize the sheer magnitude of this idea. She wondered if they would be able to keep up with the demand. Already after the first day there were close to seventy orders, and they hadn't even started shooting the videos.

She told Julianne the news when she arrived at the booth.

"It's a good thing Andre is getting a studio facility secured this week so we can get right to work when we get back to Salt Lake," Julianne said. "I'm glad we've already hired those six other instructors to help us. We can't waste any time."

"The response is marvelous, but don't be surprised if we see knock-offs of our idea within the next month or two. Even with a copyright, someone will find a way to tweak our idea just enough to duplicate it. I've picked up on some interesting conversation as I've wandered around the other displays and I can tell, this has caused quite a stir." Alex glanced down at her watch. "I'd better go change for my next lecture. When are you finished today?"

"I'm done. I was just going to hang out here for a bit, then I'm free the rest of the day."

"Let's go over to the Horton Plaza tonight. I've heard it's a lot of fun."

"What's the Horton Plaza?" Julianne asked.

"There's all kinds of shopping and entertainment and a lot of great places to eat. We can also walk around the Gaslamp Quarter and look at all the art galleries and speciality shops."

"Sounds fun. I'm game for anything." Julianne smiled at some women waiting to ask questions about the *Just for You* video.

"I'll meet you back at the hotel room then," Alex said with a wave.

Meandering through the three hundred or more booths, Alex made her way out of the Expo Hall to the women's locker room so she could change her clothes from workout gear to a more suitable attire for her nutrition lecture.

She dressed quickly, then with her notes in one hand and her gym bag in the other, she headed for the conference room where her lecture was to be held. In the distance she heard the steady beat of music from a class in one of the larger halls.

On a bench outside the room, she took a minute to sit and gather her thoughts and review her outline. She'd given this lecture many times but liked to refresh her memory before each presentation.

Halfway through the first page, she stopped. Once again, she had the feeling that someone was watching her. This time she raised her head slowly, letting her eyes quickly take in her surroundings. Except for several women gathered at the end of the hall taking a break with a quick snack between classes, and the regular hustle and bustle of a busy convention, she saw no one. At least, no one who would give her a reason to feel the goose bumps that covered her arms and shivered up her neck.

This is ridiculous! she scolded herself for being so jumpy. But the odd feeling stayed with her until she turned her attention toward setting up for her lecture. Once inside the classroom she greeted participants as they came through the door and rechecked her overhead transparencies to make sure they were in the correct order.

"Hi, Alex. Sorry I'm late. I was getting those extra copies of 8x10 glossies for your booth. I knew you'd run out," Dylan said. "You're everyone's favorite presenter."

"I don't know about that," Alex said. "But thank you for taking care of that for me."

"Do you need any help setting up?"

"I think I've got it." At the flash of disappointment on his face, she reconsidered. "Oh wait, would you mind checking to see if the overhead is working? And the microphone. Then I think I'll be ready to start."

"No problem," he said happily and bounded away.

Alex groaned to herself. She felt like she was babysitting, the way she had to find things for Dylan to do. She didn't have the heart to tell him to get lost or that she'd call him if she needed him. *I guess all I can do is put up with him for now,* she decided. *It's only a few days and then I'll never have to see him again.*

* * *

That evening Julianne and Alex wandered around Horton Plaza, stopping to watch a street magician who amazed and delighted the crowd of onlookers. The Plaza swarmed with tourists and crowds and the girls ended up waiting in line for half an hour for their chance to eat. They decided on Mexican food, figuring that this close to the border it had to be good.

Over cheese laden enchiladas and nonalcoholic strawberry daiquiris, Alex and Julianne ate outside on the terrace where the lights of the San Diego-Coronado bridge stretched across the harbor and moonlight reflected on the ocean.

After dinner they walked around the Gaslamp Quarter even though the shops were closed. As they followed the sidewalk, Alex felt the same strange sensation she'd had earlier. Someone was watching them, following them.

"Julianne," she said quietly, as they continued down the path. "Don't look yet, but in just a minute will you casually glance back and see if someone is behind us. Someone suspicious-looking." Alex knew she sounded like she was out of her mind, and was grateful when Julianne simply nodded. As they stepped to one side of the sidewalk to allow a group of people to pass by, Julianne looked back and studied the people behind them.

"Okay," Julianne said. "There is a mom and a dad with three children; one is in a stroller. There's a young couple holding hands, and a group of teenagers, five or six of them, carrying skateboards and talking loudly. That's pretty much it."

Alex was relieved that there was no explanation for her strange feeling, but she was also confused. *What was going on?*

"Are you going to tell me what this is about?" Julianne asked, puzzled.

Feeling foolish, Alex laughed and said, "It's nothing. I'm just being a little paranoid, I guess. I thought someone was following us."

"Really?" Julianne looked behind them again. "I didn't see anyone out of the ordinary—you know, sinister-like."

"I'm a little jumpy. I think I must be tired. It's been a long day." Alex didn't want to tell Julianne about the other times she'd had similar feelings. She just wanted to forget the whole thing. Obviously it was her imagination. "Are you ready to go back to the hotel room?" Alex asked. "I'm exhausted."

"I'm tired, too," Julianne acknowledged. "I think I still have a little jet-lag from last week. We can come back when Rich and Andre get here. Rich might enjoy seeing all the galleries."

That was all Alex needed to hear. She was anxious to get back to the safety and security of the hotel room and call Rich. Maybe hearing his voice would calm her down.

* * *

The phone was ringing when they opened the door to their room. Alex rushed over and answered it. "Hello?"

A familiar, well-loved voice asked, "Alex, is that you?"

"Rich!" Relief filled her immediately. Things like this happened often between them; she would be thinking of him and he would call, or he would show up at her door just as she was about to invite him to come over.

"I've been a little worried about you," he said. "How are you feeling?" Rich knew Alex had been concerned about coming to the conference because of her recent discovery about her health. She didn't want to have to go to the hospital because of a ruptured cyst.

Alex sat on the bed and slid her shoes off her aching feet. "Just my regular stomach pain, but as long as I take my pain medication, I do okay."

Alex told him about her day at the convention, not mentioning the strange feelings that had plagued her at odd moments. Then Rich updated her on how their house was coming.

"You know how we heard horror stories about contractors never showing up when they're supposed to? My problem is just the opposite—everyone seems to show up at the same time. I feel like an orchestra leader trying to keep everyone in the symphony playing the same song." Rich sounded tired and Alex was sorry he had the burden of overseeing the construction of the house. But before she could say anything, he added, "Guess what? Andre called today, and he's found a studio here in town we can use to film your video."

Rich had met Andre when he and Alex had stopped in London on the way home from Europe after Alex's Supertour. Rich had flown to Austria to meet Alex, and on the way home they had stopped to see Julianne in England. Andre had come over from France to be with her when she began her eating disorder treatment, so the foursome had been able to spend some time together. Rich and Andre had hit it off from the beginning, and before they parted ways, the two couples had made plans to get together again. This weekend they would be able to do just that.

"Andre's been a little discouraged trying to line up a crew," Rich said. "I told him I had time to make calls and help him a little. We want to have everything in order when we get back from California."

As Alex listened to Rich, she realized that she'd been very ungrateful. Her frustrations over their disagreements had kept her from seeing that above all he was a very kind and considerate man. She just needed to learn to appreciate his thrifty nature more. "Thanks for helping, Rich," she said softly. "I can hardly wait for Saturday to see you, either. I miss you."

Rich's voice was tender as he said, "I miss you, too, honey."

Alex hung up reluctantly. When Rich became her agent, she reminded herself, she wouldn't have to go anywhere without him.

"Hey," she said, noticing a bouquet of flowers on the table near the window. "Who sent you flowers?" She walked over and inhaled their sweet fragrance.

Julianne was standing at the bathroom, wiping the toothpaste from her lips. "I was waiting until you got off the phone to ask you. They're not for me."

"Oh, darn it," Alex grumbled. "And I didn't even notice before I hung up with Rich. I could have thanked him." She sighed. "Oh, well, I'll just have to call him back, won't I?"

Julianne reached for the phone. "Not until I make a quick call to Andre. I told him I'd ring him at his hotel tonight."

"Find out about the studio he's arranged for the video shoot," Alex asked. "I'm curious to know if we can get the set pulled together that quickly."

Alex took the card with her name on it from the envelope and read:

This is just the beginning of the many surprises that await you.

There was no signature. Alex read the card again. It didn't make sense. Why would Rich send her such a strange note? And why didn't he sign it?

After Julianne got off the phone, Alex read the note to her. "Why don't you just call Rich?" Julianne asked. "Maybe he's planning to come a day early, or he's arranged for some romantic cruise around the harbor while an airplane writes 'I love you' in the sky."

Alex rolled her eyes. "I'm sure that's exactly what he has planned, Juli." She dialed his number.

Rich picked the phone up on the first ring. "What's up?"

When Alex asked him about the flowers, he confessed that he hadn't thought to send flowers. "If you didn't, then who did?" She was sure it wasn't Nicko. Red roses were his style. There was someone else who had given her white flowers, but Jordan Davis was in Palo Alto—at least, he had been living there up to the time Alex had first gone to Idaho to be with Jamie.

"Well, I'd like to know who's sending my fiancée flowers," Rich grumbled.

Alex looked at Julianne, who shrugged her shoulders. Where did they come from?

"I guess I'll just have to wait and see. I'll let you know as soon as I find out anything. Maybe Sandy sent them."

"How is Sandy, by the way?" Rich asked.

Alex smiled. She'd never seen Sandy looking so good or acting so excited about anything before. She hated to admit it, but she had decided that this move was just what Sandy needed.

"We had a good talk at dinner about genealogy, if you can believe it," Alex laughed. "I swear I've never seen a person go as nuts over genealogy as she has. She's done research on both my father's and mother's descendants, and it's made me think that this is something Mom would get excited about."

Alex and Rich talked a few minutes more. Before they said good-bye again, Rich said, "Don't worry about the flowers. You've probably got a secret admirer. Just enjoy them, and I'll see you soon, okay?"

The weekend seemed forever away. Once Rich got there with her, she'd feel a whole lot better.

Chapter 11

Judith put one last pinch of salt in the gravy and gave it a stir. Just as she put the lid back on the pot, the doorbell rang. Wiping her hands on a dish towel, she rushed to the front door and greeted her guests. She'd invited the sister missionaries over for dinner again before she left for Salt Lake City. They'd come for dinner once before, and Judith had enjoyed their company so much she invited them again.

"Girls, come in. How are you this evening?" she greeted. "I hope you've had a good day."

The two sisters exchanged humorous glances, and Sister Bond said, "Well, except for taking the wrong subway, getting stood up at two appointments, and my curling iron going out on me, it's been great."

"Oh, dear. One of those days," Judith sympathized. "I hope it wasn't a problem making time to come over this evening."

"Are you kidding?" Sister Bond said. "It was the only thing that kept us going. We knew you wouldn't stand us up and that you'd be friendly to us."

"And," Sister Corlett added, "we haven't forgotten how wonderfully you cook."

While the sister missionaries washed their hands, Judith set the pot roast, mashed potatoes and gravy, and vegetables on the table. To keep the orange rolls warm, she waited until after the prayer was said to take them out of the oven.

While they ate, Judith asked each of the sisters questions about their home and family life. She found out that Sister Corlett came from a family of thirteen children and that she was the only girl in her family. "My mom cried and cried when I left," Sister Corlett said. "She was sure we'd never see each other again."

Sister Bond explained that she came from a nonmember family and was being supported by members in her ward. She had joined the Church when she was sixteen, and after high school she had spent two years at BYU before deciding to go on a mission. Her family had been very opposed to her leaving. "They haven't written at all in the nine months I've been out," she acknowledged. "But I'm still praying for them. Someday . . ."

Judith's heart ached for both of the girls, but she was moved by their conviction and sacrifice to serve missions and spread the gospel. The sweet spirit they brought with them when they were in her home was almost tangible.

They, in turn, asked Judith to tell them about herself. Their first dinner had been more formal, and their discussion hadn't been very personal, but they felt more comfortable with each other this time. Judith told them about her first husband, about Jamie and her miscarriages, and about Alex and her upcoming wedding. She also told them about her upcoming move to Salt Lake City, her new job, and David Rawlins.

"I met Dave over a year ago," she said. "He was Jamie's doctor for years and has treated her and my other daughter, Alexis, like his own daughters. He's been a wonderful friend to our family, and we've all grown to care about him very much. My girls adore him and wish that Dave and I would make our situation permanent."

Neither of the sisters spoke, but their genuine sense of caring prodded Judith to open her heart even further.

"You see girls, I'm in a bit of a spot and I'm not sure what to do about it. Maybe you can help me." She smiled nervously at them. "Dave has hinted several times about getting married. He hasn't come right out yet and asked, but I'm afraid he will. Soon."

"How wonderful," Sister Corlett exclaimed.

"Yes, it is wonderful," Judith echoed. "*He's* wonderful. But it's not that simple." Judith explained how her first husband had joined the Church against her wishes and how it had torn them apart. Then when he died in a car accident a year later, it had nearly killed her, too. "The only thing that kept me going after that was my two daughters. I knew I was all they had, so I had to go on for them." Her voice trembled but she managed to keep her emotions in control.

"Anyway, now that I've met Dave, I find that I have been able to love again, something I thought would never happen. But I am not a member of the Church, and I don't want to get into a relationship like that again. I don't know what to do," she concluded looking at them, a frank appeal for help her in eyes.

"Have you ever thought about joining the Church?" Sister Bond asked directly. When Judith admitted that, yes, she had, Sister Bond's face registered surprise. "You have?"

"Oh yes. In fact," Judith continued, "I've thought about it many times. I believe the teachings of the Mormon church. I've felt the Spirit many times, and I've grown to love the scriptures. They give me great peace of mind. I've always believed in prayer; it was the only way I got through those first years after my husband died."

"Then I don't understand," Sister Bond said, a perplexed expression on her face. "If you believe the teachings of the gospel, why don't you just get baptized and marry Dave?"

"Because I'm afraid," Judith admitted, looking down at her hands in her lap. The sisters were silent, waiting for her to explain. "I've learned a lot about your temples and eternal marriages and families," she said, "and I realize that I can only be sealed to one man while I'm alive. I still love my first husband with all my heart, and nothing would make me happier than to be sealed to him and have my daughters sealed to both of us. But now I've grown to love Dave as well, and I feel that would hurt him. I don't know what to do."

"Is that what's keeping you from getting baptized?" Sister Bond asked, finally.

Judith nodded her head. "I've been thinking I'd like to be baptized. But I'm just so confused."

The sisters were quiet for a moment, absorbing the ramifications of what Judith had just said. Sister Bond was the first to speak. "Have you talked to Dave about this? Have you told him what's in your heart?"

Judith shook her head, admitting that she hadn't felt comfortable bringing it up.

"I'm sure the concept of faith is nothing new to you, is it, Judith?" Sister Bond asked.

"No, of course not," Judith answered.

"There are many things in life that become complicated and cluttered because of our limited earthly knowledge," Sister Bond explained. "The Lord only asks us to do our best and he will bless us. The love and companionship you have with Dr. Rawlins may not become a marriage sealed in heaven, but I believe there is a purpose to your relationship. He's been sealed to his first wife, hasn't he?"

"Yes, I'm sure he was."

Sister Bond continued, "Perhaps you two have been brought together to help you during this life, so you can be happy, so you can have companionship, someone else to love and cherish and take care of. Who knows? Dr. Rawlins' wife and your husband up in heaven may even have had a hand in bringing you together because they knew how lonely you both were. Even though you'll be sealed to your first husband, that doesn't mean you can't still marry for time only and have a rich, rewarding marriage together. You can still do a lot of good in the gospel and in your own lives for the rest of your time on earth."

Judith's mouth fell open. "I never thought of it that way," she said, stunned.

"I agree," Sister Corlett added. "My aunt's husband died very young and left her with three small children. She met a man whose wife had also died, who had four children. They married in the temple, not for eternity, but for this life, and together they've raised all seven children in the gospel. All seven of those kids, five boys and two girls, have served missions and been married in the temple. My uncle and aunt are on a mission right now in Australia. Together their family has taken the gospel to many different people in many different nations. I would say that even though they haven't been sealed together for eternity, they will share an eternal bond that will be a part of them and their family and their spouses in heaven forever."

Looking at the two sisters, Judith knew without a doubt that they had been sent to her by the Lord. Was it really possible to marry Dave and still be sealed to her first husband and her children? Was it possible for Dave to actually consider that arrangement, knowing that it would only be for this life?

Whether or not the answer was completely clear, Judith realized that these two sweet sisters had finally given her the hope and the courage to believe that, somehow, things between her and Dave would work out.

"I don't know how to thank you," Judith whispered as tears filled
her eyes. Suddenly she could hardly wait to see Dave again and talk
with him.

* * *

When her flight touched down in Salt Lake, Judith eagerly made
her way through the connecting tunnel into the airport. The flight
had never seemed so long.

She saw Dave before he saw her and felt her heartbeat speed up.
He looked striking in tan Dockers and a coral polo shirt, open at the
neck. His face, neck, and arms were bronzed from games of golf and
morning jogs. *He is such a handsome man,* she thought. *I never thought
I'd love anyone else again. How lucky I am.*

His gaze searched the crowd of passengers anxiously. She noticed
a worried expression on his face as if he was afraid she hadn't made it
on the flight. When he finally saw her, his whole face brightened with
a smile that made her heart leapfrog.

He waved at her excitedly. She waved back and pushed her way
through the crowd. As he took her in his arms, they held each other
tightly, just a few moments longer to make up for lost time. They'd
been apart over two weeks. That was two weeks too long.

"I've missed you terribly," he said, and hugged her again. Dave
asked about New York, and when she told him she needed to find a
storage unit for her furniture, which would be arriving later that week,
he offered to take care of it for her.

She squeezed his hand in hers as they walked toward the baggage
claim. "Thank you, honey. It's so wonderful to have someone to help.
You're so good to me, you've completely spoiled me."

"You deserve to be spoiled," he said firmly. "I would do anything
for you. All you have to do is ask."

Judith heard something in the tone of his voice that made her stop
and look at him. Unaware of the busy terminal and swarms of passengers surrounding them, they stood staring at each other, caught in
the arc of electricity that enveloped them both.

"That's quite an invitation," she said, searching his face, trying to
read the meaning behind his words. "I mean, if you're serious."

"I'm very serious." There was a depth in his eyes, when he spoke, a tone of sincerity which convinced her that this was a moment in time she would always remember.

He took a deep breath and began to speak a little more rapidly than was usual for him. "I know this probably isn't the best time to ask—I can't even get down on one knee—but I've missed you so much, and I've realized . . . well, I'm tired of having a long-distance relationship. Judith, I love you, and I believe you love me. Would you marry me?"

She couldn't help the tears that quickly filled her eyes, or the smile that lit up her face. "Dave, are you serious? I can hardly believe this."

"I couldn't be more serious," he said quietly, stepping toward her to narrow the gap between them. All around them people scurried about, but the noise and confusion seemed very, very far away.

"Judith, I love you," Dave insisted tenderly. "I miss you so much when we're not together."

Judith reached up and stroked the side of his face. "I love you, too. I'm always happier when I'm with you. You know that, don't you?"

"Then how about it? What do you say?" His eyes searched hers, as if trying to read the answer before she could say it.

A million questions and doubts filled her mind all at once. All the way from New York, she'd thought about her visit with the sister missionaries. She knew that the things they'd told her were true, and she had prayed she would have enough faith to put her belief into action. She loved him. There was no doubt about that. But . . .

But nothing! she decided suddenly. Knowing that she did love him with all her heart, she looked him straight in the eye and said, "Yes, Dave, sweetheart. I would love to marry you."

Without warning, he dropped her carry-on bag and swept her into an embrace that lifted her off her feet. Laughing and hugging, they celebrated the moment, sealing their commitment with a kiss.

Secure in the warmth of his embrace, Judith knew she would be very fortunate indeed to have Dr. Dave Rawlins for a husband.

Chapter 12

Alex sank wearily into a beach chair overlooking the bay. It had been a busy day, and she was exhausted. She'd given several back-to-back lectures and presentations at the convention, and the day wasn't over yet. Although she'd given her last lecture, she still had an awards dinner and ceremony to attend that night to honor the efforts and achievements of people in the fitness industry. She closed her eyes to relax for a moment. A shadow fell over her, and she groaned inside. Couldn't she have just a moment's rest? she thought.

"Alex! I've been looking for you." Oh bother, it was Dylan. He'd been at her elbow nearly the entire day.

"What is it?" she asked, trying not to speak sharply. After all, he was just doing his job.

"I wondered if you'd like an escort to the dinner this evening," he invited her very formally. "I'd be happy to serve as your dinner companion."

Stifling her sigh of relief, Alex said, "Thanks, Dylan. That's nice of you to offer, but I'm going with my friend Julianne."

"Oh," he said. There was a long moment of silence. She could tell he was disappointed.

"You're still going, aren't you?" Alex asked. "I mean, you know lots of people there, and it should be fun."

The young man shrugged. "Yeah, I guess." There was another silence. "So what are you doing right now?" he asked.

"Relaxing. Thinking." Alex closed her eyes and sat back, hoping he'd take the hint. Instead he sat down in the chair next to hers.

"About what?"

"Oh . . . lots of things." She didn't particularly want to get into it, but she had a feeling he wasn't going to leave. "I still have a lot of things left to take care of before my wedding." *And a few matters to clear up with my fiancé about our house,* she added to herself silently.

"So it is true," he said. "You really are getting married." Alex thought she detected an odd note in his voice, but she couldn't say exactly what it was. Passing it off as just another one of his peculiarities, she nodded.

"On July 16th, to be precise. We're supposed to start moving our furniture into our home on the 14th, but I'm not sure it will be finished by then. We've had so many problems."

"With the builder? That happens a lot," he said. This time his tone was clearly sympathetic.

"No, actually, it's been with Rich—my fiancé," Alex admitted. "We've had some disagreements about the house."

Dylan looked momentarily pleased, before he quickly arranged his face into a suitably empathetic expression. "I've heard that building a house can cause stress in a relationship," he said.

Alex thought Dylan's face was remarkably open. He was so easy to read. It was obvious—he had a crush on her and maybe he even thought she wouldn't be getting married after all. *No such luck,* she told him silently. *It's Rich or nobody.*

Aloud, she said, "It's just strange that two people who get along as well as Rich and I do could have such a difference of opinion about some things."

"It's bound to happen," he reasoned. "I mean, men and women are from different planets, you know."

Boy did that ever seem like the truth. Alex sighed, remembering her last discussion with Rich about the additions she wanted on the house. It was like they were speaking different languages.

"Well, Rich is much more practical than I am about things," Alex explained. "And he's completely analytical when it comes to decision making. I tend to be very emotional when I make a decision."

"That's understandable," Dylan responded. "Especially with an upcoming wedding and a new house. You're feeling stressed at all there is to do, and he's probably feeling the weight of responsibility of being a husband and a provider."

"Maybe," Alex shrugged, regretting that she had opened up to her assistant, but then, as she considered his words, she recognized there was more than a grain of truth in them. Rich had said he was worried because he didn't have a firm job or a brilliant career carved out for himself yet. And although Alex herself wasn't worried, she knew Rich was. With a flash of insight, she realized that it probably bothered him that they were using most of her money to pay for things with the wedding and the house, since his money was tied up in his artwork and the business that had burned down.

"You know what, Dylan?" she said. "I think you're absolutely right." She shook her head as she pondered his words another few seconds. "In fact, I know you're right. I'm glad I talked to you."

Once again a pleased expression crossed Dylan's face. "I'm glad I could shed a different light on the situation and help you see things from his eyes."

"In fact," Alex said slowly, evaluating the events of the past several weeks in light of her new understanding. "I've been pretty obstinate about my feelings. I haven't been very cooperative for him to work with, either."

Dylan shook his head. "Now I find that very hard to believe," he said, smiling companionably at her. He reached out his hand and laid it on hers. "You're a very nice person, Alex. I'm glad I've been able to get to know you."

The gesture seemed innocent enough on the surface, but Alex suddenly felt extremely uncomfortable. What had she been thinking discussing her personal life with him? She hadn't meant to encourage him.

"Well, uh, it's getting late," she said, jumping suddenly to her feet. "I guess I ought to get to my room and get cleaned up for the dinner. Thanks again for talking."

"Anytime," he said blankly, obviously surprised by her sudden movement. "You know I'm here for you anytime."

As Alex hurried toward the hotel, she could feel his gaze on her back until she was out of his sight. Later, as she and Julianne made their way back to the convention center, Alex told her about her talk with Dylan. "I don't know, Julianne, he's just so eager and intense. I'm flattered that he thinks I'm so wonderful, but the fact of the matter is, he's making me crazy. Will you trade assistants with me, please?"

Julianne laughed. "I wish I could help, but I wouldn't know what to do with him anymore than you do. Face it, Alex, the price for fame is sometimes having to put up with the Dylans in this world." Alex wished she could think of a nice way to tell Dylan that he didn't need to help her anymore, but she couldn't come up with anything. He was starting to get on her nerves. Maybe she'd talk to Sharla, the conference administrator, and let her take care of it.

As Alex and Julianne entered the ballroom, they saw that it was bursting with people. Several tables toward the front were reserved for the convention presenters. Taking their places at their table, the two young women exchanged casual conversation with the presenters around them.

Dinner was served and for the next hour they socialized and ate the delicious meal. Sandy sat with them, and continued to rave about the potential for their new personalized videos. Already the response had exceeded their expectations, and Sandy was certain that once it was made available to the working woman or man, or the busy housewife, there would be an even greater response.

Soon the president of the National Fitness Association stood and started the awards presentations. Three years earlier at this same convention, Alex had received the honor of "Fitness Instructor of the Year." It had established her career and given her a boost that set her apart from others in her field. This year many of Alex's close friends and associates received awards for their work and efforts in raising money for charitable organizations and for their efforts in the field of fitness.

But no one was more surprised than Julianne when her name was called to receive the honored award for "Fitness Instructor of the Year." Julianne made her way to the pulpit to receive the award as the presenter described her struggles to overcome her eating disorder and her great example and commitment in the face of her challenges. Alex clapped so hard her hands hurt.

Julianne accepted the beautiful crystal trophy, and the presenter asked her to say a few words. Clearing her throat, Julianne began, "This is a great surprise and a great honor. I would like to thank the NFA for their support and encouragement this last year, and I'd like to thank the many friends and fellow instructors who've stood by me through my recent challenges. In particular, I would like to thank

Alexis McCarty, my dearest friend. I can't imagine where I'd be now if I hadn't had her to help me. Without her encouragement, I might never have had the strength or courage to seek help. Thank you, Alex, and thank you all for everything you've done for me and for this special honor. I will treasure it always."

Alex blinked quickly to clear the moisture that collected in her eyes. Julianne had given her more credit than she deserved. She was grateful she'd been able to help Julianne and hoped that between them they could help educate others who struggled with eating disorders of any kind.

Alex greeted Julianne with a hug when she got to the table. Julianne was busy accepting the whispered congratulations from those near their table, so Alex didn't even hear when her name was called to receive the award for the "Year's Best Workout Video."

"Alex!" Sandy shook her shoulder. "They just announced your name."

"They did?" Alex didn't believe her.

"You got the award for 'Best Workout Video.' Get up there."

The announcer said something about the theme for the evening being overcoming trials and challenges since many of the award recipients were great examples of doing exactly that. He told about Alex's cookbook and the section she'd written on her struggle with anorexia nervosa as well as her recent workout video, which had included weight training and athletic conditioning.

At the microphone, Alex accepted her award and tried to gather her thoughts. "This was very unexpected," she said, looking across the large room full of health professionals. "I've had a very rewarding year and there are so many people to thank. First, I want to thank my manager, Sandy Dalebout. She's not only a wonderful manager but a good friend, and I love and admire her a great deal."

Alex went on to name the people involved in making the video who had helped make it a success. "I feel very honored to be in the midst of so many people I respect and admire and am humbled to receive this award. Thank you."

Applause exploded around her as she made her way through the crowded tables toward her seat. Many of her colleagues and friends congratulated her on her way back. She waved and smiled until, without warning, a face among the sea of faces caught her eye. A face she'd hoped she would never have to see again. Jordan Davis.

* * *

Giving Julianne a terse explanation, Alex left the ballroom quickly with her friend right behind her. "Alex—wait! Listen. I'm sure you don't have to worry about running into him. After all, we've been here three days and this is the first time you've seen him."

Alex's heart raced. "I really thought I was past all this," she said, looking nervously around the lobby of the convention center. "But actually seeing him again just made my skin crawl. How did I ever find him attractive in the first place? What was I thinking?"

"We all have someone weird in our past," Julianne said, hooking her arm through Alex's to slow her pace. "In fact, I have three or four. You can't blame yourself. Fortunately, you realized he wasn't right for you, and you ended the relationship. *That's* what counts. Some women never do, and look what happens to them."

Alex nodded as she pushed open the heavy glass door. "You're right," she said, as they followed the path that led from the convention center to their hotel room. Suddenly she stopped. "You know, all those times I've felt like someone was watching me, following her, I'll bet it was him, keeping an eye on me," she exclaimed.

"You think so?" Julianne asked thoughtfully. "He does sound like he has problems."

They had only taken a few more steps when a voice stopped them cold. "Good evening, Alex."

Both women nearly screamed as a tall, muscular form stepped out of the shadows in front of them. It was Jordan, the very person Alex had been hoping to avoid. She could see immediately that he'd continued to bulk up since she'd last seen him, almost two years ago. She didn't doubt he took steroids. A competitive body-builder, he was clean shaven and his skin was deeply tanned.

He flashed them a winning smile. "My congratulations—to both of you." When Alex said nothing, her eyes wary, his face hardened. Fortunately Julianne came to the rescue.

"Thank you," she answered for both of them. "And your name is . . ."

"Jordan Davis." He inclined his head slightly. "And, of course, I already know who you are. Congratulations, Julianne Leighton, 'Instructor of the Year.' That's quite an honor. And Alex—" He narrowed his dark eyes and studied her face. "Impressive as always. Life must be treating you well."

Alex lifted her chin. "It is," she said. *Especially since I dumped you!*

He nodded. "I'm glad to hear it, although I've followed your career, and I already knew that. Still, it's been a long time, and there's so much to catch up on. I know a great coffeehouse not too far from here—that is, unless you'd prefer a drink."

"We don't drink coffee or alcohol," Julianne answered quickly. "But thanks for asking." She grabbed Alex's arm. "In fact, we were on our way back to the hotel. We've got some, uh . . . some stuff to do."

"Oh, that's too bad," he said. A slight smirk crossing his handsome face with its straight nose, full lips, and clefted chin. He still kept his head shaved, smooth and bald. "I was hoping to hear all about your trip to Europe—and your engagement?" He lifted an eyebrow as he looked directly at Alex.

Alex nearly jumped. *How did you know about my trip and my engagement?*

"You've been a very busy girl this last year." Jordan shook his head in amazement. "And on top of all your success with your career, you've got a wedding on July 16th."

He even knew the exact day of her wedding?

Julianne apparently decided to take action. "Jordan, it's been nice meeting you," she said, pulling Alex with her as she started off down the path, "but, really, we have to hurry along. We've got some important phone calls to make."

Jordan watched them go, his face expressionless. "Well, I certainly wouldn't want to keep you," he called after them.

Without a backward glance, the two hurried off to their hotel room.

* * *

Julianne scowled. "It's obvious that he thinks he's pretty special. I mean, sure, he's attractive in an intense sort of way—but what an ego! Was he that bad when you knew him?"

Alex shut her eyes, wishing they hadn't run into him. "I didn't realize it at first, but when I got to know him better . . . yeah, he has a pretty high opinion of himself."

Julianne gave her friend a concerned look. "You know, he still has something for you. There's a look on his face that says he hasn't let go."

Just then the phone rang. Alex gave her friend an exasperated look. "You don't think he would try to call, do you?" Julianne shrugged. "Just in case, would you answer it?"

Julianne picked up the phone. "Hello!" she barked into the receiver. "Oh, hi, Sandy." Her tone relaxed considerably. "She's right here. Hold on." She handed the phone to Alex.

"I'm sorry if I worried you by rushing out like that," Alex apologized.

"What happened? Are you sick?" Sandy asked anxiously.

Trust Sandy to keep an eye on me, Alex thought. *I'm sure going to miss her when she goes to Paris.*

"I wish that's all it was," Alex groaned.

"Then what is it?" Sandy spoke quickly, the pitch of her voice rising with her concern.

As Julianne set both of their awards on the table next to the bouquet of roses, Alex sat on the edge of her bed. "Sandy, do you remember that guy I dated a few years ago?"

Sandy was silent. It was the last question she would have expected. She relaxed a little. "You've dated a lot of guys, Alex. Can you be more specific?"

"He was arrogant, conceited, jealous, and obsessed with me."

"Ahh," Sandy said. "You must mean Jordan."

"Exactly."

"What about him?"

"I saw him tonight at the dinner and on our way back to the hotel." Alex told her business manager about her odd feelings of being followed, and then how she and Julianne had run into him as they left the building.

"Sounds like a Hitchcock movie," was Sandy's response. "I'll bet he's just curious to see if you look the same, if you've changed now that you're such a success and you're famous. And to tell you the truth, I don't think he really ever got over you. I mean, it was you who finally broke things off. Right?"

"How could I have been so stupid as to fall for him in the first place?" Alex groaned, hating to admit that she'd been blind to his faults.

"It was a difficult time in your life, remember?" Sandy pointed out. Alex didn't need any reminders. Her career hadn't really started to take off, and she had suffered some big disappointments. In fact, she still remembered how it felt when she was nearly chosen as the hostess for a fitness program starting on a new cable fitness station but had been turned down almost at the last minute. An inside source had revealed that an executive's niece had ultimately been given the job, but Alex could never have proved it. It had been a painful rejection, especially when she'd been told she was the best candidate and they were getting ready to make her an offer.

"Let me see what I can find out about Jordan and what he's doing at the conference," Sandy offered. "He can't just hang out here without being involved somehow. In the meantime, double bolt your doors and windows, and steer clear of him as much as you can."

* * *

Alex didn't fall asleep until around three o'clock in the morning. Between the stomach pains that seemed to hit without warning and her memories about Jordan, her thoughts had been riding an emotional merry-go-round—worrying about her health, Clint Nichols, Jamie's pregnancy, Julianne's baptism, the house she and Rich were building, and of course, the wedding. She had herself worked into quite a frenzy until exhaustion finally took over and she slept.

Julianne finally woke her at a quarter after eight. "Alex, what time are you supposed to be at the booth?"

"Sometime around nine," she said groggily, her mind still thick and heavy from lack of sleep.

Julianne's voice was crisp and no-nonsense. "You'd better get moving then. You don't have much time."

"Are you going out?" Alex mumbled.

Julianne picked up her purse and tucked her room key inside. "Some publicity person called earlier this morning. I'm supposed to meet with a reporter from the NFA's newsletter. They want to do an article about me for the next issue."

Alex remembered all the publicity that followed receiving such an award. "What else do you have?" she asked, throwing off her covers and forcing herself to sit up. Julianne had a lecture at two and since Alex would be done after her one o'clock workshop, they made plans to meet at the pool that afternoon. With a wave, Julianne was gone, leaving Alex alone in the room.

After a quick shower she felt more alert and revived, her mind filled with plans for the day and the excitement of knowing that in two days, Rich and Andre would be with them.

With her nerves still on edge, she kept a sharp lookout as she walked to the convention center. Feeling the muscles in her back and shoulders tighten, she slowed down and breathed deeply, letting the mild San Diego weather soothe her nerves. In the Expo hall, several conference participants were taking time out of their schedule to visit booths and purchase workout shoes and clothes, aerobic music, video tapes and equipment. Alex's booth was surrounded.

The morning flew by. Alex spent all of her time answering questions about the personalized workout videos and explaining the philosophies behind their product. She was grateful when Julianne joined her around eleven o'clock. Alex left the booth at noon to give herself time to grab a bagel and talk to Sharla about Dylan.

"I'm sorry he's not working out," Sharla said. "I thought he'd be so much help to you. He was so eager to help, and he was willing to do anything to be assigned to you."

Alex felt embarrassed to even bring it up. "He's been very helpful," she acknowledged, "but he's just a little too helpful, if you know what I mean. Almost to the point of making me feel uncomfortable."

Sharla asked Alex if she could put up with him one more day, and Alex nodded, reluctantly. At this late date, she figured she could if she had to.

"Let me talk to him," Sharla said. "I'll explain to him that you need a little more space and that you'll contact him if you need him. I'll find him some other responsibilities to keep him busy."

With a sense of relief, Alex headed out of the Expo Hall for her next presentation. But the feeling immediately evaporated when she heard a voice call her name. It was Jordan again. She broke through a crowd of participants in an effort to escape another meeting with him, but she wasn't that lucky. She made a dash for the exit, but a hand grabbed her arm and stopped her.

"Alex, didn't you hear me calling you?" Jordan spun her around to face him.

Alex felt herself tense up. With all the women who flocked around him and begged for his attention, why was he wasting time on her, an old girlfriend who had dumped him years ago and who was engaged to be married to someone else?

"Sorry," she said insincerely. "I have a workshop at one and didn't realize how late it was. I've still got some things to do to get ready for it."

"You know, I almost get the idea you're trying to avoid me," Jordan said accusingly. "I just thought it would be nice to talk, to catch up. After all," he added, "there was a time when we meant something to each other."

Alex looked into his dark gleaming eyes. "We really don't have anything to talk about," she answered directly.

"Sure we do," he contradicted her. "We've always had a lot in common. And I'd like to show you my new line of nutrition supplements and workout gear. I've got a booth here at the Expo with all my new products," he boasted. "I've built quite a business since we parted ways."

Obviously she didn't give him the gushing response he was after because he kept trying to impress her.

"My products have become quite successful and we've even gone international," he continued, not seeming to notice Alex's obvious irritation. "I have a lot of connections in Mexico and throughout South America."

When Alex realized the only way she was going to get away from him was to act suitably impressed, she said quickly, "Wow, Jordan. That's great," then glanced at her watch. "I'd better go or I'm going to be late."

"Maybe I could take you for a ride in my Ferrari while you're here," he said as she started to walk away.

A Ferrari? That was Jordan all the way, Alex thought. "Gee, thanks for asking," she said, "but I'm booked for the next two days solid, then my fiancé comes to town on Saturday." She shrugged and turned away. "Sorry."

"I've really been wanting to talk to you, Alex," he said, his voice tinged with annoyance. "Don't you think you owe me at least that?"

I don't owe you anything, Alex said silently. "I'll look you up if I get any free time in my schedule," she called over her shoulder as she raced through the exit to the safety of the crowded hallway.

Alex would have been happy to file all her memories of Jordan in the round file. She could still feel the constriction of the possessive vines he'd wrapped around her when they'd dated. It hadn't taken more than a few months for her to realize his motives—to completely control her life and manage her time and her affairs. He told her who to spend time with, where to go, and what to do. At first she'd actually believed him when he said it was just because he cared about her so much and wanted to spend every waking moment with her. He'd overwhelmed her with compliments and gifts, and she'd been flattered by his attention. But when he started questioning her every action, and her other relationships, she'd realized that his jealousy wasn't normal.

People had tried to warn her about Jordan when she'd first started dating him, but she hadn't listened. And she'd learned to regret it. She'd decided to end the relationship quickly, but Jordan had resisted her attempts to end it civilly. By the time he finally understood that she was serious, the end had become quite ugly.

Alex bypassed lunch and headed for the safety of the classroom where her workshop was scheduled. She still had twenty-five minutes before starting, but was glad to have the time to shake off the meeting with Jordan and concentrate on her outline. Soon, class members started filling up chairs and she did her best to push Jordan out of her mind. She hoped he wouldn't be as hard to get rid of now as he had been the first time.

Chapter 13

Feeling unusually tired, Jamie was grateful when Nikki went down for her afternoon nap. It would give her some time to lay down and maybe catch some sleep herself.

She couldn't stop thinking about the man claiming to be Andrea Nicole's biological father. She'd even tried to see some kind of resemblance. This man had a narrow chin and small mouth. So did Nikki, but it was still a stretch of the imagination to find any exact similarities.

Lying on the couch, Jamie shut her eyes and tried to force the unpleasant thoughts away that nagged her night and day. So what if he was her father? What then? Did the man think that a single father who was on the road a lot could provide a better home life and upbringing than she and Steve could provide? Didn't he realize how traumatic it would be to uproot a small child from the only environment she had ever known and the people she trusted? And the most important question—If you really loved someone, truly loved that person, didn't that mean you wanted what was best for them?

Jamie tried to breath deeply and relax. She reminded herself that Steve had been spending some time with an attorney, trying to find some kind of legal angle that would protect them, in the event the man did receive a positive paternity test and wanted to take her back.

The thought made Jamie's heart clench with fear. She couldn't believe that the Lord had done so much to help bring Nikki to their family, just to take her away to live with someone who looked like he grew up with the "Hell's Angels" and spent eleven months of the year on the road. No—she wouldn't believe the Lord would do that to her little family.

The cordless phone next to her on the coffee table rang. Praying it wasn't Clint Nichols, she answered it quickly so it wouldn't wake the baby. It was Judith. She and Dave wanted to come visit and take Steve, her, and the baby out to dinner. Jamie propped herself up to a sitting position. "What is it?" she asked

"We'll tell you when we get there—around five o'clock" was all Judith would say.

Jamie set down the phone feeling relieved and encouraged. There was a great amount of comfort just knowing that her mother's strength and support would be there to help her deal with the situation. And Dr. Rawlins always provided wisdom and stability when it was needed.

With those comforting thoughts, Jamie relaxed back into the cushy softness of the couch and finally allowed a moment of peace to lull her to a much needed sleep.

* * *

Alex and Julianne spent a relaxing afternoon by the pool, lounging in the sun, sipping icy cold fruit drinks with little paper umbrellas, and talking with great anticipation about the fun-filled week ahead of them with Rich and Andre.

Alex kept sitting up and looking around to make sure Jordan wasn't anywhere near while they were at the pool. But eventually she relaxed and allowed the sun to bathe her nerves with its calming warmth.

Sandy met them later for dinner. After they placed their order, she said, "Well, I found out why Jordan is here."

"So did I," Alex said, hoping this would be the last time they talked about him.

Sandy's face showed her surprise. "You know he's a vendor and has a booth?"

"Yes, and that he's very successful and has an international business, and drives a Ferrari," Alex said dryly. She told Sandy about her second encounter with Jordan and added, "I wish I knew why he felt like we needed to talk. There is nothing for us to talk about. Why can't he get that through his head?"

Sandy remembered only too well her few encounters with Jordan. He had resented her relationship with Alex and positively oozed resentment whenever they met. "Probably because he's only interested in what he wants," she said. Sandy had talked to Alex's friend Randy who managed the gym where she used to work out. It was Randy's opinion that Jordan was just the type who would risk his health, taking steroids and experimental drugs, just to get bigger and better than anyone else.

"It's almost like Jordan's starved for attention and acceptance," Sandy continued. "Randy also said something very interesting. He said that Jordan disappeared for a while and when he resurfaced, he had an expensive car and jewelry and clothes. Of course, Jordan attributes it to his success with his new line of supplements, but Randy knows you can't make that kind of money that quickly. Especially to buy a Ferrari. Randy should know, he promotes his own brand of supplements."

Julianne looked up from her dinner across the table. "So, how'd he make all this money?" she was determined to know.

"Probably drugs," Sandy said, and repeated what she had told Alex earlier about Jordan's arrest.

Alex remembered her last conversation with Jordan before they broke up. His words hadn't made sense at the time, but now she thought she understood. When she had told Jordan it was over, he said she would regret breaking up with him. He planned to be very wealthy and very important one day and she would always regret what she'd done. *Well*, she thought to herself, *I've never regretted it. And that's the truth.*

When Julianne suggested that Alex might do better not to show up at the booth the next day, in case he tried to locate her there, Alex shook her head. She didn't like the idea of letting Jordan intimidate her and keep her from doing the things she came here to do. She'd rather stand up to him than be a coward and hide.

"No!" she said adamantly. "I'm not about to stay in my hotel room and let him ruin everything."

"Good girl," Sandy cheered.

* * *

Alex breathed a sigh of relief as the last participant left the workshop. The combination workshop and lecture had been three hours long and she was exhausted. It would be a pleasure to spend the rest of the day at the booth, then tomorrow Rich would arrive. She couldn't wait.

Sandy met her after the presentation to escort her to the Expo Hall. She was planning to meet with Rich to describe his duties as Alex's business manager when he arrived.

"I'll give him my files on all the fitness organizations," Sandy said, looking at her clipboard and list of notes. "He'll also need copies of your contracts and future obligations. But we've kept your schedule open for the next few months so you can devote your time to the personalized videos. And of course, so you'll have time for your wedding and honeymoon. You're still planning on coming to Paris, aren't you?"

"Absolutely," Alex promised. "I can't wait to take Rich to the museums and galleries there. He'll think he's died and gone to heaven."

Sandy was as excited as a little girl. "It will be so fun to have you meet Jean Pierre. You and Rich will love him."

As they walked into the Expo hall, Alex forced herself to remain calm. She was still afraid that Jordan would jump out of nowhere and haunt her, but she'd decided she wasn't going to let him determine her actions and frame of mind. He was a pitiful, insignificant part of her past and she was through letting him unnerve her like some adolescent bully.

"There's Julianne," Alex said when she saw her friend talking with a group of women who'd attended the conference.

The women were thrilled when Alex joined them, and several had been waiting for her so she could sign their cookbooks before they left. Once that was done, the commotion died out and left them time to catch up on what had been happening at the booth.

"I let Pam and Kristi take some time for lunch. We were busy most of the morning and through the lunch hour," Julianne explained, "then it slowed down, so I let them go. Of course, just as they left it got busy again, but nothing I couldn't handle. I'm glad you two showed up when you did, though."

Sandy noticed that Julianne's collection of videos was nearly gone. "Looks like receiving that award helped boost sales of your video," she observed. "It will also help the success of your new project. The timing couldn't have been better."

Julianne caught Alex's eye and said quietly, "Don't look now but your favorite assistant is on his way over."

"Dylan?" Alex tried not to pull a face as she said his name. "What in the world could be possibly want?"

"You're about to find out," Julianne said under her breath. Then changing her tone, she greeted him. When Alex said hello, he drew her aside.

"Could I talk with you for a moment, Ms. McCarty?" he said stiffly. She wondered why he was acting so formal.

"Sure," Alex said. "We can talk over here."

When they found a private spot away from the crowds, Dylan came right to the point. "Why didn't you just talk to me and tell me there was a problem?" he asked, looking embarrassed.

Alex's heart dropped. What had Sharla said to him? Had she actually told him everything they'd talked about? "Dylan, I'm sorry," she tried to smooth it over. "I didn't—"

Dylan interrupted her. "I know I can come on strong, but I just wish you would have talked to me about it," he insisted.

Alex felt caught.

"I'm sorry, Dylan," she said. "I should have. That was wrong of me."

Dylan looked as miserable as a high school sophomore who'd just been rejected for a first date. Then he tried to smile. "That's okay. I hope we can still be friends."

Alex was relieved. "Of course we can," she assured him. "I'd like that."

"You know, a group of us are going to Sea World tomorrow— some of the assistants and some presenters too. Would you and Julianne like to come?" he invited.

Alex was torn between relief and frustration. Relief that she wouldn't be seeing him again, and frustration that he didn't seem to realize that. Fortunately, she had a ready excuse. "That's nice of you to ask," she said. "But my fiancé is flying in from Salt Lake City with Julianne's boyfriend. They're coming to spend a few days with us."

"Your fiancé?" he said, frowning slightly. "He's coming here?"

"Yes, tomorrow."

"So, you're still getting married?" he asked slowly, as if her words hadn't sunk in completely. "I thought maybe those disagreements you've been having with this guy were a signal that things aren't right."

"We've been engaged almost a year," Alex laughed. "I think we've spent enough time together to know for sure. I was just upset with him about some house decisions. But I'm sure it's nothing we can't work through."

"Oh . . ." His voice was subdued. Alex pretended not to notice anything wrong. *Leave him some dignity*, she thought.

"But hey, thanks for the invitation to go with you tomorrow," she said lightly. "Who knows we might end up at Sea World ourselves."

There was a silence for a moment and Alex was getting ready to excuse herself when Dylan spoke up.

"What else are you going to do while they're here?" He spoke as if it was an effort. Alex appreciated that he was trying to act normally and not put her on the spot. He really was a decent young man. She might even have dated him a few years before, although she probably would have felt suffocated before very long. *It's just a crush*, she thought to herself. *He'll get over it and find someone he can have a real relationship with.*

Alex had been so busy just anticipating being with Rich again, she didn't really care what they did. "We'd talked about chartering a sailboat and going sailing," she answered Dylan, "but I don't know if it will work or not." Her eyes darted over to the booth where her friends waited for her. She didn't want to be rude, but she wasn't interested in furthering the conversation.

He lifted his eyebrows. "This is a busy time of year for sailing. You may have some trouble getting a boat."

"I kind of hope so, actually," Alex admitted. "I'm not sure I want to go sailing. Andre, Julianne's boyfriend, has done a little sailing, but the rest of us haven't even been on a boat before. To be honest, it scares me—the thought of being on the ocean in a tiny little boat."

"Really?" For the first time, Dylan looked amused, even superior. "That surprises me. I wouldn't have thought you were afraid of anything."

For some reason, his smile irritated her as much as his puppy-dog eagerness. "I just don't want to take any chances or do anything risky this close to my wedding," she said shortly.

Dylan could tell from her tone that he had offended her somehow. He tried to appease her, to regain the ground he had established with her. "I can imagine," he said, nodding to show he understood. "Although people go sailing every day and nothing happens to them, and I think you'd like it. The trip to Catalina is supposed to be very enjoyable."

"I'll keep that in mind." Alex could see Julianne trying to get her attention. "It looks like my friends are getting ready to leave," she told him. "I'd better go. Thanks for all your help, Dylan."

"Sure," he said with a slightly embarrassed smile. "Sorry I drove you nuts."

Alex waved her hand as if to brush away his apology. "Hey, no problem. Have a nice trip home."

"Oh, I'm not going home," he said cheerfully. "I've taken a job as a cruise ship activities director. I'm heading to Orlando for training."

"That's sounds like a perfect job for you," she said sincerely. "Good luck."

"Thank you," he said, gazing deeply into her eyes.

They didn't speak for a moment, then he stretched out his hand. "Friends?"

"Friends." She accepted the handshake, which to her surprise, somehow turned into a hug. He wrapped his arms around her and squeezed her tight. Over his shoulder, Alex noticed Julianne's expression turn from surprise to amusement.

Finally he backed away. "I'll never forget the time we spent together," he said.

He was making far too much out of the situation, Alex thought. "I doubt I will either," she answered honestly. "Well, good luck to you, Dylan."

She gave him a wave then darted off to meet Julianne and Sandy. "Come on, let's get out of here," she said.

Julianne hid a slight smile behind her hand. "What was that all about?"

Alex sighed heavily. "I'll tell you on the way back to the hotel," she said. "All I know is that between Jordan and Dylan, I must be a total weirdo magnet."

"You shouldn't be too surprised, Alex," Sandy said. "You've had other guys in the past get carried away like this. It just comes with the territory of being in a high-profile career. Movie stars get this all the time."

That was true enough. Alex could recall two separate instances in the past when she'd been the object of attention from overzealous guys. Both of them had worked out at the gym where she taught. One, she'd actually had to confront with the fact that she didn't want to date him and they had nothing in common. Luckily he had moved on. But the other fellow had become quite aggressive, to the point where the management had severed his contract and told him he was no longer welcome at the gym. She had been ready to get a restraining order against him, but he too eventually found someone else to shower his affections upon. Yes, as Sandy said, it came with the territory.

"I had a chap in England who took a fancy to me," Julianne said. "At first I was flattered by all the gifts and attention. He sent me something every day for nearly six months. It started out with small items—cards, candy, flowers. Then, as time went on, his gifts became more expensive and more personal. When he began sending me lingerie, I started to get nervous. And I'd find him showing up everywhere I went."

"How awful," Alex sympathized. "That must have been frightening."

"It was. It came to a head right before I left for the European Supertour last summer." Julianne's face was somber as she reflected on the memory. "That was when my bingeing and purging went completely out of control."

'You've never said anything about this," Alex remarked, surprised her friend had never mentioned it.

"It's in the past and I'd just as soon leave it there," Julianne said matter-of-factly.

"But what happened?" Alex couldn't help wanting to know the ending of her story.

Reluctantly, Julianne told them the rest of the story. "Luckily a good friend of my father's is a policeman and took a special interest in what this fellow was doing. John was actually patrolling our neighborhood the night this fellow tried to break into our flat in London."

"He actually tried to break in?" Sandy looked alarmed. "Julianne, you must have been terrified."

"Fortunately I wasn't home at the time," Julianne said. "He's in jail now and it's over. So can we please change the subject?"

Alex and Sandy quickly complied and all three decided to go get a frozen yogurt and relax in the shade. But as they walked to the snack bar, Alex couldn't help thinking of Julianne's close brush with danger. As Sandy had said, this kind of thing came with the territory, but that didn't make it any less frightening. Alex hoped she never had to deal with a situation as awful as Julianne's. Dealing with overattentive fans like Dylan was bad enough. And thank goodness—he had finally moved on and out of her life.

Chapter 14

At last! Rich and Andre would be arriving that morning. Both girls were as excited as two children at DisneyWorld. Impatiently they waited in the lobby, watching for the shuttle that would be bringing their men from the airport.

Several women who had attended the convention came through the lobby to check out of their rooms and saw Alex and Julianne. When they recognized Alex and Julianne, they created a minor fuss, asking for autographs, digging through their suitcases for convention itineraries for them to sign. One even had Alex's cookbook and asked her to sign it.

As they were finishing up, Alex happened to glance up and across the room. There stood Jordan with a cold expression as he watched the fans showering attention on Alex and Julianne.

An empty shuttle pulled up at the front door, and with excited thank you's and farewells, the satisfied fans grabbed their bags and raced for the van. Alex didn't have time to even catch her breath before Jordan approached them. Why was he still hanging around? she wondered. What did he want from her?

"My, my," he said, "Aren't you two popular. How would it be to be so adored by fans?" he mocked them.

"Hello, Jordan," Alex said calmly. Although Jordan had moments of charm, he also had a bitterly sarcastic edge. That was the side Alex remembered best. "I thought you'd be gone by now," she said calmly. *Actually I was hoping you'd be gone by now.*

"Business has been so good I stayed on an extra day," he said loftily. "I just had a breakfast meeting this morning with a client who's thinking of becoming a rep. In fact," he checked his watch, making sure he flashed the Rolex plainly enough for the girls to notice, "I have another meeting in an hour across town. So I guess I'd better be going."

Alex looked at Jordan curiously. He'd been someone she'd been close to for several months and she'd spent many hours in his company, but now he seemed like a total stranger. Yes, he annoyed her and she wanted him to leave her alone, but she also felt pity for him. He was trying so hard to impress her, wanting some kind of approval from her.

"Well," she extended her hand, hoping to close this chapter in both of their lives for good, "good luck to you."

He grasped her outstretched hand and shook it slowly, staring pensively into her eyes. There was something so desperate, so longing about his gaze, Alex quickly withdrew her hand. She had a sudden impulse to flee his presence.

"Excuse me," a young clean-cut man in a Marriott uniform said. "Are you Alexis McCarty?" When Alex nodded, he held out an envelope. "This message just came for you."

"Thank you," Alex said, accepting the envelope, wondering who it was from. A thought flashed across her mind. Was it Jamie? Was something wrong with the new baby? Or was it Rich—had he been delayed? She ripped open the envelope, dreading to read the contents.

Alex—

Just in case you still wanted to go sailing, I got the name of a guy who might be able to help you.

Once again, I really enjoyed meeting you and getting to work with you. You're incredible.

Love,
Dylan

Enclosed was a slip of paper with a phone number and the name *Captain Rex Porter* written on it.

"Alex, what is it? Is something wrong?" Julianne asked, concerned.

Alex chuckled and shook her head, "No, thank goodness. It's just a note from Dylan. He found someone who might be able to help us if Andre still wants to go sailing." Jordan, still standing beside them, lifted an eyebrow.

Julianne placed a hand on her heart. "I got a little nervous there for a minute, thinking that Rich and Andre had had a change of plans and weren't coming."

"Rich and Andre," Jordan repeated the names. "I believe Rich is your fiancé," he said to Alex. "So Andre must be your friend." He looked at Julianne.

"Yes and they'll be here any minute," Julianne said quickly. "So we'd better say good-bye, Jordan." Alex appreciated Julianne's effort to get rid of him.

But Jordan wasn't ready to leave them yet. "You're interested in going sailing?" he asked.

"Rich and Andre are," Alex said curtly. "We're not sure of our plans yet."

"May I see who he recommended?" Jordan snatched the paper out of her hand before she could answer. "Hmmm, Rex Porter. Must be a private charter outfit. I'm sure he'll be fine for a short excursion." He held out the paper to Alex in such a way that she was forced to touch his fingers. "I hope you enjoy yourselves." Both his expression and the tone of his voice suggested otherwise.

Another shuttle pulled in front of the building. Alex started to turn away from Jordan, thinking the shuttle might hold her fiancé if it was from the airport. Then she noticed it was just a delivery van.

Jordan described some of his own nautical travels, trying to impress them, Alex thought, but not achieving any success whatsoever.

Finally Julianne pointed. "There's the shuttle!" she cried. "We've got to go," she said to Jordan. Grabbing Alex's hand, she took off for the front door.

"Bye, Jordan," Alex called over her shoulder. The girls raced outside just as the shuttle doors opened. Julianne hollered Andre's name as he stepped from the van. Alex thought she was going to die from anticipation, but sure enough, Rich was the next passenger to exit.

She opened her mouth to call his name but her throat was choked with emotion. His gaze quickly found hers and he smiled broadly. Time stood still as they raced to each other and hugged tightly.

"I can't believe how much I missed you," he said.

Alex still couldn't talk. She was trying hard not to cry, but she was failing miserably.

"Hey," he pushed her away from him gently to look at her face. "Are you okay?"

She nodded, then crushed herself against his chest again. Nothing felt better than his strong, protective arms around her. He led her off to the side of the hotel entrance, out of the way, and held her a moment longer. "Alex, is something wrong?" he asked. "Has something happened?"

Wiping at her eyes and sniffing furiously, Alex tried to dry her tears. She felt stupid for crying, but the emotion sprang from her unexpectedly and she couldn't control it.

"I'm sorry. I'm just so glad you're here," she managed to say. She would tell him about Jordan later.

"So am I," he agreed softly. "This has been a long week with you gone."

"Where did Julianne and Andre go?" Alex looked around but couldn't see them anywhere.

"They must've gone inside already. Let's grab the luggage and find them."

But Julianne and Andre had already taken the luggage in with them. Alex and Rich found them sitting on a couch together. Andre jumped up when he saw them. "Alex, it's so nice to see you again." His sincerity, coupled with his French accent, made him hard to resist. Alex greeted him with a hug.

"It's good to see you too, Andre. How are you? I heard you found a studio already."

"Oh yes," he nodded vigorously. "I was just telling Julianne how impressed I am with Salt Lake City. I had a nice visit there and managed to line up most of the equipment we need for the video shoot when we get back in a week. And I also found—" he paused dramatically— "a new cameraman while I was there." Andre waited for her reply, but when she didn't speak, he asked, "Aren't you going to ask who it is?"

"I doubt I know him," Alex replied slowly. "I don't know many people there yet."

"But I think you do," he said slyly. "It's your fiancé, Rich."

"Isn't that great," Rich said. "I'm so excited to learn about filming."

"He will do a great job," Andre pronounced, "and I've got a couple of others lined up who have some great experience and happened to be available. The way everything has fallen into place so easily, you would think this was all meant to be."

Julianne and Alex smiled at each other. They'd said the same thing many times themselves.

"Well, come on," Rich said. "We can talk about all of this later. Let's get everything settled, then we can take off and have some fun. There are a million things I want to do while I'm here."

* * *

An hour later the two couples were on their way to Sea World. It was close by and since Alex was the only one who'd ever been there, the other three wanted to go. Alex didn't care what they did, as long as she was with Rich.

She was grateful the park was busy enough they didn't run into Dylan and his friends. She wasn't up to seeing him again. Later that evening they went to Belmont Park, on the Mission Bay Boardwalk, and rode on the wooden roller coaster and ate cotton candy, hot dogs, and nachos. Afterwards, they ended up in the lounge at the hotel to talk about their plans for the next five days. They needed to be back in Salt Lake City by the following Saturday.

The talk skipped back and forth between Julianne's and Alex's awards to Andre's experiences in New York and Los Angeles.

"So . . ." Alex said, brightly. "We haven't decided yet what we want to do. We'll go to church tomorrow, then go for a drive to the temple and do some sightseeing, but what about the rest of the week?"

Rich spoke up first. "We talked before about chartering a boat and sailing to Catalina Island or somewhere. I understand we can do that in a day. That might be kind of fun."

"If we decide to go sailing," Andre added, "I talked to a man in L.A. who said it's a nice trip to Ensenada. You don't need a passport and it's only about a ten-hour trip."

"Mexico! That sounds great!" Rich exclaimed. "We could sail down one day, stay overnight, spend a day there, and return the next."

Alex kept silent. She wasn't fond of the idea, but Julianne spoke up, "It would be very adventurous. But I've never been out to sea before. What if I get seasick?"

"There's all kinds of medicine you can take. We'll make sure you don't get seasick," Andre assured her.

"Alex?" Rich said, "You haven't said much. What do you think about the idea?"

She searched for the right words, not wanting to sound like a party-pooper but not feeling good about the idea. "I . . . uh . . . ," she stammered. "I . . . well, we only have seven days here. Tomorrow is Sunday, so we can't really do too much then. Since we leave on Saturday, that really only gives us five days to do everything we want. This three-day trip would take pretty much the entire time."

"She's right," Julianne said. "Do we want to spend all our time here out to sea?"

"We don't need to go to the zoo *and* the wild animal park, do we?" Rich asked practically.

"I don't," Andre said and looked at Julianne. It was obvious that both men were pushing for the trip. Then he added, to Alex's relief, "I wonder if it would be difficult to arrange a trip like this without a lot of advance planning."

"Maybe we ought to call tomorrow and see if it's even a possibility," Rich offered. "We can make our decision then." The others nodded enthusiastically while Alex prayed silently that a boat wouldn't be available.

It was getting late, so the four of them returned to the rooms, passing by the front desk to ask about chartering a boat. The woman who gave them a list of charter companies wasn't encouraging. "Most people make their reservations months in advance so if you're looking for a boat now, your chances of finding one aren't very good." She shrugged. "You might get lucky if there's a cancellation or something."

This news encouraged Alex. She prayed that all the boats would be reserved and they'd have to give up the cause. She didn't know exactly why, but she just didn't want to go. Of course, she couldn't tell if it was her inner voice telling her or the paranoia of the last few days still hanging over her. Whatever the reason, she decided to keep it to herself until they found out whether they could even go or not.

Chapter 15

Jamie tiptoed from her daughter's room and pulled the door closed. Andrea Nicole had been worn out with the excitement of having Grandma back in town. Judith had given her granddaughter a huge stuffed bear from New York. The bear was just as big as Nikki, who was nevertheless determined to drag it with her everywhere she went. The two barely fit in the crib together.

Jamie rejoined the others in the front room as they were talking about Steve's upcoming LSAT test. Sitting beside her husband, she leaned her back against his shoulder and lifted her feet onto the couch. Somewhere at the bottom of her legs were her ankles, she was sure of it, even though she couldn't see them any more.

"I'm as ready as I'll ever be," he said. "I've done everything I can to prepare for it. All I can do now is hope for the best. If I don't get into law school, you just might be looking at the next guy who delivers pizza to your house."

"You've worked hard," Jamie said encouragingly to her husband. "I know you'll do well, honey. And don't forget about your fortune cookies. You should be hearing from Delaney's sometime this week, right?"

"How is that going?" Judith asked. Dave Rawlins sat beside her, holding her hand.

"I'm waiting to move on the project until I know what their decision is," Steve answered. "I'm a little nervous, though. I found a similar product at a gift shop in the mall. But I didn't really like the packaging or the fact that most of the sayings were either off-color or downright filthy. So I'm hoping they like my idea better."

"Of course they will. I think it's a wonderful idea. It's a novelty item people would have a lot of fun with," Judith said. "Don't you think, Dave?"

"Absolutely," he replied.

Jamie liked the way they sat by each other on the love seat, holding hands. They seemed so right for each other, so perfectly suited. What were they waiting for? They should be married and living happily ever after by now.

"So, Jamie, how are you feeling?" Dr. Rawlins asked her.

"I've been a little tired lately and I'm retaining a lot of water, but other than that I'm fine." Her doctor had been watching her for signs of toxemia, but her blood pressure was still good. Compared to her other pregnancies, this one was going extremely well.

"How are you doing, Mom?" Jamie said. "Is it strange to think you're not going back to New York?"

"It's wonderful to be here," Judith said. "I didn't even feel sad when I left the city. As much as I liked my apartment and friends and my job, it wasn't hard to leave it because, well, everything I love most in the world is here. And I'm excited for all the new beginnings and changes that are about to happen in our family. Now we just need to get you to relocate permanently," Judith said, nudging Dave gently.

Jamie looked at them both curiously. Something was going on with them. "Hey you two," she asked. "What's up?"

Judith tried to smile, but tears formed in her eyes and she couldn't speak for a few moments.

Dave spoke up. "I have asked your mother to marry me and she said yes."

Jamie let out a cry of excitement and rushed over to hug her mother and her soon-to-be father.

"Congratulations!" Steve jumped up and shook Dave's hand, then hugged Judith. "This is great news. We're so happy for you."

Judith and Dave hugged, then he kissed her tenderly. Jamie blushed seeing them openly affectionate with each other, but couldn't help being pleased to see them both so happy.

Wiping her eyes on a tissue, Judith explained to her daughter and son-in-law, "There's something else. I've also decided that I'm ready to get baptized." She turned to Dave. "I want to be a member of the Church before we get married."

At the look that passed between them, Jamie felt as if she was intruding on something very special and personal. Jamie wished somehow she and Steve could sneak into the kitchen to give them some privacy. Sensing the sacredness of the moment, Steve wrapped his arm around her and pulled her close. He kissed her on top of the head and then rested his chin there.

"I wonder," Judith said, wiping her nose and regaining her composure, "would it be out of line for me to ask for a blessing? I could use a little heavenly help and reassurance about all of these decisions." Dave and Steve both assured her they would be pleased to do so.

"I used to think that they were just for special occasions, like sickness and things like that. But every time I've seen someone receive a blessing, there's so much power." She crumpled the tissue tighter in her hands. "And right now I could use some of that. This is quite a big step for me and I'm a little bit scared."

Steve set a chair in the center of the room, and Dave helped Judith to her feet. When she was seated, Dave and Steve rested their hands on her head. As Dave began the blessing, he told Judith how much Heavenly Father loved her and how proud he was of her for being such a loving and devoted mother and for the decisions she'd made. He assured her that she would have a confirmation and a peaceful feeling that would tell her without a doubt the decisions she had made were the right ones. Even though the adversary would try to stop her, she would have the strength to overcome his influence and all would be well.

Jamie peeked out of the corner of her eye, watching her mother and the two men who were performing the blessing. It was an image she had never thought she would witness. The look of peace and serenity on her mother's face moved Jamie to tears. Gratitude filled her as she realized that the Spirit had truly worked a miracle in her mother's life.

Dave finished the blessing, saying, "You have a mission of importance to fill during your journey upon the earth. Many will be influenced by you and your testimony. Opportunities will be placed in your way, and you must be at your spiritual, moral and physical best to be ready at all times to take advantage of these opportunities, having faith that the Lord is guiding you every step of the way.

"You will also have the opportunity to serve and share with others that truth which you hold sacred in your heart. The future will contain many challenges, but you will walk with a peaceful heart and glad countenance, giving faith and hope to others."

Dave closed the blessing, but Jamie barely heard the words. The thought struck her that her mother and Dave could very well be missionaries together. Imagine that!

* * *

"What did you just say?" Alex pressed the phone to her ear, hoping but not sure that her mother had just said what it sounded like she said.

"I've decided to get baptized and I've accepted Dave's proposal," she repeated. "We're going to get married."

"Mother!" Alex shrieked into the phone. "This is wonderful. It's incredible! I can't believe it!"

Julianne came running from the bathroom, her mouth foaming over with toothpaste. "Wha'," she garbled through her mouthful of suds, "wha' happen'?"

"My mother's getting baptized—and *married,*" Alex said excitedly.

Julianne gasped and started choking. She ran back into the bathroom to clear her mouth.

"I am so proud of you, Mom," Alex enthused. "I'm so happy, too. This is the best news you could ever tell me. I wish I could be there with you."

"I know, honey, I wanted to wait until you got home to say something, but I just couldn't hold it in any longer."

Judith wanted to schedule the baptism for the following Sunday. Alex and the others planned to be back in Salt Lake by Saturday afternoon, so Alex assured her mother that Sunday would be perfect.

"I'm just sorry it's taken me such a long time to finally have the guts to make a decision," Judith tried to explain her reasoning for moving so quickly. "But now that I have, I wonder why I didn't do it sooner."

Judith told her that she and Dave hadn't set a wedding date yet, and Alex was aware of her mother's concerns, but she also knew everything would be fine. All of this was a dream come true. She couldn't wait to tell Rich.

* * *

The next day was Sunday. The foursome went to church, then drove to the temple. Alex wasn't prepared for the majesty and beauty she found when the temple came into sight. Holding hands, they walked the grounds that could only be compared to the Garden of Eden itself. Alex felt as though she were in paradise. She ached to go inside, wanting to be surrounded by her loved ones and knowing that they would share eternity together.

"Just think," Rich said, pulling her close. "It's only another month and we'll be going to the temple."

"I wish it were this one, today," Alex said, laying her head on his chest. "Sometimes I get afraid. We've made it this far, we're so close, and I start worrying that something's going to happen. Is it just Satan, throwing doubt into my mind, challenging my faith, or do you think . . . ?"

"Nothing's going to happen," Rich said reassuringly. "There's no doubt in my mind that we were brought together by something heavenly. I'm positive that we are going to get married, have lots of babies, and be very old before we have to worry about any of that." He sealed his promise with a smile and a kiss.

"We just have to have faith, Alex. Remember your patriarchal blessing? The Lord has already promised it would happen. Now we just have to exercise the faith to make it happen."

He spoke with utter conviction, without a hint of doubt in his voice. Even though there was still a tiny corner of worry in her mind, her heart was filled with that promise and with Rich's strength.

She couldn't help saying, "I just wish I knew, one way or the other, about having children. It's the not knowing that's nearly killing me."

Rich lifted her chin with his fingers and looked into her eyes. "Alex, no matter what, it doesn't change how I feel about you. I love you and we will deal with whatever happens as we come to it."

Once again, Alex drew upon his faith and optimism. "I don't know what I'd do without you, Rich," she said, laying her head on his shoulder. "I'm so sorry that I've been so emotional and so difficult about some of the decisions about the house. I want you to know I trust your judgement completely, and if you feel we shouldn't make those changes, then I agree with you. I'm going to love the house just the way it is. The important thing isn't the house; it's who I'm sharing it with."

Rich stroked her hair tenderly. "I've been just as difficult, actually more difficult than you ever could be," he said. "I'm sure we can find a compromise. We can talk about it when we get home. Let's meet with the contractor and look at the figures."

Although Alex had been willing to give up her bay window and the fireplace, she felt enormously comforted that Rich was willing to hear her side after all. "You know what?" she said.

"No, what?"

"I love you, Mr. Greenwood."

"And I love you, too, Mrs. Almost-Greenwood." The warm breeze gently caressed them with the sweet scent of hyacinth and azaleas.

Taking Alex by the hand, Rich led the way down the path to find their friends. This was how she always wanted it to be. Them together, with Rich leading the way. Not only did she love him with all her heart, she had a profound respect and admiration for him. His conviction to the gospel and his unwavering testimony strengthened hers and assured her that they would indeed be together in all things: of one heart, of one mind, of one belief.

At times she felt overwhelmed with gratitude for her blessings. She almost felt guilty. She didn't deserve everything the Lord had given her, yet He continued to shower blessings upon her. And Rich was willing to discuss her ideas about the house! She fell in love with him all over again.

Chapter 16

That afternoon before Sandy returned to her home in Palo Alto, she met with Alex and Rich to give them a feel for what she did for Alex as her business manager. Alex knew she would miss Sandy greatly, both as a friend and a manager, but she had no doubt that Rich was capable in every way of handling her business affairs. In fact, when it came to financial matters, Rich was even more qualified than Sandy.

As she gathered her notes and planner and placed them in her briefcase, Sandy reminded them that even though she would be in Europe, they could e-mail her anytime they had questions.

"Thanks for everything," Alex said, hugging her friend good-bye.

"Hey, you too," Sandy said. "Just think where I'd be now if you hadn't given me that set of scriptures. My whole life has taken a different course. It seems like doors of opportunity have swung open for me in every direction. And I have you to thank. I don't know if I would have had the courage to approach me about the gospel, like you did."

"Believe me, I was scared," Alex admitted. "But I was actually more frightened not to. I didn't want to be held accountable for not giving you a chance to learn about it for yourself."

"You've been a good example for me. I intend to do my part in sharing the gospel," Sandy declared. "When I see what it's done for me, I want to give everyone the same chance for happiness that I have."

Sandy's blue eyes glowed with excitement and her face was even more beautiful with the new light shining from inside her. Sandy had always been striking, a woman who received a second look from men; she had a kind of beauty that caused both men and women to take notice. Not just her physical beauty, but a love and warmth that drew people to her. Alex knew that wherever she went, she would make a difference in people's lives.

That evening before going to bed, Alex gazed out the windows over-looking the harbor, noticing the string of lights on the bridge that stretched to Coronado Island, and the silhouette of the city laid out in the distance. She was excited for the week of fun ahead, but part of her wished she could be at home, sharing in her mother's excitement, supporting Jamie through her challenges. Alex had been tempted to talk to Rich about going home a day or two early, but didn't want to shortchange Andre and Julianne.

The week will go fast, she consoled herself. They would keep busy, and before she knew it they would be on the plane back home.

Her gaze dropped to the roses on the table that had long since bloomed and wilted, their edges crisp and dead. Whisking the roses from the vase, Alex crammed the bouquet into the garbage can. "Ouch!" she muttered as one of the thorns scraped her finger, and she grabbed a tissue from a box on the night table. As she applied pressure to her finger, she sent a heartfelt prayer heavenward that the Lord would not only make the week go quickly, but that He would also keep them safe.

* * *

Alex and Julianne met Rich and Andre downstairs at the restaurant the next morning for breakfast. The girls ordered juice and toast, the men helped themselves to the breakfast bar.

"So," Andre said to Rich and Alex, "how does it feel to only have barely a month left before you get married."

Alex and Rich looked at each other, then Rich said, "Well, all I can say is, if you ever decide to get engaged to someone for a year, my best advice is, *stay in separate countries!* It's too hard when you're together!"

Everyone laughed, but Alex knew Rich wasn't exaggerating. The last year of their engaged lives had been very difficult and had tested their limits. But they had remained committed to their goal and never allowed the adversary to tempt them. They'd learned early to avoid any situation that could risk them letting down their defenses, even once. And even though it had been extremely difficult, there was no doubt, they had been blessed and it was definitely worth the wait.

"We may not have a choice about it," Andre said, looking at his sweetheart sadly. "I'm planning on relocating to America, maybe even to Salt Lake, depending on how this personalized workout video project turns out. Julianne's going back to England."

"Don't be too sure about me being in England the whole time," Julianne said. "Reebok is sponsoring a national tour this coming year and since I'm 'Instructor of the Year,' they've asked me to join them. I could be in America for six months or more, if I want."

Alex remembered all of the offers that rolled in after she received the award. Julianne's career was easily on the brink of becoming very big. And as talented as she was, Alex wouldn't be surprised to see her on ESPN with her own show within the year.

"Honey, that's great news," Andre said, leaning over to give her a peck on the cheek. "We can set up rendezvous all over the United States."

"Sounds romantic," Julianne said with a smile.

"Speaking of romantic," Andre said, "I called around to boat charter places and I'm not having any luck, even just for a quick jaunt up to Catalina Island. There's only one place who hasn't been able to confirm a reservation for Thursday, but they won't rebook until twenty-four hours before. We won't know if it will work out until Wednesday morning."

"That's too bad," Julianne said. "I know how much you wanted to go sailing."

"I don't know what I was thinking," Andre said, shaking his head. "I should have known we would've needed advance reservations."

"Wait a minute," Julianne turned to Alex. "Do you still have that phone number Dylan gave you?"

Alex had been hoping that Julianne would've forgotten about the number. "I think so," she answered reluctantly.

Andre read the name Dylan had written on the card. "Porter's Charters." He jumped out of his chair. "I'm going to call right now."

Rich had been observing Alex's face. "You don't seem to be too keen on this idea, Alex. Don't you want to go sailing?"

Alex didn't want to be the one to ruin everyone's fun, and she wasn't opposed to an afternoon on the ocean, but she wasn't excited about spending three days at sea.

"I don't know," she said hesitantly. "I just thought we might spend time sightseeing and shopping and going to the beach. It's already Monday and we have to be home on Saturday."

To Alex's relief, Julianne said, "I agree. Maybe we should just do the Catalina day trip so we don't spend all our time sailing."

"Well," Rich conceded, "If that's how you feel, I'm sure Andre won't mind. It doesn't matter to me, I can go either way."

Alex was glad to hear Rich was open to her feelings.

"Great news," Andre said when he returned. "This guy just had a group cancel. They were supposed to go to a place called Guadalupe Island, which is a four-day trip, so he's got plenty of time to take us to Ensenada if we want."

Rich looked at the girls then back to Andre, who immediately sensed something wasn't right.

"Is there a problem? I thought you guys would be excited," he said, looking around at their faces.

"It's not that," Rich said. "We just talked about some of the other things we could do in the same amount of time. There's so much to do here in San Diego."

"But you can go to the San Diego Zoo any time. You can go shopping in Salt Lake. But you can't go sailing on a sixty-foot schooner every day! Now that's something to get excited about."

"That is a pretty big ship," Rich said.

"It's incredible. This guy, Porter's his last name, recently spent a fortune remodeling the inside. It has two large staterooms for guests, then a room for him and the other crew member. He says it's really luxurious and if we let him know by early this afternoon we can have anything we want for meals—lobster, steak, Chinese. I guess he's quite a gourmet and loves to pamper his guests with fancy cuisine and accommodations. Believe me, this would be one luxurious cruise."

"It sounds great," Rich said. Alex detected the yearning in his voice. She could tell he wanted to go as much as Andre did. And in a way, Andre was right, they could go to the zoo any time and shopping too. If the boat was as nice as this guy said, it would be kind of fun to relax and sail and sit out under the stars at night.

"Also," Andre added, "we can even go fishing, and when we drop anchor in the evening we can swim."

"Did he say how the weather was supposed to be?" Alex asked, not wanting to leave anything to chance.

"He was going to check while I talked to you guys. We need to get right back to him with a decision because he's already had a few other calls wanting day trips. But he'd rather go out for a nice three-day excursion. He's been sailing all his life. In fact, he spent time in Le Havre, France, working on the docks there, going out on fishing boats. I guess this guy has had quite a life at sea. He says he's too old for all of that now and is content taking tourists out for short trips."

Rich and Andre both looked at the girls, and Alex and Julianne looked at each other.

"It does sound kind of fun," Julianne said to her, "especially if the boat really is that nice."

"He actually said we could have steak?" Alex asked Andre.

"Anything we want," Andre answered.

Alex looked at the three eager faces in front of her and realized that not only did they all want to go, but she did too.

"Then what are we waiting for?" she said. "We better hurry and call before someone else beats us to it."

Andre flew out of his seat and headed for the phone.

Rich looked at Alex suspiciously, "Alex, are you sure you want to do this?"

She nodded slowly, "Yes, it sounds like fun. We'll have a good time together."

"I want you to say something if you really don't want to go on this boat," he persisted.

"It doesn't really matter what we do." Alex took hold of his hand. "As long as we're together, it will be fun."

He leaned over and kissed her forehead.

The decision was made. They were going sailing.

* * *

Back in their room Alex and Julianne repacked all their clothes and separated what they didn't need to take on the boat with them. The hotel said they could store their luggage since they would be spending Friday night at the hotel before going back to Salt Lake.

"Alex, are you sure you're okay with going sailing?" Julianne asked as she tucked her "Instructor of the Year" award between several sweatshirts inside her suitcase.

"Yeah," Alex answered, "I'm fine with it, really." She knew she was still trying to convince herself as much as she was everyone else. In all honesty, it wasn't so much the sailing, but something inside of her that didn't feel quite right about the trip. She was sure it was just nerves and the fear that she didn't want to take any risks this close to the wedding. But she also knew she was being overparanoid and extra cautious. Nothing was going to happen.

"We ought to run down to the gift shop and get some Rook cards or something," Alex said. "That might be fun to play at night."

"Andre said the guy has a television and video machine on board so we can watch movies if we want," Julianne suggested.

Julianne needed to get some film for her camera and wanted to get something for nausea in case any of them got seasick. That reminded Alex to double check and make sure her pain medication was in her bag. Then she called Jamie.

At the sound of Jamie's voice and Nikki's jabbering in the background, Alex felt a twinge of homesickness in her chest. "How are you, and how's the baby doing?"

"You should see this house," Jamie said, wearily. "It's a wreck. Nikki loves to go around unloading my kitchen drawers. I repack them a dozen times a day."

Alex asked her if they hadn't any child-proof locks. Steve hadn't yet gotten around to it, Jamie said.

"You sound tired. Are you feeling okay?" Alex was especially concerned about her sister given that her luck with full-term pregnancies wasn't good.

"I'm okay. I'm sure it's nothing to worry about but I've been having a lot of false labor today."

"Have you been overdoing it?"

"Not really. Nikki and I watched Barney videos most of the morning and she'll be going down for a nap here pretty quick, so I'll be fine."

"Have you had any spotting, or anything like that?" Alex didn't know a lot about complications with pregnancy but last time Jamie was having contractions, she had started bleeding.

"No, thank goodness. Alex, I don't think it's anything to worry about. Besides I have a doctor's appointment Thursday, I'll be fine."

"Good," Alex was relieved to hear that. "But you'll call your doctor if you need anything before then, won't you?"

"Of course," Jamie answered. "Alex, I wish I wouldn't have said anything. It's normal to have contractions like this in the last stages of pregnancy. Hold on, I have to get Nikki. She's standing up in one of the drawers." Alex heard her sister in the background talking to the toddler.

"If only parents had as much energy as their children," she sighed when she came back. "I swear this kid is part mountain goat, she loves to climb so much. I just gave her a bottle. She's lying in on her blanket in the living room. With any luck, she'll fall asleep."

"I'd better let you go, I just wanted to talk to you before we left." Then she remembered. "How's Mom doing? Is her baptism still set for Sunday?"

"Yes, she's getting really excited. The stake missionaries came over last night and visited with her. They want to make sure she's ready. Boy she about knocked them off their chairs. They couldn't believe how much she already knew about the Church."

Alex was still surprised and excited about the fact that her mother was actually getting baptized. "I wish I could be there to help get everything ready."

Jamie replied that the missionaries were doing most of the work on the program and Judith had the refreshments afterwards covered. She added that their mother would then start teaching at the "U" on Monday morning. "She's a little nervous, but very excited. She has no doubt that this is all the Lord's will. It's kind of weird having her talk in spiritual terms, but it sounds good. Does that make any sense?" Jamie asked. Alex knew exactly what she meant.

Changing the subject, Jamie asked, "So, what are you guys doing? I'm surprised you're calling in the middle of the day."

"We're getting ready to go sailing tomorrow."

"That's sounds fun," Jamie said enthusiastically.

"I hope it is. We're going to Ensenada for a few days."

"Ensenada, Mexico? Wow. That could be a real adventure," Jamie remarked.

"That's what I'm afraid of."

Jamie picked up on Alex's hesitancy immediately. "You don't want to go?"

Alex shrugged. "I don't know. I've never been sailing before. What if I hate it? Then I'll be stuck on a boat for three days." Alex knew she was being negative, but she could be honest with Jamie.

"I bet you'll be surprised at how fun it is. Oh, there's the doorbell. I'd better get it."

About the time Alex hung up the phone, Julianne returned. Slipping off her sandals, she sat down on the bed across from Alex. Holding up a large bag from the gift shop, she dumped the contents of the bag onto the bed. There was everything from junk food to motion sickness pills.

"I just figured that we might want some snacks," Julianne said airily. "I know the men will, especially at night. Plus I just thought I'd pick up some extra medications like pain pills, stuff for muscle aches, along with these." She held up the box of motion sickness pills. "The guy down there said they work like a charm."

"Looks like you've got everything covered." Alex couldn't believe all the stuff Julianne had bought, but in a way she was glad. Just in case there was any kind of emergency or illness, Julianne had it covered.

"Have you heard from Rich and Andre?" Julianne asked, loading the items back into the bag. Just then the phone rang.

"Hey, you girls about ready?" he said.

"Ready for what?" Alex mouthed to Julianne that it was Rich on the phone.

Rich and Andre planned to take the ferry over to Coronado Island. From there, they thought they would go to the beach and rent some bikes and ride around. They could also stay and have dinner.

"That sounds wonderful. Just a sec, let me ask Julianne." Alex told Julianne about Rich's and Andre's plan. "We'd love to," Alex said. They agreed to meet in the lobby in fifteen minutes.

Spending the rest of the day on Coronado Island was more like what Alex had in mind. Quickly she changed her clothes into something more festive and packed a bag with beach gear. Her excitement to go to Coronado Island almost overshadowed the deep nagging concern she had tucked away in her heart about the sailing trip.

* * *

Jamie hurried to the door before the doorbell rang again. She stopped cold when she opened it to find Clint Nichols standing in front of her.

"Mrs. Dixon, I know you don't want to see me, but we need to talk," he said.

Jamie pulled the door in closer so he couldn't see Nikki behind her, sleeping on her blanket on the floor. "Mr. Nichols. I don't mean to be rude but I would rather not speak to you without my husband present."

"I understand," he said, "but I'm having some trouble with this paternity test and I wanted to talk to you about it."

"Like I said, Mr. Nichols, I'd be more comfortable with my husband here." Jamie kept a tight hold on the door knob, just in case the man tried anything funny. She didn't trust him and was prepared in the event he tried to enter their home.

Jamie wondered if he wasn't listening since he went on with his problem as though she hadn't said anything.

"It's just that since I don't have a birth certificate proving I'm the father, they have to have tissue samples of the mother so they can get some blood for the DNA test."

And how they would do that without digging up the mother's body, Jamie didn't know. Maybe when this guy saw how much trouble he was causing he would give up and go away.

Jamie stared at him. What did he want her to say?

"Mrs. Dixon, I'm just trying to do what's right."

Jamie's emotions escalated with her heartbeat. "Doing what's right is letting this little girl stay with the only parents she's known since birth and giving her a chance to grow up in a home with love and security." She didn't even try to keep her voice down. This man was a threat to her and her child, and she wasn't going to allow him to walk in and ruin their happiness.

"But I have a responsibility and I can't just run away from it," he insisted. "If this is my child, I have to know."

Jamie felt a surge of unbridled anger tear through her veins so strongly it frightened her. "Mr. Nichols, I have to go now," was all she dared say. Slamming the door and locking the dead bolt behind her, Jamie scooped up her sleeping daughter and cradled her in her arms. Her tears ran down her cheeks onto her daughter's blanket.

No one could take her daughter. No one.

Chapter 17

Julianne was looking for her sunscreen, so Alex went downstairs to meet Rich and Andre. As the elevator descended, Alex rummaged through her bag for her lip balm, only looking up when another hotel guest stepped inside. To her horror, it was Jordan.

"Well, what a small world," he said with a sly smile.

"Jordan! I thought you'd gone home." She put the chapstick back in her purse without using it.

"I've had some business to attend to," he said. He didn't take his eyes off of her. "Looks like you're headed to the beach."

"Uh . . . yeah," she mumbled, shifting her bag on her shoulder. "Yes, we are."

"It seems I've finally got you alone after all," he said with a strange smile. "I'm almost tempted to stop the elevator so we can catch up with each other. It's a shame we haven't had time to visit."

Alex felt a jolt. The last thing she wanted was to be stuck in an elevator with Jordan for who knows how long. "My friends are downstairs waiting for me," she said coolly.

Jordan shook his head. "I'm disappointed in you, Alex. When I learned you'd be here, I was so looking forward to talking to you. But you've been very obvious about your feelings." The elevator bell dinged announcing their arrival to the lobby. "I can take a hint," he finished.

"Good-bye, Jordan," Alex said as she shot out of the elevator the second the doors opened. Rich and Andre were right in front of her. Masking her anxiousness with enthusiasm, she raced up to them. "Hi," she excitedly, as she latched onto Rich's arm. "Julianne will be right down."

She noticed Andre look behind her, his face registering curious interest. She didn't have to turn around to know who was standing in back of her and Rich.

"May I help you?" Andre asked.

Jordan appeared at her side. "My name is Jordan Davis," he said extending his hand. Alex felt Rich stiffen beside her. "I'm an old friend of Alex's."

Realizing it was the best way to keep the encounter smooth and brief, Alex spoke up. "Jordan, this is Andre Marquard, and my fiancé, Rich Greenwood."

Rich extended his hand and shook Jordan's.

"Congratulations on your engagement," Jordan said to Rich. "I hope you two will be very happy together." He seemed sincere, and Alex hoped he was ready to let go.

Jordan made no move to leave. "I understand you're hoping to go sailing while you're in town," he said. "Were you able to find a charter company? If not, I've got a couple of names you could try."

"Actually, yes," Rich told him. "We've been able to make arrangements with a private company. But thanks anyway."

Jordan glanced down at his watch. "I've got an appointment downtown, so I'll say good-bye. Nice meeting you." He smiled at Rich and Andre. "Again, congratulations on your upcoming marriage, Alex."

"Thank you, Jordan," she said, still not sure what to make out of his appearance. Was he sincere or just putting on a show for Rich and Andre?

It didn't matter, because a moment later he was gone. Finally he was out of her life.

* * *

The two couples took the ferry across the bay and docked at Ferry Landing Marketplace on the island of Coronado. Julianne still couldn't believe they'd run into Jordan in the lobby and was mad that she'd missed the whole encounter.

They hopped on a tour bus that looked just like an old-fashioned trolley car, riding it along Orange Avenue, the main artery of the town. Alex noticed all the darling shops and boutiques lining the street and at one stop the four decided to jump off and go window shopping.

Orange Avenue reminded her of Cape Cod, with its clapboard houses, small restaurants and stores. It was just like New England, especially with its nautical atmosphere and shops filled with sailing equipment and clothes.

The early afternoon breeze filled the air with the scent of outdoor grills and the tang of salty seawater. The brisk, invigorating aroma put them all in a festive mood. Carefree and relaxed, the two couples strolled leisurely down the Avenue, stopping for a tantalizing scoop of homemade ice cream on sugary waffle cones. Licking their cones as they walked, they soon realized they weren't far from Silver Strand Beach State Park.

The beach, strewn with high rise hotels, tall stately palm trees, and hundreds of tourists, was a long stretch of silver-white sand as far as they could see. The water rolled in on azure blue waves and lapped the shore with a foamy rush.

After some scouting they found a place to change into their swimsuits and by mid-afternoon they were relaxing under a clear blue sky in the warm summer sun.

Peeking under the brim of a straw hat, Alex looked around and admired the beauty of the ocean and the beach. Not too far in the distance, she could see the cluster of buildings making up the famous Hotel Del Coronado she'd read about in a travel brochure—a historic hotel built in 1888, the world's first electrically lighted hotel, lit by Thomas Edison himself.

Many famous people had stayed at the hotel, including dukes, presidents, and hundreds of celebrities. In fact, it was a setting for many movies, and for good reason—its ornate Victorian gingerbread architecture was breathtakingly beautiful, especially surrounded as it was by the lush tropical setting of palms and ferns and bright flowers. Alex felt like she'd just fallen into an episode of *Fantasy Island*.

While Rich applied sunscreen to her back and shoulders, Andre and Julianne tested the water. Alex quickly sat up when Julianne started yelling for Andre to put her down. He had picked her up and was threatening to throw her into the surf. However, a rather large, unexpected wave swept Andre off his feet, and both went tumbling into the water. They both came up sputtering, but before too long they were playing and frolicking in the waves. Alex and Rich couldn't resist and within seconds, Alex and Rich were in the brisk water with them. They splashed and chased each other, trying to jump over the waves and body surf onto the beach.

Alex admitted defeat after she was carried by a wave and slammed onto the shore, finding her swimsuit filled with sand and her mouth with seaweed. Tired and shivering, she ran for her towel and dried off, then lay in the sun, letting the strong rays warm her. Moments later, Rich pounded up the beach toward her.

She kept an eye on him, just to make sure he wasn't going to surprise her with a gallon of water or a creature found crawling around the shore, but he had no such designs. He showered her with some refreshing sprays of water as he shook water from his hair, then he flopped down beside her, obviously exhausted from fighting the powerful waves.

"Hey there, beautiful." He leaned over and kissed her lips. They each tasted of salt. "This is heaven, isn't it?"

"Mmmm," Alex sighed. "It sure is." She felt as if every bone had turned to putty.

"Hard to believe people actually live here, isn't it?" he asked.

"This would be a tough life," she agreed. "Perfect surroundings, perfect weather. Hey, where'd Andre and Juli go?"

"I don't know," Rich said lazily. "They were right behind me."

Alex raised herself up on one elbow and saw them, hand in hand, walking down the beach. She glanced at Rich, as he lay stretched out on his towel, his legs extending beyond the towel's length. Then she noticed a dark smear on the back of his leg.

"Hey, Rich, bend your right leg. You've got something on the back."

He bent his knee and she peered closely. "You've got a huge gash on your calf," Alex said. "Can you see it?"

He sat up and looked. "Man, I didn't even feel it." He wiped at the wound with the corner of his towel.

Alex dampened the corner of her own towel with bottled water. "Here, use this."

Rich wiped at the cut, revealing a deep gouge in the muscle.

"That looks serious," she said. "You ought to get some stitches."

"You think?" He turned his leg so the sun shone directly on it. It had stopped bleeding. The wound was two inches long and looked about a half an inch deep. "I must've cut it on a shell or something."

He examined it by pulling the gash open with his thumbs. Not one for blood, Alex felt her stomach lurch at the sight of his raw flesh.

"I think it's okay," he decided. "It's pretty deep but I don't think it needs stitches. I'll just put some antibacterial ointment on it and a nice tight bandage to pull it together. It'll be fine."

"I'd hate for it to get infected," Alex worried aloud. "Are you sure you don't want to get it looked at?"

"Nah, it's okay. It doesn't even hurt." Rich lay back down, making sure his wound was on the clean towel and not in the sand.

When Julianne and Andre returned, Alex asked her if she had any bandages. She had, in fact, several helpful items in her bag and was able to clean up the wound and dress it nicely. Just to be safe, Rich didn't go back into the water and by late afternoon they'd all had their fill of sun and fun.

Aware that they weren't in any state to go to a nice restaurant, they cleaned up as best they could and found an outdoor café. Alex had never tasted lobster so good.

Andre tapped his knife of the side of his water glass, then raised it up to propose a toast. "Here's to good friends, good food, and good fun," he said. They all added their "here, here's," and clinked their glasses together.

After stuffing themselves at dinner, they walked lazily back to the landing where they could catch the ferry to their hotel. Onboard, Alex looked out over the expansive San Diego skyline across the harbor and admired the beauty of the lights and the starlit sky.

Rich stood behind her, his arms wrapped around her waist, as they drank in the view and breathed in the refreshing night air. She rested her head back against his shoulder as the soft motion of the waves rocked them gently.

"It's beautiful isn't it?" he said softly in her ear. "Did you have fun today?"

She nodded. "It was perfect. I hate to see it end."

The colors on the horizon intensified as the sun slipped from view. Blazing crimson and brilliant orange lit up the sky, turning wisps of clouds into streaks of fire.

They watched in silence, wrapped in each other's arms, as the colors faded and softened to a warm glow, dimming slowly to night.

Alex was grateful that soon she and Rich could spend all their evenings, and the rest of their days, together, forever. They would have an eternity of sunsets to share.

* * *

Early the next morning, Alex awoke to the annoying sound of her alarm clock. Her sleep had been anything but restful. She didn't know why, but for some reason, her dreams had been shadowed by nightmares.

She'd never considered herself a paranoid person, but lately she felt as though she overreacted to everything.

She climbed out of bed and walked to the sliding glass door, unlocked it and went out on the balcony. It was dark, the stars still glittering in the sky.

The captain had told them to report at the boat *before* sunrise, explaining that they needed an early start to make it to their destination on time. There weren't many things that seemed important enough to get up for at four-thirty in the morning, but if that's when the boat sailed, they needed to be there.

Alex breathed in the crisp morning air, filling her lungs and clearing her head. One good thing about going on this boating excursion—she would have plenty of time to discuss the final details and plans of their wedding and her European honeymoon with Rich. They could also talk about the personalized video project, especially now with Rich involved, and they could have fun relaxing, eating, and enjoying each other's company.

Wishing she would have slept instead of worrying all night, Alex yawned, filled her lungs, and stretched her arms overhead, hoping to clear the thick heaviness in her head.

Just as she was about to head for the shower, the phone rang. Julianne groaned and pulled her pillow over her head. Alex reached for the phone, wondering if it was Rich.

It was Sandy. "You mentioned you were leaving early this morning and I wanted to talk to you before you left," she said.

"But it's so early," Alex protested.

"I wasn't able to sleep," Sandy explained. "I've got so much to do before I leave for Paris. I'm trying to get my schedule arranged. When are you heading back to Salt Lake?" Sandy had been thinking about joining them for part of the video shoot if her schedule permitted.

"Oh, we're still taking the ten-twenty-three out of San Diego on Saturday. Andre says we can be in the studio Wednesday morning. If you could come on Sunday though, you could attend my mother's baptism."

Sandy's response was just what Alex expected. "Your mother's what? That's wonderful news. But why didn't you tell me she was thinking about joining the Church?"

Alex laughed at Sandy's enthusiastic reaction. "Because she just barely decided to do it. Isn't this exciting?" Alex asked. "I just wish there was some way Mom could come through the temple with me when I get married, but I can't wait another year until she can go through."

"I don't think she'd expect you to," Sandy laughed. "I don't know many people who've attempted a two-year engagement."

"So how are things going?" Alex asked. "I guess you haven't changed your mind about Paris."

Sandy laughed. "Sorry, everything's pretty much in place there. I'll be back for your wedding, of course."

"And we'll be over to visit you on our honeymoon. I can't wait to show Rich Paris," Alex sighed happily.

"So, are you guys doing anything fun while you're there?" Sandy asked.

Alex explained that they were sailing to Ensenada and leaving that very morning.

"Oh, really?"

Alex noticed a strange tone to Sandy's voice. "Is something wrong, Sandy?"

"Well, no, not really. Personally I don't do well on sail boats. I get very seasick."

Alex didn't like hearing that. She didn't know whether she got seasick or not. She sure hoped those pills Julianne bought worked. "This is a pretty big ship, plus we've got some good medicine. I think we'll be okay. Don't you?"

"Of course. But will you please call when you get back, so I'll know you made it safely?" she insisted before they said good-bye.

"Was that Sandy?" Julianne asked, wiping the sleep from her eyes. "And what was all that talk at the end? Is she worried about us going on this boat?"

Alex nodded. "And now I know where I've gotten all my paranoia from—*from her!*"

"Well, I think it's going to be fun, and very romantic," Julianne said loftily. Then she glanced at the clock. "Good grief, look at the time. We're supposed to be downstairs in forty-five minutes."

While Julianne showered, Alex took the opportunity to kneel by her bed. *Heavenly Father,* she began, *am I just being overly sensitive and paranoid, or are these uneasy feelings I'm having an indication that we shouldn't go on this boat? Right now I can't seem to tell the difference between a prompting and my own insecurities. Help me please to know for sure. Please bless Rich that if we shouldn't go, he too, will know. And no matter what, please bless us and protect us.*

She remained on her knees for a moment, waiting for the sure answer, the solid feeling of "yes" or "no," whether they should go, but nothing came. She didn't feel strongly either way.

With a sigh, she got to her feet and grabbed her bag, hoping that when the confirmation came it would be before they headed out to sea.

Chapter 18

As the faint rays of morning blushed the sky, the two couples wound their way through a maze of planked walkways, among rows of ships bobbing gently in the water. Overhead, gulls called and flapped as they scavenged for food.

"There she is." Andre pointed when he found the vessel among the other boats in the harbor. "The *Sea Queen*. What a beauty."

Barely able to see in the dim light, Alex searched through the tangled view of masts and riggings to see which boat he pointed to but couldn't tell which one was theirs. The group followed the walkway past other boats of various shapes and sizes until they came to a stop.

"What a beauty," Andre said again. "Sixty feet of grace and power."

Andre had spent time on sailing ships as a youngster with his grandfather. He had a great love for sailing and claimed that once it was in your blood you could never get rid of it. Judging by the excited look on his face, this trip was a dream come true.

As sailboats went, Alex could see that the *Sea Queen* was one of the larger ships docked in the harbor. Standing before the boat, Alex felt dwarfed.

"Ahoy," a voice called. "Come aboard, mateys."

Alex looked up and saw a man on a rope ladder, halfway up the main mast.

"Are you Captain Porter?" Andre yelled.

"That'd be me," the man hollered back. "You can stow your gear below. I'll be right down." From high above, the man made an awful noise in his throat, then expelled a glob of chewing tobacco over the side of the boat.

"Yuck," Alex whispered.

"How disgusting." Julianne pulled a face.

"C'mon," Rich quickly said. "Let's take our stuff down below." They followed him aboard, allowing him to search for the hatch that led below deck.

Alex was surprised to find the boat tidy and in good order. It looked well cared for and was indeed a beauty. The weathered wood was polished and clean. It was nothing like its captain.

Andre took the lead and the others followed him down the companionway to the belly of the ship to a large common area where the kitchen, or galley, as Andre called it, was located. The appliances were stainless steel; the counters were of black granite and the floor, polished teakwood parquet. Directly across from the galley, next to the stepladder leading to the deck, was a chart table with radio and electronic equipment, Alex guessed, used for navigation.

Further into the room was a seating area, where they could eat and relax.

"Wow," Julianne remarked with surprise. "I didn't dream it would be quite so luxurious."

"You know," Alex voiced her thoughts. "This boat and Captain Porter aren't really a match."

"What do you mean?" Andre asked.

"Captain Porter doesn't exactly seem like the classy kind of captain I would've expected on this type of boat." She nearly added that the captain looked like he'd be more comfortable on a raft on the Mississippi River, but was glad she didn't.

"Welcome aboard," the captain's booming voice startled them. His large frame filled the hatch as he clamored down the ladder. He wore a sweat-stained captain's hat over the shaggy gray-blonde hair that curled around his neck; his skin was as leathery as an old saddle. He smiled showing yellow tobacco-stained teeth, with one tooth missing right in the front. "Glad you could make it."

He reached out and shook hands with all of the passengers. They introduced themselves to him. "As soon as my first-mate, Donovan, arrives, we can raise the anchor. So," he asked, "how do you like her?"

"She's a beautiful boat, Captain Porter," Andre answered. "We're happy you had a cancellation so we could sail on the *Sea Queen*."

"She's quite a lady, tough as they come. We've ridden out many a gale together, but she holds fast and never gives up," he said, his gruff voice a perfect match for his straggly appearance. Alex was standing close to the captain and she wasn't sure, but she could have sworn she'd caught a whiff of alcohol on his breath. It wasn't even six-thirty in the morning. Maybe it was left over from the night before, she tried to rationalize.

His comment reminded Alex of a question she had. "What is the weather forecast, Captain?"

"Well, little lady—" he looked her directly in the eyes. "We might have a spell of rough weather but nothing we can't handle. If we keep her about eight or nine knots, we can get ahead of the storm. But the sea is very unpredictable. She's a lot like a woman, always changing her mind."

There was something in his eyes that made Alex squirm. "Yer not worried now, are ya?" he asked.

"Uh, no," she said, then added, "Should I be?"

The captain laughed. "We've laid in plenty of supplies and have this vessel in ship shape. We could survive for a month in a hurricane."

Alex felt a little better.

"How long have you owned the *Sea Queen,* Captain?" Rich asked.

"Oh," the captain drew out the word, as if he were mentally counting the time. "I'd say it's close to six, seven years now." He pulled on his cap and said, "There's a forward cabin and a berth next to the galley. You folks git yerselves settled, then we'll shove off shortly."

The passengers thanked him and watched as the man climbed the companionway to get back out on deck.

"I don't know about him," Alex said softly. "Are we sure we want to trust out lives in his hands?"

"He's just an old sea dog," Andre said. "We're probably safer with him than some unseasoned sailor in a snappy outfit."

"I hope you're right," Alex said, trying to ignore the nagging feeling inside. "He smelled like alcohol."

Rich looked at her. "This early in the morning?"

"That's what I thought. Maybe you ought to go check him out, just to make sure he's sober enough to drive the boat."

"It probably wouldn't hurt," he agreed. "Come with me, Andre."

While the men checked on the captain, Alex and Julianne checked the accommodations. To their relief, they discovered the berths to be comfortable. The V-berth, at the front of the ship, was big and roomy. It had a large bed in it, hanging lockers and plenty of space. This was the girls' room.

The side berth was located next to the bathroom, or the forward head, as Andre had called it. This was Rich's and Andre's room.

At the rear of the boat was the aft cabin, where the captain and his crew member would sleep. There was another bathroom, the aft head, next to it. Next to the captain's quarters was the engine room. Andre had explained that the engine was used mainly to get the boat out of the harbor or back into port. The ship's generators were also found in the engine room.

"Well?" Alex said, when Rich poked his head inside their room a few moments later.

Rich and Andre had been satisfied with the captain's explanation. He had apologized profusely, saying that he had gone to a bar the night before and someone had spilled a large mug of beer all over him. He had got in late and hadn't yet had a chance to change.

"This boat isn't so big we can't keep an eye on the captain," Rich said. "I don't think we have anything to worry about."

"Me either," Andre said. "So come on, let's get out on deck and enjoy the sunrise as we leave the harbor. It's beautiful out there."

* * *

"I got it!" Steve shouted as he hung up the phone. He ran to Jamie and gave her a hug, dancing her around the kitchen. "Delaney's wants to carry my fortune cookies! Isn't that great?"

"Oh, honey, I'm so excited!" She hugged him again. "This couldn't have come at a more perfect time."

"We've got to start production immediately. And they suggested we come up with a holiday line of fortune cookies—for Halloween, Thanksgiving, Christmas, Easter—and then also something for parties and family gatherings."

"Steve," Jamie said, breathlessly, "I can't believe it. They must really like your idea."

"They do! They want to offer me a six-month exclusive contract and are willing to pay more before I approach any other companies with the product."

"Do you think it's wise to limit yourself?" Jamie asked cautiously. "I'm sure it's something I need to look at closely before I sign," Steve acknowledged. "Rich is so good with finances and contracts, I'm sure he'll be able to help me know what to do." Jamie stroked her husband's cheek proudly. "That's terrific, honey. You never gave up and now look, you're going to be a fortune cookie magnate."

"Ahhh sooo," Steve said in an exaggerated oriental accent. "Confucius say—" he held up one finger "—Good luck smile upon man with good idea, and," he said, pulling Jamie close, "man who has beautiful wife." Jamie giggled and let her husband shower her with kisses.

The phone rang breaking up their romantic interlude.

"Hello," Steve said cheerfully.

Jamie could tell by the change in his tone that he wasn't happy about who was on the other end and what was being said.

Steve didn't say much except for "yes," "no" and "I see."

"I guess we have no choice," he said at last. "Tell your attorney we'll take care of that within the next week. But, Mr. Nichols, while we're waiting for the results, I suggest you think about this child—our daughter," he emphasized in a louder voice, "and not yourself. I admire the fact that you feel a sense of responsibility, if in fact Andrea Nicole is your child. But she has lived with us almost a year, and we are her family now. With us she has two parents, a wholesome environment, and all the love and stability she'll need. Perhaps you should think about what you have to offer her, what kind of a life she would have with you—a single man, a truck driver who spends ninety percent of his time on the road."

Jamie closed her eyes and prayed for strength, asking the Lord to help them, to be with Steve as he spoke, so the words he said would touch this man's heart.

"Mr. Nichols, this is about what kind of life this child deserves. She'll have everything she needs and wants with us, a good home, a family, love, and a future. She can have a college education and every opportunity the world has to offer. Doesn't that mean anything to you?"

Steve listened for a moment.

"I see," he said. "Well, like I said, we'll discuss it when we find out the results of the test. Until then, I don't think we have any further reason to communicate." Without even waiting for a response or a good-bye, Steve hung up the phone.

Jamie blinked at the film of tears in her eyes.

Steve took one look at her and wrapped his arms around her. "Honey, don't cry. Everything's going to be okay." He rocked her gently, letting her release her emotions.

After a moment, Jamie dried her eyes and listened as Steve repeated the conversation. "Even though it's hard to accept, this man is only trying to do what he thinks is right," he told her.

"But—" Jamie began.

"I know what you're going to say," he interrupted. "But let me explain. He said he never knew his own father. His father abandoned his family when he was a child. All his life he's had to struggle and work to help his mother and his brothers and sisters. He feels like he has to do this. He never wants to be like the man his father was. He says if he has to, he'll quit his job and find another one where he can stay in one place. His sister is more than happy to take charge of Nikki while he works, and he vows he will make any sacrifice he can to make Nikki's life happy."

Jamie struggled between pity for the man and her own pain and heartache. How could anyone take her child from her? Jamie loved Nikki more than she could say. She would give her life for her child. She felt it would literally kill her to have to give her up.

"But how can they even run the test?" she asked, her voice shaking. "I thought they needed the mother's blood to get the DNA."

"Apparently they did an autopsy after she died to determine if any controlled substance was being used," Steve said. "They keep the slides with tissue samples for years. They can get the DNA from those."

"And the money?" Jamie insisted. "Where's he getting the money for the test?"

"He sold his motorcycle," Steve said.

"Oh, Steve." Jamie's tears returned. "What are we going to do? We can't lose Nikki. We just can't."

"I know, honey. And we won't," Steve spoke gently. "The Lord performed a miracle to bring her to us. He won't let someone take her away from us."

Jamie sniffled. "What did you tell him we would take care of?"

"We have to take the baby in and give them a sample of her blood for the test."

"What?!" Jamie cried. "I'm not going to do it."

Steve shook his head. "We don't have a choice. He's retained an attorney and was advised that we can cooperate and keep this out of the courts, or they can force us to cooperate and then it gets ugly."

"Oh, Steve. This is getting worse and worse. I can't bear the thought of that man taking her. It will kill me," Jamie wailed.

Jamie let her husband hold her as she sobbed with his arms wrapped securely around her. The test couldn't come out positive—it just couldn't.

*　*　*

"I don't think those pills are helping," Julianne said as the ship dipped and rose through the continuous ocean waves. They'd been out to sea for an hour, and already Julianne's face was the color of pea soup. She lay on her bed, hoping the nausea would go away.

Alex had suggested Julianne go up on deck, thinking the fresh air would help her feel better. She was grateful that she herself wasn't having any severe reaction to the constant roller coaster motion of the boat, but she was sorry to see Julianne struggling to even stay upright.

"Maybe we should turn around," Alex said, "before we get out too far. I don't think you want to spend the next three days with your head over 'the head,'" she said, trying to make a joke to lighten her friend's mood. But Julianne didn't laugh.

"I'm sure fresh air and sunshine will help," Alex suggested. "Maybe it just takes a while for the pills to work."

Julianne pressed her hand against her stomach. "I think these pills are making me sleepy."

"You're going to be fine," Alex reassured her. "You just need to rest and get that stuff in your system."

Julianne relaxed back against the pillow on her bed. Alex sat next to her. "Juli, we won't make you stay on the boat. We'll just turn around."

"And ruin Andre's and Rich's fun. I can't do that." She lay back and shut her eyes, pulling in long slow breaths.

"Well, I'm going to go talk to them, just the same," Alex decided.

"I'm sure they wouldn't want you sick the entire time. Call me when you're ready and I'll help you out on deck."

The two men were at the helm with the captain, talking about sailing. "Hey you guys, Julianne isn't feeling very well. I don't know if those pills are helping much," she announced.

"Tell the young lady there're plenty o' crackers in the galley. She needs to keep her stomach full and fresh air in her lungs. She'll get her sea legs soon," the captain said as he steered the ship.

"I'll go find those crackers for her," Andre said before he disappeared down to the galley.

After he left, Rich explained to Alex that the captain was just telling him about the electronic and navigational equipment used to run and steer the boat: radar, chart plotters, compasses, digital tach/synchronizers, and automatic bilge pumps, besides the fax machine, computer station, and hi-tech radio equipment down below.

"I guess my question would be," she observed, "what do you do when you lose power and can't rely on your electronic equipment to guide the boat?"

The captain looked at her with surprise, then smiled. "That's a good question, miss. 'Twould be pretty sad if the captain couldn't sail a boat without the help of technology, now wouldn't it?"

Alex nodded.

"I'll be right back," Rich said. "I'm going to run downstairs and get my videocam." Alex stayed and listened intently as the captain gave her his detailed answer.

"Of course I have instruments on board to help me stay on course. And to ease your pretty mind, I haven't yet encountered such a problem, but you must always be prepared, right?"

"Right."

"There are many ways to get your bearings." He pointed to the position of the sun. "Since we are on a course due south, you know that the San Diego harbor is in the opposite direction. Land is due east and open ocean is to the left. Even in the middle of the ocean a seaman can still find his way back to port. It's amazing, isn't it?"

"Yes," Alex agreed. "It is amazing." She was glad to learn that even though the man looked like a barnacle-encrusted relic, his nautical knowledge appeared adequate.

"The sun rises in the east," he continued, "so the sunrise can provide you with a rough determination of where east lies from your position. The sun bears due south at noon. If your goal is to sail north, you could simply keep the sun behind you throughout the middle part of the day. Err to the west during the morning, err to the east by the same amount all afternoon. This will keep you on a fairly good course to the north."

Alex heard Rich coming up the companionway. "Sorry I took so long," he said stepping through the hatch. "I stopped to check on Julianne."

"How is she?" Alex asked, hoping her friend had found some relief from her misery.

"She's feeling a little better," Rich responded. "Andre's feeding her crackers right now."

"I think I'll go see if there's anything I can do." Alex turned to the captain. "Thank you for explaining all of that to me. It was very interesting."

"My pleasure, miss. And if you ever have any more questions, I'd be happy to oblige." He tipped his captain's hat and smiled. Even so, the squinty look in his eyes made her uncomfortable. She had every intention of staying as far away from him as she could.

As she walked away, she heard the captain telling Rich that he didn't like to be on film, claiming that his ugly mug would break Rich's camera. Alex smiled to herself knowing that no one was a match for Rich and his camera. When he wanted to shoot something, he made sure he got it.

Holding tight to a side rail, Alex stopped to look out at the ocean and clear sky. She felt a tingling rush as a wave slapped against the side of the boat, sending a salty spray over the railing. The stiff breeze held the tightly trimmed sails, tugging and pulling the ship through the rolling sea. It was indeed exhilarating.

For a moment, Alex was caught up in the experience, understanding just for a moment the thrill of what sailing was all about. The freedom, the loss of time, the carefree, childlike newness she felt as the ship gracefully but powerfully made her way through the unpredictable waves.

"'Scuse me, Ma'am," someone said behind her. It was Donovan, the first mate. Rich had nicknamed him "Gilligan," but she didn't see any resemblance. Donovan had several piercings in each ear, and both his arms were covered with tatoos. He wore his long hair pulled back with a piece of leather. If Porter made her uncomfortable, Donovan made her downright nervous.

His unshaven face and brooding eyes had made Alex uneasy. She knew it was wrong to prejudge him, but her gut instinct told her to watch out for him. She was grateful she hadn't brought anything of great value with her on board. Rich, however, had his expensive video camera with him. She made a mental note to remind him tonight to put the camera in a safe place, just in case.

Alex stepped aside, allowing Donovan to pass by, and watched him secure one of the lines. The confusion of masts, sails, and lines made her head spin. If he knew how to maneuver all of this, then she had to at least give him some credit. She didn't think any amount of sailing would help her understand how to raise a sail or steer the boat. It all seemed to her that they were at the mercy of the sea and the wind. But it appeared that these men knew how to set a course for a final destination and actually get there.

Andre and Julianne emerged from inside the boat and came out on deck. Alex was glad to see that Julianne had some color in her cheeks and was able to stand upright. They found a comfortable spot on the cushioned benches and rested in the early afternoon sun. Andre kept his arm around her and Julianne rested her head on his shoulder.

They made a cute couple, Alex thought. Julianne's hair had grown to her shoulders and was a glossy honey-blonde. It had natural curl and hung in soft waves. Andre, on the other hand, had medium brown hair that was stick-straight, which he kept short. Alex liked the playfulness of his bushy brows and warm green eyes and the constant smile on his face. He was fun to be around because he was always in a good mood and made the best of any situation. He was upbeat and positive, and his mood seemed to lift the spirits of anyone around him.

Alex decided to let them relax in private so she went down to the galley and started lunch. The captain had a steak dinner planned for them, but told them they were free to fix their other meals. Alex couldn't help but be skeptical of the captain's cooking skills. She knew it was rude, but she hoped it was safe to eat the food he prepared.

As she searched through the refrigerator and cupboards, she pulled out rolls and lunch meats and attempted to make submarine sandwiches for them all. But every time she set out to slice the pickles for the sandwiches, the boat rocked and sent the gherkin flying. *I need a dozen hands, just to hold things in place,* she thought in disgust. With increased creativity and determination, she finally completed the task of making the sandwiches, losing one tomato in the battle.

She found potato salad and juice in the fridge and a bag of chips and clam dip to go along with the meal. When it was ready she went to find the others, hoping everything would still be intact when they returned to eat it.

She found Rich with Julianne and Andre. "You guys hungry?" she asked.

"Starving," Rich replied.

Even Julianne felt like eating a little, and they settled down inside the galley to their lunch, laughing and eating as Alex tried to explain how difficult it was to prepare. Rich extended an offer to the captain and Donovan to eat with them, but they declined until the passengers were finished.

"That Captain Porter is quite a seaman," Rich said. "He was telling me about some of the hair-raising experiences he's had on some of these fishing boats."

"How hair-raising can fishing be?" Julianne asked, holding tightly to her glass as the motion of the boat started it sliding to the edge of the table which, thank goodness, had a raised edge to help keep items from sliding off.

"These weren't just regular fish they were after. He went for swordfish, one of the most dangerous types of commercial fishing there is. In fact, except for being a lumberjack, being a commercial swordfisherman is the most dangerous occupation there is."

"Really?" Alex said, somewhat skeptical.

"I believe him," Rich stated. "Did you notice he's missing two fingers on his left hand?"

Alex had noticed but hadn't thought it polite to ask how he'd lost them.

"That's from getting his fingers caught in one of the lines as they were pulling in a load of swordfish. He said his hands were so cold and frozen that he didn't even know it happened until another member of the crew pointed it out."

"Oh, sick," Alex said, setting down her sandwich with distaste.
"Wow," Andre said, fascinated. "Where do they go for swordfish?"
Rich was happy to oblige with an answer. "Off the coast of Maine toward Nova Scotia. It's called 'The Grand Banks.' On this particular trip there was a freak storm, early in the fall. They had blizzard-like conditions for over twenty-four hours. Everything froze, including the men."
Even though it was a warm, balmy day, Alex shivered. "Why would they go on these trips, if it's so dangerous?" she asked.
"The money. Most men made between ten and twenty thousand dollars in less than a month." Rich placed another scoop of potato salad on his plate. "Captain Porter said that after staring death in the face as many times as he has, he finally retired and started sailing for pleasure. He says he loves the sea but doesn't want to be buried there. It's much safer taking passengers like us out for pleasure trips than risking his life fishing."
"I wonder if he's married?" Julianne questioned.
"I'll give you one guess," Alex said, just a little sarcastically.
Rich had that information as well. "He said his wife left him, claiming she couldn't compete with his love for the sea. He was gone nearly eight months out of the year, then home for less than a week between fishing trips. I guess that's where he and Donovan met, on one of those fishing boats. They both decided there had to be a better way to make money. But I can't imagine they make much taking tourists on day cruises to Catalina Island."
"I'm not sure about Donovan," Alex said quietly. She looked toward the hatch to make sure they were alone. "Does he make anyone else nervous besides me?"
"I didn't really get to meet him," Julianne said. "I was a little preoccupied when he came on board." Julianne had gotten nauseous almost immediately, before the ship even left the harbor.
"Seems like the typical sailor to me," Rich said.
"Me too," Andre answered. "I've been around a few shipping yards. Those men are rough. They live a very hard life."
"I guess so," Alex conceded. She didn't comment that he looked more like a drug smuggler than a sailor to her.
Rich gave her a somber look. "You aren't sure about either of them, are you, Alex?"

"I can't explain it," she said in her defense. "But I'm not. And it doesn't help when I smell alcohol on the captain's breath."

"I've smelled it too," Andre said. "I wouldn't be surprised if he did have an occasional drink now and then. But he does know how to handle a boat."

Alex shrugged. "I'm probably just being oversensitive, but I'd feel better if we weren't in the middle of the ocean with them in charge."

* * *

Later in the afternoon, while the four passengers relaxed in the sun, Rich noticed the captain tie off the helm, then disappear down below. About fifteen minutes later, he returned.

"What is it, Captain?" Rich asked as Captain Porter headed for the helm.

"Nothin' to be concerned about, mates," he answered. "Just a summer storm ahead. We'll get plenty o' rain, but it'll blow over before ya know it. You'll be wantin' to stay below when it hits, so you don't end up overboard. Donovan and I can handle it."

"I've got to get some footage of this," Rich said, running for his camera. "I want to get a picture of this storm cloud."

Alex was surprised Rich could get so excited about the whole thing. In contrast, she and Julianne looked at each other with trepidation. When the captain said "rough weather," did that mean "rough" according to what he was used to? Or "rough" according to what they were used to? As far as Alex was concerned, the ocean was rough enough the way it was now.

They scanned the horizon, looking for the storm. To Alex, the sky was completely clear, not a cloud to be seen. Nothing had changed. She fully expected to see a dark cloud looming in the distance, but it was a stunningly beautiful day.

"Captain," she asked, "how do you know there's a storm coming?"

"When there's static on the radio, I know somethin's brewin'," he pronounced solemnly. "And when you've been at sea as long as I have, you can feel it in yer bones. But I've checked the weather reports and the radar. You don't need to worry, miss. We'll have a lot o' wind and rain, but that's about it. This is just an afternoon thunderstorm, not a storm front. We won't even get a lot of waves out of it. These storms can be violent, but they blow over quickly. Now it would be different if we were facing a whole storm system. Yessiree. Be glad this is just a cumulonimbus cloud."

Alex looked again at the sky, but there was nothing threatening about the white, puffy clouds in the distance.

"O' course," the captain went on, "I remember a time when I was sailing in the South Pacific, and we got hit by a squall that nearly rolled our boat."

"Did you capsize?" Alex couldn't imagine how terrifying that might have been.

"No, but we lost nine men that day. Half our crew."

Alex gasped. "Wasn't there anything you could do?"

He shook his head. "A squall isn't detectable on radar. You don't see it coming. In seconds the wind can triple from fifteen knots to fifty. We had ten-foot waves and higher, some breaking over the stern, but we got hit by a rogue wave, and there was nothing we could do. Just hang on and pray."

"What's a rogue wave?" Alex asked, fascinated by his story.

"You see, miss, there's a pattern to the sea, almost like a rhythm. About every seventh wave is an odd wave, and in nasty weather it's not uncommon to get a twenty- or even a forty-foot wave, unexpectedly. That's what we call a 'rogue' wave."

Alex shuddered at the thought. Her first instinct was to tell the captain to turn the ship around immediately and get them back to land. As much as she enjoyed the beauty of the sea, and the thrill of the wind and water, the experience didn't seem worth the risk.

Sure enough, in less than an hour the formation of clouds on the horizon began taking on a new and ominous shape. The passengers watched as the anvil-shaped cloud grew to enormous heights and towered ahead of them in the distance. The darkening cloud, dirty gray on the bottom, sent gusts of wind their direction.

"This is incredible," Rich said, capturing the developing storm on camera. "It's really beautiful."

Alex couldn't see any beauty in what lay ahead of them. All she could see was a menacing storm cloud ready to beat down on them at any minute. The boat seemed small and insignificant in the face of the storm, and she realized that she had absolutely no control over the situation. They couldn't avoid it and their welfare lay in the hands of Captain Porter and Donovan. Not a comforting thought.

As the wind gusts increased, the captain began shouting orders.

"Donovan, I'll reef the sail. You put up the storm jib." The captain tied off the helm, then flaked the mainsail onto the boom, shortening the sail. Donovan completely dropped the front sail, then raised a smaller one in its place. All of this was done quickly and efficiently.

When he finished the captain yelled, "You passengers put on life jackets and get below. Close all hatches, ports and windows. Secure your gear. We're in for a wild ride."

"I don't think I like this," Julianne yelled over the bursts of wind and commotion.

"Let's get down below," Alex hollered, heading for the stairs, as droplets of rain started to fall. She'd known something was going to go wrong. Sending a prayer for help and protection heavenward, she hurried inside with Julianne close behind her. They found the life jackets and helped each other put one on.

"Where are Rich and Andre?" Julianne asked anxiously.

"They were right behind us," Alex answered, feeling panic rise in her chest.

A loud crash of thunder sounded, causing the girls to lunge for each other and hold on tightly.

"I hope Rich and Andre are okay," Alex worried aloud.

"I'm going to go get them," Julianne said.

"I'm going with you."

It took the strength of both girls to open the hatch. Dark rain greeted them. Cautiously the two girls held on as they fought to get on deck. Through the heavy rain, Alex could see Andre several feet before her, hanging onto the rigging.

"Andre!" Julianne hollered. "Get inside."

"I'm coming," he called back. "I'm helping Rich get his camera gear."

Leave the crazy camera! Alex wanted to yell. A flash of lightening, followed immediately by the deafening boom of thunder, caused Alex's heartbeat to race. Andre's face showed his alarm as the rain came harder, pounding down in sheets. The boat rocked and lurched, making it difficult to stand, even while holding on.

Then, to her relief, Alex saw Rich as he handed his camera bag to Andre. Finally they were coming inside. Alex and Julianne scrambled below and waited anxiously for the men.

She thought she heard some yelling going on and strained to make out the noise, trying to separate voices from the sound of the shrieking wind and crashing waves. Andre and Rich still weren't coming inside. Something had happened.

"Julianne," she cried, "something's wrong. We have to go back out." Alex headed for the door and steeled herself against the elements pounding down upon them.

Up on deck, each step was physically challenging as she fought against the gale force wind and struggled to keep her balance. Keeping hold of the sturdy lines that held the sails in place, she forged ahead. She could barely see to the stern of the boat through the drenching rain, but she kept going until a shape became the back of a man.

"Get inside," someone yelled. It was Donovan coming up from behind her.

"What happened?" she demanded.

"Man overboard. Get inside!"

Man overboard? Who? Andre? Rich? Terror struck her heart.

She saw someone ahead pulling at a rope stretched over the rail. Her question was answered when the man in front of her turned. It was Andre.

Rich had been swept overboard.

Chapter 19

"Rich!" Alex yelled, her words lost in the fury of the storm. The dip and roll of the waves threw her back against the door, but she held onto a guideline, the threads of the rope digging into her flesh.

She managed to regain her footing and find her balance, then lunging for the rail, she grabbed on. In the angry, churning water, Rich clung to a life preserver as Donovan and Andre labored together to pull him back to the boat.

The power of the waves seemed to suck Rich under, but he always emerged back on top. Slowly, they tugged, pulling him closer to the boat until they could finally reach out to him.

Every nerve in Alex's body sparked and her muscles clenched as she watched, fearing Rich would fall back into the water at any moment. Finally, Andre and Donovan hefted his limp body back on board. Staggering and swaying, Alex made her way to him, praying with all her might that he was alive. She fell to his side and assessed his condition. His lips were blue, his skin stark white, but, thank goodness, he was conscious.

"Rich!" she hollered so he could hear her. "You're safe now." She turned to Andre. "Help me get him inside."

It wasn't easy, but they managed to drag him to the hatch and down the stairs, where they laid him gently on the floor. He lay there shivering uncontrollably, his body temperature dangerously low, his muscles fatigued from the fight to stay above water. He could barely speak but managed to say, "Camera. Where's . . . the camera?"

Alex's lips curved involuntarily into a smile. It was just like Rich to be more worried about the videocam than himself.

"I've got it, old boy," Andre answered. "It's safe. Let's get you dry now." Julianne had watched everything from the hatch and had a warm blanket waiting for him when they brought Rich inside. She dashed to his room to get dry clothes. Alex held the blanket around Rich while Andre helped Rich out of his wet clothes. Soon they had him in dry clothing and wrapped warmly.

The boat continued to lurch and reel side to side and back and forth, the storm unleashing its energy upon them. Because Rich had swallowed a lot of water, the chaotic movement of the boat caused him to throw it all up, but once his stomach was empty, he felt much better. Color returned to his lips and cheeks, and Alex breathed a sigh of relief. He was going to be fine.

Just to be safe, they slipped into life vests, and Andre sat close to Julianne as they held onto the furniture while the boat pitched and swayed with every wave. When Alex had helped Rich with his life vest, they clung silently to each other and to the bench seat around the dining table. Both couples sat wide-eyed and quiet, not knowing what to say or do.

Then, it ended.

The boat stopped all motion. An eerie stillness settled in. They all looked at each other in wonder, curiosity, and some fear.

They heard Captain Porter yell at the top of his lungs, "YEE-HAW! That was a doozie! HOO-WEE! I thought we were goners there for a minute."

A smile broke onto Julianne's face, then Andre's.

"Donovan!" the captain yelled. "Raise the mainsail and check for damage."

The clomp of footsteps made them all turn in expectation. The captain was coming downstairs. "Yo-ho, mateys," he bellowed, "Any survivors down here?"

"Barely," Andre answered.

The captain looked at Rich. "You the one that went overboard?"

Rich nodded sheepishly.

"Good for you! Now you've got something to tell your children and grandchildren about," he said enthusiastically. "Nothin' like a good drenchin' in a storm, is there?"

Rich didn't answer, Alex was sure he didn't know what to say.

"Anything broken?" the captain asked him.

"No," Rich said.

"Imagine that." The captain shook his head. "You took quite a blow. I thought for sure you'd broken a bone. Well!" He took in a long breath. "Glad to see you're all alive. I'd best get back to my post." He headed back outside, leaving them speechless.

"'Nothing like a good drenching'?" Alex asked with disbelief after he was gone. "Is he serious?"

"I think he's a bit bonkers, if you ask me," Julianne said.

"I had no idea a storm could hit so suddenly, with such fury," Andre observed. "Rich, are you sure you're okay?"

Rich nodded. "I'm fine. I'm exhausted, though. I was swimming like mad until you got that life preserver to me. I couldn't keep above the water."

"What happened?" Alex asked. "How did you end up overboard?" She had to force the image of Rich fighting for his life out of her mind. It made her heart race in fear when she thought of how close he'd come to drowning.

"It all happened so fast, I'm not sure," Rich said with a shrug. "I remember a big flash of light, followed by a loud crack of thunder. Then it was like this enormous gust of wind tipped the boat, smacked into me, and knocked me over the rail. I literally felt myself being lifted off my feet."

"I saw it all," Andre said. "That's exactly what happened."

"I thought the captain said there wouldn't be many big waves," Alex reminded them.

"Maybe in his book, those weren't big waves. He's probably used to seeing twenty- and thirty-footers," Rich said.

"Probably," Alex said. "But still, that was a close call." She reached over and stroked Rich's face, grateful to feel its warmth again. She decided now was the best time to offer a suggestion, one she wasn't sure would go over very well, but she had to try. "I know how much you all wanted to go sailing," she said cautiously, "but I've had enough. After what just happened, I think we ought to turn around and head back to San Diego."

None of the others said anything; they just looked at each other then back at her. Even though she knew they probably wouldn't go for it, she had to try. She didn't want to take any more chances of anyone getting hurt. She realized now she should've listened to her gut instinct in the very beginning, then they wouldn't even be in this situation.

"Actually," Andre finally said, "I was having the same thought. Even though the chance of another storm like this isn't likely, I'd hate for anything serious to happen to one of us."

"I agree," Julianne said.

"Me too," Rich said.

Alex was relieved. They could go back to San Diego and enjoy the rest of their time together.

"Besides," Andre said, "after that wild ride, I'll admit, I took my turn at losing my stomach out there."

They decided to tell the captain right away, hoping they might even be back in the San Diego harbor late tonight. Or at the very most, in the morning. Rich was feeling stronger so he accompanied Alex topside to talk with the captain. She noticed Rich favoring his right leg. She stopped him, her hand on his arm. "Rich, does your leg hurt?"

Rich looked down. "Yeah, it's starting to bother me a little."

"Did you injure it when you fell?"

"I'm not sure," he said. "I haven't had a chance to look at it really. I probably banged it on the side rail when I went over the edge. It'll be fine."

Alex took his hands in hers and swallowed the emotion that quickly tightened her throat. "I can't tell you how scary it was to see you in the water today." Tears filled her eyes. "I was so afraid I was going to lose you."

Rich pulled her close and wrapped his arms around her. "Honey, I'm sorry I scared you." He chuckled. "I was pretty scared myself."

"Don't *ever* do that to me again." She pulled back and looked up into his face. "I don't think I could live without you."

"You won't have to." He hugged her tightly. "You have my promise. And soon you are going to be stuck with me forever."

Those words were music to her ears. "I'm looking forward to that day. As far as I'm concerned it can't get here quick enough."

"I agree," Rich said. "It seems like this last month is going slower than the first eleven."

Alex laughed and agreed wholeheartedly, then followed him through the hatch in search of the captain.

"Beautiful evening," the captain said when they joined him. Donovan was nowhere to be seen. Except for the rescue, Alex hadn't seen much of him that day. But, she decided, it was probably just as well. She didn't like how she felt around him.

Rich scanned the horizon. There wasn't a cloud in the sky. "Hard to believe an hour ago we were in the middle of that storm," he said. The heavy sun hung lazily in the west against a calm sea while copper shadows glinted and danced on silver ripples.

The captain nodded. "That's how those summer cloud bursts are. Unpredictable and sudden."

"Captain?" Alex cleared her throat nervously. "We've been talking and we've decided that instead of going on to Ensenada, we'd like to turn around and go back to San Diego."

The captain looked at her, but not with surprise.

"Of course, you can keep the money for the entire three-day trip," she added.

She expected him to come back with an argument, in an effort to convince them to continue on, but to her relief he didn't. With a nod, he said, "If that's your wish, we can anchor here tonight, and be on our way back to port first thing in the morning."

"Thank you," Alex said sincerely.

"Why don't you folks relax and enjoy the beautiful evening?" the captain suggested. "I'll go downstairs and make you a steak dinner you'll never forget. After a good meal, you'll all feel much better."

Alex had forgotten about the dinner that came with the excursion. Her mouth watered at the thought of a scrumptious meal. She realized all the excitement had made her quite hungry.

"I'm going to get my video camera and catch this sunset on film," Rich said. "I'll tell Andre and Julianne to come up and join us. It really is a beautiful evening."

After Rich left, Alex sensed movement behind her and expected to see her fiancé again. Instead, it was Donovan. How long had he been standing there? He didn't say much, just stared at her, then hurried down the hatch and left her alone on deck.

As far as Alex was concerned, they couldn't get back to dry land fast enough.

* * *

"Hi, Mom," Jamie said, answering the front door. "Thanks for coming over on such short notice."

"Honey, is everything okay?" Judith asked anxiously. "What did your doctor say?"

Jamie had been having early contractions for some time, but not until they had become downright painful had she finally called the doctor, who had told her to come to the hospital immediately so she could check her. Judith would stay with Nikki while Steve drove her.

"Have Steve call when you get settled. I'll be anxious to hear—" Judith stopped as she noticed her daughter holding the sides of her swollen stomach and taking measured breaths. "Are you sure you're okay?"

Jamie nodded, then began to relax after another minute. "Sorry, just a contraction."

"I'm ready," Steve rushed into the room. "Hi, Judith," he said, "thanks for helping us out. Where's Dave?" he looked around. "Did you say he was coming with you?"

"He's coming over later," Judith said as they headed out the door. "Now don't forget. Call me!"

At the hospital, Jamie was ushered into an examination room where her doctor gave her a brief but thorough exam. Then she said briskly, "Your body is not responding to the medication. We can't stop the labor."

"But it's too soon. I can't have the baby tonight," Jamie protested.

Dr. Chandler stroked Jamie's arm in an effort to calm her. "I know you're concerned about losing the child, but I assure you, Jamie, everything's going to be just fine. You're almost thirty-seven weeks. This baby is very healthy, and so are you."

"But . . . but . . ." Jamie couldn't pull her thoughts together. She couldn't bear the thought of having the baby early, of the possibility of losing another child. Why was her body doing this to her?

"I'm going to get your husband in so you can tell him that we're going ahead with the delivery. I'm sure he'll want to make some phone calls to your family." Dr. Chandler stood to leave. "Jamie, I don't want you to worry."

Jamie nodded, her emotions too charged for her to speak.

Within seconds after the doctor left the room, Steve entered and rushed to his wife's side. "How are you, sweetie?" He kissed her forehead.

"Oh, Steve, can you believe this?" Jamie moaned. "Not again."

"Honey," Steve said soothingly, "Dr. Chandler told me we have nothing to worry about. You have to be strong now. You have to have faith."

"But I'm so scared," she whimpered. "What if . . . ?" She couldn't even say it.

"I'm going to call and ask Dr. Rawlins to come over and help me give you a blessing," he promised. He leaned closely to her, "Everything is going to be fine. Just think, soon we'll be able to see our little baby. I'm still hoping for a boy, you know."

Jamie and Steve had agreed earlier that they didn't want to have an ultrasound to identify the sex of the baby. They wanted it to be a surprise.

Now Jamie smiled at her husband's excitement over the thought of having a little buddy to take to ball games and fishing. She didn't want to tell him that she felt very strongly that they were having a girl. But Jamie knew either way it wouldn't matter. The minute they saw their new baby, she knew it would be love at first sight.

Chapter 20

The captain wasn't kidding. He really did know how to make a delicious steak dinner. He grilled some tender, juicy T-bones and served them with steamed vegetables and new potatoes, with cheesecake for dessert. Alex hadn't even seen all the ingredients for such a meal in the refrigerator, but it didn't matter to her. Wherever it came from, the food was incredible.

To their delight, there was a beautiful moonlit sky that evening. The two couples sat out on deck and let the cool night air, the soft lapping of waves, and the star-filled sky lull them into a relaxed and enchanted mood.

The captain and Donovan had cleared away dinner and retired to their cabin, leaving the two couples to themselves.

"You know," Andre said, slipping an arm around Julianne's shoulders, "except for the storm, this trip really has been a lot of fun."

"Except for the storm and the motion sickness," Julianne added.

"Yeah," Andre laughed. "I guess I forgot about that."

"Actually, once I got that medicine figured out, it wasn't so bad," Julianne said.

"Speaking of medicine," Rich said, "is there any chance one of you has something for aches and pains?"

"I have some prescription pain medication," Alex said. "Aren't you feeling well?" After his near drowning, he hadn't seemed quite like himself. He hadn't even finished his meal—something Alex had never seen.

"I'm feeling a little flushed and achy," Rich admitted, "and I'm really exhausted."

"I'm sure it didn't help swallowing all that seawater," Andre said. "You'll probably feel better after a good night's sleep."

Julianne rose to her feet. "I've got some Tylenol. Why don't you try that first?"

Alex reached up and felt Rich's forehead. He did feel warm.

"Is there anything I can do?" she asked, trying to suppress the worry that crept into her mind.

"I just need a pain reliever and some rest. I'll be fine." He patted her knee and relaxed against the cushioned bench.

The quarter moon cast silver shadows upon the water, and Alex thought how strange it felt to have no land in sight and absolutely no idea where she even was. They'd only been out to sea since that morning, but it seemed like they'd been gone for days.

When Julianne returned with a glass of water and some capsules, Rich accepted them gratefully. "The captain and Donovan sound like they're remodeling their room downstairs," Julianne said, as she returned to her place beside Andre.

"What do you mean?" Alex asked

"They're being so noisy—doors opening and closing, things banging around. Almost like they were looking for something. I don't know."

"Hmmm," Alex mused ironically. "Maybe Donovan lost an earring and they're looking for it."

"One of them will be up here soon," Andre said. "Someone has to keep watch all night."

"Really?" Alex asked. "Why?"

"The captain told me earlier that even a boat this size is no match for one of the tankers that haul through the water. By the time we showed up on their radar, if in fact we ever did show up, they wouldn't be able to change course. They could plow right over us and not even know they'd hit anything."

Alex felt better knowing that someone was keeping an eye on things. "I just hope the captain stays sober while he's on watch," was all she said.

Rich drank the last of the water from his cup and thanked Julianne again for the Tylenol.

Julianne explained that her mother was very big on keeping emergency supplies handy, as well as extra food and water. "She's a nurse, you know," she said. "Plus, I think it's because she grew up in the aftermath of World War II. No one wanted to be caught unprepared ever again."

Andre added that the war had destroyed much of his country and had devastated the French people. "My parents are a lot like Julianne's," he told Alex. "They like to keep extra supplies on hand, just in case." He nodded his head toward Rich, and Alex turned to see that Rich was breathing heavily, his hands hanging limply to his sides. She nudged him gently, but he didn't respond.

Sure enough Rich had drifted off.

Alex looked back at Andre. "Would you mind helping me get him to bed? He's obviously checked out for the night."

"Not at all. In fact, I think I'll turn in with him. We'll probably be starting back as soon as the sun comes up." Andre stood and stretched, then stepped over to his friend. "C'mon, buddy. We're going to bed."

Rich, groggy and half-asleep, accepted Andre's help and together they made their way to their cabin, with the girls close behind.

* * *

Something wasn't right. Alex sat straight up in bed and listened. She heard someone moaning. Somebody was in pain.

She pulled a robe on over her pajamas, pausing to steady herself against the movement of the boat. It was early morning and soft light poured in through the portholes in their quarters. Stepping outside her cabin, Alex listened again. A groan from the next room caught her attention. The sound was coming from Andre and Rich's room.

Softly she tapped on their door and waited for an answer, but there was none. She knocked a little louder.

"Rich? Andre?" she said. Another groan, this one louder, forced her to turn the knob and peek inside. Andre was sleeping like a log on his side of the bed, but Rich was thrashing about, his covers twisted around his feet.

"Rich?" Alex said. He didn't respond. "Rich, are you okay?" She stepped closer, trying to discern why he wasn't answering. On closer inspection, she could see clearly that Rich was covered in sweat; his hair was wet and glued to his forehead, his t-shirt drenched and crumpled.

She reached out to calm him, but the moment her fingers touched his skin, she realized he was burning up with fever.

"Rich!" she demanded. "Can you hear me?"

The thrashing stopped as he recognized her voice. "Alex?" he whispered weakly.

"Rich, I'm here. What's wrong?"

"Hot . . . I ache . . . all over," he rasped. "Need something to drink . . ."

"I'll get you a glass of water and another Tylenol," she responded urgently.

A million thoughts filled her head as she rushed to the galley. What was wrong with him? How could Andre sleep through all that movement next to him in bed? And why did the boat seem to be rocking so much?

Maybe the captain was already up and had them sailing back to San Diego. With all her might, she prayed that was the case. The sooner they got back to dry land, the better. Especially if Rich needed a doctor.

She quickly got his drink, grabbed two of the pain capsules, then raced back to his room.

"Here," she said. "I'm back, honey. Everything's going to be okay." She helped him lift his head and gave him a sip of water to moisten his mouth and throat. "You need to take this. Can you swallow these pills?"

He nodded slowly. She gave him one at a time, then followed each with another sip of water. She poured the rest of the water on a cloth and pressed it against Rich's forehead. Trying to help him relax, she assured him that he was going to be fine, even though she didn't know for sure herself. What in the world was wrong with him? Why was he sick? What did he have? Could he have salt poisoning from swallowing so much seawater?

She needed to talk to the captain. "Andre," she said loudly. "Andre, wake up."

"Huh?" Andre stirred in his sleep.

"Andre, it's me, Alex." She waited for him to open his eyes and look at her. "You have to wake up. Rich is sick. I need you to watch him while I go find the captain."

"Sick? Who's sick?" he said groggily, his eyes slowly closing again.

"Andre, listen to me," Alex demanded. "Rich is very sick. Please watch him while I go talk to Captain Porter."

Andre opened his eyes again and pushed himself up on his elbow. "What's the matter with him?" His eyes weren't all the way open, but at least he was awake.

"I don't know," she said, "but he's burning up with a fever and says he's achy all over. I'll be right back. Please keep an eye on him."

"Okay." Andre finally forced his eyes open, leaned over, and felt his friend's forehead. "Wow, he really is hot."

Not wasting another moment, Alex charged out of the room, up the companionway through the hatch, and emerged onto the deck of the ship.

"Captain!" she hollered. "Donovan!" She ran around the walkways, but didn't see them anywhere. The captain wasn't at the helm, the anchor was still in the water, and the deck was empty. She noticed something else in her search. There were storm clouds in the distance, covering what was left of the morning sunrise.

"Oh, great," she said out loud. "Another storm."

Please, Heavenly Father. Don't let it storm on us right now. We've got enough to worry about without that.

Clamoring back through the hatch, she practically slid down the stair ladder and raced for the door to the captain's quarters.

Banging on the door, she hollered, "Captain Porter, we need you. Could you get up please?" She waited for what seemed like an eternity. There was no answer.

How could people sleep so soundly on a boat? And wasn't someone supposed to be on watch twenty-four hours?

"Captain!" She pounded again.

Finally, desperate, she cracked the door open and poked her head inside. "Captain Port—"

The cabin was empty.

Where in the world were they?

They weren't in their room. They weren't on deck. There was nowhere else they could be.

"Captain Porter!" she screamed, panic filling her chest. "Donovan!" She searched the room thoroughly for the men, then stopped. All their clothes were gone. The room was devoid of any personal items. She hadn't seen their luggage, but she assumed they'd brought some things along with them.

"What is going on?" she said. Racing from the room, she burst into her own stateroom. "Juli, wake up. Julianne!"

"What?" Julianne sat up. "Alex, what is it?"

"Rich is sick," she cried, "and the Captain and Donovan are gone."

Julianne looked bewildered. "What do you mean, they're gone? How can they be gone?"

"I don't know, but I can't find them anywhere," Alex wailed in frustration.

Julianne jumped out of bed. "That's ridiculous. They've got to be here somewhere."

The two girls looked in every possible place below deck, searching the captain's quarters and engine room thoroughly. They even leaned over the edge of the ship to look in the water around them, but came up empty.

"I don't like this," Julianne said, her eyes wide with concern. "Where are they?"

"I don't know," Alex said in exasperation. "This doesn't make any sense."

"Look, Alex," Julianne pointed at the darkening sky closing in around them. "That doesn't look like the thundershower we had yesterday, does it?"

Alex shook her head dismally. "I don't know what's going on," she said. "But it looks like we're in for a very bad storm."

The first thing to do, they decided, was to tell Andre and check on Rich. Then they'd get the life vests and rain gear from the storage locker.

"Maybe we should find the radio and send out an S.O.S. or a May Day or whatever you send for a distress call," Julianne suggested.

"Good idea," Alex agreed.

When the two girls told Andre about the captain and Donovan, he almost didn't believe them. In fact, he wanted to go look again, positive he could find them, but Alex and Julianne assured him that the boat was empty except for them.

"How's Rich?" Alex asked.

Andre gave Rich a worried glance. "I think he's a little delirious.

He's mumbling words, but not making any sense. At least, the fever reducer is helping. He seems to have calmed down."

Andre suggested that Rich might have taken in so much water into his lungs when he fell overboard that he had developed pneumonia or something similar.

"Wait a minute," Julianne said, crouching down closer to Rich's leg. "Look at this." She pointed to his right calf. Rich's wound from the Coronado Island beach had become red and swollen. The wound itself was open and oozing puss.

"I don't think Rich's condition has anything to do with him falling overboard," Julianne said. "I think he has an infection."

"Does he have a red line going up his leg?" Andre asked.

Alex and Julianne looked closely.

"Not that I can tell," Alex said. "Last night I noticed he was limping. I asked him what was wrong, and he said he thought he'd bumped his leg going over the boat. He had long pants on so he couldn't see."

"We'd better keep an eye on it," Julianne said. "I had an uncle who cut his hand chopping wood. It wasn't even that bad of a wound, but within forty-eight hours after the infection set in, he died."

"Forty-eight hours?" Alex's heart nearly stopped. "Do you think . . . ?"

"He's going to be fine, Alex," Julianne assured her, regretting her hasty words. "We just need to keep his fever down and give him plenty of liquid so he doesn't dehydrate. We should change the dressing on his wound often, and it would help to put some ice on the swollen area."

"How do you know things like this?" Andre asked her, impressed.

"I told you. My mother's a nurse," Julianne grinned. "I guess I picked it up by watching her all these years."

"Well, thank goodness you paid attention," Alex told her. "I'll go get some ice."

"And I'll clean up the wound and put a bandage over it. I have some antibiotic ointment but I hope there's some alcohol in the first-aid kit."

Alex ran for the fridge. Then, as if the boat had slammed into the side of a building, she felt the storm hit. The cabin rocked to the side, then back the other way. As Alex clung to the counter, she had a strange feeling. It didn't require an expert seaman to know that this storm was going to get very ugly.

Then she opened the freezer and saw immediately that there wasn't any food. Suppressing the panic that filled her chest, she grabbed some ice and wrapped it in a dish cloth. She stopped to open several food lockers and discovered they were also empty.

All their food was gone. What was going on?

Another wave crashed into the boat. Bracing herself against the bank of lockers on the wall, she allowed the boat to straighten itself again, then raced back to Rich's room.

"What's going on?" Julianne cried when she burst through the door.

"The captain told me about storms like this," Alex said. "He called them squalls."

Andre's face looked pale. "I grew up with my grandfather's stories about these unexpected storms that catch sailors unaware. We just have to stay calm," he said, "and keep our heads together. I'm going up on deck and see what's going on. You girls stay here with Rich."

"Hang on," Alex yelled as the crash of another wave slammed against the boat with a deafening bang. Again the boat lifted and tilted. Complaining loudly, the boat creaked against the strain of the powerful storm.

Alex felt relief fill her chest as once again the ship regained its position.

With wide, frightened eyes, and a tremor in her voice, Julianne said, "That was a bad one."

"We're going to be fine," Andre said confidently. "I'll be right back."

"Wait," Alex said before he left, wishing she didn't have to tell them. "We don't have any food."

"What!" Julianne said so loudly she startled Rich. "What do you mean there's no food?"

"I just checked the fridge and the lockers. There's no food."

The three looked at each other in confusion. "What is going on?" Andre muttered. "I'll be right back."

"Be careful," Julianne said. "We don't want you going overboard."

Andre made his way from the room, then Alex had a thought that seemed absolutely preposterous. Almost as preposterous as their situation.

"This whole experience seems too calculated to be an accident," Alex said, thinking aloud. "You don't think Porter and Donovan are scam artists, do you?"

"But why would they abandon their boat?" Julianne asked reasonably.

Alex was silent, pondering. *Why would someone abandon an expensive boat like this along with its four relatively inexperienced passengers?* A thought suddenly occurred to her. "I wonder . . . what if someone put them up to this?" she said slowly.

"But who?" Julianne asked. "And why?"

"I'm just thinking there might be a connection . . ." Alex paused. "Do you remember that bouquet of flowers in my room in San Diego?"

"And the strange card that came with it," Julianne remembered.

"It gave me such a creepy feeling," Alex recalled. "Just like I feel right now." She repeated the words on the card: *"This is just the beginning of the many surprises that await you."* She looked at Julianne and her eyes narrowed. "I know I can't prove it, but something tells me Jordan had something to do with this," she said.

Julianne was astonished. "Jordan? You haven't seen him for two years, except at the convention. Why would he do something so drastic?"

Alex sighed. "I know. You're right. But who else do we know who's capable of doing something like this."

Another wave, this one with the blast of a cannon, rocked the ship, causing Alex and Julianne to scream as the nose lifted up, then tipped to the side. Alex thought for sure they were going over.

Andre burst into the room with an armful of life vests, "Here," he yelled. "Put these on." He threw them each one and one for Rich. "I've been trying to reach some help on the radio."

Alex was grateful Andre had taken charge. She was so frightened, she didn't know what to do. They helped Rich into his life vest, then went to check Andre's progress with the radio.

Julianne explained to him Alex's theory about Jordan, and Andre looked at Alex questioningly. "Do you think Jordan is capable of something like this?" he asked curiously.

Alex remembered Jordan's ego that could never accept rejection. "Yes," she said definitely. "Then again, no. Oh, I don't know." She shrugged. "I just can't believe that our crew would just abandon us for no reason. Someone or something is responsible for this."

The boat shuddered against the onslaught of waves.

"Right now none of that matters," Andre said. "We just need to concentrate on getting ourselves rescued."

"That's right," Julianne told her. "It doesn't matter how we got into this situation. The important thing is that we keep our heads and find a way to get back to shore."

Still, Alex felt responsible for getting them into their predicament. She remembered the awful feelings she'd had about going on this sailing trip and the promises in her patriarchal blessing, telling her she would know in whom she should place her trust. She hadn't trusted the captain, and she hadn't felt good about Donovan.

The signs and indicators were there; she'd just ignored them. She'd been prompted not to go—even Sandy had told her not to go—but she hadn't wanted to disappoint the men and ruin the fun. And, she admitted to herself, the luxury of the ship had captivated all of them.

"Alex, this isn't your fault," Julianne assured her, as though she could read Alex's thoughts. "Now, c'mon—" she made her way to the food lockers. "We're not going to just sit here and drown." Scouring them one more time, she gave a shout of triumph. "Look! A box of crackers and a tin of tuna fish. And I've got a bag of red licorice and a bag of peanut M&M's in my suitcase."

Andre rose and motioned to Julianne. "Keep trying the radio. I'm going back on deck. I want to check the lifeboat."

"I'll come with you," Alex volunteered. She wanted to see what was happening outside.

Buckets of rain flooded in when they opened the hatch. They couldn't even see to the helm from the companionway.

"Here." Andre grabbed a coiled rope hanging beside the ladder and tied it about his waist. "You hold this line while I go out."

"Okay." Alex's heart beat wildly in her chest. "Be careful."

Andre inched his way out on deck, the force of the storm knocking him against the outside of the cabin. Alex held tightly to the rope as it slid slowly through her hands. More frightened than she could ever remember being, she sent a pleading prayer heavenward for their safety.

Despite her fervent prayer, the boat pitched and careened with the turmoil of sea. Waves broke over the rail flooding the deck. With the rolling of the boat, the unsecured hatch swung open and water poured inside. Alex heard Julianne's scream as an avalanche of water dumped over her.

"Close the hatch," Alex yelled to Julianne, but the storm's fury swallowed her words.

Alex worked her way toward the cabin, but each step was precarious on the slippery deck surface. Then, without warning, a giant wave hit, sending a mountain of water on board, washing Alex's feet from under her. She felt herself sliding across the deck, the rope slipping through her hands.

"Help!" she screamed, but her words were lost in the thundering storm.

Chapter 21

Momentarily stunned, Alex quickly grabbed onto a cable so the crashing waves didn't send her flying overboard. Her shoulder throbbed where she had banged into the side of the boat. Clawing her way to the helm, she found her footing and pulled herself to her feet. Rain stung her face and the wind whipped her from side to side, but she clung to the steering wheel, wanting to confront the rogue storm that threatened to end their lives. She felt as if the very jaws of hell were gaping open and waiting to swallow her and the rest of her friends whole. Again she prayed, *Heavenly Father, where are you? Please, help us!*

A flash of lightening split the sky followed instantly by a clap of thunder.

"Alex, get inside!" It was Andre, pulling her toward the hatch.

Another bright flash of lightening sent them both scrambling below as the force of another wave knocked the boat to its side and sent a shudder through the entire frame of the ship. Down below they found Julianne still working the radio, with no success. There was too much static.

Static. Just like the captain had said. Static on the radio meant a storm was coming. Well, it was here and it was scaring them all to death.

With renewed determination, Andre went back to the helm, steering the boat into oncoming waves, trying to save the boat from capsizing. Alex and Julianne took turns at the radio, trying desperately to signal help. They checked on Rich periodically, but he'd become completely disoriented and weakened by his feverish state. Alex gave him two of her prescription pain relievers, hoping they would give him some relief.

Soaking wet and chilled to the bone, Alex sank to the floor and leaned her back against the wall, watching Julianne at the radio. Seeing Rich so disoriented had shaken Alex more than anything she'd ever experienced, and she was overwhelmed with the hopelessness of their situation.

"Julianne, I don't get it," she said wearily, "Here we are only weeks away from getting married, and we may not make it through today. After waiting almost an entire year, I can't believe this is how it's going to end."

"Alex," Julianne assured her, "we are not going to die at sea."

"Well, it certainly looks like it," Alex said grumpily. She knew she should be an example of faith to her nonmember friend, but she couldn't pretend. She had never been afraid of dying, never even thought much about it, and now . . . well, even if they all didn't drown, Rich would likely die if they didn't get help. And there was no sign of help in sight.

"Well, I'm not drowning, I know that for sure," Julianne said firmly. "And I'll be hanged before I let any of you drown. Alex—" she said, sitting down beside her friend and putting an arm around her, "—we have too much to live for. We're fighters, we're survivors. We both still have too much ahead of us to accomplish. We can't die!"

Alex stared at Julianne, impressed with her determination. Here she had the added comfort of the Holy Ghost, and the promises of her patriarchal blessing, and it was her friend who had neither who was the stronger one.

"I'm sorry, Julianne," she said, "I'm just so mad at myself for not paying attention when I knew there was something wrong and we shouldn't take this trip—"

"Hey," Julianne interrupted her. "Stop kicking yourself about that. It's over. It's done. It's not doing any of us any good for you to blame yourself. Let go of it. We need to put all our strength towards getting out of this situation, and not waste it beating ourselves for not seeing through that creepy Donovan and that beer-swilling captain."

Alex laughed in spite of herself. "Okay, I'm convinced. I'll try to forget it."

"Hey," Julianne said adamantly, "I'm going to be standing next to you at your reception, looking incredible, I might add, in my lavender bride's maid dress, and anticipating my own wedding someday—"

The boat rocked deeply, and the two girls gasped and hung onto each other, praying the boat would right itself again. Around them the books flew off their shelves and crashed across the floor, sliding into the wall with a thud. The plastic dishes in the lockers rattled noisily against each other in the cabinet.

How's Rich handling this? Alex wondered, imagining him thrown across the room. As the boat leveled off, she made her way to his room. She found him clinging to the headboard.

"That was a bad one," he said with a nervous laugh. "Who's sailing this ship anyway?"

They hadn't had a chance to tell him their situation. She debated whether she should or not.

"We ran into another storm," she told him. The storm had already lasted for over an hour. Certainly it couldn't keep up this intensity much longer. Could it?

"How are you feeling?" she asked anxiously.

"I've been having some crazy nightmares," he groaned.

"Rich," Alex said earnestly. "Listen. The sore on your leg is infected. You've had a high fever."

Rich looked blankly at her, not understanding.

"Remember that cut you got at the beach?"

"But that was nothing," he said, leaning on one elbow to see.

"Remember you said your leg was hurting? Well, it was your wound. Here," she went over to him, "let me help you."

She peeled back the edge of the bandage and exposed the moist, oozing wound, red and swollen and warm to the touch.

He pulled a face. "That's sick. Why didn't I notice it earlier?"

"I wish you had, because it's pretty serious," Alex scolded him. "We need to get you to the doctor right away."

"Does Captain Porter still think we'll be back in San Diego this afternoon?" Rich asked, laying back and closing his eyes.

"Uh, well . . ." Alex couldn't go on. The boat rocked wildy, forcing them to hang tight.

Alex held her breath and closed her eyes, praying the boat wouldn't go over. Her stomach rolled and pitched with the boat. Julianne had already lost the contents of her stomach, but since there was no food, there was nothing left to throw up. The timbers creaked, the frame complained and groaned against the strain, but the ship continued to hold together. *Please, Heavenly Father, calm this storm. We have to get Rich to a doctor.* "How's your stomach, Rich?" she asked when she felt confident they weren't going down. "We've all been taking Julianne's motion sickness pills. This storm is enough to turn anyone's stomach."

"I'd take a cracker or two and a drink of water, if you don't mind," Rich said feebly.

"Sure. I'll go get some. Just hang on, okay." When she returned, Rich ate a few bites of a cracker, and then worn out by the effort, he dozed off again.

Alex left the room and found Julianne and Andre gathered around the radio. She was glad she'd avoided telling Rich about the captain and Donovan abandoning ship. He needed his energy to get better, not to worry about their situation.

"Andre, what's going on?" Alex asked.

"It's bad," he said anxiously. "The waves are breaking over the bow. She's starting to take on water." Seeing Alex's worried, questioning look, he explained, "It means this storm had better end quick or we might just be going swimming."

Alex and Julianne shared a concerned look.

"We're still afloat," Andre said, "but I had to come inside. I don't even know if I'm doing any good out there anyway."

"Hey," Julianne cried. "I hear some voices."

All three gathered around the radio. A faint, crackling voice was heard.

"I can't understand them," Alex said. "What are they saying?"

"I think they're speaking Spanish," Andre said.

"We ought to try and contact them," Julianne said. "I'm sure they'll understand some English."

Andre tried every possible way he could think of to communicate their need for help. But without coordinates to give them some idea of their location, he wasn't hopeful. They listened for some reply, but the voices had faded to static. There was nothing on the radio.

Finally Andre gave up. "We can try again, later," he said. "How's Rich doing? Do you think a blessing would help?"

"Yes," Alex answered, "and I think it would make me feel a lot better, too."

In Rich's room they surrounded the bed, and while Rich continued sleeping, Andre lay his hands upon Rich's head to gave him a priesthood blessing. He blessed Rich with a strong body and the ability to fight the infection. He prayed for the Lord to watch over and protect them and to bless their boat to remain strong and solid. He also prayed for increased faith for each of them that they might be able to call upon the powers of heaven to help them.

Andre's words penetrated deep into Alex's soul, and she felt a tangible increase of the Spirit with them. She still didn't understand why they had to go through this, but she did feel that the Lord was aware of them.

The blessing ended just in time. Another crash sounded and the side of the boat lifted sharply, angling their world, but this time, it didn't stop.

"Hang on!" Andre hollered, "I think we're going to roll."

Alex and Julianne dropped to the floor and grabbed a bed post as the boat seemed to raise up out of the sea.

Chapter 22

"Okay Jamie," Dr. Chandler said. "It's time to push. I want you to take a deep breath, hold it, and bear down."

Jamie looked quickly at Steve, trying to gather courage and strength. Even though they'd had several ultrasounds to check the baby, Jamie knew from sad experience there could still be problems.

"You can do it, honey. The baby's going to be fine," Steve said. "Let's find out if we're having a quarterback or a ballerina."

Slipping his arm beneath his wife's shoulders as the doctor had instructed him, Steve helped Jamie sit up, thus allowing some leverage, which would make her efforts more effective. Grateful for modern medicine and epidurals, Jamie gripped the rails of the bed and bore down.

"Jamie, push!" the doctor ordered.

With all her might, Jamie took a deep breath, held it tightly, and pushed.

"Okay, good. Take a deep breath and do it again," Dr. Chandler coached.

Again and again, Jamie pushed until she felt her eyeballs were about to explode, until she knew her strength was completely exhausted.

"Hang in there," Steve said encouragingly.

"Nurse," Dr. Chandler ordered. "I want you to stand at Jamie's shoulders and push down on her stomach at the same time she pushes. Okay, Jamie. I know you're getting tired. But here comes a contraction, so get ready. We're going to help you."

Mustering strength from somewhere, Jamie drew in a deep breath, held it, and pushed. The nurse standing over her nearly lay on top of her as she pushed on Jamie's swollen stomach. Jamie felt every pound of the nurse's frame on her abdomen.

"Again, Jamie, quick. Another breath," the doctor said.

And again, Jamie obeyed, bearing down with all her might. Finally, the contraction ended.

"I don't think I can keep going," Jamie gasped.

"The baby's moving down," the doctor said, examining their progress closely. "The baby's head is right there. I think we can do it this next time."

Tears filled Jamie's eyes. She didn't have any strength left. But when Dr. Chandler told her a contraction was coming, she managed to find the strength to push again.

"I can see the head, honey," Steve cried. "You're doing great."

"The baby's crowning," the doctor said. "Again, Jamie. Push!"

An agonizing groan tore from Jamie's throat as she gave her final effort. With all the strength she had left, she pushed, then collapsed against the bed.

It was enough. Within mere seconds, she heard the cry of a baby. Her baby.

Exhaustion and emotion took over and she began to sob. The baby was okay. The baby was alive!

"It's a boy!" Steve cried. "Jamie, it's a boy!" He leaned down and kissed his wife on her sweaty brow. "He's beautiful, honey. You should see him. He's got a ton of dark hair."

Steve stepped away for a minute then came right back.

"And his hands, oh honey, you should see his hands. Those are the hands of a quarterback."

Jamie smiled, feeling new strength return to her body.

"Here," Steve said. "Let me put a pillow under you, so you can sit up." He helped her raise up slightly then slid a pillow beneath her.

The doctor efficiently stitched her up, and the nurse placed a small, warm, bundle in her arms. Jamie blinked furiously, trying to clear her vision so she could see the baby. She pulled back the edge of the blanket and exposed the tiny face of her newborn son. His eyes were swollen shut and his tiny lips were pursed and puckered. She touched his miniature nose and stroked one soft, pink cheek. Tears trickled down her own cheeks.

He'd made it safely into the world.

Gratitude filled her. Finally, she was able to complete the beautiful cycle of childbirth.

"Hello, son," she whispered.

He felt so snug and safe in her arms. She'd just witnessed a miracle, been a partner with God in bringing a sweet spirit to earth. Never before had she been so grateful to be a woman. To have this divine opportunity and power to actually give life to another human being.

She shut her eyes and held her infant close to her chest. The immediate, increased love in her heart filled her chest until she thought it would burst. They had a son. Nikki had a little brother.

Reluctantly she handed the baby to the nurse who was waiting to give the newborn a thorough check up. Steve followed the nurse, anxious to know that his future all-star was healthy and strong.

Jamie shut her eyes and took a deep breath. Everything was going to be okay. Her baby had made it here safely.

Everything was going to be all right. It had to be.

* * *

"Do you think it's over?" Alex asked. She released her white-knuckle grip on the bed post and looked around the room. The lamp hanging in the corner of the room swayed drunkenly on its hook while Rich's and Andre's belongings were strewn everywhere, some floating on the twelve inches of water that sloshed at the bottom of the boat.

"It seems to be," Julianne said, her voice hopeful although she still clung to the other bed post. Andre had thrown himself across Rich, to keep him from getting tossed off the bed, and Alex looked at them, soaked with sea water and cold. The boat hadn't rolled over, but it had come close. A fervent prayer ran through Alex's mind as she thanked the Lord repeatedly for protecting them. She couldn't deny it. Without heavenly protection they could have easily capsized.

"Is everyone okay?" she asked, reaching out for Rich's hand. "Rich? Andre?"

"Hangin' in there," Rich said, pushing himself up to a sitting position. Alex had told him about their predicament when he had awakened, and he was as bewildered as the rest of them why the captain would have abandoned the ship.

"I'm going to take a look outside and see what's going on," Andre said. "Stay here." He waded through the water and out the room.

"I can't believe this," Alex said. She felt like crying but fear had frozen her emotions into a state of numbing disbelief.

"You guys will never believe this," Andre yelled from topside. "Come on up. I think it's over."

"Is he kidding?" Julianne asked. "He wants us up there?"

"I think so," Alex answered. Rich was still pale but wanted to go with them to see the damage to the ship. So with Julianne on one side and Alex on the other, he made his way through the cold water to the step ladder leading above board.

Outside, the sky was still overcast, but the threatening black clouds from the storm were in the distance. The wind came in gentle puffs, and the waves, still choppy and whitecapped, seemed like nothing compared to the one that had nearly rolled them.

The ship was a horrible mess. The life raft, their only hope in the event they capsized, was long gone. The sails hung in tatters, the lines and rigging knotted and tangled. A brave but shredded American flag still flapped in the breeze.

"We made it," Julianne yelled at the top of her lungs. She hugged Alex with one arm. "We're still alive! Can you believe it?"

Andre was at the helm, looking at what was left of the instruments. "The storm's destroyed everything."

"And until we get some help from the sun," Rich looked skyward, "we can't really get our bearings to sail back."

"Sail?" Julianne asked, her eyebrows arched high with surprise. "Are you thinking we can still sail this thing?"

"I'm sure one of these sails is still functional," Rich said, matching Andre's determination. "We have to try. Don't we?"

Julianne and Alex looked at each other, then at Andre. Julianne said, "Are you sure that's the best thing to do? Shouldn't we stay put and wait for help?"

"What help?" Rich said. "Who's going to help us?"

"I don't know, but what if we go the wrong direction and head farther out to sea?" Julianne asked.

"That's probably just where we're drifting now," Rich replied. They'd lost the anchor in the storm.

"He's right," Andre agreed, then added, "We have to do something. We don't have any food and who knows how much fresh water we still have." Andre left to check the engine room. They needed the engines in order to start the bilge pumps. Rich limped over to the helm and looked at the broken compass.

"How are we ever going to find our way back?" Alex asked. She tried to muster some optimism, but the reality of the situation was bleak at best and she'd never been so wet and miserable in her life.

"No problem," Rich said. "I can make a compass."

"You can?" Alex and Julianne asked together.

"Hey, I'm an Eagle Scout," he defended himself. "I remember a few things from all those camping trips."

All it took was a paper clip and a piece of plastic straw. Rich looked inside the cupboard doors and grinned at the sight of the magnets that kept the doors shut during the movement of the boat. He briskly rubbed the paper clip over the magnet to increase the magnetic pull of the clip, then they threaded the straightened paper clip through the straw and floated it in a bowl of water.

Staring intently at the bowl as if it were a scientific experiment vital to humanity, they watched as the paper clip shifted and settled in the water. Even though it moved with the gentle rocking motion of the boat, it remained determinedly in one position.

"It works!" Julianne exclaimed, then added doubtfully, "Almost."

"What do you mean, 'almost'?" Rich looked at her, feigning offense. "It's doing what it's supposed to do."

"But which end of the paper clip is north and which end is south?" Julianne asked.

"That way is north," Alex said, pointing one way, then after a moment, she pointed the other way and said, "Or is that way north?"

"See what I mean?" Julianne said.

"All we have to do is wait for a break in the clouds so we can see the position of the sun," Rich explained. "Once we determine which direction is east and west, we're in business."

"I wonder if the radio still works?" Julianne asked.

"It would be a miracle if it does," Alex sighed.

"Why didn't we tell someone where we were going or what we were doing?" Julianne said, sinking to a bench that had lost its cushions during the storm. Everything that hadn't been lashed down or bolted to the boat had washed overboard. The poor boat looked like its next stop would be the wrecking yard.

"I didn't talk to anyone about our trip before we left," Rich said. Then Alex remembered. "But I did."

"You did?" Rich asked. "Who?"

"Jamie and Sandy. Sandy called right before we left."

"That's right," Julianne said. "You actually told her we were going to Ensanada and that we'd be back Thursday night." Julianne's face brightened.

"Alex, that's great," Rich said, "I mean, at least we know someone will notice when we don't show up on schedule."

With a sigh, Alex said, "I hope so." As worried as she was about being stranded, she was even more worried about Rich's condition. Would he be able to hang on until someone noticed and came looking for them?

"Let's go check the radio," Julianne said. "Maybe our luck is finally turning around."

The girls helped Rich down the step ladder. They heard Andre in the engine room along with a strange *ka-wooshing* sound followed by a deep creaking.

"How's it going?" Rich asked trying to keep his leg up out of the water. He leaned on Alex, using her as a crutch to help him.

"The manual pump still works, at least," Andre answered breathlessly, but with his ever-present optimism. Alex wondered how long it would take them to clean out all the water, if that were even possible.

"I guess that means without power, we have no radio?" Julianne asked.

"Radio's shot," Andre said between pumps. "Everything is soaked."

"Rich, why don't you go into the captain's room where it's dry and lay down for a bit," Alex instructed. "You need to get off that leg and get some rest."

"I feel like such a wimp, though," he replied. "I haven't done anything to help."

"Listen," Julianne said, taking him by the arm, "Your body needs you to rest and take it easy. We don't want you to get any worse."

"She's right," Andre said. "We're fine. Go get some rest."

Rich disappeared into the captain's cabin at the back of the boat, and the rest of them took turns pumping.

Julianne wouldn't give up on the radio and tried several times to bring it to life. While she sat at the instrument panel, she found a few books and documents that had survived the storm.

"You guys, come here, quick," she called out. "I found something."

"What?" Alex joined her first. "What is it?"

Julianne showed her some sort of legal papers that looked like the boat's current proof of insurance. Alex scanned the paper then stopped when she located the name of the owner. The names listed were "George and Bertha Higgins, joint owners."

"That's strange," Alex said. "Why doesn't it have Captain Porter's name on it?"

"Look at the date," Julianne said, pointing with her finger.

"This is good until April of next year," Alex exclaimed. "This is a current insurance form. He told us he'd owned this boat for almost seven years."

"What are you looking at?" Andre stepped up behind them.

"This," Alex handed him the paper. He glanced through the paper and drew the same conclusion. "Porter didn't own this boat; George and Bertha Higgins do. And they live in Las Vegas, Nevada."

"This boat is stolen!" Julianne declared. Then she said, "Maybe this had nothing to do with Jordan or anyone else."

"What do you mean?" Alex asked.

"Maybe Porter and Donovan stole the boat and set up this excursion just to make a quick wad of cash, then split before they got caught," Julianne insisted.

"You know, that does make sense. Those two sure did seem like the type that would do something like that," Alex said. "But I just can't shake the feeling that there's some connection to Jordan."

Julianne had only met Jordan a few times but she couldn't believe he would deliberately set Alex up like this. "Really—" she began.

Alex held up her hand. "No, listen, Juli. He knew we were going sailing; he even saw the name and number Dylan gave us."

"Well then," Julia said, "what about Dylan? He knew our plans, too. In fact, he's the one who told us about these guys."

Alex shut her eyes and let her chin fall to her chest, taking in a deep breath. Nothing made sense and yet everything seemed possible. She was so confused how any of this could have happened. "You're right, at this point I'd believe anything. But Jordan has the criminal connections. Anyway, Dylan has a job in Orlando on a cruise ship."

"I guess we're not going to know anything until we get back to San Diego and get the police involved," Julianne said.

"Aren't Porter and Donovan going to be surprised when we make it back to San Diego and turn them in," Andre said with a satisfied smile.

"Let's just hope the police believe our story," Julianne said ruefully. "What's happened is so outrageous I'm not even sure I can believe it."

The others agreed, but decided to cross that bridge when they came to it. For the moment, Andre wanted to check the sails. Julianne offered to take her turn running the manual pump while Alex looked in on Rich.

Rich looked up at her when she walked through the door. "What's going on?" he asked.

Alex explained the new evidence they'd found and their suspicions. She couldn't mask her concern.

"Honey," he managed to scoot up so he could prop his back against the pillow, "we are going to get home. I'm feeling stronger and the storm is over. Man, if we could survive a gale like that on the high seas without sinking, I'd say someone is watching out for us, wouldn't you?"

She had to agree. "But still. . ." she paused, remembering Julianne's scolding earlier but needing to express her feelings to Rich, ". . . I wish I would have listened to the Spirit more closely. I had the feeling we shouldn't have come."

"Well, if anyone's to blame, it's me," Rich said firmly.

Alex looked at him in surprise. "You! What did you have to do with any of this mess we're in?"

Still exhausted from the effort required to go on deck earlier, Rich closed his eyes for a moment and Alex wondered if he was in pain. "I didn't listen to you when you told me you were nervous about this trip. You tried to tell me, Alex, several times, even. And I didn't listen." He opened his eyes and looked at her. "I'll never doubt your instincts again, that's for sure."

"Don't put too much stock in my instincts," she warned him. "I don't feel real close to the Spirit right now. Besides the Lord's going to quit giving me promptings if I don't figure out how to listen better."

Rich gave her hand a gentle squeeze. "That's something we all need to work on, not just you." It was silent for a moment and when he spoke again, it was so softly that she could barely hear him. "I felt so close to the Spirit on my mission, sometimes, even so much that it was as if the Lord Himself were leading me and my companion by the hand. It was an incredible feeling. And it was a feeling I promised myself I would never lose." He looked away, swallowing hard, then said, "I've lost that closeness, but I haven't forgotten how it felt. I yearn to have the Spirit in my life like it was. Not just every once in a while, but daily."

"Me too," Alex said, giving him an encouraging smile and squeezing his hand in return.

"We'll work at it together, won't we?" Rich said, nodding his head. "Mrs. Almost-Greenwood, we have a whole life together to learn to get it right."

Alex leaned closer to him and pressed a kiss to his forehead. "I sure hope so."

Chapter 23

While Rich rested and Andre pumped water, Alex and Julianne spread all their belongings out in the sun to dry. Then they sat on deck, staring out at the broad expanse of ocean wondering where they were.

Alex thought about her conversation earlier with Julianne. Since the storm had cleared and her clothes had dried, she was feeling much more positive about their survival. She still had her doubts but she couldn't deny that they had been spared from the storm.

"Julianne," she said sheepishly. "I'm sorry for what I said earlier. Thanks for helping me keep my perspective."

"It was pretty scary," Julianne admitted.

Alex sighed. "It's just that everything's gone wrong. I had this image of how this vacation would be, you know, fun and romantic, and it hasn't been at all like I thought. Nothing's like I imagined it would be."

Julianne was silent, listening.

Alex continued, "I thought Rich and I would get married and start a family right away and live happily ever after. But now even that's not going to happen."

At Julianne's continued silence, Alex looked at her friend. "What is it?" she asked. "Is something wrong?"

"I just don't think I've ever seen you feel sorry for yourself," Julianne said. "I guess I thought you were too smart to waste energy on self-pity. It seems odd to hear you talking like this, as if you think you should be immune to trials. Your sister had a terrible time trying to have a baby. Your mother lost her husband and had to raise two children without any help. Everyone has something, Alex. Why should you be any different?"

Julianne's voice wasn't judgmental or harsh, just honest. She had never spoken like this to Alex before, and Alex realized she was absolutely right.

Julianne wasn't through yet. "Doesn't your Doctrine and Covenants talk about how we're supposed to act when we have trials and tribulations?"

Doctrine and Covenants? Alex thought. "Probably. I can't remember where, though."

"Well, I've had trials too, Alex," Julianne said. "In fact, I don't know many people who haven't, and anyone who expects their life to be 'trial-free' isn't being very realistic."

Alex thought of Julianne's life and the accident that forced her to give up ballet, her parents' reaction, her struggles to defeat her own eating disorder. She had to admit that everything Julianne said was painfully true.

Julianne went on. "I don't know why this is happening but I do know that we have to stay strong and have faith and everything will turn out. I know it will."

Alex's mouth dropped as Julianne practically quoted Alex's patriarchal blessing where it told her to stay strong in trials and to have faith, and all would be well. How quickly she'd forgotten.

"So what does it say in the Doctrine and Covenants?" Alex asked, ashamed that she didn't know which scripture Julianne was referring to.

Julianne picked up her triple combination, which had survived the ordeal with minimal damage. "Here. It's in section 122." She started to read, *"If thou art called to pass through tribulation; if thou art in perils among false brethren, if thou art in perils among robbers; if thou art in perils by land or sea . . ."*

"That's us," she paused to say, with a brief flash of humor, then went on to read several more passages, ending with, *". . . and above all, if the very jaws of hell shall gape open the mouth wide after thee, know thou, my son, that all these things shall give thee experience, and shall be for thy good."*

With a start, Alex realized she'd been thoroughly chastised. The Lord had been very generous to her during her lifetime. She'd received blessings in great abundance, especially during the last year, and although she'd been grateful, how quickly she'd forgotten about those blessings when things got tough. And here was sweet Julianne, not even a member of the Church, reminding her to not give up, to stay strong, to have faith.

Alex felt tears prick at her eyes and she squeezed her eyes shut to say a quick thanks to Heavenly Father for her friend's strength. Then, opening her eyes to look at Julianne, Alex whispered, "Thank you, Julianne. I needed to hear that."

Alex knew now that the Lord hadn't forgotten them. She also knew she needed to repent for doubting Him.

* * *

"Honey, he's beautiful," Judith said, as she held the newborn in her arms. Even though he'd been born three weeks early, except for being a little jaundiced, he'd tested perfectly and was a healthy six-pound two-ounce baby.

Jamie smiled proudly from her hospital bed, where Nikki sat next to her snacking on a cookie off her mother's lunch tray.

"Baby," Nikki said, pointing to the infant.

"That's right," Jamie said, "You're a big sister, Nikki."

"Sis-ther," Nikki repeated, her mouth full of chocolate chip cookie.

"He's got so much hair," Judith remarked, slipping off the little stocking cap the nurses had on the baby's head to keep him warm. "I can't decide who he looks like."

"Steve thinks he's got my eyes and nose, but he's definitely got Steve's mouth," Jamie explained. "Those lips are just like his dad's."

Wiping her daughter's sticky fingers with a napkin, she asked, "Have you had any luck contacting Alex?" Judith shook her head and Jamie shrugged. "They're probably having the time of their lives. Some of those boats are really elegant. I bet they're sunbathing and fishing and having all kinds of fun," Jamie decided.

"I hope so," Judith patted the baby gently as she rocked side to side. "I guess there's been a pretty bad storm system off the Pacific Coast. Sandy said she was sure it wasn't giving them any problems, but she hated the thought of them out on the sea in bad weather just the same."

Jamie heard the concern in her mother's voice. "Is there anything we can do to find out if they're okay?"

"Sandy said something about calling the Coast Guard to see if they could contact the boat. You'd think that these ships would have to stay in contact with someone." Judith sighed, then tried to speak more positively. "I'm sure everything's fine. There's probably nothing to worry about."

Jamie knew her mother was trying to be optimistic, but the fact was, she could tell her mother was concerned. Frankly, so was she.

* * *

Even though the sore on his leg was red and swollen and oozing, Rich was feeling well enough to come out on deck. Julianne had taken the responsibility of keeping the bandage fresh and clean, and she felt there was some improvement in its appearance. The first-aid kit that had been stored in the bottom of one of the lockers held some meager but essential supplies. Julianne kept the wound cleaned with fresh bandages, but without alcohol, there wasn't much else she could do.

"According to my watch, it's almost three in the afternoon," Andre said. "The sun should be on a course due west, shouldn't it?"

"Right," Alex agreed, looking overhead.

"So, if we put the sun on our left, north should be straight ahead." Andre held the makeshift compass in his hand. He positioned himself according to the sun and checked the compass. "It's lined up straight ahead. I think we've got our bearings. North is that way," he pointed behind them. "We need to turn the boat around and sail in a northeast direction. That will take us toward land and toward San Diego." He looked at his friends, then added, "I think."

"Sounds right to me," Rich said from his position on the cushionless bench.

"So," Andre said, "we don't have a sail on the main mast, but we can still raise the jib on the foremast. Any sail, at this point, is better than nothing."

None of them could argue with that.

"I don't know how far we are into Mexican waters, but I'd feel better a little closer to American shores," Alex said.

"Me too," Julianne said.

Alex stood at attention. "The crew is ready, sir." She saluted. "Ready to hoist the sail."

Andre smiled. "Alrighty, mates. I think I remember how they did this yesterday. We need one person to guide the sail as it goes up the mast, and the other two can pull on the line to raise it. Then we have to secure the line."

"Aye, aye, Captain," the girls said together.

Julianne took her place at the mast, ready to guide the sail, and Andre untied the line. Alex stood behind him, ready to pull on his command.

"Ready?" Andre said. "Go!"

Luckily the breeze was light and gentle, and the sail rolled off the boom and slid smoothly up the mast. Fluttering in the breeze, the sail waved like a welcome flag to carry them home. It was a beautiful sight against the clearing sky.

"Okay," Andre said, securing the line. "Now we need to catch the wind and turn this thing around." He took his position at the wheel and told the girls to maneuver the boom until the sail caught the breeze.

"Once we fill the sail this direction, we'll have to swing the boom to the other side. Got it?" he hollered.

"Got it!" Alex yelled.

She and Julianne leaned into the horizontally positioned pole and pushed it outward until suddenly, as if inflated by magic, the sail stretched with a whoosh and a snap and grabbed hold. Alex's breath caught in her throat as the boat responded. It was a beautiful sight.

"Okay," Andre yelled, "Now tighten the line while I turn it around, then get ready to change from the port side to the starboard side."

"We're ready," Julianne yelled.

"Coming about," Andre yelled and turned the wheel.

To everyone's amazement, even Andre's, the boat curved slowly around.

"Take it just a little further," Rich said. He'd assumed the position of navigator, holding the bowl containing their compass. Andre continued turning the wheel.

"Okay, stop," Rich yelled. "Right on course."

The girls strained and held the sail that tugged against the stiffening breeze. They remained on the starboard side, ready to tighten the line and secure the sail in position.

"Hold 'er steady," Andre called. "Okay. Secure the line. I think that does it."

Quickly the girls wrapped the line and tied a knot.

"Good, but I think we need to tighten the sail just a little," Andre instructed. "She's flapping too much."

"Why is everything on a ship a female?" Julianne muttered under her breath to Alex.

"Because if anything goes wrong, then they can blame it on 'her,'" Alex answered.

The girls laughed.

"Juli!" Andre yelled, "you need to tighten that hoisting wire through the winch so the sail is more taut."

"Yessir," she hollered back, jumping to the task. "He's certainly become bossy since he took over this ship," she said, looking at Alex.

Alex didn't answer but turned her head away so she could laugh. Julianne was right. He was being bossy, but he was also helping them get back to San Diego. It was a fair trade.

"I thought he didn't know much about sailing except for what he learned from his grandfather when he was little," Julianne said, turning the winch, winding the wire tightly around the metal drum, cinching the sail even more securely. "But he's pretty impressive, I have to say."

"Good work, Juli, I think that does it," Andre called.

She gave him a courtesy smile.

"He studied Porter and Donovan when they were here," Alex said. "He does seem to have a genuine love for sailing."

"Well, I hope this cures him of wanting to pursue it too seriously, because I doubt I'll ever go on another boat in my life," Julianne said.

"Look at that," Andre yelled to them, "You did it. We're sailing."

She and Julianne whooped and hollered and danced around the deck. Andre and Rich laughed and joined in the cheering.

Alex looked up at the sail, pulling the boat through the water and felt tears come to her eyes. Yes, they had done it. Working together they were going to survive. *Thank you, Heavenly Father. Thank you. I'm sorry I doubted.*

Jubilant, the passengers-turned-crew-and-captain nibbled on licorice and crackers for dinner and continued their course due northeast. The setting sun enabled them to keep a constant check on their position and Rich's compass remained reliable.

Rich had gone to bed early, still not feeling well, but they all felt confident that they were making headway in the right direction and would reach help soon. Even so, Alex could see her prescription medication running low. She prayed help would arrive before the pills ran out.

Andre kept the ship on course, and Alex and Julianne couldn't help but notice that he seemed to be thriving on the challenge of guiding the ship, with the wind in his face, and commanding a crew.

As dusk approached, they knew they'd have to lower the sail when it got too dark to see. They hated the thought of stopping, since it interrupted their progress, and they had no anchor to secure their position. But without sunlight they didn't dare continue. They could start again early in the morning.

Chapter 24

What's wrong? Alex thought as she looked down at Rich, who lay mumbling and feverish. Although he had retired early, feeling a little tired and achy, he had seemed better. But, when Alex and Julianne checked on him around 2 A.M., his fever had shot back up. Even worse, a red streak had begun to stretch from his infected wound upward along his calf. If they didn't get help soon, Alex was afraid of what would happen.

Alex tried to give Rich a few sips of water. Some of it ran down his throat, some of it trickled down his chin. Julianne mopped his brow with a damp cloth, trying to keep his temperature down.

"He's sweating more than he's drinking," she whispered to Alex. "I'm sure he's going to dehydrate if we don't get enough water down him. And this is the last of our water."

"Maybe there are some purification tablets in the first-aid kit," Andre suggested. "I'll go check." The moon was barely a sliver, lending them little light to see by. Fortunately, the first-aid kit had held a flashlight, which they kept with them to find their way around the boat.

A few minutes later Andre came back into the room. "I didn't find anything," he reported. "That's all the water we've got. How's he doing?"

"Not good," Alex said. "I'm really worried about him."

Julianne rinsed the cloth in a bowl of water on the nightstand. She applied the cool compress to Rich's cheeks and neck. Rich groaned in his sleep.

"I have a feeling this is going to be the longest night of my life," Alex said.

"I guess it's the only way to end the longest day of our lives," Julianne countered ironically.

"It has been a long day, hasn't it?" Alex said, keeping her eyes on Rich's flushed face.

"I'm going back on deck for a while," Andre said. "I'd hate to have a run-in with a tanker or something."

Alex smiled gratefully at him. He'd taken charge and managed to keep them thinking they actually could survive, although Alex still had moments when she honestly couldn't see how. They'd never be able to survive another storm like the one they'd had, and it was only a matter of time before the lack of food and worse, the absence of fresh water, took its toll.

"Why don't you go up and keep Andre company?" Alex told her friend. "I'll sit here with Rich."

"You sure?" Julianne asked. Alex nodded. "Okay. Just holler if you need me."

Before leaving her friend, Julianne paused to give her a supportive squeeze on the shoulder. "I don't know how, but we're going to make it and so is Rich. He's strong, and his body is fighting the infection. Okay?"

Alex appreciated her encouragement, even though she herself doubted her friend's words. Alex continued to sponge Rich's face, neck, and arms with the cloth and a small amount of cool water from the last of the storage tank, but nothing seemed to be helping anymore. His temperature continued to soar.

She'd tried everything to help him; there was only one place left to turn.

With a groan she kneeled at his bedside. She'd given him the last of her pain medication during the night, and all they had left was the tiny travel-size bottle of Tylenol, half-empty. Her own stomach pains had returned and she'd felt a constant, steady pain for the last several hours. She moved carefully, not just because it hurt to move but because her abdomen felt tight, as though an abrupt movement would cause something to tear loose. But she felt Rich needed the medication more than she did.

There was one last ounce of hope left in her. Even though she didn't feel worthy to approach her Heavenly Father, she bowed her head humbly. Holding onto Rich's hand, she began to pray, harder than she'd ever prayed in her entire life. *Please, Father, spare his life. Please send help to rescue us.*

With every fiber of her being, she pleaded for their deliverance, and she apologized to the Lord for doubting, for losing faith, and for forgetting the many ways he had blessed her life. She continued praying until she fell into an exhausted sleep, on her knees, with her head resting on the bed.

* * *

As she had the previous day, Alex woke to the sound of moaning. Although she'd gone back to her room and slept an hour, two at the most, she was thick headed as she slid off the mattress and stepped onto the damp floor. They'd managed to pump most of the water from the cabin, but the floor was, by no stretch of the imagination, dry.

She ran directly to the aft berth where Rich slept on the captain's bed. Judging by the agony in his voice, she knew he'd taken a turn for the worse.

Terror held her heart paralyzed before she even entered the room. What were they going to do? He desperately needed medical attention; without it, she knew, beyond any doubt, he would die.

"Rich! I'm here, Rich." She rushed to his side to calm him. His flailing arms fell limply to his sides at the sound of her voice and he rolled his fever-stricken head from side to side. Alex knew Rich was becoming dehydrated; if that happened, his fate would be sealed. *Surrounded by water, but with nothing to drink,* she sighed.

"What's wrong?" Julianne burst into the room.

"Juli, I'm worried. I don't think he's going to make it." Alex tried to stay strong but a wave of tears caught in her throat and filled her eyes.

"We have a drop or two of drinking water left," Julianne said. "But somehow we have to get him cooled off. Do you know if Andre is still up on deck?"

Alex nodded. "As far as I know." He'd stayed up there all night to keep watch.

"I'll go find him. Maybe he has some ideas." Julianne hurried from the cabin.

Alex prayed the entire time Julianne was gone. If ever she needed the Lord's help it was now. Rich was at the brink of death; surely the Lord wasn't planning on taking him now, was he?

Moments later Julianne returned. "We're surrounded by fog," she announced.

"You're kidding?" Alex's heart sank. What was next? Getting run over by a tanker?

"No, but that's good news. There's dew everywhere. It's collected on everything." Julianne searched the room for bedding and other material to take upstairs. She ended up ripping the bed sheet into strips. "I'm going to go get these wet. Andre is trying to figure out a way to gather the water so we can drink it."

"Is it clean?" Alex asked.

Julianne shrugged. "I don't know how clean it will be, but it's better than seawater. We might just have to take our chances." Gathering the armload of cloth strips, she said, "I'll be right back," and left the room.

"Rich, hang in there," Alex whispered, leaning over him. "We're going to take care of you. You're going to be fine. Keep fighting, honey. I need you." She couldn't imagine how he must be feeling. She hoped that he wasn't in pain. It broke her heart to think he might be.

Closing her eyes, she continued her prayer, the one that she had repeated in her heart and mind for the last two days. Pleading for strength, faith, and deliverance, she poured her heart out to the Lord. It was going to take a miracle for them to survive this ordeal, and the only way they would get one was with the Lord's help.

"Look," Julianne announced excitedly when she charged back into the room. "These cloths are absolutely dripping." She had them inside a bucket and indeed they were dripping with water. The fog was so thick, she said, all she had to do was lay the rags on top of the cabin and soak up the dew that had already collected. Andre was worried that anyone passing by wouldn't see their boat, or would run into them, but Julianne was thrilled. "This just might save Rich's life," she said as she pulled the rags from the bucket. "I thought we had thick fog in England, but it's nothing compared to what's out there right now."

Alex preferred to look at the situation from Julianne's perspective and went straight to the task of sponging Rich's forehead, cheeks, neck, and chest with the damp material.

"He's really burning up," Julianne remarked as she moistened his arms with the cloths. "I also brought the last of the water." She motioned to the small bottle of water next to the bucket with the wet sheets. "That's all we have left until Andre collects some of the dew so we can drink it."

Alex fought the whirlwind of hysterics that wanted so badly to become a tornado inside of her. But she knew she had to maintain control. All the emotion in the world wasn't going to change anything. She had to stay calm. But it was so hard when her chest felt like it would explode.

Rich calmed down considerably after they had sponged him for several minutes. They even managed to get him to drink several sips of water and take more of the pain reliever they hoped would help bring down his fever. Other than that, there was nothing they could do.

"Come on, Alex," Julianne said, after they sat for several minutes, in silence, watching Rich lay there, breathing. "Let's go up on deck. You need a breath of fresh air."

Alex hated leaving Rich's side but welcomed Julianne's suggestion. She was beginning to lose perspective. Her whole grip on reality was slipping.

From the hatch door, it was difficult to see through the fog even five feet ahead.

"Wow," Alex exclaimed, "this is creepy."

"It's always something isn't it?" Julianne remarked. "If it's not a storm, it's a rogue wave. If it's not pirates, it's fog. We've had it all this trip, haven't we?"

"I'd say we certainly got our money's worth," Alex said ironically.

Julianne called for Andre and he responded from somewhere near the fore mast. The girls made their way to the front of the boat and found him inspecting the jib.

"Is the sail okay?" Alex asked, hoping something else hadn't gone wrong.

"It looks fine to me. As soon as this fog burns off, we can get her raised and get sailing for home." He stood from his crouched position and stretched his back. Alex could tell he was completely exhausted.

"Why don't you go get some sleep, Andre? We can keep an eye on things here," Alex suggested.

Julianne seconded the motion. "We'll call you if we need you."

Alex grabbed his arm and tugged him toward the rear of the boat. "Go get some sleep. We don't need our captain falling asleep at the wheel."

"All right, but call me, for any reason," he insisted. "Oh, and don't be surprised if this fog plays tricks with your ears. I've heard all kinds of strange noises."

"What kind of noises?" Julianne asked.

Andre shook his head. "I can't really explain it. But I'm sure you'll hear them."

"We'll be on the lookout," Alex said. "Now go."

"Thanks, girls." He dragged himself to the hatch and disappeared below.

"Poor guy," Alex said, "He's so tired he's hearing things."

They walked to the helm of the boat and found a place to sit.

"Hey!" Alex's foot kicked something. "What in the world?" She leaned over. "Julianne, here's the flare gun. Why haven't we shot off any of these flares?"

Julianne didn't have a ready answer. "I don't know."

Alex loaded the gun and said, "I'm going to shoot one."

"Do you think someone will see it in this fog?"

"The fog can't be everywhere. Maybe there's someone in the distance who will see it."

"Then what are you waiting for? Shoot it!"

Alex raised the gun directly overhead and bracing herself for the recoil, squeezed the trigger. A loud explosion followed.

Alex and Julianne looked at each other, then tilted their heads back, trying to see overhead into the dense fog.

"I guess it worked," Alex said.

"Shoot another one just in case no one saw the first one."

"You want to shoot it this time?" Alex asked her.

"Sure." Julianne took the gun, reloaded, then raised her arms overhead and—

"What's going on?" Andre's voice called from the hatch as he tumbled out on deck. "Is something wrong?"

"No, Andre," Alex assured him. "Everything's fine. We just shot off the flare gun."

"And I'm shooting another one." Julianne raised her hands and shot the gun.

Again, a loud boom echoed off the fog.

"Hey, that's kind of fun," Julianne said, eyeing the other flares.

Andre gave a tired smile and told them to holler if there was any response. Then he went below deck.

"I guess we can shoot more later," Julianne said.

"So, what do we do now?" Alex asked.

"I guess we wait until the fog lifts, then we can raise the jib and keep sailing. I sure hope that happens soon."

"I wish we had something to eat," Alex said. "I'm hungry."

"Yeah, me too," Julianne replied.

Alex looked at Julianne, then burst out laughing.

"What's so funny?" Julianne asked.

"I don't know. It just struck me funny that you and I starved ourselves on purpose for so long, and now here we are, hungry and wishing we could eat."

Julianne chuckled. "It is ironic, isn't it?" She jumped to her feet. "Did you hear that, Alex?"

"Hear what?"

"Shh, listen."

They both strained their ears, trying to pick up the noise, but the only sound they heard was the slapping of waves against the boat.

"I guess it wasn't anything," Julianne said, as she sat back down with a disappointed huff.

"What did it sound like?"

"I don't know, some kind of low humming or something." Julianne lifted her hands uselessly.

"If it is something, I'm sure we'll hear it again," Alex said hopefully. They sat, shrouded in the fog blanket, shivering against the damp coolness, hearing nothing.

"I must be losing my mind," Julianne said disappointedly.

"This trip would be enough to make any person crazy," Alex replied.

From below a voice called, "Alex! Julianne!"

"It must be Rich." Alex hit the ground running. She was terrified of what she would find, but knew Rich needed her.

"Please, Heavenly Father," she prayed out loud as she ran for his room. "Don't let him die."

Chapter 25

"I'm sorry about the timing, honey," Jamie said to her husband who was spending the evening with her at the hospital. He sat in a chair next to her, holding the baby. They had already decided to name the baby Steven Tyler Dixon and call him Tyler if it was a boy.

"Jamie, it's okay," he reassured her. "Hey, if I don't know all that stuff by now, one more day of studying isn't going to make the difference when I take the LSAT." Steve nuzzled his son's neck with his nose then kissed his forehead. "He's incredible, Jamie. I still can't believe I have a son."

Jamie smiled at her proud husband. What a pair those two would be. She glanced over at the shoebox on the chair containing a newborn pair of athletic shoes. They'd cost a fortune but Steve couldn't help himself. Visions of the NFL and his son's face on the cover of Wheaties boxes had made him completely irrational.

"Don't sign him up for Little League quite yet, though," Jamie laughed. "Let's get him beefed up first."

"I wish Rich and Alex were here," Steve crooned to his new son. "I can't wait to show this little guy off to them."

"They said they'd be home Saturday afternoon." Jamie shifted positions in the bed. She hadn't realized how painful the delivery was until the anesthetic wore off.

Steve looked up from little Tyler to smile at Jamie. "They are going to be so surprised when they find out you've already had the baby."

Jamie still couldn't believe it either. After three previous pregnancies, all ending tragically, she was grateful that this baby had been born strong and healthy. He was little, just over six pounds, but his lungs were good, he was keeping his body temperature, and he had even nursed a little that afternoon. His pediatrician, Dr. Shepard, said Tyler was doing so well he could go home the next day.

"Honey," Jamie said, unable to let go of the nagging fear at the back of her consciousness, "What do you think is going to happen with this paternity test?" She didn't mean to shed a negative light on the day, but she'd continued to worry about it. She couldn't bear the thought of losing Nikki.

"I don't know." Steve sighed. "My friend at the 'U' said as soon as they got the results we could find out. But I don't know what to think. I have a hard time believing the birth mother actually knew who the father was, you know, given the fact that she spent time with so many men."

"I keep hoping that's the case," Jamie said. "But what if it does turn out positive? Do you get the feeling he'd actually take her?"

Steve met her eyes soberly. "I wish I knew, Jamie, really I do. But I don't. All we can do is hope and pray the test is negative."

"I do pray," she said. "Constantly."

Steve stood and carried the baby over to his wife and placed him in her arms. Then he leaned down and kissed his wife gently. "We've had too many experiences telling us Nikki's supposed to be with us. Remember when we had her sealed to us?"

Jamie would never forget that special day. It had been one of the sweetest, most spiritual moments in her life. The Spirit had been so strong that there was no doubt in her mind angels had indeed been in attendance. It was also the first time she'd felt Tyler move within her. They were a family, meant to be together, sealed for eternity. Nothing on earth could break that heavenly bond.

Jamie smiled at her husband, grateful for his strength. He was still her sweetheart, the man of her dreams. She loved him even more than the day they were married.

"Everything will work out," Steve said softly.

"You're right," Jamie sighed. "I'm sorry I worry so much."

"That's okay. I guess you're entitled to one flaw." He kissed her forehead. Then he kissed her again, a little harder and not on her forehead this time.

* * *

"Baby!" Nikki squealed when she saw the newborn in his clear, hospital bassinet. The toddler ran to the side of the bed and peeked over the edge. Reaching on tip-toes, she tried with all her might to touch the baby's head, but her arm wouldn't reach.

"Baby!" she demanded.

From her hospital bed, Jamie reached out and steadied the bassinet so Nikki didn't pull it over.

"Here, punkin'," Steve scooped his daughter up in his arms, "You want to touch the baby?"

"Baby," Nikki shrieked with delight. "Baby."

"You have to be gentle," Steve said. "Very soft."

Ever so delicately, Nikki stroked her brother's forehead. She giggled as the infant scrunched up his nose and let out a dove-like coo.

"Your brother has a surprise for you," Steve said.

"Pwize?" Nikki said excitedly.

"Yes." Steve set his daughter down so he could retrieve the gift from the pile. Jamie's bags were already packed and stacked by the door. She was anxious to get home and settled.

"Thanks, honey," Jamie said, grateful that her husband was finding something to keep Nikki occupied for the moment. She knew it would take some adjusting for Andrea Nicole to get used to having a baby around, and she realized she would have to keep a constant eye on her. Jamie could see how easily an accident, like tipping over the bassinet, might occur.

"What time did they say they'd release you?" Steve asked, as Nikki ripped the paper off her gift.

"Ten o'clock. But I'm ready now." It was barely eight thirty.

"Well, honey," Steve said patiently "We can't leave until your mother gets here anyway. She wants to video everything. Alex and Rich will feel bad if we don't at least get something on tape."

"True," Jamie answered, but she still felt like she'd been in the hospital for two weeks instead of two days.

"Here we are," Judith announced when she and Dave entered the room.

"Hi, Mom," Jamie exclaimed, noticing how vibrant and happy her mother looked. "Hi, Dr. Rawlins."

"Good morning, sweetie. How did you sleep?" Judith walked right to her daughter's bed and brushed a kiss on her brow.

"Not too good," Jamie answered, "but I'm sure that's going to be the story of my life for the next year or so."

"I plan on taking a turn at night, too," Steve said in his defense.

Nikki let out a cry of pleasure as she discovered the cute little Cabbage Patch Doll that had her same dark, curly hair and lavender-blue eyes.

"Now you have a baby all your own," Steve said. "Just like mommy."

Nikki hugged her new doll to her chest.

"You haven't heard anything from Alex, have you?" Jamie asked.

"No. The Coast Guard hasn't been able to contact their boat. They are supposed to return today though, aren't they?"

"I think that's what Alex said," Jamie answered. "I'll sure be glad when they get back. I'm so anxious for them to meet Tyler."

"And how is my handsome little grandson doing?" Judith said, switching her attention to the squirming newborn. "He is so sweet," she remarked. "Yeeessss," she cooed to the baby in a tiny voice, "you're a handsome little guy, yes you are."

"So, Judith," Steve said as he gathered up shredded wrapping paper and stuffed it into the trash can, "are you ready for your first day of school?"

She didn't even look up from her little grandson. "I'm as ready as I'll ever be," she answered.

Judith would be teaching three classes. The classes met on Mondays, Wednesdays, and Fridays, the first one at eight o'clock, the second at ten o'clock, and a third at noon. There was a possibility of a fourth class on Tuesdays and Thursdays at four o'clock but it hadn't yet been decided. It would be a very demanding schedule, but Judith was filled with anticipation.

"Are you nervous, Mom?" For the tenth time, Jamie checked the clock in her room, wondering where the nurse was so she could go home.

Tyler had decided to take a nap, so Judith looked at her daughter. "I feel fairly comfortable with the class material," she said. "I mean, I've spent the last fifteen years practicing what I'm going to be preaching, but it's getting up in front of three hundred students that has me a bit nervous."

Jamie couldn't imagine standing in front of a crowd that big and having to teach a subject. Personally she knew she couldn't do it, but she knew her mother was going to be great, and she told her so.

"I hope I'm as good as you think I'll be, sweetie," Judith replied. "I'm sure it will take a few days to get rid of the nerves. To be totally honest, though, I feel more excited for this than I have for any of the projects I've worked on the last few years."

Nikki thrust her baby doll up to her grandma and said, "Baby." In response, Judith fussed over Nikki's new doll, and the little girl looked pleased at the attention her "baby" was receiving.

"How are you feeling?" Dr. Rawlins asked Jamie.

"A little sore," she said, "but I feel fine otherwise."

"You scared us there for a minute," he said, smiling that wonderfully loving smile of his.

Jamie realized that she'd known Dr. Rawlins almost five years, and in that time she'd been through some of the hardest experiences of her life with him right there by her side. He could never take the place of her father, but since her father couldn't be there with her, she couldn't think of anyone she'd rather have in her life than Dr. Rawlins.

"Pretty amazing, isn't it, doctor?" Jamie said. "I almost had myself convinced I could never do this."

"I can't think of anyone who deserves it more than you," he smiled at her warmly.

While Nikki happily pulled all of the tissues out of a box and made pretend diapers for her doll, Dr. Rawlins and Judith ooh'd and aah'd over Judith's second grandchild. Jamie's joy was full. Having Tyler, strong and healthy, was an answer to years of prayers and heartache. She knew she didn't deserve all the blessings she received and she was humbled by the depth of the Lord's love and generosity.

For a moment her thoughts slipped to her father. Had he spent time with her newborn son before he came to earth? Had he been there when Tyler left his heavenly home to come to earth? The thought warmed her and touched her heart. Many times she'd thought of her father as a guardian angel. She knew he was busy with his heavenly callings, but she hoped at times when his wife and daughters *really* needed him, he was able to bless them with his guardian spirit. She felt that way because there were many times she felt his presence near. He was still very much a part of his family's life.

Keep an eye on Alex, would you? Jamie asked her father. *Take care of her if she runs into any trouble.*

Chapter 26

"Rich!" Alex ran into Rich's cabin and knelt beside him. She placed a hand against his feverish cheek. "Rich! Can you hear me?" There was no response.

Andre, too, tried to rouse him, "Rich, wake up!"

"I can't revive him, Juli," Alex said. "Why won't he wake up?"

"His body is so weak from fighting the infection, he's lost consciousness," Julianne answered. "You feel how hot he is?"

It was no use. He had gone from bad to worse and Alex was afraid of the next step for him. Coma? Or even . . . death?

"Nothing is helping. Nothing!" Alex broke down into tears. The man she loved was dying right in front of her eyes and she couldn't help him. Except for praying, there was nothing she could do.

Julianne wrapped a comforting arm around her shoulders.

Through her tears, Alex said, "I'm so afraid . . ."

Julianne patted her back and rocked her friend in her arms. "He's going to make it. You have to believe that," she said. Speaking soft words of hope and encouragement, Julianne held her as Alex's tears flowed freely, Within a few minutes the well ran dry, leaving Alex weak and empty. For several more minutes, they sat in silence, as Rich, lost in a state of semi-consciousness, lay completely still, his chest barely moving with each breath.

The only prayer Alex had the energy to muster was a simple plea—*Lord, please help us.*

Then, muffled and faint, she heard a sound, low and long. She raised her head and met Julianne's eyes.

"Did you hear that?" Julianne asked hesitantly.

"Yes," Alex said. "I heard it that time."

They both looked at Andre. "I heard it too," he agreed.

"It sounded like a fog horn," Julianne said.

"That means—" Andre began.

"That means we'd better get out on deck!" Julianne cried.

They nearly collided, hurrying through the door so quickly. Scrambling up the companionway, all three emerged on deck where they saw that the fog had thinned considerably and begun to lift.

"Where's the flare gun?" Andre shouted. He searched frantically around the captain's seat.

"Right here," Julianne said, snatching it up off the deck and handing it to him. Quickly he loaded the gun, pointed it skyward, and shot.

Breathless, they waited for some reply, some sign of life beyond their own boat.

Nothing came.

"Shoot another one," Julianne suggested.

Not wasting a second, he loaded the gun and shot another flare.

"Please," Alex pleaded heavenward, "let someone see it."

Several seconds passed before Andre lowered the gun, disappointment filling his face. Just as he was about to toss the gun back into its box, a loud, low horn bellowed through the fog.

Startled, they all screamed together.

"It's a boat," Alex cried. "It's getting closer." She tried to jump up, but was yanked back by a searing pain in her stomach.

"Alex, what is it?" Julianne asked, leaning towards her.

Alex waved her away. "Just a pain, I'll be okay."

Julianne looked doubtful. "Are you sure?"

Alex nodded.

"Wait a minute." Julianne froze. "What if they don't see us? What if they run over us?"

"Surely they must have radar," Andre said.

"Maybe we should honk our horn," Alex suggested.

Andre shook his head. "It needs power to work."

"There's a bell up front," Julianne remembered. "I'll go ring it."

But she didn't have time. Another blast came from the other boat, which sounded like it was right on top of them.

"Where is it?" Julianne cried. "It's so close."

"Let's hope they're slowing down," Andre said, trying to peer through the fog. "Julianne," he urged, "find that bell and ring it!" He reloaded the gun and shot another flare while Julianne ran to the front of the ship and began ringing the bell. It sounded out loud and clear. Alex shut her eyes and prayed. When she opened them, she saw the nose of a ship slowly emerging toward them through the thin veil of fog. "There it is!" she cried. Then she noticed an emblem on the nose of the boat. "It's the Coast Guard! We've been saved!"

Andre grabbed her in a hug and swung her around. Julianne left her post and joined them. Then they stood, side by side, arm in arm, waiting for the gap to close between the boats.

"Ahoy, there," they heard a voice over the loudspeaker.

Alex, Andre, and Julianne waved wildly.

"Are you the *S.S. Sea Queen?*"

"Yes," Andre answered. "We need help."

"Stand by, *Sea Queen.*"

Relief flooded Alex's entire soul. Their ship had come in. Their miracle had arrived. The Lord had helped them in their darkest hour. Rich would get the help he needed.

Their prayers had been answered. The nightmare was over.

* * *

"We'll need to keep him here at least three days," Dr. Winston said. "He's on a strong antibiotic and he's severely dehydrated. We'll need to monitor him closely for the next twenty-four hours to see if his condition stabilizes."

They'd all received medical attention upon arrival. Alex was grateful to have something for the pain in her stomach. It would help until she could have surgery.

"But he is going to survive, isn't he?" Andre asked the question that had tormented Alex's soul.

"He's young and strong," the doctor said to the group gathered around him in the waiting room. "But I won't lie to you. His condition is very serious."

"What are you saying, Dr. Winston?" Alex asked, afraid to know his answer.

"I'm surprised he's made it this far," the doctor said. "I think you have every reason to be hopeful, but I also want you to be aware of how serious this is. Let me put it this way—he got here just in time." Dr. Winston's beeper sounded. "I'll have the nurse keep you informed of his progress," the doctor said. "Excuse me."

"Wait!" Alex blurted out. "Can I see him?"

"He's being taken from emergency to the ICU. I'll tell the nurse to let you know as soon as he's settled." Dr. Winston's smile was kind. "But keep your visit short."

"I will, doctor," Alex breathed gratefully. "Thank you."

The doctor hurried away down the corridor.

"Detective McBride is down in the lobby waiting," Andre reminded them. "He's anxious to talk to us."

They still hadn't had a chance to shower and change since their arrival back in San Diego. A helicopter had airlifted Rich from the Coast Guard boat which had rescued them, sixty miles off the coast, still hours away from the harbor. A police squad car had been waiting at the dock to meet Alex, Julianne, and Andre and transport them to the hospital as soon as they arrived. Except for mild dehydration and a serious case of "sea legs," they were all fine. Alex still felt motion, especially in the elevator, but the solid ground beneath her feet had never felt so good. After a warm meal and plenty of fluids, they'd all felt dramatically improved. Now all they needed was a shower, clean clothes, and some rest.

"How's your friend doing?" Detective McBride asked them.

"He's in serious condition," Alex answered.

"He's in good hands," the detective assured them as he motioned for them to take a seat.

"I'd like you to come down to the station and give me a sworn statement after you've had a chance to get cleaned up and get some rest. For now, would you mind giving me a brief overview of the situation?"

Both of the girls looked at Andre, visually electing him to be their spokesman.

Andre took a deep breath and gave a brief accounting of their experience, concluding with the ownership papers they found, and descriptions of Porter and Donovan.

After writing a few more notes, the detective looked up. "The *Sea*

Queen was reported missing from the Santa Cruz harbor almost a month ago."

Julianne and Alex gasped.

Seeing their surprise, he nodded. "To be honest we've never had a case quite like this, but I'll run these names and see if I come up with some connection. From the sound of it, they're professionals. Chances are they already have a record. I'm sure something will come up."

"Thanks, Detective McBride," Andre said, extending his hand. "We're glad this whole ordeal is over."

The detective looked at Alex. "You've got your friend Sandy Dalebout to thank. It took her persistence and constant badgering to get the Coast Guard to keep looking each time they came up empty."

Good old Sandy, Alex thought. She was going to call Sandy as soon as she could. They owed her their lives.

When they had finished speaking with the detective, Alex hurried to the ICU. At the nurses' station, she stopped in front of the nurse on duty, who was slurping a diet Coke and eating potato chips.

"Excuse me," Alex said, "Dr. Winston told me I could visit a patient in the ICU. His name is Rich Green—"

The nurse gave her a bored look. "Are you a family member?" she asked.

Alex shook her head.

"I'm sorry. We don't allow visitors that aren't family into the ICU," the nurse droned.

Alex wasn't about to let this woman stand in the way of seeing Rich. "But Dr. Winston told me I could go in for just a moment," she protested.

The nurse shook her head. "Rules are rules and we specifically don't allow visitors. I'm sorry."

"Then could you please page Dr. Winston?" Alex asked desperately.

"Dr. Winston has gone off duty." The nurse turned her attention back to her potato chips.

"But you don't understand," Alex said, quickly losing her patience and composure. "My fiancé is very sick. I have to see him."

The nurse sat up stiffly. "Listen, lady," she snapped. "I'm not about to break hospital rules and lose my job."

Alex took a deep breath, knowing she wouldn't get anywhere if she got upset. "I understand the rules, but Dr. Winston said—"

"I don't care what Dr. Winston told you," the nurse said impatiently. "He didn't tell me anything."

Alex stood helpless and trembling with frustration. She needed to see Rich now. Tonight.

She heard a voice behind her. "Is there a problem here?"

From the look on the nurse's face, Alex knew immediately who was standing behind her. She whirled around. "Dr. Winston, I'm so glad you're still here. I was wondering if I could see Rich."

"Of course, come with me," he invited.

Alex fought the desire to stick her tongue out at the nurse, but instead followed the doctor to another station where he instructed her to put on a face mask, gown, and sterile gloves.

"He still hasn't regained consciousness," he warned her, "but the nurse has informed me his condition has become more stable. You can stay with him for fifteen minutes. That's all for now," he said as he led her to Rich's room.

As she walked inside the door, she didn't gain much comfort seeing Rich hooked up to monitors and an I.V. and wearing an oxygen mask. He lay motionless, his chest barely rising with each breath. Tears stung Alex's eyes as she thought about how close he had come to death and how far he still had to go.

"Rich," she whispered. "I'm here, honey." She wrapped her gloved fingers around his hand and held it lovingly. "Dr. Winston's taking good care of you and we're all praying for you. You just need to rest and get better, okay?"

She watched him sleep for a moment, hoping that each tiny muscle twitch would become movement, that his eyes would open and he would regain consciousness. But he remained still.

She told him about the rescue and Detective McBride, hoping somehow her voice would reach that spot in his mind that would trigger him to awaken, but there was no response.

Before she knew it her time was up. She left the room, looking back several times in hopes that he'd stirred or moved even a fraction of an inch. With a heavy heart she left the room. The battle wasn't over quite yet.

* * *

Resisting the urge to take a shower first, Alex telephoned Sandy, who nearly broke her eardrum when she heard Alex on the other end of the line.

"Alex! You're back. Are you okay? How's Rich? What happened?"

After the barrage of questions ended, Alex filled Sandy in on the details of their experience, still not sure she could believe it had actually happened herself.

"I knew you were in trouble, Alex," Sandy said. "The Coast Guard kept telling me that there was nothing to worry about, that there hadn't been any reports of any craft in trouble, but I knew. I just knew."

Alex was overcome with appreciation for her friend. "I can't even begin to thank you enough," she said. "Rich isn't out of danger yet, but the doctor said we were rescued just in the nick of time. And the rest of us wouldn't have lasted too many more days without water."

"Did you tell the detective about Jordan?" Sandy asked. "I still think there could be a connection to him." She paused, thinking. "Too bad you don't have a picture of those other men. I'm sure that would help."

"Yeah, it would be—" Then as if a bolt of lightning struck her, she remembered. "Sandy, I can't believe I forgot about this. I think Rich got them on video."

Sandy was incredulous. "Alex, you're kidding? I'll hang up. You call the detective right now."

Alex couldn't believe that she'd actually forgotten all about Rich's video footage of their voyage. She'd never been so grateful for technology as she was right at that moment and for Rich's annoying hobby. His video just might crack this case.

* * *

"It's a miracle this video camera survived," Julianne said as they watched the video footage from Alex and Julianne's hotel room.

Somehow the camera had been above the water line the whole time. Even though the camera bag had gotten soaked, the plastic liner inside had protected the camera.

"It's obvious Porter did everything he could to dodge that camera," Andre observed. "Look how he managed to keep his head turned. See, he keeps looking away, every time Rich approaches."

"Darn! I don't know if they're going to be able to get a good look at him," Alex said, disappointed. "And Donovan hasn't even been near the camera."

Julianne grabbed her arm. "Wait a minute . . . Look!" she cried. "Rich is going to the front of the ship. Maybe Donovan won't suspect the camera's on and—"

"There he is!" Alex shrieked when a full, but brief view of Donovan flashed on the camera. The scene changed abruptly, as if Rich had had to quickly stop recording, but the image was there for just a moment. "Rewind and freeze it, so we can see what we've got," she directed.

Andre rewound the tape and played it again, stopping just as Donovan stepped into view.

"Perfect," Julianne said, clapping her hands. "Detective McBride isn't going to believe this."

There was a knock at the door.

"That's probably the detective right now," Alex said, jumping to her feet.

"Good afternoon," she greeted Detective McBride. "Come on in. We have something to show you."

The detective took a seat expectantly and watched as they replayed the video of the Captain and Donovan.

"Can I take this tape and make a copy?" he asked. "I'd like to have it for evidence. We'll be able to make a match without any trouble with it—that is, if they're in the computer."

"Even for Porter?" Andre asked.

"Even for Porter," the detective affirmed. "With this much detail, the computer can generate a full composite we can work with. Good work. This video just might be the link we need in catching these guys. I'm glad you got them on tape."

"We have Rich to thank," Andre said, anxious to give credit where it was due.

"Well, I hope to thank him in person real soon," the detective said.

Chapter 27

Alex remained glued to the side of Rich's bed. He was responding to the antibiotics, his fever had finally broken, and his vital signs were strong. He'd even been moved out of the ICU, but for some reason he still hadn't awakened.

Alex's stomach churned as she watched him sleep. Why didn't he wake up?

A movement behind her caught her attention. She looked up to see Sandy standing at the doorway.

"Sandy!" She jumped to her feet. "What are you doing here?"

Sandy gave her a hug. "I couldn't concentrate on anything I was so worried. I figured I could do more here than I could at home."

Even though Sandy couldn't do anything more than sit back and watch and wait, like everyone else, Alex appreciated her coming. She felt the added comfort, support, and strength that came from just having another loved one nearby to help carry the burden of concern. Even though Rich's mother had wanted to fly down and be there, they'd decided to wait another day and see if Rich's condition changed.

"You're supposed to be in France," Alex said.

"Paris isn't going anywhere," Sandy said, walking over to the bed and looking at Rich. "How's he doing?"

Alex reported what the doctor had said. "His condition has improved. We're just waiting for him to wake up."

Sandy shook her head. "I can tell he's been through a lot. He looks so pale and thin."

"He hasn't eaten for three days," Alex explained.

With a reassuring smile, Sandy took Alex's hand in hers and gave it a squeeze. "He's going to be fine, Alex. Don't you worry. He's strong and healthy and he'll bounce back in a hurry. You'll see." As they sat down near the bed, Sandy asked, "Has he been given a blessing?"

Alex nodded. "One of the nurses is LDS, and she asked her husband to come in and help Andre give him a blessing."

"And?" Sandy prodded her.

"And in the blessing they said he would recover fully." Alex had been clinging to these words, waiting for them to be fulfilled.

"Then he will," Sandy said resolutely. "Alex, you don't doubt that, do you?"

Alex was quiet for a moment. Then she said, "It's just that our luck has been pretty crummy lately. I'm a little skeptical, I guess."

Sandy had been the first nonmember friend Alex had explained the gospel to. She had been impressed at Alex's strength when confronted with Sandy's "friends" who had offered to set Alex straight. In the last year, she had seen Alex blossom and grow as never before in the entire time they had known each other. This experience had evidently given Alex's faith a beating, but Sandy had no doubt that her friend would grow from it. Tactfully she changed the subject.

"What's happened with the case? Are the police having any luck?" she asked.

Alex told Sandy everything she knew. "They made a positive identification with Donovan and Porter and they have a few leads," she began. "The boat's owners have been notified of its return, and although the boat is in terrible condition, they do have full insurance coverage—thank goodness. And they still haven't been able to connect Jordan with any of this," she concluded.

Sandy gave Alex a dark look. "I'll bet somehow he's connected."

Alex agreed. "These two losers, Porter and Donovan, didn't seem bright enough to pull something off like this on their own," she said. "I spoke with Detective McBride about Jordan's possible connection with the case. He says Jordan shows a lot of the characteristics of a stalker's profile, but there's no hard evidence to go by."

Alex had learned from the detective that her experience with Jordan wasn't unique. Eight percent of all women in the United States were victims of stalking. The only way they became free was when the stalker found another victim to prey upon.

Sandy shook her head with disbelief, and Alex reached out for

Rich's hand, hoping somehow her touch would awaken him. "I don't know what part Jordan played, but whoever is responsible for what happened to us needs to pay for what they did."

"The deeper the detective digs the more he's going to uncover," Sandy assured her. "They'll solve this case. I know they will."

Alex smiled her thanks for her friend's support. She hoped Sandy was right. But somehow, in her heart, she wasn't convinced she'd ever learn for sure who had been behind this whole bizarre experience.

* * *

"Hey," a groggy voice said.

Startled, Alex lifted her head. "Rich?" she cried. "You're awake!"

"Where am I?" he muttered, barely able to open his eyes or move his lips.

She leaned over the bed, close to him. "We're in San Diego, at the hospital."

"Oh," he murmured. Then it registered. "The hospital?"

"You've been pretty sick," she said, reaching up to stroke his hair.

"I've had some wild dreams," he said. "It all seemed so real—a boat, the ocean, water everywhere."

She hated to tell him it wasn't a dream, but that could wait. "How are you feeling?" she asked.

"Lousy," he said.

She took his hand and pressed it gently. "You realize you're lucky to be alive," she said.

Not comprehending, Rich looked at her. "I am? Why? What's wrong with me?"

She explained briefly about his injury and the infection that had set in while they were on the boat.

"But you're going to be okay," she assured him. "The doctors are pleased with how quickly you're responding to the medication. In fact, I need to tell the doctor you're awake."

"Wait . . ." Rich's eyelids fluttered as he tried to stay awake. "I want to tell you something first . . . In my dream," he said, taking several shallow breaths, "a lot of crazy stuff was going on. None of it made sense. But you were always there by my side." He stopped talking for a minute to gather his strength. "You never left me." He reached for her hand. "Thank you."

Alex blinked the tears that stung her eyes.

"I'll always be by your side, Rich. I'll never leave you," she promised.

He gave her hand a weak squeeze and whispered, "I love you."

Those were words Alex feared he wouldn't live to tell her again. "I love you, too," she whispered, not trying to hold back the tears that threatened to spill over.

As Rich drifted back into his slumber, Alex too closed her eyes with a grateful heart. The Lord always been there for her, yet on the boat she'd questioned whether He had even cared.

She asked the Lord to help her remember the lessons she'd learned throughout their ordeal. Just like her patriarchal blessing had said, she needed to stay faithful and things would work out.

* * *

The first thing Alex saw as she and Rich stepped off the plane was the huge "Welcome Home" sign that her mother, Dr. Rawlins and Steve held. Next to Steve was little Nikki, holding so many balloons Alex thought she'd be lifted right off the ground.

Filled with warmth at the thoughtful gesture, Alex waved to her family with her free hand, but held firmly to Rich's elbow, helping him through the crowd of passengers. He was able to walk on his own, but he was still a bit weak and shaky.

"Welcome home, honey." Judith was the first to hug her daughter. "Rich, it's so good to see you. How are you feeling?" She embraced him as well. Alex had called her earlier and described the whole ordeal.

"I feel a lot better than I did," he chuckled, "although, really, I'm doing quite well."

"Good to have you back, buddy," Steve said, pulling his friend into a hug. "Man, that must have been some wild trip, huh?"

"You'll have to ask Alex. I don't remember much of it," Rich laughed again.

"We want to hear all about it," Steve said. "Jamie's dying for us to get you home so she can see you."

"How's my new little nephew doing?" Alex asked.

"He's great," Steve managed to answer before Nikki made her presence known.

"B'loons," Nikki replied. "Pwetty."

"Yes they are," Alex said, scooping Nikki up in her arms. "I hear you have a new brother. I'll bet you're a big helper to Mommy, aren't you?"

"Baby!" Nikki said. "Baby."

Alex watched as Dave took Rich aside to discuss his condition. She was grateful to have Dr. Rawlins available, just in case Rich needed him. Even though the doctors in San Diego had assured her repeatedly that he was going to be fine, she still worried about him.

"Everybody ready to get going?" Steve asked.

Alex was more than ready. All she wanted was to get back to life the way it was, normal, predictable, and far away from the ocean. It had taken her several days to get her land legs back, and sometimes she still felt the rocking of the boat. She was grateful and relieved to put all of that behind her now and look forward to the future—Rich's and her future—together.

Chapter 28

Judith's baptism had been rescheduled so Alex and Rich had another day to recover from their trip and it gave Julianne and Andre a chance to get back from California. They'd taken an extra day to go to Los Angeles so Andre could meet with some people about their video. Alex was grateful for his dedication to the project and that she didn't have to worry about it. She had enough to worry about.

By now Sandy was in Paris. They'd said a tearful good-bye in San Diego and one more over the phone before she flew to Europe. In Alex's estimation, Sandy was one incredible lady and Alex prayed that her friend would find someone equally as incredible to spend her life with. Sandy was lonely and had so much to offer a husband. He would be one lucky guy, whoever he was.

"Okay, Mom," Alex said, helping her zip up the back of her baptismal dress. "I think you're set. You look beautiful."

"Thanks, sweetie," Judith said, turning to look at herself in the mirror. "I don't know why, but I have butterflies. Were you nervous before your baptism?"

"I was until the opening prayer, then I calmed right down," Alex answered.

"You'll be fine, Mom," Jamie assured her. "I'm so proud of you." She blinked quickly, her eyes filling with tears.

"Thanks, honey. Thanks to both of you." She put her arms around them both. "This is a very special day for me and I'm so grateful to have you here with me."

Judith went on. "I don't know how to explain it, but I feel in my heart that not only is your father here with us, but he's very pleased about this decision." Alex had felt her father's presence with them also.

Judith had explained to them earlier her feeling that her first husband approved of her decision to marry Dave. In a year's time, they could go to the temple and Judith would be sealed to Samuel and Alex and Jamie to their parents. "Dave is very supportive about it," Judith said gratefully.

"He's a wonderful man," Jamie said.

"He really is," Judith answered. "I have a feeling that even though he and I won't be married for eternity, there will be something very special that we'll all share forever."

There were few things in life that made a person feel as good as Alex felt right at that moment. And once again she knew that the power of the Spirit in their lives provided them with the sweetest moments they could share on earth.

* * *

Alex had scheduled her surgery for the following day. Even though she dreaded the procedure, she was anxious to have it over with so she could get on with her life.

She found she wasn't as nervous as she'd expected. Rich had given her a beautiful and powerful blessing the night before. Once again, the blessings of the Spirit had taken her fears and replaced them with feelings of peace. Rich had blessed those performing the surgery as well, and Alex felt confident that she was in good hands, both physically and spiritually.

He'd also blessed her that her body would respond well and recuperate fully. He had spoken with such power and conviction, her doubts had flown.

Just before they wheeled her into surgery Alex had searched for the right words to express her feelings of love and gratitude for him and her family. But no words seemed to describe the depth of her feelings.

The best she could come up with was, "I love you, Rich. Thank you for being my best friend."

"I love you, too," Rich had said. "I'll be here when you wake up." He kissed her one last time before they wheeled her down to surgery.

His kiss was the last thing she remembered before going to sleep.

* * *

"Alex, wake up." Rich brushed the hair off her forehead and ran his finger down her cheek to her jaw. "Alex?"

She stirred and mumbled something in her sleep as the voice penetrated her subconsciousness.

"Riccchhh?" she said slowly, drawing it out into two syllables.

"I'm here, honey. Wake up. Time to wake up." He jostled her arm gently.

"But I'm so sleep—" She drifted off.

"Come on," he said, "you can do it. Open your eyes," he insisted, patting her hands and cheek.

She heard the words but her eyes just wouldn't respond. With the little strength she did possess, she tried with all her might to lift her lids. Finally she opened one eye.

"There you go," Rich said encouragingly. "Now open the other one. You can do it."

Her eyelids felt like they weighed fifty pounds each.

It took another hour to get her to fully respond and understand where she was and what was going on. Finally she shook off the drug-induced sleep to find Rich waiting anxiously at her side.

"Hi," she said groggily.

He leaned forward. "Hi, honey. How are you feeling?"

"Okay," she answered.

As the anesthetic continued to wear off, Alex's thoughts became clearer. "Where's the doctor?" she asked.

"She was here a few hours ago," Rich replied. "She said she'd come back when you wake up."

"Did she say anything—" her words still slurred "—about the surgery?"

"She found some cysts and endometriosis, like she suspected, but she said she's seen other women in your condition, or worse, still conceive." Rich delivered this news happily.

"She did?" Alex was vaguely aware that this was good news, but she was still too groggy to feel excited about anything except going to bed for the rest of the day.

Rich continued, "If you're not pregnant in three months after we get married, there are some medications she wants to talk to you about."

"I've heard about the medication," she mumbled. "I'll grow hair and get fat."

"Honey—" Rich began.

"It's true," she said stubbornly. "I don't want to take the medicine."

Rich patted her hand. "We don't have to worry about that now," Rich said. "Besides, we won't need it. You wait and see."

She smiled as she drifted off again. Rich's optimism was contagious. He believed it so strongly himself that she believed it, too.

* * *

In response to the knock at the door, Jamie got up slowly from the couch. Her tail bone was still sore from giving birth to little Tyler, and as she walked across the room she leaned forward, pressing one hand against her lower back. Opening the door, she saw the last person she wanted to see. She was in no mood to talk to Clint Nichols again.

"Mr. Nichols, what could you possibly want now?" she said impatiently, with only the thinnest veneer of civility. "The results of the test aren't back yet. I know because I've checked."

She hadn't slept more than half an hour the night before, it was two in the afternoon, and she was still in her pajamas. If he expected cordiality, he wasn't going to get it from her.

Realizing that he hadn't come at an opportune time, he spoke apologetically. "I don't mean to bother you, but I came to tell you I'm leaving town for a while."

"Oh, really," Jamie said caustically.

"I don't know when I'll be back. I've been offered a job back east and I start in three days," he explained.

What in the world was this man trying to tell her? She didn't have time to sit and visit; her milk was coming in and she could feel the drips running onto her stomach. "So?" she demanded.

He shrugged. "I just thought you should know."

Jamie took a deep breath. "Mr. Nichols, can I be honest with you?" she said, trying to speak calmly.

He nodded.

Jamie's words were crisp and to the point. "I appreciate you wanting to be noble and live up to your responsibilities, I really do," she said. "In most cases, that would be very admirable but, frankly, I don't see what you being my daughter's biological father has to do with anything.

She has a father and mother who love her very much and a new baby brother she adores, and we aim to give her a life of happiness and opportunity where she can grow up and have a good education, a nurturing home life, and a bright future. What, Mr. Nichols, do you have to offer her except fulfilling an obligation no one has even asked you to fulfill?"

He didn't say anything for a moment, as if he were thinking about these things for the first time. Jamie felt bad that she'd gone straight for his jugular, but this was her child he was messing with and she wasn't giving up without a fight to the death.

"I understand what you're saying," he finally said, "but all my life I've run from responsibility, just like my father. I've had the freedom to do whatever I please, to go wherever I want to . . ."

"A child would certainly change all of that," Jamie said dryly.

"I know," he said. "I've thought about the burden that comes with having a child."

"You see, that's the difference between us, Mr. Nichols," Jamie quickly responded. "I don't consider my children 'burdens.' They are my whole purpose in life, and I'm thrilled about it. Everything I do revolves around them and their well-being."

"But it's time I began facing up to my obligations," he insisted stubbornly.

"But why start with my daughter?" Jamie felt a welling up of tears forming. She fought for control. "If you really understood what being a parent was all about, you'd realize it has nothing to do with what *you* want. It's all about what's best for your child. Your responsibility and obligation are deciding what's best for *her*, not for *you*. How can you feel good about tearing an innocent child away from the only family she's known?"

He hooked one thumb in his belt loop and shrugged a second time, apparently searching for a reply, but seemed unable to find one.

"Mr. Nichols," Jamie repeated clearly, "like I said, it is very admirable for you to feel responsible for a child you might have fathered, and if she is yours, I am forever grateful to you for helping her into this world. She is the joy and light of our lives, and we love her more than anything. But I'm asking you to do what's best for her. A life on the road, with a father who's gone constantly, isn't the way to raise a child."

He was silent, listening, before he finally spoke. "Well, I'll send you my address and phone number when I get settled, and I'll think about what you've said." He turned to leave, then stopped. "Don't get me wrong, Mrs. Dixon. I'm grateful you folks took this little girl and gave her a good home. I had an alcoholic mother and an abusive father, and I always longed for a home like you have." He cleared his throat and looked away for a moment. "I . . . I . . ." He swallowed hard. "I'll be in touch." Quickly he turned and walked down the stairs.

Jamie watched for a moment as the man left. Her heart was split in two. She resented him terribly for what he was trying to do, but another part of her pitied him and even yearned to help him.

Then she shook her head to clear her mind. It had to be hormones and lack of sleep that made her so sappy. He was a threat to her family. How could she feel sorry for him?

But she did.

Chapter 29

Soft music with a gentle beat played as Alex led the group in some stretching moves. Just as the doctor had promised, she could barely tell that she'd recently had surgery.

"Reach the right arm up, and over and hold it there," Alex said. "Exhale and stretch your arm further . . . and hold . . ." The group adjusted their position. "And . . . relax."

Finishing the workout with several deep breaths and applause from the crew, Alex smiled proudly, feeling confident that the first rehearsal had gone even better than expected. She felt great and the crew and instructors were great. Everything had fallen neatly into place. And because of her continued relationship with ProStar International as spokesmodel and representative, Alex had received workout gear, clothes, and shoes for the project for her whole crew.

The instructors—two men and three women—taught at different health clubs in the Salt Lake Valley. Finished for the day, they gathered their gym bags and water bottles and waved good-bye to Alex and Julianne, who had taken seats on one of the podiums and were discussing changes that needed to be made in format or presentation. Out of the corner of her eye, Alex could see the crew busily taking care of the equipment. Rich was talking to one of the other cameramen and Andre was working with the sound crew.

"So, what do you think about changing Eric and Debbie's places?" Julianne asked.

Alex agreed. "I'm glad you mentioned it. The set will definitely look more balanced."

"I like the other instructors having microphones so they can add their comments to the workout," Julianne said. "It makes it seem more interactive I think."

"I do too. That Cami sure has a cute personality. I can see her having her own show someday. She's a lot of fun," Alex said.

"Great job, girls," Andre said, taking off the headset he wore around his neck to communicate with the sound and lighting booth and the camera men. "We could have put it down on tape and used it. We'll shoot first thing in the morning, and if all goes this well, we may even finish early."

Julianne's eyes gleamed with excitement; her fears had been left behind long ago as their dream was becoming a reality.

"I've just got a few bugs to work out with my crew," he said, "so we're going to stay a bit later tonight. We'll meet up with you for dinner around seven. How would that be?" He kissed Julianne briefly in farewell.

Alex wanted to check on Rich to make sure he was holding up through the long hours. He'd seemed to gain his strength back, but she didn't want him overdoing it. He still looked a little peaked and hollow-cheeked to her.

"Hey there," she said, coming up behind him. She circled her arms around his waist and gave him a hug.

"Well, hello," he turned, and greeted her with a kiss on the cheek. She pulled a face. "I'm all sweaty."

"Mmmm." He licked his lips. "A little salty, but still very delicious."

"I like having you on the set," Alex confided. "It's kind of fun being able to see you behind the camera. But you better quit pulling faces and blowing kisses at me," she said. "I almost forgot my routines."

He held up three fingers. "No more, I promise. Scout's honor."

Alex explained the plan to meet later, and Rich nodded in agreement. "Do I get one more salty kiss for the road?" he teased.

Their kiss lingered. After coming so close to losing Rich, Alex cherished every moment with him. Several days ago she wondered if she would ever feel his arms around her again as he had struggled to fight the infection that had invaded his body. His speedy recovery was no doubt a product of his own body's strength, but also many hours of fasting and prayer.

She found Julianne and together they stepped into the beautiful June evening. The days were growing warmer and longer and the air was filled with the sweet fragrance of flowers and a barbecue off in the distance. They chatted cheerfully on the way home, finding humor in the mistakes they'd made during the shoot, and giggling as they remembered how Julianne had gotten her body parts mixed up on some of the toning exercises.

"Hey," Alex said, checking the rearview mirror. "Don't look now but this car has been behind us almost the entire way home."

Julianne gave Alex a startled look. "Do you think he's following us?"

"I don't think so," Alex said, her eyes still looking in the mirror. "But it's odd that he's taking the same exact route we are."

"Maybe he lives near you, or even at the same apartment complex," Julianne reasoned.

"I guess that's possible," Alex said. "Can you see who's driving?"

Julianne glanced back. "It's definitely a man. He's wearing a baseball cap and sunglasses." Julianne turned sideways so she could look directly at Alex. "Why don't you take a side road or a different route and see if he follows? There's a good spot. Turn there." Julianne pointed to a small street leading down a narrow tree-lined road.

Alex slowed, and turned while Julianne watched behind to see what the other car did.

"I don't see him," Julianne said. "I guess it was nothing."

"Wait," Alex said watching the rearview mirror. "Look! There he is."

Julianne gasped. "He turned! He *is* following us."

"What do we do now?" Alex forced herself to remain calm.

"We could call the cops on your cell phone," Julianne suggested.

"But the guy hasn't done anything," she argued. "They'll think we're nuts, won't they?"

Julianne frowned. "Maybe we should go to the mall or someplace where there's a lot of traffic and confusion. We could lose him there."

"Yeah, maybe." Alex was trying to think. "Or we could let him get really close so you could get his license plate and the make and model of his car." She gripped the steering wheel tightly. "I sure wish I knew where the police station was located, I'd take the car straight there."

"Okay, I can see his license plate," Julianne said. "It's a Utah plate, H-C-V-9-9-7."

Alex had a sudden thought. "I'm going to cut through the University and see if we can ditch him there."

Alex accelerated and headed east. As she approached an intersection, the yellow traffic light turned to red. Looking both ways quickly, she sped through the light, then checked her mirror. The compact, metallic blue car came to a stop at the red light.

"We made it!" she exclaimed. "I think we can get far enough ahead that he won't be able to follow."

"Hurry," Julianne cried. "If a cop pulls us over, we can tell him what's going on."

Alex stomped on the gas pedal and they screeched around the corner, speeding down Foothill Boulevard toward her apartment. Julianne kept a steady watch behind them for the silver blue car.

"We're almost there," Alex said, her heart racing faster than the speedometer.

Whipping into the parking lot, she sped toward her stall, pulled in, and quickly shut off the lights. They waited anxiously, the suspense mounting as they saw a car round the corner and pull into the complex. Alex held her breath as the car traveled their direction, its headlights illuminating a path through the dimming evening shadows.

They both sighed with relief as a black BMW continued past.

"I think we're safe," Alex said, then added, "Besides, do we even know for sure that car was after us? I mean, if he wanted to follow us, wouldn't he have just run that red light?"

"You're right. We're just overreacting," Julianne agreed. "I think that boat trip made us both a bit jumpy."

"Me too," Alex sighed. "Come on. Let's go shower. Rich and Andre will be here any minute and we don't want anything to spoil this evening."

Feeling secure once again, they let themselves into Alex's apartment and deposited their gym bags on the couch. "You can go first," Alex said. "I'm going to call Jamie and see how she's doing."

While Julianne showered, Alex poured herself a cold drink of water and relaxed on a bar stool. She was ashamed of herself for getting so jumpy over the car behind them. Really, if he'd wanted to catch up to them, he easily could have.

The phone rang at that moment, catching her off guard and nearly sending her to the roof. Laughing nervously at herself, she picked up the receiver. It was Detective McBride calling to tell her they'd apprehended Porter and Donovan and had them in custody.

"Where were they? How'd you find them?" Alex asked.

The detective was happy to relay the details. "We've followed several leads, all dead-ends, until early this morning, someone spotted them in Oregon. They were in a dumpy motel on the outskirts of Portland."

Alex was filled with relief.

"We're still waiting to interrogate them, but I wanted you to know that they are in custody."

"I'm so glad you called to tell us," Alex thanked him. "I hope they confess to what they did, then we'll be able to find out if Jordan has any connection to the case."

"We'll do our best to find out everything we can," he promised. "And we do have several men trying to locate Davis."

The detective promised to call the next morning after speaking to the two men. "I'm going to do everything in my power to see these two behind bars," he declared. "Someone needs to be responsible for what happened to you folks out there on the ocean."

Alex was curious. "Please don't take this wrong, but I'm a little surprised to see you so involved in this case. You seem to have a personal interest in it."

"Well," he hesitated a moment before he explained, "if you feel strongly that your old boyfriend could be connected, I want to follow that lead. You see, my daughter was killed by a stalker, Ms. McCarty. I live daily with the regret of not taking her seriously enough in the beginning to do something about the scumbag who killed her, before he had a chance to take her life."

Alex felt a pang in her heart for the detective. "I'm so sorry," she said.

"Yeah," he said, "Me too. I'm sorry every minute of every day. The only thing that makes me feel better is trying to catch the rest of those deranged lowlifes who torment other innocent people, like yourself."

Alex thought about the car they'd suspected of following them. "Detective McBride, do you think we're in any danger now?"

"My honest opinion?" he asked. "For now I think you're safe. Davis would be a fool to come anywhere near you. His presence alone would prove his connection to the case, and he has to know that we're looking for him. No," he said matter of factly, "for the time being, I think you're safe. But I've worked with these fruitcakes for enough years to know, they don't usually give up until they get their way."

Alex shifted nervously on her chair. "Is there anything I should be doing to help?"

"There's a Detective Hardcastle there in Salt Lake. I've notified him of your case. He's a good friend of mine, and I've asked him to keep an eye out on his end. If you notice any suspicious characters around or strange occurrences I want you to contact him there. He's a good man," the detective added. "We were partners when my daughter was killed. He feels as strongly about stalking cases as I do. You'll be in good hands."

He gave Alex a phone number, and she jotted it down on a pad next to the phone.

"It wouldn't be a bad idea to take some extra precautions," he said as a final warning. "Don't go anywhere alone. Get yourself some pepper spray. Keep a charged cell phone with you at all times—things like that."

Alex already had some spray on her key chain and in her home, and she kept her cell phone charged and in her purse always. "I'll be careful. Thanks again."

She decided to call Detective Hardcastle first thing in the morning to tell him about the car following them. It was probably nothing, but just in case, she was going to follow Detective McBride's advice and play it safe.

Maybe it wasn't over yet, but at least they had Donovan and Porter in custody. She felt better just knowing that.

* * *

"How could this happen!" Alex cried. "Who would have done this?"

Alex looked around the studio and shook her head in despair. They had come in this morning, excited for the final shoot, only to find utter devastation. Anything not nailed down in the studio had been broken or turned upside down. It looked like a tornado had ripped through there.

Julianne looked at Alex, her expression matching Alex's own feelings—anger, confusion, and fear. They didn't say, but both had a feeling it had something to do with Jordan.

* * *

Within the hour Detective Hardcastle, with a team of officers, was on the scene gathering facts and fingerprints, taking pictures, and asking questions of the cast and crew.

Alex gave him as much background on Jordan and their experience on the sailboat as she could. She also told him about the car following them.

Detective Hardcastle looked thoughtful. "To be honest, Ms. McCarty, this is probably just an unrelated case of vandalism. We've had a lot of problems with gangs in this area of town. This seems typical of something they'd do, but to be on the safe side, until we gather the rest of the evidence and examine our findings, I want you to take extra precautions. I especially don't want you to be alone at any time."

"Thank you, Detective." Alex shook the man's hand. He was in his fifties, a kind, gentle man who reminded her more of a school teacher than a law enforcement officer.

The policemen finished their search while everyone else stood around wondering what to do next. Andre immediately took charge.

"It will probably take the rest of the day to repair damages, but I think we can put this place back together," he said, addressing the group of crew and cast members who'd shown up on schedule for the taping. "We should be able to have this cleaned up by the end of the day. If you can stay and help, we'd appreciate it. Plan on staying a little longer tomorrow afternoon to help make up for lost time today. Crew members need to stay and check out their equipment. There's no telling what kind of damage has been done to the sound system or the cameras."

Alex looked once more at the set, wondering how in the world they would ever be able to get everything put back together before tomorrow morning, but she appreciated Andre's optimism and energy. It was exactly what she needed to get her mind off her fears that danger was close by, and possibly had been in this very room.

Chapter 30

As the final beats of the music faded, Alex gave the camera one last smile and told the group behind her and the future participant who would be working out with the tape that they did a great job. She wished them a wonderful day and said good-bye. The other instructors also said their farewells and Andre gave the cue to fade out.

"And . . . cut!" Andre shouted. "That's a wrap. Good job, people. We made it." He clapped his hands and the rest of the cast and crew joined him. There was a sense of triumph after the setback from the previous day. "Same time tomorrow morning, all right?"

"Good job, Alex," Cami said as she wrapped a towel around her neck and blotted the sweat on her face.

"Thanks, Cami, you too," Alex complimented her. "Now that I'm going to be living here in town, I'll have to come to your studio and work out." Cami was the director of Salt Lake Valley's hottest aerobic and weight training studio, The Sweat Shop. Many members of the local professional basketball team worked out there, and any celebrities who passed through popped in for a workout when they were in town.

"You wouldn't be interested in teaching any classes, would you?" Cami asked.

"Actually, I might," Alex said. "After the wedding when I get settled, I'll come and talk to you. We can discuss the workshop you're putting together."

"Do you really think it's possible for me to become a national presenter?" Cami looked at Alex hopefully.

"Absolutely," Alex assured her. "If your workshop's as good as it sounds, you won't have any trouble lining up conferences, and I'd be willing to help you get your foot in the door. Being such a success at your own club and being in this video will help, too," she added.

Cami smiled broadly. "I've enjoyed working with you and Julianne. I appreciate all your help."

"I'm glad to do it," Alex said.

Cami left with the rest of the cast, and Alex found Julianne, Andre, and Rich watching a replay of the tape on the monitor. It hadn't been easy recreating the set, and they'd been up until early in the morning, but they'd managed to do it. Alex was relieved to see it looked even better on film.

"So," Andre asked her when she joined them, "what do you think?"

"It doesn't look too bad." She watched for a second. "Is it just the screen, or do we all seem to have really long heads and necks?"

"It's the monitor," Andre said with a laugh. "I promise, this isn't a conehead workout."

"I, for one, am just glad we didn't have any problems filming," Julianne said gratefully. "I was nervous when we first started, thinking something was going to fall on us, or explode."

Alex laughed. "Me too. Like someone had sabotaged the stage or something."

Andre looked up from the screen. "Officer Gooding, one of the policemen who came yesterday, told me he would have one of his men patrol all night."

"Didn't he say they'd keep watch for the next week or so?" Rich asked.

Andre nodded. "We won't have any more trouble, I'm sure of it. Officer Gooding said he's convinced this was gang related."

Alex wasn't convinced, however, "Isn't it odd that the kids didn't take anything, though?" she asked, not wanting to be negative, but wanting to get at the truth.

Andre shook his head. "Gooding said that sometimes these kids are looking for specific items—stereos, televisions, things like that. They want something they can grab and run with. I don't see them hauling off one of our cameras or a panel of electronic equipment."

"So, why all the destruction?" Julianne asked.

Andre had a ready explanation. "Retaliation that they weren't able to get anything off of us. Officer Gooding said they would have grabbed the goods and been gone, but were probably on foot and couldn't carry the heavy equipment, so they trashed the place."

As the two couples left the studio, ready to enjoy the success of the day and what was left of the evening, Alex thought about Officer Gooding's comments. Everything he said made sense, but it was as if a low-gauge warning device inside of her wouldn't let her rest assured that all was well. She'd ignored a prompting once before and it nearly cost them all their lives, but this time she was going to listen. Because this time, she wasn't sure they would survive.

* * *

Even though they'd lost a full day of work with the vandalism, under Andre's disciplined leadership they were able to catch up to their original schedule and finish shooting on time. That night the cast and crew celebrated at a nearby restaurant. Alex felt a mixture of exhilaration at the accomplishment and a twinge of sadness that the project was complete. Andre had been so impressed with Rich's ability to work the camera so well he'd asked him to help him with his next project. Rich was even talking about taking some classes at the "U" in film making.

The next morning, feeling revived and energized, Alex lay in bed thinking that in less than two weeks, she and Rich were getting married. She was grateful to have the bulk of the video project out of the way so she could concentrate the next week on the final plans for the reception. She was especially glad to have Julianne there to help her. Julianne had a knack for detail and a flare for entertaining. With Judith busy at the University, Julianne was the perfect one to take the place as wedding coordinator.

Which reminded Alex that she needed to discuss a few things with her mother about the reception center decorations and sending out the invitations. Climbing out of bed, she glanced out of the window and saw that it was a gorgeous summer morning, and she marveled at the brilliant blue of the sky. If they weren't so busy with the wedding it would be a perfect day to go to the mountains for a picnic.

Alex was puzzled when she opened the door to her mother's room and found it empty. The bed was made and nothing was out of place. Where had her mom gone so early in the morning?

Maybe over to Jamie's. She'd give her a call.

"Steve, hi," she said on the phone. "Is Mom there?"

"Your mother?" Steve sounded surprised. He told Alex that Judith had stopped by with Dr. Rawlins after her class the day before. They had stayed to visit for a while, but he hadn't seen her since. "Have you called Dave? Maybe they went to breakfast or something," he suggested.

"You're probably right," Alex said. Those two spent every possible waking moment together, and she wouldn't be surprised if they'd gotten up early to have breakfast then spend the day combing antique stores and shopping.

Alex searched the counter for a note from her mother—she usually left one when she went out—but there was nothing. Dialing Dave's number, Alex waited for him to answer, but the machine picked up instead.

She hung up without leaving a message. She wasn't worried about her mother, especially if she was with Dave, but it wasn't like her mom to take off without telling Alex her plans.

"Good morning," Julianne said with a yawn and a stretch as she came into the kitchen. "What are you doing?"

"Trying to find my mother. She's off with Dave somewhere."

"So early?" Julianne was mildly surprised.

"I guess. They're both not home so I'm assuming they're together," Alex answered with a flustered lift of her hands.

At the ringing of the phone, Alex looked relieved. "Maybe that's them," she said. To her surprise it was Sandy, calling from Paris. "How are you doing?" Alex asked.

Sandy's voice was positively ecstatic. "I can't even begin to tell you how wonderful everything is over here. It already feels like home and things have worked out perfectly so far. Right now I'm standing in my lovely flat in Paris, looking out at an incredibly beautiful sunset. My apartment is incredible, my job is incredible, Jean Pierre is incredible and I know, without a doubt that I'm supposed to be here. Am I blessed or what?"

Alex laughed. "I'd say you're pretty blessed. I repent for my selfishness in wanting to keep you here. What's up?"

Sandy asked about Rich and how he was doing, then about the video shoot, and Alex told her how everything had gone and how impressed she had been with Rich's and Andre's professionalism. She also told Sandy about the break-in and the vandalism. She didn't mention Jordan, figuring that until they knew for sure, there was no sense complicating the issue. Sandy commiserated with her and then said, "I have some news for you. Are you sitting down?"

"Yes," Alex answered, wondering what other surprises Sandy had in store for her.

"Good, because I have something to tell you that's going to knock you right off your feet. I met an old friend of yours."

"You did? Who?" Alex couldn't think of anyone she knew in Paris.

"Not only did we meet, but we ended up having dinner together and spending the entire next day going to museums," Sandy warbled enthusiastically.

Alex was intrigued. "Will you tell me already? Who was it?"

There was a brief silence, then Sandy said, "Does the name Nickolas Diamante ring any bells?"

Alex was stunned. "Nicko! You went out with Nicko?"

"I did," Sandy assured her. "And he is every bit as handsome and charming as he's always been." She marveled that Nickolas was such a gentleman but not so formal that she felt uncomfortable.

Alex couldn't help smiling and shaking her head at the same time. What a small, small world it was.

"He was happy to know you were getting married in a few weeks and that you're doing so well," Sandy went on. "He thinks the world of you, Alex."

"I think a lot of him, too." Alex smiled, remembering him. "There's no one like Nicko, that's for sure. But tell me about you two. Did you hit it off?"

"Would it be okay with you if we did?" Sandy asked quietly.

"Sandy, are you serious?" Alex demanded to know.

"I wouldn't want you to feel bad, or be mad at me for—"

"Sandy Dalebout, I can't believe you're even asking my permission for you to date Nicko," Alex scolded her. "I think that's wonderful."

Beside her, Julianne was going nuts. "Is she really dating Nicko?" she whispered.

Alex nodded and listened as Sandy said, "I didn't know if you still had feelings for him or anything."

"Listen, Sandy," Alex said sternly. "I am in love with Rich. Nicko is a dear, sweet friend, but I have no romantic feelings for him whatsoever. I can't think of two people who would appreciate each other's finer qualities as much as you and Nicko would."

"Really?"

"Really," Alex said. "But don't forget, he's not a member of the Church. I think you should be careful."

Sandy's enthusiasm waned a little. "I know," she said. "I mean, we've only been out together twice, but already I feel a strong connection to him. He was in town for some business, and Jean Pierre and I happened to go to lunch at the same restaurant where he was dining. He recognized me before I recognized him. Then one thing led to another and boom! There we were, going to dinner and dancing, then strolling through museums and admiring art. He certainly has a vast knowledge of art." Alex acknowledged that was true.

"We did discuss religion while we were together," Sandy told her. He had asked if Sandy was a Mormon. When she said she was, he told her that Alex had given him a Book of Mormon while she was in Europe. He didn't even look at it for several months. Then one day, for some reason, he picked it up and read a passage Alex had challenged him to read—the promise in Moroni 10:3-5.

"And?" Alex asked anxiously.

"And he liked what he read," Sandy reported. "He hasn't had much time to read lately, but he had a lot of questions. We spent several hours just talking about the Church. Alex, I would say that the seed you planted has taken root and is starting to grow."

Sandy had also told Nickolas about her experiences doing genealogy work and the spiritual experiences she had had finding names and tracing her ancestors. Sandy's voice was warm with conviction as she said, "I think genealogy is the key to his conversion. He's got a strong sense of family, and he's incredibly interested in finding out who his ancestors are. He wants to learn more about where he came from. Of course, he still needs to read the Book of Mormon and gain a testimony of it, but I think he'll do it."

Alex was amazed at what she was hearing. She'd known Nicko possessed a profound spiritual side, but didn't know if it would ever be given a chance to be nourished. Perhaps the Lord had been preparing him for Sandy all this time. Maybe this was the reason Sandy felt she needed to move to Paris.

Nickolas had returned to Rome, but was coming back to Paris in a few days. Sandy was planning to do some research for him so she could have his four-generation chart done when she saw him again.

"You're really something, you know that," Alex told her.

"Hey, when the Spirit moves you, you can't just sit there. Believe me, I've learned to listen to those promptings."

"Absolutely," Alex said, fully aware of what Sandy was saying. "So have I."

"Listen, kiddo, I've got to run," Sandy said abruptly. "I just wanted to check on you and tell you about Nicko. I'll see you soon. Is there anything you need from Paris for the wedding?"

"Just you," Alex said, "As long as you're here, that's enough. And tell Nicko hello from me. I'm very happy about all of this, Sandy. I think that maybe there's been some divine intervention going on in all of this."

"Me too," Sandy said with a laugh. "Who would have thought the Lord was in the real estate and employment business?"

"Not to mention a romance counselor," Alex added. "Let's just be grateful He is. Take care of yourself and let me know if I can help on my end. We've got the genealogy center right here, you know."

"I know, and I plan on spending some time there when I come for your wedding," Sandy assured her. "I'll talk to you soon."

Alex hung up, still a bit dazed from the conversation. Julianne immediately bowled her over with a million questions.

Alex recounted her conversation with Sandy, all the time hoping that her mother and Dave would show up or call soon. *Where were they?*

Chapter 31

"I know you guys don't think there's anything to worry about, but this just isn't like Mom and Dave to take off and not let anyone know where they are," Alex announced, hoping that someone would show some concern.

She and Rich, along with Julianne and Andre, were sitting in Jamie's living room later that afternoon watching Nikki play with her collection of dolls. Tyler slept peacefully in his bassinet.

"I just think they took off early this morning and went for a drive and shopping," Steve countered. "They probably just lost track of time."

"But neither of their cell phones are on, which I find very unusual. Mom is always in contact with both of us every day, isn't she, Jamie?" Alex wasn't going to drop the issue. Something strange was going on and she didn't like it.

"I have to agree with her," Jamie said. "Mom's been worried about me and the baby, and I don't think she'd take off without letting us know her plans."

"I think it's like Steve said," Rich added his vote. "I bet they've just lost track of time. They'll call or show up soon. And if they don't, we'll start making some calls and try to track them down."

Alex wasn't sure where they'd even begin to look for Dave and her mother, but at least Rich had offered to try and help. That gesture made her feel much better. With all the strange things going on around her, she couldn't help but feel a little uneasy about the situation.

There was some talk about going out to a movie, but they decided to call in for pizza and rent a video to watch that evening so Jamie and Steve could join them.

"Why don't you show us the new house?" Andre asked Rich. It was nearing completion and he and Julianne were anxious to see it. But for the first time since work on the house began, Rich didn't jump at the offer. Alex looked at him with surprise. Here were two people actually requesting to go through the house, and he wasn't already out the door with his video camera.

"Rich, we can be back in an hour," Alex said. "Now would be a great time to take them to see the house. We can stop and pick up the movie on the way back."

Rich was strangely reluctant. "Dan's been doing some work today that won't be done until Tuesday or Wednesday. It would be better if we can wait until then."

Alex didn't understand what work he was referring to. The construction was all but completed, the cabinets had been installed, and the tile put down. In fact, by next week the paint was supposed to be done and the carpet laid.

"It's no problem," Andre said. "We'll wait until then."

Alex looked at Rich curiously. He'd never turned down an opportunity to show off the house. What was up? Had something gone wrong? She would ask him about it later.

"Andre," Jamie spoke up, "how is it that you speak such good English?"

Andre inclined his head. "Thank you. I'm glad you think so. In France we are required to take English in school. I had English classes for almost eight years. I took more classes at the University, and I also worked in a film lab. My boss was from America and he helped me with my conversational skills. I served a mission to Sweden, which helped me learn Swedish, but since I had many English-speaking companions, we often spoke English. That allowed me to practice everything I learned at school. Since I've moved to England, I have become much more fluent. Living in the country is definitely the best way to learn a language."

"You speak like an American," Jamie commented. "You have just the slightest accent."

"It's almost impossible to be in any international business and not speak English," Andre explained. "It has helped me a great deal to know the language, especially now that I'm trying to start my own production company here in the United States."

"Now that you've almost finished with the personalized exercise videos, what's your next project?" Steve asked.

"I've got a commercial shoot lined up, but I've actually been toying with the idea of writing a screenplay of our experience in San Diego and making a movie out of it," he announced to their surprise.

"Really?" Julianne was as surprised as the rest of them. "You haven't said anything until now."

He smiled at her. "I've been thinking about it for a few days, and I'm beginning to think it would make a great story."

"It would be an incredible story," Jamie agreed. "I could see it as a 'Movie of the Week.'"

Andre looked at Alex and Rich. "How do you feel about it? Would you be okay with it, if I did?"

"Sure," Rich said. "As long as you get Tom Cruise to play my part."

They all had fun trying to figure out which movie stars would play each character. They were talking and laughing so hard they almost missed the doorbell.

"I think Jack Nicholson would make a great Captain Porter," Steve said as he went to the door. "He can be so mysterious and sinister." He swung the door open wide, and there stood Dave and Judith, arm in arm, both grinning from ear to ear.

"Mom!" Alex jumped to her feet. "Where have you two been?"

The couple stepped through the door. Alex noticed something different about them immediately. She couldn't put her finger on it, but it was there.

The two didn't say anything for a moment, then suddenly Judith burst out, "Dave and I got married!"

"What?!" Alex screamed. She didn't mean to startle the baby, but he began to wail. Nikki didn't know what was going on, but all the commotion and the baby's crying got her started crying, too. It took a minute for the news to sink in and for the children to settle down.

Alex was grateful Jamie had the presence of mind to congratulate her mother and Dave, and to hug them. It wasn't that Alex wasn't happy for them, it was just so unexpected, she could hardly take it in.

Steve ran into the kitchen and grabbed some more chairs.

"Sit down and tell us everything," Alex demanded. "Why didn't you tell us?" She had always thought when her mom remarried, if she ever did, she and Jamie would naturally be there.

"Well," Judith began, her cheeks flushed and her eyes sparkling, "yesterday afternoon Dave and I went for a ride. You know how we like to drive around and look at the scenery. We just got driving and realized we were almost in Nevada." She took her new husband's hand in hers and smiled at him lovingly. "Dave said, 'Wouldn't it be a kick if we surprised everyone and got married tonight?'"

Dave looked at them innocently, although the twinkle in his eye revealed that he was fully aware of his role in the adventure.

Judith went on, "Of course, he meant it as a joke when he said it, but I told him I was game if he was. Then, somehow, we realized how serious we both were. I know this isn't how we meant to get married—believe me, I never pictured myself doing something like this. It just happened. So I guess that means we eloped," she finished, looking at everyone as if quite proud of their little adventure.

Alex said nothing, still trying to accept what her mother was saying, but Steve stepped forward. "Congratulations," he said. "We're very happy for you."

"Thank you, son," Dave said accepting Steve's handshake. "We hoped you kids wouldn't be upset with us."

Jamie moved toward her mother and gave her a hug. "Of course we're not upset," she said. "We've wanted you two to get married for months now. I was just hoping we could have a nice wedding at the Church and be able to attend the ceremony."

"I'm sorry, darling," Judith apologized, "We got caught up in the idea and completely lost our heads. I would never want you kids to run off and do something like this, but . . . well . . ." She looked humorously at her new husband. "I guess we can't go back in time. And I wouldn't want to," she said, leaning forward to give him a kiss.

"That's the important thing," Alex said, giving her mother a supportive hug.

"Thanks, sweetie," Judith smiled at her oldest daughter.

"We'd still like to have some sort of celebration for you," Jamie said. "A reception or open house or something."

"Maybe after Alex's wedding, we could do something," Judith said. "We'll worry about mine later."

The evening turned into a small-scale celebration for the newly-weds, but they were tired and anxious to be alone, so the party ended early. Judith stopped by the apartment to grab a few things before she went to Dave's place with him.

"This is just temporary until we find a house of our own," Judith said filling a suitcase. "I can't believe how nervous I am."

Alex smiled at her mother. "He's a lucky man."

Judith tipped her head thoughtfully. "Thank you, sweetie. I don't know which one of us is luckier. The main thing is that I know this was the right thing to do. Maybe not the right way to do it," Judith said, shaking her head as if she still couldn't believe it herself, "But still, he and I are supposed to be together. And I appreciate all your support, honey."

"Dave's been the closest thing I've had to a father since Dad died," Alex said honestly. It would take a bit of getting used to, but she was grateful her mother had found such a wonderful man. And she liked the idea of having a father figure in her life. Soon, she would be married to Rich and then her family would be complete. In one short year, they could all go through the temple together and she could be sealed to her mother and father and sister, something she'd never imagined would happen.

So much had happened in the last year, and she'd been so worried something would prevent her and Rich from being able to realize their dream, but here they were, barely over a week away. They were going to make it!

* * *

The voice was familiar, but unexpected. "How are you doing, Alex?" Detective McBride asked. "I'm calling because I wanted to keep you posted. We've located Jordan's whereabouts."

Hearing the name of her old boyfriend sent a chill up her spine. "Where is he?" she asked.

"Back in the Bay Area. We've had two different sightings reported. I know you've got a wedding to get ready for and I thought you might appreciate having one less thing to worry about." After the detective had offered his best wishes for her future and her wedding day, Alex thanked him and hung up the phone. *If they find a connection to Jordan, they can put him behind bars soon,* she thought, *and I won't ever have to worry about him again.*

Chapter 32

"Who did you say wanted to meet us at the studio at seven?" Julianne asked when they stepped inside the empty studio and noticed they were alone.

"It was Kevin, I think," Alex said, looking around. "When he called, he said that Rich and Andre were here and wanted us to meet them to go over some editing."

"Why so early?" Julianne questioned. "It doesn't look like anyone is even here."

"They must be expecting us—the doors were open." Alex tried to find some light switches. The studio seemed extra dark inside.

"So where are they?" Julianne asked, covering a yawn.

"Maybe they ran to grab something for breakfast," Alex suggested. "They'll probably be here any minute."

"You try and find some lights, and I'll go call them," Julianne suggested. "They'd better be on their way, that's all I can say."

In the faint light from a small outside window, Alex stepped carefully around each dark obstacle as she worked her way through the studio, trying to find some sort of switch to turn on the lights.

"Ouch," she exclaimed, bumping her shin on a sharp corner. She felt her way along boxes and film equipment and finally found the back wall where the switches were located.

Running her hands along the wall, she searched for anything that felt familiar. "Julianne," she yelled. "I can't find the lights. Are you having any luck?"

Julianne didn't answer.

Alex continued sliding her hands on the wall, when finally her fingers touched a switch. "Juli, I think I found one." She flipped the switch but nothing happened.

"Hey," she said. "Why isn't this light working?"

She tried the switch again. Nothing.

"Juli!" Alex yelled. "Are you having any luck? I found some switches but they don't seem to be working."

Julianne still didn't answer her. *She must be on the other side of the studio,* Alex decided. *Or maybe she's on the phone by now.*

"There's got to be another switch here somewhere," Alex mumbled as she continued her search for light. The strap of her fanny pack was digging into her hip bone so she shifted its position and squinted through the darkness, trying to make out shapes and images.

"Juli!" she yelled. "What are you doing?" She knocked over a cardboard box and sent it crashing to the floor. The noise echoed through the large building.

As the last echo faded away, Alex remembered that last night she'd taken her cell phone out of her car and slipped it into her fanny pack. She'd been using the pack instead of a purse lately; she'd had so much on her mind she managed to misplace her purse almost daily. She was grateful the phone was still there so she could give Rich a call for herself and find out what was keeping them. But before she could unzip the pack and get the phone out, something struck her in the back of the head and everything went black.

* * *

Alex's first thought was to wonder why she was having such a hard time breathing. The air seemed thick and heavy, and it was difficult to fill her lungs. Her head throbbed painfully and when she opened her eyes she was surrounded by darkness. Confusion and panic filled her at once. Why couldn't she see or breathe? And except for a jostling bounce that intensified the ache in her head, there was nothing.

Where was she? What was going on?

She lay uncomfortably on her side, her hands tied in front of her and her feet bound tightly together. Where was she? And then she realized, she was in the trunk of a car.

Questions flew through her mind; panic and fear collided inside her chest and exploded into pure terror. Who was driving the car? Why had someone kidnapped her? And the most terrifying question of all, what were they going to do to her when the car stopped?

Then the answer came. Jordan! He'd fooled the authorities, going to San Francisco. He must have come here next, looking for revenge. Revenge for something she hadn't even done or intended to do. She'd done nothing to deserve this. Except make the mistake of getting involved with him. But because he was unstable and desperate, she could die unless she thought of something quick.

"*No!*" she couldn't help crying out loud. Not now. *Please*, she prayed, *don't let me die now.* What about Rich, their wedding, their future, her children, her family?

With every ounce of strength she possessed, she placed her faith and her life in the Lord's hands. She was not giving up or giving in. The Lord had given her promises and she knew He would stand by those promises. He'd delivered them from drowning at sea, He would help her now. She knew He would.

Not knowing how much time she had, she began thinking of her options. She was at a disadvantage in every sense, but she was not going to let this man take away her life.

Wait! She had her phone. She could call for help. Almost fearfully, she felt for the fanny pack, praying that it was still around her waist, but not daring to hope.

It was. She was saved.

With her hands tied, it was difficult to unzip the bag and rifle through the contents. *Please let it be here. Please, Heavenly Father.*

Sheer relief filled her as her hand circled the precious object. Who should she call? What could she tell them? She didn't have any idea where she was, or what kind of car she was in.

All she knew was that something had to happen fast. It was hot inside the trunk, and the air was getting thicker.

She pushed three buttons. 9-1-1.

"Nine-one-one. Do you have an emergency?" a woman's voice asked.

"Yes," Alex said desperately. "I am calling from the trunk of a car. I've been kidnapped, and my hands and feet are tied up."

"Excuse me, did you say kidnapped?"

"Yes. But I don't know where I am, or what kind of car this is."

"What is your name?"

"Alexis McCarty."

The phone beeped. Her battery hadn't been charged.

"Miss," Alex said, panic striking her from every direction. "I don't know how much power I have left, but you have to help me. The person who's done this is named Jordan Davis. Detective Hardcastle knows everything. You have to contact him and my family." She gave the woman Jamie's name and number and Rich's name and number.

The car hit a large bump, grinding over what sounded like railroad tracks. The movement threw Alex against the side of the trunk, and her shoulder rammed into a steel box. The faint light of her phone key pad gave off just enough illumination to allow her to see it was a emergency repair kit for the car.

"Wait," she said into the phone, which again beeped a warning, "I think we just went over a railroad track, and it feels like we're heading down a hill. And I think—" she strained her neck to the side and saw a label, "—I found it. An emergency repair kit for a 1998 Ford Taurus."

"Good job, Alexis. Anything you can tell us will help," the woman on the other line assured her. "I've sent out an APB. We've got everyone on alert."

Then Alex remembered something else. "I think the car may be metallic blue." The car that had followed her and Julianne the other night had been a Taurus, the same color. She thought there was a good chance it was the same car.

"You need to check on my friend," Alex said, wondering how Julianne was. She hadn't answered any of the times Alex had called her. Was she all right?

Alex told the woman where the studio was located.

"We'll have someone go over there right away."

The phone beeped again.

"My phone's probably going to go out any second," Alex said. "I . . ." She choked on a sudden lump of fear in her throat. "You . . ." She couldn't help crying. "Please help me."

"Don't panic," the woman said. "We will do everything we can. Every available officer in the county is on alert. We have a description of the vehicle and a point of origin. We'll find you."

"Wait!" Alex made another connection. "I think I just heard the roar of an engine. I can't be sure, but maybe it was an airplane."

"That's great, Alexis. Can you tell if the car is traveling at a high speed, fast enough for the freeway?"

"Yes, I'm sure of it."

The phone beeped again and went dead.

"Hello!?" Alex cried. "Hello, are you there!?"

But the phone was dead. And Alex was afraid she would be next.

Chapter 33

Julianne held an ice pack over the large bump on her head, while Andre cradled her in his arms. Around her a swarm of officers combed the studio inside and out, looking for some shred of evidence to help them locate Alex.

"I can't believe she's out there with him," Julianne moaned, her tears dampening Andre's shirt sleeve. "Andre, what if the police don't make it? What if he kills her?"

"Shhh," Andre soothed. "They'll find her. Thank goodness she had her cell phone with her."

Julianne remembered the last time she and Alex had encountered Jordan in the lobby of the hotel. She had glanced behind them as they ran for the van carrying Rich and Andre. Jordan's face had been dark with anger as Alex had made clear her preference for her fiancé over him. "I know it's Jordan," Julianne said aloud. "I know it is. He's the only person who would do something like this."

"Then they'll find him," Andre assured her. "They have a description of the car and a description of him. All the authorities are on the lookout."

They had left a message with Detective McBride to let him know what was going on with Alex and find out why his men hadn't apprehended Jordan. They were waiting for him to return their call.

Julianne buried her head against his shoulder and prayed. In her mind she imagined how terrified Alex must be. The police had told her about Alex's phone call, and Julianne pictured her friend tied up in the back of a car trunk, headed for some desolate destination where anything could happen. The police had to find Alex before . . . Julianne hated to think what could happen.

"Detective McBride is on the phone," Rich told them. "He's talking to Detective Hardcastle right now."

Rich, Andre, and Julianne gathered around the detective as he finished his conversation. Rich noted a distinct look of confusion on the man's face when he hung up the phone.

"What is it? Is something wrong?" Fear stilled his heart.

"I don't know how to tell you this," Detective Hardcastle said. "They have Jordan in custody. He's with them right now."

"What!" Julianne cried with disbelief.

"If they've got Jordan," Rich said, "then who's got Alex?"

* * *

Even though Alex felt as though she would pass out any minute because of the heat and lack of air, she knew as long as the car was moving, she would remain unhurt and alive. But just as she feared, the car began to slow and then come to a complete stop. Her heart beat so wildly in her chest she wondered if she'd have a heart attack before Jordan had a chance to hurt her.

It seemed like forever that she waited, straining to hear every movement, every footstep. But it was quiet. What was going on? What was he doing?

A wave of nausea washed over her. She forced herself to calm down and breathe slowly, steadily. It was difficult to draw in any air, but she knew that in order to survive she had to remain calm.

Then she heard the squeak of the car door opening and felt the car shudder as the door closed with a bang. Footsteps came closer until she knew he was standing in front of the trunk. She wanted to scream and cry and beg, but pure willpower and an inner strength from somewhere allowed her to remain calm as she awaited her fate.

The keys jangled in the lock and the trunk lifted.

Her vision blurred against the brightness of the day. Then it cleared. With a shock, she looked into the face of her abductor. "Dylan!" she gasped.

"Oh, shut up!" he hissed. He reached in and pulled her from the trunk as if she were a rag doll. He threw her to the ground, and pain shot through her hip and shoulder as she slammed into the dirt.

There was nothing in sight except for low rolling hills of sage brush, scrub oak, dirt, and rocks as far as Alex could see. All she could tell was that they were somewhere west of Salt Lake. No one would hear her if she screamed.

Standing above her was a different Dylan than the one she had met in San Diego. Gone was the puppy-like eagerness to please, the annoying adoration he had showered her with. Now he stared at her with cold, hard eyes. "You've ruined my life, you know" he said in a measured tone. "You and every other woman I've ever known. And just like the others, you'll have to pay."

Alex struggled to think of everything she'd heard about trying to establish a bond with an abductor. "I'm sorry, Dylan," she tried to infuse her voice with warmth and caring. "I never meant to hurt you. I didn't understand. I'm sorry."

"It's too late!" He kicked her square in the ribs, and a sharp pain ripped through her body. She groaned and gasped for air.

Standing directly in front of her, practically on top of her, he lashed out at her. "You're just like my mother. All of you. I'm not good enough for any of you. Someone has to teach you that you can't treat people that way."

Alex couldn't talk; the sharp pain in her side stabbed at her with every breath.

Dylan looked down at her, his eyes softening momentarily. "I thought you were different, Alex. I was willing to devote my life to you." Then his eyes hardened. "But no, just like the others," he kicked at her again, this time striking her in the thigh, "you thought you were too good for me."

"It wasn't like that," Alex managed to say. Clutching her leg, she fought against the lightheadedness that washed over her. "I didn't understand. We'd just met."

"I would have done anything for you." He swore at her, calling her names she didn't even understand.

"I'm sorry, Dylan. Let me make it up to you," she pleaded, hoping she could reach that part of him that had cared for her once, that was willing to do anything for her.

"Didn't you hear me!" he screamed. "It's too late!" He kicked her again, this time in the back, causing her to cry out in pain. Tears streamed from her eyes, but she fought with everything she had to stay in control, not wanting to add fuel to the fire of his wrath.

"You don't deserve to live," he screamed. "You're good for nothing. NOTHING! Do you hear me?"

Alex hugged the ground, wishing she could sink underneath its surface and hide.

Help me, she prayed as she'd never prayed before. *Father, help me!* She braced herself for another blow, but instead, Dylan stood back, looking down at her strangely. "I have to hand it to you, Alex. You've been tougher to kill than the others." His voice held an odd tone, almost one of admiration. "I had devised the perfect plan for you," he nodded, "A burial at sea. A ship full of novices, lost in a storm . . . the ship would go down and take you and your stupid boyfriend with it. I knew if your friends wanted to go, you'd do whatever they wanted. When I learned from Porter that several storms were forecast for the week . . . well, everything seemed to fall into place."

So it had been Dylan, not Jordan, who had masterminded the boat trip. Why hadn't she suspected it?

"Somehow you managed to survive," he observed, "which just means that this time we can't leave anything to chance. So I'll just have to deal with you myself—just like I had to with the others."

Alex wondered how many others there were. She could barely swallow, her mouth was so dry. Her body screamed with pain, and her head throbbed from the blow Dylan had given her earlier when he had knocked her unconscious. She could feel where her hair was blood caked and matted at the back of her neck. Her wrists and ankles throbbed where strong cords held them bound.

As Dylan stared off in the distance for a moment, Alex hoped it was at an approaching vehicle. She glanced swiftly around her for any kind of stick or club she could grab, but there was nothing. She brought her wrists to her mouth and tugged at the knot on the cord with her teeth. It budged, but she still didn't get it untied.

Dylan turned toward her. "It's time, my pretty, perfect Alex."

"Dylan" she begged. "Please!"

"Please what? Spare you?" His laughter became lost in the empty expanse surrounding them. "So you can marry your precious Rich?"

He lunged toward her, his hands grasping her neck. His fingers pressed inward, squeezing until she could barely breathe. Dylan wasn't a large man, but he was solid. He had a grip like a steel vise.

"Tell me, Alex," he whispered as his face drew close to hers. "How does it feel to know you're about to die?" Then, with one abrupt movement, he lifted her and threw her against the ground. Rocks dug into her back. He knelt beside her.

"I loved you, Alex." His voice was wounded, full of pain. "Only you. I was your number one fan, and I gave you my heart." His agony appeared to deepen as he leaned over her, his face an image of raw pain, then in a split second his features were distorted with rage and he leapt on top of her and encircled her neck with his hands. "And what did you do, Alex?" he whispered.

Alex shook her head, unable to speak with his weight nearly suffocating her.

"You crushed it," he answered softly, his face next to hers. "Now you're going to pay for your callousness."

"Dylan, no," she whispered hoarsely. "I'm sorry."

"Oh, shut up!" He slapped her across the face. Her cheek stung, her jaw felt as though it had been pulled from its joints. "You make me sick."

He stood up and in apparent disgust stomped to the car. She wasn't sure what he was getting, but she knew this was the only chance she'd have. With everything she had, even though her jaw screamed in pain, she chewed at the knot on her wrist, pulling and tugging until the cord gave. But Dylan had secured it several times, so she pulled and tugged again, loosening the next loop. At last the bands felt loose enough she knew she could slide her hands out and free herself. She just had to wait for the right time.

Next, before he came back, she had to work the knot free that kept her ankles bound, but leave the cords in place. If Dylan saw her bands loose, there was no telling what he would do.

She untied herself just in time. As he stepped from behind the vehicle, Alex was puzzled to see him carrying a shovel. She'd expected a gun, or a knife, but not a shovel.

"You know, Alex," he spoke almost calmly to her. "It was torture having you turn me away in San Diego like you did. I felt so alone. Your rejection made me feel like I was dying a very slow death." He smiled, looking deeply into her eyes. "That's how it will be for you. A slow and lonely death . . . so you will know exactly how you made me feel."

He rammed the shovel into the ground and lifted a mound of dirt. He was going to bury her alive!

The heat of the late morning sun beat down on both of them, scorching Alex's skin, cracking her dry lips. Sweat ran on her dirt-covered forehead, stinging her eyes.

Dylan's fury grew with each shovelful. Alex could see that the hole he was digging, between a boulder and a scrub oak tree, would be undetectable to an unknowing eye. Once she was under the ground, she would remain there. Unless she could escape.

Could she make it to the car and get away? If she could get inside and lock the door, she might have a chance. Lying as still as possible she waited until he was focused on his task before she slid the bands off her feet. Slowly, she slid her bottom foot from the rope. Her timing had to be perfect.

Now!

Her right leg buckled as she sprang to her feet, but she ran for the car. He'd actually left the driver's door open.

Dylan swore when he saw her sprint for the automobile.

She closed the door just as he reached her. She slammed down the lock and reached for the keys. They were gone.

Then she heard him laughing. She looked out the window and saw him dangling the keys in front of her.

"No!" she screamed, pounding the steering wheel. "No!"

Before she had a chance to search the car for a weapon, he slid the key in the lock and opened the door. She scrambled for the other side, but he grabbed her and pulled her kicking and screaming from the vehicle. He pushed her to the ground and threw himself on top of her. With every ounce of strength, she scratched and clawed at him. He managed to pin her once, but she wiggled free. Cursing and swearing, Dylan dug his knees into her already damaged ribs. She screamed in agony, which only made him laugh.

"Have it your way, Alex," he taunted her. "Either way you end up dead."

She kicked her legs, trying to hit him in the back with her knees. The movement caught him off guard, and he released his grip on one of her arms. She grabbed a handful of sand and using every bit of strength she had left, threw it in his face.

"Aaaaaghh!" He covered his face with his hands, attempting to clear the dirt from his eyes. Alex clawed at the ground behind her, trying to turn over so she could break free, but he refused to loosen his hold on her.

Then her hand located a rock, about the size of a baseball. It wasn't much, but maybe, just maybe . . .

Swinging as hard as she could, she sent a stunning blow to the side of Dylan's head. He cried out in agony, blood spilling from the open gash as he fell face forward on the ground. With a strong push, Alex rolled out from under him and ran for the shovel. It was now or never. Without another thought except to save her own life, Alex swung. The head of the shovel connected with the back of Dylan's head.

Her first thought was to hit him again while he lay still on the ground, but something stopped her. She didn't know if he was dead or not, but she couldn't deliver another blow.

* * *

"We've had a lead," Officer Gooding told the group of family and friends gathered at Jamie and Steve's house as they waited together for the police to find Alex. "We just received a report that a car fitting that description was seen earlier traveling westbound near the airport."

"Where could he be taking her?" Rich asked. He'd nearly worn the carpet in Steve and Jamie's living room bare from pacing so much. It was killing him to have to wait around while someone else looked for his fiancée. He'd give anything to be doing something, anything constructive, to locate her. Judith and Jamie clung to each other, their tearstained cheeks revealing the anguish and worry in their hearts. Would the police find Alex before it was too late?

"We're doing everything we can, folks. Every available man in three counties is helping us with the search," Officer Gooding explained. "We're also sending out a search and rescue helicopter. It will cover a wider territory faster than ten squad cars."

Dave shook the man's hand. "Thank you, officer. We appreciate you stopping by."

"I'll keep you updated on our progress. In the meantime, if you need anything you can call this number and you can get in touch with me. There is a chance she may be able to contact you."

After Officer Gooding left, a heavy silence hung in the room like a dark cloud.

"I still can't believe this," Jamie said. "All my life I've watched stories on the news, all the strange and awful things that happen to people. I never thought anything like this would ever happen to us."

Every television station and newspaper in the valley had contacted them, wanting to get more on the story, to get all the details. The family had discussed the matter, feeling primarily that the press was just anxious to land a good story, but realizing also the benefit of making as many people as possible aware of the situation. Maybe someone out there within reach of the radio or television would be able to give them a tip that would help them find Alex.

Neither Judith, Jamie, or Rich felt they could answer any questions without getting emotional, so Steve became the family spokesman. Even though he did become quite emotional during the interviews, he did a wonderful job expressing their concern about Alex's safety. He asked the public to be on the lookout and to report anything that might help the police.

They sat under that dark, dismal cloud of gloom and waited. It was enough to make a person crazy. Rich continued to pace. "I'd give anything to be in that helicopter!" he said.

"Why couldn't you go?" Steve said. "You worked with Search and Rescue in Idaho for five years. You could be a lot of help."

Dave rested a reassuring hand on Rich's shoulder. "It's worth a phone call, son," he said.

Without another thought, Rich grabbed the phone and dialed the number. Dispatch put him through to Officer Gooding immediately. It took a great deal of convincing and pleading but when Rich hung up it was apparent, he was going on that helicopter.

"I need someone to drive me," Rich said. "I think I'd have an accident trying to get there. Officer Gooding said there's still a chance I might not be able to go, but he's going to call right now and see if they'll bump one of their other rescuers to make room for me. He didn't want to let me, but then, for some reason, he changed his mind."

"Come on, then." Steve grabbed the keys off the coffee table. "Let's get you down there."

When the two men left, the reverberating slam of the door emphasized the emptiness the others felt.

Chapter 34

While Dylan lay still, Alex ran to the car and popped open the trunk. She quickly searched inside, knowing she didn't have much time.

The cords that had held her bound weren't going to be strong enough to keep Dylan captive. His wrists were much thicker than hers; the cord would barely wrap around them twice. She needed something else. Something stronger.

Keeping one eye on him at all times and the shovel right next to her, just in case, Alex scoured the trunk for something to use. Opening the emergency car repair kit, she nearly screamed for joy when she found a roll of duct tape. After living alone as long as she had, she knew duct tape was a girl's best friend. Her hopes of surviving had just increased twenty times.

Something else caught her eye. A tire iron. Grabbing it, along with the tape, she summoned all of her courage and turned. Eyeing Dylan suspiciously as she crept closer to his large motionless form, she readied herself to bind his feet and hands.

When she was hit by a mental image of him suddenly jumping up and grabbing her, she realized she'd seen too many Hollywood movies. Still, the thought terrified her and it took everything she could to get within ten feet of him. But she had to tie him up. It was her only defense.

Peeling away a strip of the tape, she knelt down beside his feet and wrapped the duct tape around them. Ten times around would have probably been plenty, but Alex wrapped the tape twice as many times, just to be safe.

She kept her breathing as shallow as she could so she wouldn't exacerbate the clenching pain in her ribs that accompanied any movement, especially breathing. Every part of her body ached and she felt as though she'd been hit by a semi truck, but even though she felt like collapsing, she forced herself to go on. Her survival depended on it.

Knowing she wasn't safe yet, but feeling more secure now that his feet were bound, Alex approached his hands. Trembling, she pulled off a long strip of tape and reached for one of his hands.

Wham! Alex didn't know what hit her, but she went flying. Rolling a complete somersault, she came to a stop in the dirt. Her mind grasped onto the situation immediately. Dylan had broadsided her with his legs. She wondered if the movement of her taping his feet had brought him to consciousness.

Between them lay the shovel and tire iron. She had to get to them first. Her advantage was that her feet were free. His advantage—he was seething with rage.

Without a second to lose, Alex lunged for the shovel. Her foot accidentally kicked the tire iron, sliding it in his direction. With a demonic laugh, he grabbed the sharp-ended tool and wielded it as he attempted to remove the tape from his legs.

"Thought you had me, didn't you, Alex?" he sneered.

She held the shovel like a baseball bat, ready to swing, praying for perfect aim.

He fingered the end of the sharp-edged iron. "You're very good at this," he said. "I could be tempted to keep you alive, just to have you around to *play* with." He chuckled. "Some people don't handle torture very well. They whine and beg, but you," he smiled devilishly, "you're strong and feisty. I like that."

She realized he was distracting her. In one glance she noticed he'd located the end of the tape around his feet and was starting to unwind it. She prayed that all her years of training and working out would assist her in bringing him down. What she lacked in size and strength, she asked that God would make up for.

"I'd rather die," she yelled, and swung the shovel. He dodged her attempt and laughed at her as she stumbled to one knee. She regained her footing and quickly took a ready position.

"Oh, you'll die," Dylan said. "There's no question of that."

Fearing that he would free his feet before she could knock him unconscious again, she took aim and, trying to catch him off guard, swung again. This time she nailed him in the shoulder, knocking him sideways.

He rolled toward her, one hand grabbing for her feet, the other stabbing at her with the tire iron. She had to get that weapon away from him.

"Good," he said. "I'm impressed."

She jumped back, kicking sand in his face, giving him wide berth, sizing up the situation. The tape on his feet was getting twisted and rolled. It still held fast, but she was worried he would somehow be able to slide one of his feet free.

Pushing himself back onto his knees, Dylan narrowed his eyes, reminding her of a hungry, black panther, ready to attack.

And he did. Somehow from that position, he managed to spring forward enough to catch one of her feet. She screamed and kicked wildly, managing to escape.

She knew she had no time at all to think of a strategy. Every second she wasted he used to unwind the tape around his ankles, which he did at a rapid pace.

Terrified, she watched him remove his shoe and peel the tape off his pants, sliding it down. If she didn't do something quick, he'd be free and she would die. Not knowing what else to do, she dug the shovel into the dirt and flung it his direction, showering Dylan with the hot, dry sand. He swore and coughed, but it worked and distracted him from the tape.

She tossed another shovel full, and another, as if she were stoking a fiery furnace with fuel, feeding Dylan's seething anger into a blaze of deadly rage.

Dirt kept flying as she realized this was it—she had one last chance.

Taking a huge breath, she dug in her shovel and threw one last load of dirt at him, which hit him square in the face. Alex then steeled herself for what she hoped was the final blow. Knowing her life depended on it, she took aim at his head and swung with all her might.

Her blow sent Dylan flying. He landed face down and lay motionless. Alex stood, frozen, waiting to see if he was still alive. His body shuddered and with a tremendous effort, Dylan pushed himself up on one arm and looked at Alex, his eyes smoldering. He opened his mouth to speak, but nothing came out. His eyes went wide, their expression changing to one of fear and pain. Then, without a word, he collapsed.

Alex didn't waste any time. She grabbed the tape and starting with his hands, she wrapped them so tightly behind his back that even Houdini would have found escape impossible.

She forced herself to ignore the blood that pooled around his head as she reinforced the bindings around his feet with the last of the tape. Once she had him completely bound, she bravely took a look at his head, where the sharp edge of the shovel blade had sliced it open.

The gash was long and wide. A wave of nausea overcame her and she shut her eyes, drawing in several unsteady breaths. She placed two fingers on his neck, feeling for a pulse. It was barely noticeable, but it was there.

She ran to the car and grabbed a rag from the trunk, which she pressed against Dylan's wound, not sure it was any cleaner than the dirt in which he lay. Then she stopped. What was she doing? She had a car. She was free. She could go home.

Slamming the lid of the trunk down, she ran for the driver's seat, then remembered that Dylan had the keys. Returning to his lifeless form, she searched his pockets until she found them.

She stood to go back to the car, then stopped and looked down at him. He had had every intention of killing her. He would have thought nothing of burying her alive. He had jeopardized not only her life, but Rich's, Julianne's, and Andre's as well.

Still, as much as he might deserve it, she knew she couldn't leave him there in the desert to die. She thought about putting his body in the trunk, just to show him how it felt, but she could barely move him. Even though he was close to her height, he was solidly built. Instead she toiled and dragged and pulled with all her might, despite the screaming pain throughout her body, until she crammed him into the back seat.

Not for his safety, but her own, she wrapped the seat belts around his body, one cinching his arms down, the other, tightly around his legs.

Confident that he couldn't make any sudden moves, she collapsed into the front seat and put the keys in the ignition. The sound of the engine turning over was music to her ears.

Murmuring a prayer of thanks, she put the car in gear, wondering which way to go. She hadn't seen the route he'd taken to get them there so she searched for tire tracks and followed them as best as she could. As she drove the car through the brush and dirt, each bounce and jolt sent sharp pains through her ribs, jaw, and shoulder. Gritting her teeth, she drove on, hoping she would see some sign of civilization soon.

She kept a firm eye on Dylan, glancing back every chance she could. He hadn't moved and his coloring looked washed out and pasty. For a moment she wondered if she had killed him, but she pushed the thought aside. Right now she had to focus on getting back to her family and getting him to a hospital.

Her loved ones back home were probably frantic with worry, she knew. How she wished her cell phone was still charged so she could call them and tell them she was alive and where she was.

Unsure of her route, she continued driving, hoping the tracks she followed were leading her back to a main road. Then she glanced down at the gas gauge and her heart dropped. The tank was almost empty. She had no way of knowing just how much farther the car could go. *Heavenly Father, help me! Please don't let me get stranded out here in the desert.*

Holding her breath, Alex kept driving, wondering if the car would at least make it to the main road before it quit. If the car ran out before then, she didn't know how far she could walk on her own.

* * *

"Thank you, officer," Jamie said over the phone. "We'll be waiting." She hung up and wearily sat back in her chair. Judith looked at her, her expression hopeful, but Jamie could only shake her head sadly.

Julianne looked at the two women, her heart aching for their pain and worry. She knew how they felt. Alex was like a sister to her, and Julianne was sick with fear for her. From her own experience, she knew that stalkers were beyond thinking rationally and could not be reasoned with. Julianne hated to think what Alex might be going through.

Just then Andre and Steve clamored through the front door.

"Any news?" Judith asked.

Steve shook his head. "Not yet. Rich got off in the helicopter okay and said he'd radio back every fifteen minutes or so. The highway patrol reports several sightings fitting the description of the car and the driver so they'll follow up on those first." Steve looked at the women's faces creased with worry and said, "They'll find her. Rich isn't going to stop until he does. And don't you worry about Alex. She's tough. She'll take care of herself."

"But who has her?" Jamie cried. "And why did he take her?"

* * *

"We'll let the highway patrol take care of the freeways and main roads," Leon, the helicopter pilot said. "We'll cover the side and back roads."

Rich nodded and searched the expanse below, his eyes darting from side to side trying to see everything at once, but seeing nothing that would help locate Alex.

"I wish the car was red or black," Leon said, "It'd be easier to spot than metallic blue. You can use those binoculars hanging behind you if you want."

"Yeah," Rich said, grabbing the glasses. "Maybe that will help." He liked seeing things up close, but felt he could easily miss a detail or some signal to help them find her. Preferring the use of his naked eye, still he kept the binoculars handy to get a close check on anything suspicious. As he searched, he prayed that if she were out there, he would find her.

"Once we clear these telephone wires, we can take her down a bit closer," Leon said. "We shouldn't have any problem locating a vehicle from this height though."

So they kept flying and searching and watching.

Inside Rich used every bit of willpower he had to stay calm. He wondered where she was, if she was okay, and worse, what, was happening to her. It didn't take much imagination to conjure up the worst, but he fought the images, knowing it would hamper his concentration. Right now he had to focus all his attention on the search. Alex needed him, and for her sake, he had to keep his head.

* * *

Alex didn't know how much longer she could take the heat. The inside of the car felt like it was well over a hundred degrees.

Every time she looked in the back seat and saw Dylan's motionless body, she got a sick feeling. Never in her wildest dreams, would she have imagined herself in this situation. And here she was, one week away from her wedding, withering in the heat like a sun-dried raisin, with a killer in the back seat. Possibly a dead one at that.

What she wouldn't give for a drink of water.

Maybe her mistake was sitting in the car. It had been nearly half an hour since the car died, and still there were no prospects of getting rescued. What if she sat there all day and no one came?

She knew she couldn't do that. There was no way she could spend the night out there.

With that thought, she gathered her fanny pack and started off down the dirt trail. At least she had a chance of finding the road and getting help.

Each pain-filled step made her wince as she limped through the dirt and sage brush. The sun beat down on her neck and scorched her skin through her clothes.

She walked until the car shrunk out of sight. She walked until she felt like the soles of her shoes were literally on fire. She walked until she couldn't take another step.

It had to be close to noon, judging by the position of the sun. Were they still looking for her? Would she be able to hang on until they found her? Pausing to rest in the partial shade of a scrub oak bush, she looked back in the direction she'd come from, and then forward to where she thought she needed to go. How much further? Surely there had to be a road soon.

From somewhere deep inside Alex found the strength to put one foot in front of the other. But her willpower was fading along with her strength. Each step was growing slower and heavier.

Keep going, she told herself. *Keep going.*

* * *

"Wait," Rich cried, "what's that?" He pointed up ahead and the pilot took the helicopter lower.

Raising the binoculars, Rich searched rapidly for the object. When it came into view, he released an ecstatic "That's it! We've found the car."

"Let's take her down," Leon said. As he lowered the chopper, he radioed the others, giving the specific coordinates of their position. There was an immediate response and a reply from several officers directly in the vicinity.

The helicopter touched the ground, kicking up clouds of dust. Rich's stomach tightened and knotted as he waited for the helicopter to come to a complete rest. What was he going to find inside that car?

Chapter 35

"Wait!" Leon cried as Rich leaped from the helicopter door. "He might have a gun. Rich, stop!"

But Rich couldn't wait; he couldn't stop. He had to see if Alex was okay. He ran full speed toward the car, then slowed as he came closer, seeing no signs of life. Cautiously, he crouched lower as he moved in. Maybe he should have waited for help. He couldn't rescue Alex if he got himself injured.

But he was too close to stop now. He had to see her. To see if she was okay.

Staying low, Rich approached the car, expecting any moment that someone would jump up and blast him with a gun. But nothing happened.

What if they'd left the car? Where would they have gone?

Motioning for Leon to join him, Rich carefully opened the door to the driver's side of the vehicle. It was empty. There was no sign of Alex. But this had to be the right car. It fit the description perfectly. Then he glanced in the back seat and nearly jumped out of his skin.

"What is it?" Leon asked.

Rich pointed to the back seat and Leon peered inside. "Holy smoke," he said, looking wide-eyed. "Did your fiancée do this?"

"I wish I knew," Rich said. "Who is he anyway?" Rich couldn't figure out who this stranger was and why he wanted to hurt or kill Alex.

Leon's training asserted itself. "We'd better check this guy. He looks pretty dead to me."

Judging from the injured man's bloody head and bound arms and legs, there had been a tremendous struggle between the two. Rich just hoped Alex was okay. Since it was the abductor lying securely wrapped in duct tape in the back seat of the car and not Alex, he felt optimistic. But where was she? And again, he wondered, who was this guy?

"You check on him," Rich commanded. "I have to find Alex."

"Right," Leon said. "Reinforcements should be here any minute."

"Good. We can use them, " he said as he assessed their surroundings. Which way would she have gone?

Then he noticed tire tracks and—*footprints!*

At first he walked, but her path was clear and easy to follow, and he broke into a labored jog. The day was scorching hot and dry. Even if she'd started out okay when she began walking, he doubted she had any water. She could be close to heat exhaustion.

"Alex!" he called over and over.

In the distance he heard the wail of sirens. Gratitude filled him. With more people looking, they surely would find her. Running and yelling, he continued to follow her path. Where was she?

"ALEX!" he yelled. There was no answer.

Frantically he ran, scanning every possible inch of land as he went. Then, up ahead, he saw something. A cry escaped his throat when he saw her lying in a heap in the dirt.

Swiftly he ran to her, calling her name. "Alex, I'm here, honey. Everything's okay now."

She didn't respond.

Immediately he noticed the caked blood on the back of her head. Gently he rolled her over to see her face. His heart nearly broke at the sight of the purple bruises on her cheek bone, her cracked bleeding lips, and the sweat-smudged streaks of dirt that covered her face. "Alex! What did he do to you?"

Quickly, he assessed her condition, feeling for a pulse, placing his cheek near her mouth to check for breathing. She was breathing, faintly. Relief flooded him.

He lifted her from the ground, grateful they had the helicopter to get her quickly to the hospital. Stumbling across the rocky terrain, he kept going, pushing himself harder. Every second counted. The sound of sirens drew nearer, and he could see the clouds of dust billowing as several police cars approached.

"It's going to be okay," he said to Alex. "We're almost there. Leon,

I found her. Leon!" he called as he made his way towards the abductor's blue car. The helicopter pilot was examining the trunk, and he lifted his head at the sound of Rich's voice.

"How is she?" he yelled back.

"We need to get her to the hospital *fast,*" Rich commanded.

Leon hurried toward Rich and helped him carry Alex the rest of the way. They took her directly to the helicopter.

"Let's go," Rich said.

"Wait." Leon frowned. "We can't leave that guy here. He's still alive, but he's in pretty bad shape. We have to take him with us."

Rich was hesitant. Carry Alex in the same close space with her abductor? It seemed ludicrous, but he agreed, they couldn't leave the stranger behind. Not wasting any time, they quickly lifted the lifeless form from the back seat of the car.

"He's lost a lot of blood," Rich commented as they carried the man's limp frame to the chopper.

Both observed the gash on his head. "How do you think she gave it to him?" Leon asked.

Rich shook his head. "I don't know. I'm just glad she got away."

Leon made the necessary radio calls and in seconds they were off the ground. The hospital was less than fifteen minutes air time away. Leon glanced at Rich. "I don't know how your fiancée survived the ride in that trunk," he said. "I took a look and that thing's airtight. I'm surprised she's alive."

"Let's just see if we can keep her that way," Rich said, praying harder than he had ever prayed in his life.

* * *

There didn't seem to be a spot on her body that didn't ache or feel bruised. In the comfort and safety of her hospital bed, Alex closed her eyes. Although physically she hurt everywhere, emotionally she felt numb. The trauma specialist at the hospital had told her this was normal. Her acceptance of what had happened would come in degrees, and she would have to deal with it a day at a time.

Dylan had unleashed his strength and fury upon her and she had felt every painful blow, but she was young and strong and the doctors were amazed at her resilience. Her jaw wasn't broken, though it was by far the most painful injury; the throbbing ache in her ribs where Dylan had kicked her ran a close second. Breathing was excruciating and she'd actually gotten mad at Rich for making her laugh because it hurt so badly.

Rich. He'd been a monument of strength for her. How grateful she was for him. He'd given her a priesthood blessing that she would recover quickly both physically and emotionally. In addition to comfort and understanding, he had blessed her with an increased capacity to embrace the Atonement and lean upon the Lord as she worked through her feelings and emotions about Dylan. He didn't say she would be free from the pain, but that she would have the strength to deal with it. How grateful she was that he was actually going to be her husband. She was determined to heal quickly. Dylan had taken so much from her already; she wasn't going to let him take her wedding day as well.

The trauma specialist had been deeply impressed with Alex's strength as he had talked with her. Most victims he had worked with felt a sense of helplessness after such an experience, but Alex had shown an ability to cope that the specialist hadn't seen before. He attributed it to the fact that instead of just being a victim, Alex had taken control of the situation *and* her attacker and saved her own life. She'd fought with all her might and actually won.

Alex was well aware that this experience might have a long-term effect on her; the specialist warned her that she might even have nightmares. There would be times ahead when the reality of her experience would be more than she could bear, but Alex knew she could rely on Rich and her family to help her through the rough times.

Never before had she been so grateful for the gospel and to be alive. Even as she lay there in pain, she was able to recognize how many blessings she had and how the Lord had spared her life. Knowing that the Lord had protected and strengthened her against Dylan's attempts to take her life humbled her. She knew that there must be something important for her to do on the earth or she wouldn't still be here. Her scope of vision broadened, and she was able to see the complete picture, her life stretching from her premortal life to the eternities.

She thought about the challenge of not knowing whether she'd be able to have children and realized that this was also in the Lord's hands. She believed she had enough faith to live with whatever outcome He allowed her. As devastated as she would be to never have a child of her own, she knew she would still find great happiness and fulfillment in life, through the gospel and her family. The Lord had been very good to her. One way or the other, she would have a family and she would trust in the Lord that whatever happened would be His will.

On the boat, Julianne had reminded her that no one was immune to trials. Alex had also learned that a person could still find peace and happiness in the midst of trials. It might take years for her to understand and forgive Dylan, if in fact she was ever able to. But she did understand that the Atonement offered healing for everyone. Perhaps even for Dylan, if he would accept it.

Her body would heal and grow strong and well again. So would her spirit. She wasn't exactly sure how, but she didn't doubt she would move on and life would be good.

* * *

"I don't believe this!" Jamie collapsed onto the couch, her face frozen in shock, her voice unsure.

"What?" Steve flew from his side of the room to her side. "What is it?"

"Read this." She handed him the letter and watched his face as he read the contents.

"This is incredible," he exclaimed.

"Does it mean what I think it means?" she asked him.

"We'll need to have our lawyers check it over to make sure it's binding, but in the event the paternity test is positive, Clint Nichols is relinquishing any and all rights to Andrea Nicole and gives us sole custody of her," Steve explained. "He's found a job in New Jersey and realizes that he has nothing to offer a child. He says he's grateful she's found a family who loves her as their own and that he knows she's better off with us than she would ever be with him." Steve dropped the letter and grabbed Jamie in his arms. "She's ours! It's over," he cried.

"This is incredible!" Jamie cried. "It doesn't even matter what the paternity test says now. She's ours!"

"Mommy, Mommy." Nikki ran into the room to see what all the commotion was about.

Jamie and Steve stopped hugging and looked at their precious daughter, who had somehow found Jamie's lipstick and had attempted to apply it to her lips, cheeks and eyes. With smudges and smears of lipstick practically everywhere except where it was supposed to be, little Nikki looked like a Picasso watercolor.

"Look, see," she said brightly. "Pwetty." She held up the lipstick. "Pwetty."

Jamie and Steve burst out laughing and pulled their daughter into a hug. She could have set the house on fire, and they wouldn't have cared at that moment. Nothing mattered, because they knew that, finally, there was nothing standing in their way of being an eternal family.

Chapter 36

When Alex got home from the hospital she had a hard time resting because of the many calls, visitors, and well-wishers. She'd been
the subject of the nightly news and even received a phone call for an
interview with *People* magazine.

Julianne became very protective and began limiting phone calls and
turning away visitors, but when Sandy called, she demanded to talk
with Alex. And, of course, Alex wanted very much to speak with her.

Sandy had been upset not only to learn out about Alex's ordeal, but
also to find out that it had been Dylan, and not Jordan, who had been
behind the ill-fated boat trip. And then to think, he had actually kidnapped her and nearly killed her!

Alex told her that Dylan was still in a coma, but the doctors
thought he would survive. Porter and Donovan had turned state's evidence and given the police names and details about Dylan. He'd paid
them an outlandish amount of money to take Alex, Rich, and the others sailing and then abandon them.

Jordan had had no connection with the boating trip after all, but
the police who investigated him in relation to Alex's case didn't come
up empty. When they found him, they searched his apartment, finding
all kinds of drugs as well as records of the people he was dealing with
in South America. They would be able to put him away for thirty years
with all the evidence they found.

Sandy had surprising news of her own. She'd spent the weekend
in Rome with Nicko and they'd gone sightseeing and out to dinner
and dancing. It had been romantic and fascinating and incredibly
wonderful. There was no mistaking it, Sandy had been swept off her

feet. Sandy assured Alex that even though she could easily lose her wits around Nickolas, they'd also had many talks about the gospel. She'd felt the Spirit present when they talked, and she knew Nicko felt it, too. Nickolas had admitted that he had everything in the world a person could want and realized it just wasn't enough. He was ready for the gospel.

Alex couldn't be happier for Nickolas or Sandy. She hoped this was just the beginning of something wonderful for both of them.

* * *

As each day passed, Alex felt stronger and her nightmare seemed to fade more and more into the distance. She had made a particular effort to take care of herself physically, to eat well and to get plenty of rest, grateful that Jamie and Judith were taking care of all the last-minute wedding and reception plans to take that additional stress from her. Alex could almost believe that her trip to California and Dylan's continued stalking of her had been only a terrible dream. Now and then she felt a twinge of pain in her jaw or ribs, or a flash of fear when she saw someone on the street who looked like Dylan, but when that happened, she prayed for the strength to put it behind her. Sometimes she sang a hymn to herself. One of her favorites, since she had first become familiar with the Church, was "Where Can I Turn for Peace?" She had also learned some Primary songs from Jamie and Nikki.

As Rich drove her to the house with the first load from her apartment, she hummed to herself and Rich smiled at her.

"Now I want you to shut your eyes when we go around the corner," Rich said, as he turned up their street. "No peeking.

He had promised Alex a surprise and she hoped it was one she'd be happy about. She'd reconciled herself to living without the porch and the bay window she'd wanted so much, although she had a hard time letting go of the image of a large fireplace in the master bedroom. Still, she understood Rich's position. A newly married couple just starting out really couldn't expect to have the house of their dreams, especially when they were both making changes in their careers.

"We're almost there," he said enticingly as the car followed the bend in the road. "Keep your eyes closed."

Alex felt the car stop and heard the door open as he jumped out and came around to her side of the car. Carefully he helped her step out of the car, then guided her toward the house. "Now, stop right here," he directed her.

Alex was dying to know what he was so excited about.

"Okay, open your eyes," he pronounced.

As she did, her mouth fell open with surprise. There in the front, directly ahead of her, was the porch she'd wanted to add to the entry, but had been told over and over again was just too costly. It stretched across the front of the house, adding to the charm and appeal of the home just as she had known it would. It was exactly the right touch for the Cape Cod style, with its dormered roof and cozy shuttered windows.

"I can't believe you did this!" she exclaimed. "Honey, I love it. It's beautiful." She threw her arms around him and hugged him tightly.

"I'm glad you like it." They stood back to admire the entry together. "I rather like it myself."

"What made you change your mind?" she asked, still surprised.

Rich looked embarrassed, as if remembering his obstinate refusal to even consider the idea. "I talked to Dan about it and had him draw up a plan and give me an estimate," he explained. "When he showed it to me, I could see that it really added to the look of the house and didn't cost as much as I'd originally thought it would."

"I'm so glad you changed your mind." Alex kissed him again happily.

"Me, too," he said, "I like the house much better with the porch on. Guess I'd better learn to listen to you all the time. It was a great suggestion. Are you ready to go inside?"

They climbed the steps of their new porch together, then Rich turned to her. "Wait," he said as she reached for the doorknob. "This is something I have to do." He opened the door, then turned and scooped Alex off her feet. She giggled and kissed him.

"I know we're not married yet, but it seems very appropriate to carry you over the threshold," he said. When he set her on her feet, he turned her so she would face the kitchen.

"A nook!" she cried. "You had them put in my breakfast nook." She ran over to the large bay window overlooking their backyard. "Rich, it's wonderful. Everything is perfect." The rich cherry wood cabinets, the sleek hardwood floor, the freshly painted walls, and soft, cushy car-pet—all were even more inviting and lovely than she'd ever dreamed.

They ambled leisurely through the main floor, discussing different ways to arrange their furniture and decorate each room. Then they climbed the stairs and Alex examined the two smaller bedrooms with pleasure. They were just as she had planned, with dormer windows and window seats, something she'd always wanted as a young girl.

Rich stopped before the closed door to the master bedroom. With a twinkle in his eye, he said, "I hope you like it," then swung the door open for her.

Alex gasped when she stepped inside. "Oh, Rich! I love it!"

There in front of her was the beautiful oak fireplace she'd begged and pleaded for that he had said repeatedly was simply out of the question.

"How did you manage to do this?" She ran her hand over the smooth, sleek mantle, picturing immediately how cozy it would be to have a fire burning on cold winter evenings.

Rich beamed proudly. "It wasn't easy, but Dan found a way. We hit a few snags in the process but it turned out beautifully, didn't it?"

"You're glad we have it?" she asked, feeling guilty that she'd gotten her way on everything.

"I love it," he said definitely. "We're going to enjoy it for many years, and I have to admit, I wanted it just as much as you did. I was just worried about the cost."

Even though she had wanted the upgrades and loved how they looked, Alex wondered if Rich might have gone overboard with them. "Can we afford everything?" she asked, knowing that he had considered their finances very carefully, with the conclusion that there wasn't enough for extras.

"It might get a little tight once we have a family and you're not able to work, but we'll manage." He pulled her into his arms. "But I didn't want us to have any regrets about this house. We'll take the challenges as they come and work through them together."

"It seemed like every obstacle possible was thrown in our way to prevent this wedding," she said, her voice growing softer.

"I guess that tells us one thing," Rich observed. "We must have something pretty important to accomplish together to receive so much attention from the adversary."

"But we've survived, haven't we?" She leaned against Rich's chest and rested her head on his shoulder.

"Barely," he chuckled.

"I think I'm going to like spending eternity with you, Mr. Greenwood," Alex said.

"And I think I'm going to like spending it with you, Mrs. Greenwood," he murmured, his lips against her hair. "In fact, I wouldn't mind if eternity started right now."

* * *

Before going to bed that night Julianne and Alex sat on the couch, sipping herbal tea and marveling that in less than twelve hours, Alex would be a married woman.

Julianne placed her empty cup on the end table. "Alex, I've been thinking about this for a long time, and I've made a decision."

At her serious tone, Alex looked at her apprehensively, fully aware of the many difficulties her friend had been through recently. "What is it, Juli?" she asked a little fearfully.

"I've decided to get baptized," Julianne smiled, knowing the impact it would have on Alex.

"That's great!" Alex cried, nearly dumping her tea in her lap. "Congratulations!" She hugged her friend.

"I want to set it up while you're in England on your honeymoon," she added. "That way you'll be back in time."

"That would be perfect!" Alex clasped her hands together, thrilled for her friend. "I'll bet Andre's excited."

Julianne nodded. "He's very happy, especially now that we can talk seriously about getting married." She grabbed a throw pillow and gave it a hug. "I just hope it goes fast. We'll have to wait a year, like you did."

"It will," Alex assured her. "You'll be busy with the Reebok tour, and time will fly by. "

Before crawling into bed that night, Alex knelt to pray. As she expressed her gratitude for her many blessings, she felt the tears well up in her eyes. She knew she didn't deserve everything the Lord had given her, she felt unworthy to have so much, but still He continued to shower her with blessings.

As she reflected back on the experiences of the past month, she saw plainly that the Lord had never abandoned her. He had always been there. There had been times she'd wondered where He was, and now she prayed for forgiveness for her lack of faith. *Help me to remember all the lessons I've learned this last few months,* she prayed. A scripture came to her mind, one that she'd read many times over and knew by heart from Proverbs chapter 3 verses 5 and 6:

> *"Trust in the Lord with all thing heart; and lean not unto thine own understanding. In all thy ways acknowledge him, and he shall direct thy paths."*

She finished her prayer, then crawled under the covers and double checked her alarm one more time. Her thoughts turned to her father. She knew in her heart, he would be in the temple with her the next day. He would witness this incredibly special moment when she and Rich would finally, *finally,* after so much had happened, after such a long year of waiting, be married.

Alex had been afraid she would be so excited she wouldn't be able to sleep, but before she even had a chance to have another thought, she nodded off into a much needed slumber.

Chapter 37

Alex's stomach was in knots as she approached the temple early the next morning. This had been a place she'd gazed at, dreamed of and imagined for such a long time. Finally, today, she was going inside. Grateful for the temple preparation classes she'd attended for several months earlier that year, Alex felt she had a general idea of what to expect. But coupled with the nerves of the wedding and the desire for everything to go well, Alex's jitters turned her stomach inside out and made her head ache. Her anticipation mounted until she thought she might be sick, but she managed to draw in several deep breaths and calm down.

"Hey," Jamie said, "Are you okay? You look a little pale."

"I'm fine . . . I think," she added with a nervous laugh.

Jamie slipped an arm around her sister's waist and walked with her to the temple entrance. They stepped inside the building and immediately one of the female workers approached them. Upon discovering that Alex was one of the brides to be married that morning, the fuss began and she was immediately escorted by several tiny, white-haired ladies to the bride's room where she would prepare to take out her endowment. Afterwards, the wedding ceremony would take place.

There was something so loving and calming about the sweet sisters escorting her through this momentous occasion, Alex couldn't help but settle down as the tranquil spirit of the temple took over. She glanced contentedly at Jamie beside her, knowing that in one year they would share in the same experience with their mother. Not only would Judith take out her own endowments, but their family would at last be sealed together for eternity.

As Alex took part in the temple ordinances, a powerful spirit overcame her. She realized that the eternities were open to her and that she and Rich were capable of attaining degrees of glory unimaginable. Her mind could scarcely take it all in, and she felt comforted, knowing that she could come to the temple again and again.

When she saw Rich later in his white temple clothes, her knees nearly gave way. It was almost too much for her to realize that this man was going to be her husband and sweetheart for eternity. As she approached, her eyes met his, and it felt, for Alex, as if the heavens parted and angels sang. She wasn't sure her feet even touched the ground.

Together they waited in the chapel along with the guests they had invited. There in the temple, surrounded by the beauty of the room and the reverent music from the organ, Alex looked at these people, dressed in white, gathered in her and Rich's behalf, and she knew that this was what it was all about. The purpose of life. The reason for living.

To gather inside the sacred walls of the temple with family and loved ones was a blessing and a privilege she knew was something she would never take for granted. Her vision seemed to expand as she grasped the concept of eternity, of heaven, of the chance to return to live with her Heavenly Father as a family.

Dabbing happily at the moisture in her eyes, Alex snuggled closer to Rich and prayed that she would never, ever forget this wonderful moment, this incredible experience, that she was sharing with the person she loved the very most in the world.

A quiet bell sounded and they were led to another room where they were taught sacred truths about the creation which would help them live better lives while here on earth and prepare to return someday to their Heavenly Father. As Alex made covenants with the Lord, she was moved by the Spirit to know that indeed she was partaking in one of the most sacred ordinances given to man.

When the session ended, she and Rich entered the sealing room, which was decorated in soft beige and white. The walls on each end were mirrored, their reflection a glimpse of eternity. The altar in the middle was crowned by a glittering chandelier. Alex truly felt like a queen.

Their family and friends followed them into the room, and the officiator took his place at the head of the altar. The sweet, wise man talked about the sacred nature of the sealing ordinance and the importance of keeping the covenants they were about to make. He gave them several pieces of advice, admonishing them to never go to bed angry, to always kneel together in prayer each night, and to consult the Lord at all times and make him a vital part of their union as husband and wife.

Then he asked Rich and Alex to kneel across from each other on either side of the altar. As Alex looked briefly into Rich's eyes, she knew, theirs truly was a marriage made in heaven. This was a love for eternity, one that was everlasting.

* * *

"Okay, you two, smile!" their photographer instructed them cheerily.

Alex and Rich turned to the camera and grinned. The photographer snapped several pictures of them together, then went to position himself for a group shot with the entire wedding party. The crowd of family and friends followed him, giving Alex and Rich a moment alone on the front steps of the Salt Lake temple.

"Well," Rich said, taking Alex's left hand in his and lifting it to his lips. He brushed a soft kiss on her knuckles. "How does it feel to be married?"

"Better than I ever dreamed," she answered.

"This has been a long year, hasn't it?" he asked softly.

"The longest in my entire life, but I'd do it all again if I had to, for this." She looked upward at the spires of the temple. "So many times we could have just gotten married and then gone to the temple later, but I'm so glad we made the commitment to wait and do it right."

"I love you too much to do it any other way." He kissed her forehead. "A single year isn't too much to ask for an eternity with you, Alex."

"Eternity's a long time. Are you sure you're not going to get tired of having me around?" she asked playfully.

He picked up on her teasing. "Oh, maybe after the first million years I might want to take up a hobby or start going golfing once or twice a week, but for now, you're all I need."

Alex laughed. Then Rich's laughter joined hers, their voices ringing out happily on the beautiful summer breeze, lifting higher and higher.

Epilogue

One year later

Alex watched as her mother knelt across the altar from her husband Dave Rawlins, who had graciously offered to act as proxy for Alex's father. Judith had been happily married to Dave for twelve months now, since just after her baptism, but she wanted to be sealed to Samuel McCarty, her first husband and the father of her children. When the sealing had taken place, Alex and Jamie joined them at the altar and were sealed to their parents for all eternity.

As they stood in the celestial room, together as a family, Alex felt a completeness she had never felt, like a circle finally connecting. Her family, together now, connected with her father on the other side of the veil while within her was the movement of a brand new life, ready to leave heaven and come to earth. Today, everything was complete.

"How are you doing?" Jamie asked Alex, as they stepped out of the changing cubicles in the women's dressing room of the temple. Jamie couldn't see her sister through the walls of the cubicles but she could hear her.

For the past few days Alex had been having a lot of false labor, mild contractions, just enough to give her a taste of what was to come, but not enough to be uncomfortable—yet.

"I had a few during the session today." Alex patted her large, round stomach and groaned. "I would love to have this baby early. The skin on my stomach feels like it's going to split wide open, like a ripe watermelon."

"Well, don't split here in the temple," Jamie begged. "At least wait until we get outside."

"You'd prefer to see me split on the sidewalk outside the temple?" Alex asked humorously. "I don't think so." She looked around the dressing room. "Did you see where Mom went?"

"I think she went into the restroom to fix her makeup," Jamie replied. "I hope we can get that mascara out of her temple dress."

Alex found a small waste paper basket for the wad of crumpled tissues in her hand. "Between the three of us, we sure have a lot of tears. Do you think we ought to offer to buy a few boxes of Kleenex to replace all the tissue we used?" Alex asked.

Judith appeared at that moment, her eyes red but her face glowing with happiness. "This has been quite a day, hasn't it, girls? Wasn't that sealing lovely?"

"It sure was," Jamie said, giving her mother a quick squeeze. "Being sealed together as a family is something I've prayed about for a long time. Ever since I was baptized, in fact. I'm so grateful we finally made it."

Judith deeply regretted her long-ago reaction to both her husband and daughter's conversion. If she hadn't been so hardheaded, she could have had the blessings of the gospel and the assurance of being an eternal family years before. But . . . she wouldn't waste time on regrets. "I'm sure your father wondered what it would take to get through my thick skull," she said. "I think he had a lot to do with all of this."

Alex nodded. It was her father's old journal, which Judith had found and given to her daughters, that had led Alex to read the Book of Mormon. That single act had changed her life forever.

"And now, just two years later, here we are, an eternal family," Jamie said, her voice trembling with happiness. The lonely years when both her mother and sister had resented her baptism into the Church were only a distant memory. "I felt Dad with us, didn't you?"

Judith and Alex both nodded in agreement. "I know how proud he is of each of his girls," Judith said. "And I want you girls to know how much I love you and how proud I am of you." She gave them each a hug. "Now, as much as I hate to leave this wonderful place, we don't want to keep those men waiting too long, do we? They complain enough about how long it takes us to get ready as it is."

As they gathered up their belongings, Jamie asked her mother if their bishop had said any more about her and Dave going on a mission. Judith had been reluctant at first, feeling completely inadequate as a new convert to teach anyone else. But as she had spoken with other couple missionaries, she had felt more at peace.

"Dave hopes we get sent to South Africa where he went on his first mission," she said. "He'd like to go back and use his medical expertise to help the people he already loves so much. I've gotten used to the idea and I think it would be quite a fascinating experience."

"Well, I hope you go somewhere like Europe, or Great Britain, so we can come visit you sometime," Jamie said. "South Africa is so far away."

"Great Britain would be nice. It's foreign, but you don't have to learn a language," Alex reasoned.

"I'm sure the Lord will call us where we need to go," Judith said. "It won't matter as long as Dave and I are together. And as long as I get letters with lots of pictures of my grandchildren from you two," Judith added, patting Alex's stomach.

Alex could feel her stomach slowly begin to tighten and tingle. But not wanting Judith or Jamie to make a fuss, she didn't say anything. She was tired of the false labor pains and ready for the real ones.

"Dave's a great man," Jamie said. "As much as he's done for me, I didn't think I could appreciate and respect him any more than I did. But watching him stand in today for our own father during the sealing . . ." She stopped, unable to continue as the tears started to well up again.

At that, Judith's eyes also started to fill with tears once again. "I know," she agreed. "I am so blessed. He is a great man and I feel so fortunate to be his wife. He's been so patient with me."

Alex thought of Rich and how patient and loving he'd been with her, during the morning sickness, and then later, when she'd been terrified that like Jamie, she would be unable to carry a baby to full-term, and now, in these last months, when she felt she would never feel normal again—everyday she counted her blessings.

"What took you girls so long?" Steve asked, as the women approached them in the waiting room.

"Oh, you know," Jamie said, wrapping her arm around him. "Just girl stuff."

"You've been gabbing, haven't you?" he said. "You can talk the rest of the entire day, but you stay in the dressing room and—"

Jamie kissed him quickly, stopping him in mid-sentence. "Face it honey, we'll never change. You're destined to wait for us forever."

Steve rolled his eyes. "Well," he said, "I guess you're worth the wait, but can we get going now? I'm starving."

"You guess?" Jamie elbowed him. "You'd better be a little more sure than that."

As Alex and Rich fell into line behind them, she noticed Rich staring at her.

"What?" she asked, wondering if she'd forgotten to comb her hair, or if her lipstick was smeared. "Is something wrong?"

"No," he said. "I just can't get over how beautiful you are, especially today."

Alex opened her mouth to complain about her swollen ankles, her aching back, and her huge stomach, then stopped herself. He was sincere and meant every word. It didn't matter how she felt or thought she looked; her husband thought she was beautiful.

"Thank you, honey," she said, brushing a light kiss on his cheek.

Rich smiled at her, his eyes reflecting the love in his heart. "We've been very blessed, haven't we?" He placed his hand gently on Alex's abdomen.

Alex knew what he meant. They had tried to reconcile themselves to the possibility that they might never have children of their own. They had tried not to hope or expect them, but merely to be grateful for each other. The day she found out she was expecting, that she was truly carrying Rich's child within her, was one of the best days of her life. And soon that child would leave its heavenly home and join their little family.

In fact, Alex was beginning to fear that child might arrive sooner than they had planned. The familiar tightening of her stomach started again, but this time, an accompanying ache in her lower back joined in.

Rich had noticed something wrong. "Alex? Are you okay? Are you in pain?"

Alex grabbed his hand and gripped as the sensations grew to an uncomfortable height, then slowly subsided.

"Honey, what's going on?" he demanded.

"I hope you're not too hungry," she said.

He gave her a strange look. "I'm not. Why?"

"I think we might want to stop at the hospital first. This little girl acts like she's as anxious to be born as I am to have her." They'd had several ultrasounds and been assured they were having a girl. Alex had spent the last three months decorating the nursery.

"Really? Are you sure?" A sudden look of panic crossed his expression. "What do we do? Are you okay? Can you walk? Should I carry you to the car?"

Alex shushed him and said quietly, "Let's just walk quickly outside before I have another contraction."

"But it's too early," he muttered as Alex pulled him toward the entrance.

The others were waiting outside when they finally emerged from the exit doors.

"Hey, you two, what took so long?" Steve asked, ready to remind them of his growling stomach.

"I think we're going to have to pass on lunch today," Alex said, her lower back continuing with a low, dull ache. She couldn't stand up straight. "I think I'm in labor."

The group erupted with cries of joy and excitement. It took a moment for them to realize that this wasn't the time to celebrate. In minutes they were all on their way to the hospital, with Rich and Alex in the lead.

"Are you scared?" Rich asked as he sped through a yellow light.

"Not as long as you're with me," she said. "Just promise me that once we get to the hospital, you won't leave me."

"I won't, sweetheart," he promised. "I'll be at your side the whole time. We're in this together, remember?"

Alex relaxed in her seat, breathing slowly, trying to remain calm. She didn't know what to expect or what lay ahead but she knew, no matter what, with Rich at her side, she would be okay.

"I love you, honey," she said, taking his hand. "But can you possibly drive a little faster?" A sudden pain caused her to catch her breath, and Rich gave her a worried look.

"Are you okay, Alex?"

She didn't answer right away, but continued to breath deeply and slowly. "I changed my mind," she gulped. "Can you drive *a lot* faster?"

ABOUT THE AUTHOR

Michele Ashman Bell is a busy wife and mother, who still manages to find time between car pools and her children's activities to spend time each day writing. She says that "working in the Young Women organization . . . gave me a deeper understanding of the importance and obligation to write stories that uplift, inspire, and edify readers, as well as entertain them."

A nationally certified group fitness instructor, Michele enjoys writing about characters involved in the fitness industry. She has researched eating disorders extensively in order to accurately portray the impact they can have on people's lives. Michele also enjoys remodeling her home, spending time with her family, and traveling both inside and outside of the United States.

She and her husband, Gary, are the parents of four children—Weston, Kendyl, Andrea, and Rachel. They currently reside in Sandy, Utah.

The best-selling author of *An Unexpected Love* and *An Enduring Love*, Michele has also published children's stories in *The Friend*.

She welcomes readers' comments and questions. You can write to her at P.O. Box 901513, Sandy, Utah 84090.